WHAT IF?

Compiled & Edited by
Ben Thomas & D Kershaw

The sages called him a shadow

And the light went out of the sun:

And the wise men told us that all was well

And all was weary and one:

And then, and then, in the quiet garden,

With never a weed to kill,

We knew that his shining tail had shone

In the white road over the hill:

We knew that the clouds were flakes of flame,

We knew that the sunset fire

Was red with the blood of the Dragon

Whose death is the world's desire.

The Hunting of the Dragon, Gilbert Keith Chesterton, 1922

TABLE OF CONTENTS

CLEOPATRA

By Stephen Herczeg

With her husband dead, her country invaded by the Romans, and herself imprisoned by Emperor Octavian, Cleopatra slowly brings, to her lips, the poison that will end the pain. But Cleopatra's hand is stayed by her loyal handmaiden, Na'eemah. With promises of miracles, Na'eemah has just one day to beseech the ancient gods to liberate Egypt from servitude.

Na'eemah stayed silent in the shadows of the audience chamber. She stared at her Queen as she stood on the balcony looking out over the expansive city of Alexandria.

Her Queen, Cleopatra VII, ruler of all Egypt, the most dynamic, strong and beautiful woman that Na'eemah had ever come across in her short life, was worried. For the first time, Na'eemah saw cracks appearing at the edges of her Queen's stoic resolve.

Cleopatra held out the cup in her hand. Na'eemah strode across the stone tiled floor, picked up a jug of red wine and moved out to her mistress. She filled the cup and edged back.

"Stay Na'eemah, I may need more, soon," said Cleopatra.

"Yes, your grace."

Na'eemah stepped back but stayed as close as protocol allowed. She turned and followed her mistress's gaze, across the mud huts and brick houses of the peasantry, on past the ornate gardens and terraced mansions of the gentry and finally beyond the edge of the city, where lay its docks, the grand library and the towering Pharos.

Her Queen's attention was focused on the area beyond the city limits.

Out in the sea, the final battle that would determine the fate of Egypt, and indeed its Queen, raged on.

For many years, Queen Cleopatra had rallied the forces of Egypt to fight against the oppression inflicted by Octavian, the self-imposed leader of Rome. Her consort, Mark Antony, once a close confidant of Octavian and a member of the Roman triumvirate, rebelled against his former country and joined forces with Egypt.

While the war raged, Cleopatra's armies had been decimated, leading to one final stand off the coast of Egypt. The combined forces of Mark Antony's remaining naval forces and those of Cleopatra, against the technically superior and immensely stronger Roman navy.

Cleopatra grimaced as yet another Egyptian galley was rammed by a larger Roman vessel and foundered in the calm sea.

"The Gods will protect us," she murmured under her breath.

"They will, your Grace. These Roman heathens can never defeat us, as we walk at the right hand of Ra," said Na'eemah.

Cleopatra turned and smiled at her young handmaiden. She stepped towards her, ran a hand across her dark hair and looked deep into her dark brown eyes. She kissed her lightly on the forehead and spoke.

"I wish I had the optimism of youth that so fills your soul, but even I have grown weary as I have grown older and have begun to doubt that there are any Gods at all. If there are, they certainly are not smiling down on us today," she said.

Na'eemah was stunned. Her Queen had never shown such weakness or a sense of defeat before. Such was her shock that she stood stunned while Cleopatra downed the remnants of her wine and held the cup out for more.

The hand maiden was snapped back to reality when the Queen let out a harrumph of impatience. Na'eemah quickly filled the goblet and backed away.

Cleopatra strode up to the balcony and gazed out at the battle.

Her fleet was a mess. The sea was littered with broken and burning wrecks. The only saving grace was that the distance hid the vision of hundreds of dead bodies scattered across the water.

She sipped her wine as she watched the last desperate act of the battle.

Three mighty Egyptian galleys turned towards the lead Roman ships. Their oars thrashed the sea into foam as their oarsmen stroked at a swift rate, powering them forward. The great golden rams jutted forward like proud stallions ready for their mounts, and the three drove onwards, towards the waiting Romans.

Cleopatra turned and threw her goblet, it smashed against the carved stone balustrade, shattering into hundreds of pieces. The fate of the goblet reflected the fate of her final warships. They were impaled on the great bronze covered rams of the Roman quinqueremes. Equipped with twice as many rowers, they had charged at the Egyptian galleys at higher speed and sliced through as if they were butter.

The Queen turned back to see the final moments of

her great ships as they sank beneath the waves. Her fleet was no more. Two hundred ships had been sent to their deaths. The number of men lost would be in the thousands.

As she watched, a small trireme turned away from the edge of battle and quickly moved between the burning and floundering wrecks, heading for shore.

Cleopatra turned away when she recognised the boat.

"Jabari," she called.

A tall, powerfully muscled and black skinned man stepped into the room. He bowed to his Queen.

"Yes, your Grace," he said.

"Prepare the remaining troops and house staff. The battle is lost, Mark Antony will be returning soon. The Romans will not be long after. We head for Memphis on the hour. Send my children now, we will meet them in Merimda tonight," she said.

Jabari bowed once more and said, "As you wish, your Grace." He eyed Na'eemah, nodded and left.

Cleopatra strode towards her handmaiden. Na'eemah stood wide-eyed, holding the wine jug.

"Come, leave that, we need to hurry," she said.

Cleopatra rose from her bath and allowed Na'eemah

to wrap her in a thick cotton towel.

"Do you think this was necessary, your Grace?" the young handmaiden asked, fearful of any reproach, but nervous as the sounds of battle coming from the docks increased in volume.

"I must look presentable to the population as we ride through the city. If they see me dishevelled or red with rage then rumours will spark and run through the city quicker than wildfire. Besides, I do not wish to seem to be fleeing like some thief in the night," she said.

The Queen allowed Na'eemah to completely dry her, then assist her into a comfortable, but practical set of garments for travel.

They moved into the Queen's bedchamber to complete Cleopatra's transformation, with Na'eemah finishing off hair, makeup and finally jewellery.

As the Queen stood looking back out over her city at the clash of arms happening in the docks area, a loud knocking came from her chamber door.

"Enter," she said.

Immediately, Jabari opened the door, stepped in and surveyed the room. He looked at Cleopatra who nodded. Satisfied he stepped aside and let the Queen's consort, Mark Antony, enter.

The once proud Roman general was covered in wounds and smudges of ash. His uniform was awash with blood and had deep tears across the leather.

He walked into the room and knelt before Cleopatra.

"My Queen. I am so sorry. All is lost. The fleet is decimated. The army struggles to hold the enemy at the gates of your palace," he said.

He stood up and moved to the doorway leading to the balcony. The clash of soldiers echoed up from the city. Huge troop transport galleys loomed on the horizon. Several had already docked, their gangplanks lowered, and lines of troops marched out of their holds to join the fighting.

Mark Antony dropped his head.

"We must flee the country. There is nothing left for us here," he said.

"I will not leave the country of my birth in the hands of these invaders. We will go to Memphis and reform. We can defend the city. Send out word to our neighbours. Nothing is lost until it is lost," she said, "I have sent our children on to Memphis. We shall leave within the hour on a fast chariot and join them tonight."

Antony turned and stared at her. A look of incredulity crossed his face. His shoulders slumped with realisation. He raised one hand and indicated the troops streaming into the city.

"Octavian and Agrippa will be here within the hour. We have no hope, we will both be captured. I will be executed for treason, or worse, exiled from my homelands. Left alive, but taken from you and my children forever," he said.

He walked out onto the balcony and approached the balustrade.

Cleopatra called out to him.

"Nothing is lost unless we allow it to be lost. Nothing is taken unless we allow it to be taken. The Gods will protect us," she said.

"The Gods? There are no Gods. If there are, they only have the tortures of Tartarus prepared for me."

He undid the clasps on his armour and let it fall to the tiled floor with a dull clatter of metal on stone. He stepped up to the balustrade and peered over the city as flames began to lick at the buildings lining the docks.

As he stared at the conflagration below, he saw chariots drive through the smoke and form a phalanx across the wide main street running through Alexandria. To Mark Antony, it was a taunt, a threat, directed at he and Cleopatra.

He drew his sword and held it before him in his right hand.

Cleopatra stepped up next to him and looked down at the encroaching chariots.

"They will be here soon," she said, "If we linger all hope will be lost."

She turned and stepped away. When she realised that Mark Antony wasn't with her, she stopped and looked back.

He turned the sword around and placed the tip against his chest. He grabbed the handle with both hands and began to place pressure on the blade.

"There is no hope," he said.

Cleopatra only had time to shout, "No," before he drove the sword deep into his chest.

Blood gouted from the wound and sprayed across the balustrade and down into the city below.

Mark Antony staggered back a step and fell to his knees. Blood flowed from his chest and formed a puddle beneath him. He looked up as Cleopatra's shadow fell on him, his pained expression and pleading eyes meeting her anger.

"It was all for you," he said.

"Only a fool would take such an easy escape," she said.

The once great general's eyes rolled back in his head and he fell forward to splash down in the pool of his own life blood.

Cleopatra looked down at his corpse, her expression a mix of anger and derision.

"Fool," she said.

Cleopatra stood tall and proud as Jabari led the chariot through the streets of Alexandria. The clatter of the bronze wheels on cobble stone rang through the alleyways, bringing the local peasantry out of their hovels and into the streets.

They cheered as they saw their beautiful Queen pass by.

Na'eemah watched from the following chariot, the one reserved for Mark Antony. She was to have ridden with Cleopatra but, under the circumstances, chose to trail behind.

Her Queen held her chest out, absorbing the adulation from the people. The people who had no idea that their doom followed only moments down the road.

If they resisted, they would be crushed under the heels of Roman sandals, if they didn't, they would be subjugated. The healthy young men conscripted into the ever-growing army. The women subjected to worse treatment.

After almost an hour of travel, the houses began to peter out. The groups of people dwindled to twos and threes, then single pedestrians and finally no-one. The cramped streets opened up into fields of tilled land, and as they travelled further away from the coast, a desert landscape.

They turned inland and headed closer to the green lands surrounding the delta and followed one of the outer streams that fed the great river.

Cleopatra finally relented and slumped her posture. Fatigue caught up with her and Na'eemah saw her slide down to rest in what little shade the sides of the chariot offered.

Jabari kept hold of the reins and never let his duty slip. He was the Queen's protector, a position he held with dignity and determination.

They kept to the west of the town of Naukratis to avoid the need for Cleopatra to resume her regal posturing and headed south-east. To the west the desert encroached ever further onto the green lands of the Nile delta. Towards the river, the east, the thick lush lands were a tempting oasis of green.

As the sun was starting to dip beneath the horizon, they finally arrived at the ancient but tiny city of Merimda. Jabari pulled up in a field on the outskirts where Cleopatra's retinue had made camp.

As she stepped down from the chariot, Cleopatra's eyes darted around, furtively searching for the last evidence that her life had real meaning. And they appeared.

Her three children, Alexander, Selene, and Ptolemy

stepped out from a large tent. Their eyes lit up when they saw their exhausted mother and they ran to her.

She bent down and hugged all three to her, smothering them with kisses that smeared her makeup.

"My little loves, I'm so glad you are safe," she said, tears filling her eyes and threatened to burst forth.

Alexander was first to pull away, his small slip into childlike behaviour tossed aside and replaced with a more regal stance as was his training. He peered around, an expression of confusion crossing his face.

"Where's father?" he asked.

Jabari, standing nearby, tensed.

Cleopatra dragged her face from the mess that was her daughter's hair and stared up at him. The tears she held back let loose in an uncontrollable torrent.

Alexander's face dropped from his stoic look of despair. His bottom lip trembled as he fought to hold back his own flood of tears.

Selene noticed her mother crying and joined in the conversation.

"Mummy, what's wrong? Where is daddy?" she asked, her face radiating pure innocence.

Cleopatra looked into her daughter's bright eyes.

"He's gone, darling, the Romans, they…"

Selene realised what her mother was saying. Anger and sadness exploded at the same time.

Tears ran from her eyes as she cried, "No. No. It can't be." She broke away from her mother and ran towards Jabari.

"Jabari. He can't be dead. Say it isn't so," she said, staring up at the tall black man through muffled sobs.

Jabari hunkered down to the little girl's level and took her in his arms.

"I'm afraid it is so, little one," he said, "Your father was a brave and strong man. He fought to save you, your brothers, your mother and your country, but in the end, even he wasn't strong enough. The northern dogs took him from us."

Selene's body was wracked with spasms as the full force of her grief overwhelmed her. The large man hugged her to him until they subsided. Finally, he let her go and she ran back to her mother for further comfort.

A tall, scrawny man stepped out of the shadows and approached the Queen. He wore a long purple robe, with highlights of gold and stood with a noble posture.

He stepped up to the Queen and waited until she took notice.

"Yes, Lateef," Cleopatra said.

Lateef's softly spoken voice wafted through the misery before him.

"My Queen, I have arranged accommodation with the local Mayor. It isn't much more than a hovel, but he has graciously bequeathed his estate to you for the evening. The main house is not far, as we have encamped within his gardens," he said.

After sharing a light meal with her household staff, Cleopatra, her children and maids, made their way to the house. Na'eemah helped the nurses ready the children for sleep, before turning her attention back to her Queen.

As she pulled the covers over Cleopatra, she noticed fresh tear tracks in the remaining makeup and grime from the travel. Within moments, the exhausted Queen slipped into a fitful slumber.

Na'eemah sighed, her head slumped slightly as she took in the events of the day. One that opened with a bright future but closed with the spectre of death and slavery hovering above.

She stepped out of the Queen's bedroom and found Jabari, as always, standing guard at his Queen's side.

"You need rest as well. Is there another that can guard in your stead?" she asked.

Jabari remained steadfast, he shook his head.

"None that I would trust. I will stay until dawn, then I will rest," he said.

She looked up into his brown eyes. Eyes that were fixed on one purpose and never wavered.

"Then I shall see you at dawn," she said.

Na'eemah made her way outside. The cool night

breeze brought out goose-bumps across her naked arms. She shivered. She knew it was from the cold, but deep inside she felt it was from fear as well.

She needed comfort.

As a virgin handmaiden, raised within the confines of a temple to be released only into the service of the Queen, she found no comfort in the arms of another, only in service to her Queen and her God. With her Queen asleep and in need of her rest, she could only turn to one other.

The Mayor's estate possessed a simple temple, located at the foot of the only hills in the area. Na'eemah made her way across the desolate and rocky ground of the untilled field and arrived at the front steps of the temple.

It was dark, untended by any priests.

Na'eemah had brought a torch and set light to the lamps at the entrance. They cast a pale glow on a façade of chipped and rough-hewn stone. This was not the style of temple she was used to. It was functional, dedicated not to one God but to all.

She entered and found a small flat stone-tiled floor, with a simple stone altar at one end. She set light to the lamps inside the entrance and light flooded the darkened interior. Faded and flaking glyphs of many Gods decorated the walls. She recognised many, Ra, Isis, Horus, Net and then finally the one she sought.

One picture seemed to be in better condition than

many of the others, possibly from lack of use as most of the damage was at the lower extremes where worshippers had beseeched their God by laying hands on their image, the oils from their skin soaking into the paint and causing its decline.

Na'eemah knelt beneath the painting.

It depicted a beautiful woman, with a crown of two golden cows' horns sitting either side of a red sun. The woman was dressed in a simple red ankle length dress, her face looking off to the left as was tradition.

She was Hathor, goddess of beauty, fertility, dance and music. It seemed strange that Hathor was relatively untouched, as she represented fertility, a quality much in demand amongst the farming communities.

Na'eemah had been given to the temple of Hathor, in Memphis, as a child by her parents. Their hope was to have her raised within the worship to then live in servitude to the Queen. Their hopes had been well realised. Na'eemah, however, had not seen them since that day and didn't even know if they still lived.

She did not regret their decision, as without it she would never have arrived at the place she now occupied. The handmaiden of the most powerful woman, in fact the most powerful person, in Egypt. And one that she was devoted to.

Na'eemah bowed low.

"Hear me, oh Hathor. I am and have always been your servant, as much as that of the Queen. I have dedicated a life to ensuring the Queen is served and protected, and that through her your virtues are realised. She has been fruitful. She is beautiful, a reflection of your image. Her life has been filled with music, with dance, with love."

Na'eemah looked up as a noise echoed within the chamber. In the flickering light she was sure the painting had changed, but realised it was her imagination and bowed her head once more.

"But danger comes. Our land is invaded by barbarians from far across the northern sea. My Queen has lost her lover. Her life is one of loss. She cares only to protect her children, herself and then her country. But I think that life will be short, and our country will be besieged and enslaved. The Romans will subjugate us. They will tear down our shrines and temples. Our children's children will be forced to worship new Gods, the Gods of the Romans. Your memories will be lost and with them you will be forever lost."

A wispy voice floated through the chamber as if brought on the breeze.

"What would you have us do?" it said.

Na'eemah looked about her, searching in vain for the source of the voice.

"Is there someone there?" she asked, fear growing within her.

"I asked what would you have us do?" the voice said, stronger now.

Na'eemah turned back, her eyes were drawn to the painting of Hathor.

The figure had changed position, she was facing forwards, her eyes staring down at Na'eemah.

"What would you, Na'eemah of Memphis, have me and my siblings do for you?" the voice said, the origin seemed to be the centre of the painted God.

Na'eemah fell back in shock. She crawled backwards to the centre of the tiled floor and stared back at the painting. The figure of Hathor pulled herself from the wall and stood before Na'eemah, her face resembling that of Cleopatra, the most beautiful woman in all Egypt. A fitting image for the Goddess of beauty.

Hathor said, "The people of this age have almost forgotten us. There are those that worship the Roman gods, the Greek gods, few even worship the single God, the Jehovah. Why should we help those who do not even believe in us anymore?"

Na'eemah got to her knees and bowed in supplication.

"There are those of us that still believe. Granted we are few, but our worship is strong. We keep your memory alive. I have dedicated my life to that cause," she said.

"Yes, you have been a good servant, I have watched from afar. You inspire the Queen's children with tales of the Gods. There is hope that they will repeat your efforts, but their fate has been determined and their time is short," Hathor said.

Na'eemah's face dropped in shock. The children would die, soon.

"The future can be changed. The people have lost their faith only because they have been distracted by the riches promised by these pretender Gods and their worshippers. They forget that the prosperity that has favoured Egypt for millennia is due to our Gods," Na'eemah said.

"That is true. Fear of death always makes the most heretical suddenly turn back to their Gods."

Hathor smiled.

"Perhaps the arrival of these Romans is as good for the country as it is bad for the people they slaughter. The populace will see such torment that they have only one place to turn. Us."

"They will need a sign. A miracle. Like the legends of old. Something to convince them, once again, that the Gods live and the Gods favour those who believe," said Na'eemah, seeing a spark of hope.

"Yes. I think it is time. I will admit that we have

become too complacent and kept out of the lives of man for too many years."

Hathor stood for a moment, staring at her priestess.

"I will give you a quest," she said.

"Anything," said Na'eemah.

Hathor smiled.

"I wouldn't submit to anything too lightly," the Goddess said, "You will travel to Giza. At the base of the Pyramid of Khufu there is a hidden temple dedicated to Anubis. There you can beseech the God of the Dead. I will warn him. He may help, but you will need an offering worthy of him," she said before vanishing.

Na'eemah was confused.

"What offering? Where is the temple? How will I get there?" she asked to the ether.

Hathor's voice floated out of the wall.

"You will know," she said.

The next day was hot. Cleopatra, Na'eemah and the children travelled in the largest covered wagon.

Na'eemah fought within herself to explain all to Cleopatra but knew that, as the Queen of Egypt, her own station was that of a God. To be told that other Gods did exist would have been akin to treason. Cleopatra would be well within her rights to have Na'eemah executed on the spot. Instead, she kept her mouth closed until Hathor's instructions became clearer in her mind.

Jabari rode a large white stallion nearby, keeping his eyes both on the wagon and the surrounding area. Na'eemah was worried, she didn't think he had rested or slept more than a couple of hours since Alexandria. She could see fatigue behind his eyes, but his proud stature defied it.

Hours passed and the sun was well below the horizon when they finally reached the city gates of Memphis. There were no guards on duty, no archers in the towers, no torches ablaze on the external walls.

Jabari was furious, he yelled to the guard tower but received no reply. He powered his horse inside but could find no trace of any soldiers or guards.

Cleopatra told him to simply leave it be and get them to the palace. It could be dealt with in the morning when she would call a council of the elders of Memphis and her advisors so that they could prepare the defence of the city.

The entourage finally pulled through the palace gates and unloaded all and sundry. The building was noticeably quieter than normal. Many of the oil lamps had not even been lit.

Na'eemah was a little suspicious but put it down to their absence and unheralded return. She assisted the children and told the nurse maids to feed, bathe and prepare them for bed.

Cleopatra herself drifted into the palace entrance, half asleep with fatigue and despondency. Na'eemah helped her up the stairs and into her own bedroom. A bath was run, and soon the Queen's mood lightened as she began to feel more comfortable again.

The Queen opened her shutters and stepped out onto the wide stone balcony that overlooked the capital. As with the parts of the city they had passed through, the city was very dark. Only the port area on the river bank showed any form of life. Lights blazed, people milled around, and when the breeze blew from the river, a chorus of voices and sounds of enjoyment floated by.

Cleopatra mused to herself, thinking that the city fathers had arranged a celebration at the port.

Movement on the river snatched her attention and it was then she realised how wrong she was. The noises were not celebration, they were echoes of battle.

The port was alive with soldiers. Roman soldiers. Those that had disembarked from the four Roman quinqueremes docked on the river front.

Cleopatra turned and shouted, "Octavian is here."

Her shout fell on deaf ears as the door to her bedchamber burst open and Jabari was thrown bodily into the room to land in a heap in the middle of the floor. Na'eemah ran to him and knelt down. He was alive, but unconscious.

She looked up as two heavily armoured men marched into the room, followed by a troop of soldiers.

Cleopatra's face became stern as she moved to face her oppressors.

"Octavian, what is the meaning of this?" she said, needing no answer and asking for none.

"The roads are so much slower when you can use the local population to power your ships," he said. "We've been waiting all day for your arrival, and I'm afraid that now you are here your stay will be rather short."

Agrippa nodded at two soldiers and then down at Jabari. They immediately picked him up and dragged him from the room.

Cleopatra watched the men, a look of fear for Jabari on her face.

Octavian held up a hand.

"Do not worry yourself, my Queen, no harm will befall him, unless he courts it. After all, I can always use more galley slaves and he is certainly a strong one," he said, a wry smile on his face.

"You bastard," Cleopatra said.

"Now I will leave you for the rest of the evening," Octavian said. He nodded at Na'eemah.

"Your handmaiden can stay also. She will need to help you prepare. You will have a full day of appearances as I show you off to your people to prove to them once and for all that Rome now controls Egypt. We shall tour all the major cities between here and Alexandria, where we will board my ship and you will come to Rome to officially renounce your position as Queen. After that, who knows?"

He stepped up and placed a finger under her chin.

"We have many uses for someone of your undoubted beauty," he said, a wicked smile masking his intent, "You may even join my concubines. There is still a little life left in you."

He chuckled and grabbed Cleopatra's hand as she unleashed a stinging slap towards his face.

"Careful, we wouldn't want to damage you, would we?" he said, "Besides, if you resist then I have three ways of convincing you to behave. It may only take one, but there are two spares."

Cleopatra realised he was talking about her children. Her arm went limp.

Octavian dropped her hand and strode from the room, saying over his shoulder, "Until the morning. Sleep well."

Agrippa watched her for a moment before leaving as well. The other soldiers followed. Two stopped just outside and pulled the door shut.

Cleopatra dropped to her knees and put her head in

her hands, weeping uncontrollably.

Na'eemah moved across and knelt beside her. She placed a hand around her Queen and gently spoke to her.

"All is not lost, my Queen," she said.

"Yes, it is. There is no more hope. The army is no more. My central seat of power is not mine. My lover, the father of my children, is dead. Even the Gods have deserted us."

She slowly stood up, shrugging off Na'eemah's arm and staggered across to a wooden cabinet. She opened a small drawer in the side and removed a bright green object.

Na'eemah watched her Queen step out onto the balcony and move up to the balustrade. She had seen this before and panic began to rise.

"My Queen," she said and moved to the doorway.

Cleopatra stared out across the city.

"I have failed my people. I have failed my country. I will forever be known as the last Pharaoh of Egypt," she said, pulling the small object from within her robes.

Na'eemah saw that it was a glass bottle.

Cleopatra pulled the tiny cork from the bottle and raised it above her head.

"Osiris, even you have abandoned me and all that worship you. There is nothing left for me here. My people will go on, but we will no longer be the Egypt we once were. Anubis will be my guide from here onwards," she said.

As she brought the bottle to her lips, Na'eemah ran forward and grabbed at her hand, stopping it before the deadly contents could fulfil their purpose. Cleopatra resisted, drops of poison spilt from the neck of the bottle and splashed to the ground. Small wisps of smoke rose from the stone.

"My Queen, don't, there is a way," said Na'eemah.

Cleopatra's eyes were a mix of fury and insanity. She tried to force the bottle towards her lips. Na'eemah held fast and kept the bottle at bay.

"There is no way," said Cleopatra.

"The Gods have not abandoned us," said Na'eemah, "Give me one more day to prove it."

They held each other. Cleopatra stared into Na'eemah's eyes. The handmaiden's expression was fixed and confident.

"Trust me," she said. "Have you even had reason not to?"

Cleopatra's hand relaxed slightly. She stared deeper into her servant's eyes, desperately trying to read what was hidden there. Finally, the two women unfurled themselves. Na'eemah managed to take control and corked the deadly bottle.

Cleopatra, tired, fatigued and on the edge of collapse,

looked at the younger woman and said, "One day. You have one day to conjure a miracle. If you fail, then I will die by my own hand. I will never return to Rome as some play thing for the Emperor."

"Agreed. If I fail then I will join you in the afterlife," said Na'eemah.

A smile played across her face in an attempt to diffuse the tension.

"After all, you will still need a servant," she said.

Once Na'eemah said, "I need to go to Giza," Cleopatra took control. She firstly returned to her wooden cupboard and pulled a small ivory handled knife from a draw. She handed it to Na'eemah.

"This is for your protection, until you can rescue Jabari. Give him this and he will protect you as he would me."

She led Na'eemah to an alcove in the far corner of the bedroom. A small circular hole sat half way up the wall.

Cleopatra pushed her finger into the hole. A clicking noise was followed by a section of the wall swinging out. A set of stairs led down into the cavity exposed by the doorway.

"Quickly, this leads down into the dungeon. From there follow the main corridor to the end. There is a similar hole that uncovers a passageway to the stables. Find Jabari, give him the dagger and have him take you to Giza," she said.

The Queen hugged Na'eemah to her.

"Good luck. We may never see each other again. If you fail I will be gone," she said, pushing the young woman into the stairway and closing the door once she was out of sight.

As Na'eemah descended into the darkness, the reality of her situation became clearer. She was putting all her faith in a vision of her Goddess. The more she thought about it, the more she began to fear it was all just a dream.

She stopped for a moment. Panic began to overwhelm her. Her breath came in short gasps. Her vision began to dim. The corridor seemed to tighten into an even more confined space.

The hand holding the knife went to her chest as she dragged air into her lungs, the other ran down the wall to steady her as she descended into the dark.

She finally came to a small landing and groped forward until she spied light filtering in through a tiny slit in the wall before her.

She concentrated hard and managed to drop her breath rate until it became more regular. She pushed up against the door and listened. All seemed quiet on the other side.

Na'eemah felt the wall and found a similar circular hole. She pushed her finger into it, and a hidden door opened with a slight clicking noise.

Peering through the tiny crack, Na'eemah saw rows of cells stretching off down the corridor. She watched for several moments but there was no movement.

Gently, she eased the door open and crept out into the corridor. Cleopatra had said there was hidden door at the end of the corridor. Na'eemah slowly headed that way.

The first few cells were empty. She was surprised, expecting them to be overflowing with Cleopatra's loyal guards. She realised that the absence of prisoners meant something far worse.

She hurried on and found the now familiar hole in the wall at the end of the corridor. She put her finger to the lip of the hole ready to open the door but realised she still hadn't found Jabari. She would never make it to Giza without help.

The corridor to her right was dimly lit, but she could make out more cells. She peered into the gloom, unsure if they were as empty as the ones she had passed.

A noise at the end of the corridor gelled her into action. She triggered the hidden mechanism and let herself into the dark corridor. She pulled the door closed but leant against it and listened.

The noise was a loud, and seemingly drunk, guard. He stopped and began shouting at someone in one of the cells.

Na'eemah opened the door a crack and listened.

"You're going to die in the morning, Nubian scum. Your Queen will be taken to Rome and paraded like the whore she is," he said.

Na'eemah pushed the door open and crept out. The gloom of the corridor hid her from the attention of the drunk guard.

He took a swig from the goat's bladder he held and swayed slightly as he drew breath to insult the Queen's guard once more.

Na'eemah peered around and found a small wooden stool, used by the Palace guards when they were on duty down here. She picked it up and slowly crept towards the drunk Roman.

He started once more to hurl abuse.

"When Octavian is done with her, she'll be thrown into the slave harem that satisfies the gladiators before they die in the arena. She'll be lucky to last a week, down there," he slurred.

He took another breath in readiness but was slammed to the ground as Na'eemah brought the little stool down on his head.

Jabari let out a short shout of surprise, then a longer one of glee when he saw his Queen's handmaiden standing in the corridor.

"The keys," he said pointing at the guard.

She searched him and quickly relieved him of the large set of bronze keys. She unlocked the cell and Jabari burst out and took her in his arms, hugging her close.

"I'm so glad you're alive," he said.

He placed her down.

"Our Queen?" he asked.

"She is coping, though close to breaking."

Na'eemah's eyes teared up as the reality set in. She looked up into the big man's eyes.

"She longs for death rather than become a trophy for the Romans," she said.

Jabari pushed past.

"I must go to her. I must take her from here or die trying," he said.

Na'eemah grabbed his arm.

"No. You will die before you get close," she said.

He stopped and looked down at her. His face a mass of confusion and torn emotions.

"There is a chance. A way that we can save both our Queen and our country," she said, "But we must go now."

Na'eemah pulled the knife out and gave it to Jabari.

He looked down and his eyes grew wide.

"This is the sacred dagger of Ptolemy. The Queen would never part with this," he said.

"I was to give that to you, to convince you to help me."

Jabari looked from the dagger to Na'eemah's eyes. A stern look came across his face as his sense of duty built within him.

"Then I will do everything you ask," he said.

Na'eemah knelt down and checked the guard. She realised he was still alive. Hathor's instructions came back to her.

Anubis will require a worthy offering.

She stood up and indicated the guard.

"Bring him. I think we may need his services."

"Services?"

"Well, we need him alive, for now anyway."

Jabari placed the dagger in his belt and picked up the guard. Na'eemah led him to the hidden door and they both moved down the stairway within.

The stables were empty of soldiers. To Na'eemah it seemed strange, the Romans were over confident, which was to her advantage.

Jabari prepared one of the fastest chariots, binding the

unconscious soldier so that he could neither escape or fall from the rear. He chose the fastest horse in the Queen's herd and harnessed him before they boarded and trotted out of the stables.

The city was dark and quiet. The Romans were still amassed at the port, in close proximity to their ships. Even the front gates were unmanned.

The chariot flew through the entrance archway and out into the night.

Within an hour, they arrived on the outskirts of the small town of Giza. The tops of the massive pyramids could be seen simply as black silhouettes that blocked the stars from view.

Jabari drew the chariot up to a small collection of huts at the base of the great Pyramid.

"Where is this temple?" asked Jabari.

Na'eemah shrugged.

"That was not told to me. I was hoping that providence would present itself," she said.

Jabari did not look convinced. He chose action instead and marched to the nearest shack and banged on the door.

An elderly woman wearing a bright red smock of woven cotton opened the door and smiled up at the tall black man.

"Yes?" she asked.

Before Jabari could speak, Na'eemah stepped before him and spoke.

"We are so sorry to bother you, we were sent to find the temple of Anubis. We have an offering for the God," she said.

The woman eyed Na'eemah. Her eyes fell on the handmaiden's necklace, which was all she now wore from her days as a priestess. It was a pendant made in the shape and colours of Hathor's headdress.

"Ah, you are a priestess of Hathor," she said, "Surely you need the temple of your Goddess. It is at the base of the Pyramid of Menkaure." She pointed off to the left.

"It was Hathor that sent me here. I must do as my Goddess says. The fate of the country and of our Queen depends on it," she said.

The old woman smiled at Na'eemah.

"I'm too old to be tricked," she said.

"No. No. It's nothing like that," Na'eemah said, "We have travelled from Memphis. The Romans have invaded. The Queen has been captured. Her only hope now are the Gods."

Jabari's composure was beginning to crack.

"This is getting ridiculous. We need an army not superstition," he said walking away from the doorway and heading towards the chariot. Na'eemah turned and cried out to him to stay, reminding him of his commitment to his Queen.

The old lady smiled and looked at Na'eemah. When the handmaiden turned back to her, the old woman began to change. Her face grew youthful and beautiful, her body also regaining years of lost youth and vigour.

It was the image of Hathor that Na'eemah had seen in the old temple. She was so shocked, she could hardly speak, but she managed to call out to Jabari.

He turned and spied the young Goddess standing in the doorway of the hovel. A golden corona of light surrounded the beautiful woman, lighting up the immediate area.

He stepped back towards her.

Hathor nodded at the chariot.

"You will need to bring the offering," she said.

Na'eemah and Jabari, carrying the unconscious guard, followed Hathor into the bowels of the little hovel. It wasn't just a hut but hid a subterranean entrance into a series of catacombs that wound under the area surrounding the great pyramid.

A stairwell led down into a large grotto. Hathor waved and several oil lamps erupted in flame, bathing the room in a warm yellow light.

A large statue stretched from the floor to the ceiling

and depicted the jackal headed god of the Underworld, Anubis. In the middle of the large flat floor before the statue was a stone altar. It had a vague outline of a body, with a small indentation where the head would lie. Channels had been carved into the flat stone, near the edge. Na'eemah realised the channels were used to guide any blood away from the sacrificial offering on the altar.

Hathor walked to a spot between the legs of the statue and nodded at the altar. Jabari roughly placed the guard on it. He grunted as he plonked down on the thick stone slab.

Na'eemah stood near the altar and looked up at the statue. She raised her arms and began to speak.

"Great Anubis. Your people face the greatest challenge in history. Our country has been invaded by barbarians from across the sea. They wish to rip our culture apart and replace it with their own. They will subjugate our Queen, kill our people and destroy our religion. The memories of you and your kin will be lost in the mists of time as we are forced to follow the false gods of the Romans," she said.

She waved a hand over the guard and said, "I, Na'eemah of Memphis, priestess of Hathor and handmaiden of our Queen Cleopatra, bring you one of the interlopers. We offer him to ask for your assistance."

The room remained silent. Na'eemah and Jabari

looked up at the towering statue, expecting at least some movement.

Hathor stood, a serene look on her face.

"Perhaps you need to make your offering more in line with those before you," she said.

Jabari looked at the altar. Dark stains could be seen in the ancient stone. The channels carved into the stone shared the same colours.

He withdrew Cleopatra's knife and approached the altar. Without waiting he slammed the knife down into the guard's chest.

"May your worthless life be useful in death," he said.

The guard let out one quick cry before falling quiet again.

The two humans and the God remained quiet, waiting.

Nothing moved. No sound came from the dark corners of the temple. No wind stirred.

After several moments, Na'eemah's head dropped in despair.

"We have failed," she said.

Jabari stepped forward and stood between the altar and the statue. He stared up.

"No, our sacrifice was not worthy, that's all," he said.

Na'eemah realised what he meant and gasped.

"No," she said.

Jabari raised the knife and placed the tip against his chest. He placed both hands on the hilt of the knife and readied himself.

"For my Queen," he cried as he prepared to drive the dagger into his heart.

A deep rumbling voice echoed out from all corners of the temple.

"Jabari of Argeen, there will be no need for that. Your Queen will need warriors of your loyalty in the fight to come. Lay down your dagger and know you have been heard," it said.

Jabari and Na'eemah stared up at the statue. The huge carved head tilted forward; the dark onyx eyes stared at them. The mouth moved as the voice spoke again.

"The two of you have shown loyalty above all others in these lands. While the rest of Egypt would happily join their ancestors in the afterlife, you alone have risked death to restore life and belief of the Gods back to this place. Although we bask in the death of humans, we need your faith to remain on this Earth. Otherwise we would just be spirits lost to history," the statue said.

Hathor smiled and nodded.

"Go. Return to your Queen," Anubis said, "On the morrow, you will find the miracle you seek. The power of the Gods is restored, and with it, the power of Egypt."

Na'eemah bowed.

"Thank you, Oh Anubis, thank you," she said.

Jabari bowed then wiped the dagger on the dead man's tunic and placed it back in his belt. He and Na'eemah climbed the staircase and left the chamber.

Na'eemah turned back to see Hathor once more. The goddess nodded and smiled at her priestess before disappearing from view.

As they reached the chariot and left the pyramids behind them, a great rumbling broke out underground. The residents of Giza were shaken awake and cowered in fear.

Deep below the Great Pyramid of Khufu an undiscovered chamber had been built. It housed hundreds of golden sarcophagi, laid in row upon row as if in a military formation. Upon each were lovingly laid the tools of trade of those who lay within. Swords, spears, shields, knives. All manner of weaponry.

A rumbling noise echoed through the great chamber. Then silence.

Slowly a single thump resonated across the room. It repeated until a cracking noise, as if a dry branch had snapped, reverberated out. A steady creaking followed by the crash as weapons slid from the lid and crashed to the dirt floor beneath a lone sarcophagus. A bandaged hand with fingers of dried skin covering bone poked out from beneath the lid and pushed it all the way open.

More thumps followed.

The sun shone down on Octavian's entourage as they formed up before the royal palace. The local populace of Memphis had been dragged from their homes by the soldiers and forced at sword point to line the nearby streets, with a selection led into the royal courtyard to witness the degradation and subjugation of their Queen first hand.

The assembled crowd was kept quiet and relatively calm only through the threat of violence from the nearby soldiers. Random complaints echoed out from the mob only to find an answer at the end of a steel blade.

Cleopatra appeared at the entrance to the palace and strode out into the sunshine. She stood at the top of the staircase leading up to the entrance, her hair shining in the sunlight, her beauty as radiant as ever. The throng hushed at the appearance of their Queen. Some cheered but were set upon by the soldiers and muted.

Octavian strode out and stepped up next to Cleopatra. The crowd hushed again.

The Roman raised his arm in salute to the crowd. His words drew jeers of ridicule from the people, but he continued on regardless.

"My friends, my new Roman citizens, I am Octavian. Your new leader. Your Queen has humbly relinquished her throne and ceded control of all of Egypt to the superior government of Rome."

The crowd erupted with booing and jeering, to the point that the soldiers feared they would lose control.

Cleopatra stepped forward and raised her hand. The crowd went silent, a hush of expectation ran from person to person.

"Do not despair for me, my people, know that you are always in my heart and I shall love you until the end of my days, as I know that you will love me."

The crowd cheered, the Queen waited until they quietened, she peered over and caught Na'eemah's eye. Her handmaiden smiled and nodded. Cleopatra turned back to the crowd.

"Egypt has faced worse in the past. Worse than anything the Romans can subject us to. Know in your hearts that the Gods and I will never let this country die."

The crowd cheered again, pushing forward and drawing the ire of the soldiers, and of Octavian above them on the entranceway to the palace. He turned to Cleopatra.

"Enough. You are not in command here, I am. It is time that these peasants saw that."

He took her arm and led her down to the chariot waiting at the base of the stairs. The Queen maintained her composure, ignoring her rough handling by Octavian as he dragged her to the chariot.

He pushed her to the front and her arm brushed the small bottle of poison. Her last mode of protection against any further indignity.

Na'eemah has until sundown to produce her miracle. I'm glad my final day has bloomed so gloriously.

Octavian stepped into the chariot and took the reins. The horses began to trot and took them along the wide road that led to the entrance gates. Agrippa's chariot fell into line behind them. Two others behind that.

The crowd waved and bowed to their Queen as she passed. Cleopatra maintained her composure and posture as she had in Alexandria. Her first thought was always to be the Queen.

The line of four chariots moved through the narrow gates and out into the wide-open main boulevard of Memphis. The local populace lined the streets, again, held in check by soldiers at regular intervals. The people booed when the chariots first came into view but began cheering when they caught sight of their proud Queen.

Suddenly, Octavian pulled on the reins to slow the chariot. Ahead of them, a group of figures marched out into the road and formed a line that blocked the chariot's progression. More joined them from the side until the line was several men deep.

Octavian stared at the figures. They appeared to be old men, dressed in rags and holding ancient weapons.

He burst out laughing.

"Is this the last of your famous Egyptian army? The league of retired soldiers?"

He turned towards his soldiers at the side of the road.

"Sergeant," he said to the nearest, "Form a guard and cut those men down like wheat."

The sergeant looked towards the line of men and quickly formed a squad into a phalanx. They drew their weapons and ran towards the line.

The sergeant stopped and observed the enemy. They were old. Their skin was cracked and parchment thin. He could see their bones poking through, and their teeth were exposed by their drawn back lips.

A touch of sympathy brushed across his mind, but he cast it away with thoughts of his duty.

"Attack," he yelled.

The squad stepped forward and thrust their swords into the nearest men.

The Egyptians were unmoved and unharmed. Each drew their own bronze sword from cracked leather scabbards, their muscles and bones creaking.

The Roman soldiers were so surprised when the

Egyptians' swords speared up through their chests and out their backs that they failed to even cry in alarm. Their blood washed out into the street before them.

The Egyptians withdrew their weapons and let the soldiers' bodies drop to the ground. They took a step towards Octavian's chariot.

He screamed at the other soldiers. They turned, drew their own swords and ran towards the advancing soldiers. The Romans arrived as one and were met with a clang of metal on metal, followed by their own screams as they were cut down where they stood.

Octavian's face dropped in shock. He wrestled with the reins and managed to turn the chariot around.

The sight before him made him scream in terror.

Another group of ancient soldiers stood side by side, blocking off his exit. One stepped forward, carrying the head of Octavian's general Marcus Agrippa. The general's face was frozen in a mask of horror.

Octavian stepped from the chariot. He looked around. His soldiers, his general, his army was gone. He drew his sword and held it forward.

"Put that down, you fool," came Cleopatra's voice from behind. "You don't know how to use it, and it will be useless anyway."

He dropped the sword with a clatter on the cobbled roadway.

"How?" he asked.

Cleopatra smiled. "My people asked for freedom, the Gods have smiled upon them and answered."

She pointed to the ground.

"Kneel before me," she said.

Octavian dropped to the roadway with an audible crack as his knees hit the stones. He winced in pain, but his face remained full of terror.

Cleopatra pulled the small glass bottle from her robes. She pulled the cork and held it forward.

"You have a choice, as did I," she said, "I will take you to Rome and parade you, as you would have paraded me, before deciding your final fate. Or you can take that away from me."

He looked up into her eyes. There was no sympathy there. He peered around at the damnation filled faces of the people he had tried to control and at the empty, yellow eyes of the dead soldiers.

His eyes fell back on the bottle. He reached out and took it from the Queen.

"My people will never submit to you," he said, "And neither will I."

He emptied the bottle into his mouth and swallowed.

The effect was immediate. His eyes bugged out of his head, his throat constricted, he let out an anguished cry as his air passages were cut off. Blood flecked drool spilled from his mouth. His entire face turned red with pain as the deadly poison sucked his life force from him.

The bottle smashed as it dropped to the road.

Octavian's body followed, his teeth and nose shattering as they met the stone cobbles.

Cleopatra looked down at the dead body of her enemy and smiled.

"From there our great Queen journeyed to Rome, not as a subjugated slave but as the ruler of all the known world. The Temples of the Gods of the Romans were torn down or converted to worship the true Gods. Any disbelievers were," Miss Henutsen chose her words carefully, "re-educated to a better way of thinking."

She turned and glanced through the large windows that looked out onto the modern, technologically advanced city of Roma. Gleaming skyscrapers reached for the stars. Golden chariots flew through the air ways, other sleek modes of transport ran along paved roadways below them. Tall monuments to the Gods stretched high above the people, demonstrating how important they still were.

"Two thousand years of peace has reigned since that day. All the other nations of the Earth were convinced to join with Egyptian culture. Now we stretch our wings across the solar system and beyond," she said.

Several hands shot up. Questions waited to be asked.

Edrice asked, "What happened to Na'eemah?"

"Ah, a very good question."

The teacher pointed to three identical pyramids perched on the outer hills of the city. Their outer shells formed of smooth marble as opposed to their time ravaged twins outside of Giza.

"You all know of the three great Pyramids of Rome," she said.

The students all nodded.

"They are dedicated to Queen Cleopatra, her son Pharaoh Ptolemy XV and his wife Queen Nefertakmun," she said turning and leaning in to her class.

"But did you know that whilst still a simple prince, Ptolemy took a simple handmaiden for his wife? A handmaiden who changed her name to Nefertakmun?"

She smiled as the light began to shine in the students' eyes.

"A handmaiden whose name was originally Na'eemah?"

They all gasped.

Abrax, a boy with a shock of strawberry blonde hair, piped up. "What about the mummies?" he asked.

"The legion of the dead followed our Queen to this place and stayed until their mission was fulfilled. Then one night they simply disappeared. Modern scientists have found the tomb where they wait again in eternal slumber until the day they are once again needed. It is guarded and remains untouched."

In the middle of the group, a small boy called Masuda looked up at the beautiful dark-haired woman. Her flowing red dress a bright beacon that fired off an everlasting love in his schoolboy mind.

"Miss," he asked, "Where are the Gods now?"

Miss Henutsen turned to the boy, a wry smile played across her lips. She fingered the gold and red necklace that hung around her neck. The deep red of the ruby shone as the light hit it, bathing the two golden horns that curled up either side.

"Oh," she said, "The Gods are still with us. They live among us, guiding our lives when required. They are happy now and no longer need to show themselves."

She leant forward and dropped her voice to a whisper. The children strained to hear but listened intently.

"Remember, if the peril ever becomes so great that our people, indeed our planet, is in the utmost danger, then the Gods will return."

STEPHEN HERCZEG is an IT Geek, writer, actor, film maker and Taekwondo Black Belt based in Canberra Australia. He has been writing for over twenty years and has completed a couple of dodgy novels, sixteen feature length screenplays and dozens of short stories and scripts.

Stephen's scripts, TITAN, Dark are the Woods, Control and Death Spores have found success in international screenwriting competitions with a win, two runner-up and two top ten finishes.

Stephen's stories have been published in: Sproutlings; Hells Bells; Anemone Enemy; Below the Stairs; Trickster's Treats #1, #2 & #3; Shades of Santa #1; Behind the Mask; Petrified Punks; Beyond the Infinite; Beginnings; Beside the Seaside; Sea of Secrets; Demonic Carnival; Storming Area 51; Coffins & Dragons; Through Death's Door and A Tribute to H.G. Wells.

His Sherlock Holmes pastiches have appeared in several volumes of new Sherlock Holmes stories from Belanger Books and MX Publishing.

Dozens of his drabbles have been published by Black Hare Press; Blood Song Books and Fantasia Divinity.

Later this year he will appear in: Journeys; Capricorn; Aquarius; Gemini; Sanitarium Magazine; Eerie Christmas; Pride; Bad Romance and Jibbernocky.

Connect
Amazon: amazon.com/-/e/B07916SQQS
Goodreads: www.goodreads.com/author/show/17100782.Stephen_Herczeg
Facebook: @stephenherczegauthor

ROMAN HIBERNIA

By Owen Morgan

Flames atop long poles jumped and danced in the fierce wind as sentries, outlined in the feeble light, stood to attention at the entrance to the Roman camp. Inside the commander's tent, Gnaeus Julius Agricola, Governor of Britannia, placed a stone on each corner of a flapping map which threatened to blow away. He glanced up at the sound of a challenge from one of the sentries.

He called to his aid, "Valerius, go forth and see who approaches our camp, and if it's beggars or merchants, give them a good kick up the backside and send them on their way. I'm only interested in the dethroned king of Hibernia whom we've heard about."

Agricola turned his attention back to the map of Hibernia which looked like a blob beside the roughly triangular shape of Britannia. His brow furrowed as he tried to sound out the strange place names. Valerius returned moments later with a redheaded man in tow. He was dressed in blue and green striped pants, his arms sleeved with light blue tattoos. Agricola stood to his full height, though still shorter than his guest.

Valerius, fluent in the Celtic dialect, waited to act as interpreter.

The redheaded man bowed. "My name is Túathal Techtmar, High King of Hibernia. I'm honoured that Rome would hear me. I've heard much about the power and glory of mighty Rome."

"A High King no less? Everyone knows there is a king on every hill in Hibernia. Tell me Techtmar what can you offer me?"

Techtmar's jaw trembled, and his cheeks took on a crimson hue to match his braided beard. "I have supporters, and they would be both eyes and ears. My scouts will be your scouts. If I am on the throne, then Rome has a friend, and I can stop the raids along the coasts of Britannia."

Agricola thumbed his chin. "Rome could use a friend in Hibernia. Tell me, will your people fight or shrink from battle and hide behind one of the many hills?"

Techtmar stepped back, his hand moving to his

sword belt, but the sheath was empty. Valerius pressed the flat of his blade against the High King's lower back.

Agricola smiled. "Good, that was the response I was looking for. I need auxiliaries who will stand beside Rome in the field." He waved at the Hibernian. "I forgive your reaction. Tell me more, is Hibernia endowed with anything of worth? From what I know, the island has nothing to offer but rain, hills, and bogs."

Techtmar spread his arms wide. "Romans harvest grain and Hibernia has rich soil and much rain, and many heads of cattle with which to feed larger numbers and provide leather for your sandals and belts."

Agricola turned to Valerius. "What say you?"

"We know he's a tribal chieftain. If we help crush his enemies, we could bring those sea wolves to heel, and those Hibernian pirates have been a plague on the west coast of Britannia for as long as we have been here. And we do have the necessary forces in northern Britannia and Caledonia, assuming Techtmar can guarantee the loyalty of the tribes under his banner."

Agricola tilted his head to Valerius. "See our guest out. Tell him we shall meet again on the first full moon in September. And remind him what happens to people who fail to honour their alliances with Rome."

Techtmar made an elaborate bow before leaving. Agricola frowned at the departing Hibernian king, unsure if the display was irreverent or a sign of a new alliance.

When Valerius returned, Agricola pointed to the map. "From which direction should we mount the invasion?"

"We should advance from Caledonia, as it's the shortest distance across the sea. With our mapping and conquest of the few inhabited islands off the western coast of Caledonia, we can easily cross without hindrance. I don't see why our troops couldn't complete the crossing in a single afternoon, provided we have favourable winds and a calm sea."

"I see. Make ready to send ships down the eastern coast of Hibernia and scout for anchorages and harbours. A thought occurs, why not have the XX Legion cross by the Island of Ynys Môn?" He stabbed at an island jutting out of the northwest corner of Wales.

"The island is a good place to launch the invasion from the west, but the western Welsh remain unsubdued."

Agricola chewed his lip as he contemplated the best stratagem. He produced three small wooden eagles, each representing a legion, from a pouch and placed one in Wales and two in Caledonia. "We shall be as the scorpion, one pincher from Wales to Drumanagh, and the other two toward Flower Hill and Feigh Mountain.

Then the legions can link hands and drive across the island. I predict victory by the autumnal rains."

Valerius cocked his head. "When we were in southwest Caledonia, you said Hibernia could be conquered with but a single legion. Has anything happened to change your mind?"

"No. But one of the privileges of command is the right to change one's mind. Have we any concerns in Britannia?"

"Our spies tell us all the local chieftains are content. We fear no uprisings. Though we must keep an eye on the Caledonian tribes, the auxiliaries can hold until the legions return, should this prove necessary. However, there is one thing which troubles me. We have heard about monsters which call Hibernia home."

Agricola wagged his finger. "Remember, we heard the same nonsense about how Britannia was populated with giants and great pearls? I don't think we have anything monstrous to fear in Hibernia."

"Would you permit a man who has no grey in his hair a wish?"

Agricola smiled. "Why not? What is your wish?"

"I would feel better if we made use of an auger."

"You wish to see how our expedition to Hibernia fares from a man looking at an animal's liver? I would rather eat liver than have an Etruscan look at it."

"Then, at least, permit some chickens on the voyage."

He sighed. "Very well. We'll take some chickens. They'll tell us whether the omens are good or bad."

The men of the XX Legion, attired in white cloth tunics and pants, trudged under the stinging midsummer sun, their armour swaying on poles slung over their shoulders. The men halted at the water's edge and waited for the flat bottom boats to take them across the narrow channel to what the Romans called the Island of Mona. Each legionnaire kept an eye on the farmers who laboured in the fields or to the distant trees and hillsides; the land, though under Roman occupation, was not safe. Roman garrison troops spoke of strange forms moving through the woods at night or disembodied voices whispering just out of sight. A few legionaries attributed the voices to the dead druids who they had massacred only twenty years earlier.

Agricola sat astride his black charger, watching the procession. "Valerius, do you believe the peasants are as impressed with the legionnaires as I?"

Valerius swatted at a voracious swarm of black flies with his horsetail whip. "Undoubtedly. I suspect they have not forgotten the brutality we visited upon them.

And to your point, I don't care if these benighted farmers are impressed or not. I just don't want them to stick a dagger in our backs."

"Well said. Tell me, are the signs and portents favourable for crossing the sea?"

"Both Roman and British priests speak of the two faces of Janus."

Agricola frowned. "What nonsense is this? Am I to invade either at the end of the year or the beginning of the next? I can't send the men across in winter. This is madness, what is the difference between a priest who can't give me an earnest answer and a lunatic who babbles at the moon?"

Valerius held out a coin depicting the two-headed god, Janus "I believe their message is this: the time for crossing is nigh, but returning will prove difficult."

"I'm satisfied we can cross, the fishermen who ply these waters have had nothing but calm waters and fair skies for a month. Send a messenger to High-King Techtmar. Tell him we shall land in Hibernia in four days, and his supporters had best be ready to receive us. Only that way can his tribes be assured of Rome's protection."

Four days later, a swell of sails fanned out across the rippling waters as captains brought their ships into a tight formation, not from fear of Hibernian vessels but to allow for a massed landing on a potentially hostile shore. Halfway across the waves began slapping against hulls and howling winds threatened to shred sails and collapse masts. A thunderous cracking of wood heralded the breaking up of a ship on the extreme right of the flotilla. A rocky outcropping just beneath the sea split her hull like a sword thrust into a man's guts. The ship broke apart, spilling men, horses, and crates into the churning froth. Men stretched forth pleading arms, but the storm carried away their voices then sucked them under, or dashed their bodies against ships or rocks.

Agricola, aboard the lead ship *Lion of Britannica*, swore under his breath. "Valerius, I thought the local sailors knew these waters?"

Valerius spluttered as he tried to hold down the contents of his stomach. "Yes, they did make that claim. Alas, we have no other guides. Do you wish to turn the fleet?"

Agricola slapped his palm on the rail. He spotted a horse, it's head just above the foamy surge, a victim of the foundering ship. "No, we press on. I'd rather sleep in Neptune's abode then return home empty-handed."

Cauldron-black clouds blotted out the sun, swallowing the world in darkness, the decks awash with seafoam, blood, and vomit. Sailors, below decks, pitted muscle against the sea as oarsmen moved in time to the drummer's beat. Two more vessels succumbed before the storm finished tossing the fleet like wine corks and leaving men and cargo bobbing in the angry sea.

The sea returned to a placid state without warning, the angry skies now a vivid, light blue. Agricola stood at the forepart of the ship, clutching at the soaked rigging. He observed a thin green line which coalesced into the bays and inlets of the Hibernian coast. "See Valerius, one only needs a steely resolve to conquer even the worst that the gods can throw in our path. He waved at the sea. "Oceanus, God of the Sea, I salute you, but I am the better on this day."

"My apologies. I did succumb to doubt." Valerius pointed to a large bay in the north. "I believe that is our destination."

Agricola jumped into the surf and waded through the hip-deep water, and splashed up to the beach. Only the vestiges of the storm greeted the Romans with drizzle and a light wind which caressed the tall weeds. Men, horses, and weapons poured from the ships. Within three hours, the might of Rome covered the beach. But none of the expected Hibernians greeted their Roman allies.

Valerius shook his head. "I don't like this."

Agricola folded his arms. "Now, what troubles you?"

"I thought Techtmar would have had at least a small party greet us at the beach. Where are his followers?"

"Secrets are like the wind, Valerius. You can't control them. Perhaps his force ran into enemies on their way here? In any event, I won't be dissuaded. Either a shower of coins or iron swords will give us the scouts we need. Fear not, I have brought the chickens as you requested."

Two slaves brought forth baskets filled with chickens, which darted forth once they were released. One of the slaves showered them with feed as Valerius and Agricola watched. One of the birds picked at the yellow feed.

Agricola smiled. "Are you satisfied? The birds feed, and our expedition shall meet with success—"

A cockerel spread his wings and crowed. The remainder of the chickens raced about in front of the slaves, some even took flight and disappeared into the surrounding bushes.

Valerius picked up a white feather as the slaves darted into the bush in search of the agitated fowls. "Shall we advance inland? I wouldn't want us to be caught here on the sand."

"Yes, only a fool would have his men on the beach."

The fields resounded with the tramp of iron-shod sandals as the XX Legion snaked inland, marching along what passed for roads, the ever-present green stretching beyond sight. Mounted men reported on the hour, but none found any sign of civilization. One man found the ruins of a hillfort, but the redoubt appeared abandoned for a long time.

They marched on through a tightly packed thicket which prevented sunlight from piercing the canopy. Even nature seemed to retreat before the Romans. No birds serenaded them from the trees or bushes, no deer or wolf appeared. A pack of wild dogs crossed their path but withdrew into the thicket.

Past the wood, a series of hills flanked either side of the trail. Some of the light troops mounted the knolls and scouted the area. These men returned and reported each of the mounds was a burial chamber with the doors facing toward the east.

Agricola made a dismissive gesture. "See if there are any valuables inside. If not, I want to press farther inland."

The scout paled and swallowed hard. "Begging the Governor's pardon, but all the doors are broken and—"

Agricola shook his head. "Scout, give me your report and nothing more."

"The doors are broken down. Some men ventured inside and down long passageways where they found three smaller chambers, each contained finery, and jewellry, but no bodies or bones."

"What are you saying?"

"The men, Governor...the men believe the doors were broken down from the inside...and the lack of bodies..."

"By all the gods. Forget the burial mounds. Gather your men and scout ahead for the legion and find a suitable spot to make camp for the night."

Valerius shook his head. "This is most unsettling."

Agricola rolled his eyes. "My friend, what troubles you now?"

"Surely, I'm not the only one who feels this island is touched by unworldly forces. We don't want the men speaking of spirits if more tombs are found opened and their occupants gone."

The long line of Romans trooped along the thin, dirt trail, men casting wary glances at the thick, dark woods and rolling hills. Valerius found the only life on the island, a swarm of mosquitoes supped on his flesh, leaving him irritated and red-marked. "By the gods, this island had best be worth the trip." He turned to Agricola. "Shall I consult the map?"

Agricola brought his mount to a halt. "Yes, I too

would like to know where the nearest tribe dwells."

Valerius unwrapped the parchment. "Here, we should be within three miles of the tribe known as the Eblani. As we march about twenty miles a day, this would put us within range of the Voluntii Tribe and perhaps two more. As you said, a king on every hill."

Agricola glanced at the sun. "I think it might be wise to make camp. We can meet the tribe in the morn. I have a disquieting feeling, Valerius. Techtmar is nowhere to be found. I wonder if he's betrayed us."

"Doubtful, as he knows about Rome's swift vengeance against the tribes of Britannia."

As the legion drew near a curve in the road, a man bent with age stepped out of the bushes. He leaned on his gnarled staff and eyed the invaders from beneath thick, wooly eyebrows. The first cohort came to a halt, and the lead legionnaire drew his blade and challenged the man. Agricola, frustrated by the sudden halt of his men, rode to the head of the legion. When he spotted the source of the delay, his voice betrayed his irritation. "What do you want old man? Have you had enough of this life you would cross a legion of Rome?"

The old man tried to bow, but his ancient bones refused. "My name is Arlan. I'm here to tell you to turn back, Roman. This island shall never be under the eagle."

Agricola smirked. "From which tribe do you hail old one?"

"I have no tribe. I am Hibernia, and Hibernia is me."

"I see. Do you have anything useful to tell me?"

Arlan dropped his staff, which clattered on the hard soil. He contorted his body and stood on one shaking leg, shut one eye, and jabbed a crooked finger at Agricola. "You are now cursed by the eye of Balor. Your armies shall shatter as the man who smashes his fist against a wall, and you will find no glory, only death."

Agricola turned to the first cohort. "An extra ration to the first man who rids me of this tiresome impediment to Rome's glory."

To his credit, Arlan didn't cry out when the legionnaires slipped a noose around his neck and hoisted him on a low branch. A raven landed on Arlan's shoulder after he ceased twitching. The bird scolded the Romans as they departed. The legion continued along the road, leaving Arlan swinging in the breeze.

The engineers identified a suitable place to camp and started trenching the area while soldiers placed sharpened sticks at intervals along the perimeter, and constructed wooden towers flanking the gates. Within two hours, the camp was divided by roads into four equal parts with Agricola's command tent at the centre.

At a safe distance from the tents, cooking fires brought the savoury smells of salted fish and meat. Valerius waited beside Agricola while slaves prepared the evening meal, cleaned his kit, and watered his mount.

Agricola nudged Valerius with his elbow. "Your natural pallor is returning. I didn't want to travel this island with the Green Man as my second."

"I do find myself wondering if my situation has improved, and I doubt I would do justice to one of the gods of nature. While my stomach has settled, my mind is aflame."

Before Agricola could inquire as to his distress, a sentry called out, "A rider approaches from the north."

Valerius and Agricola walked over to find a young man, his tunic dark with blood and sweat. Two soldiers helped the rider alight from his mount. A slave offered him water, and he slaked his thirst. The rider noticed the impatient Agricola and dropped the ladle into the bucket of water and bowed.

"I'm Antonio, scout for the IX Legion." He waited for Agricola to permit him to continue. "We have met with tragedy in the north. Most of the IX Legion is dispersed to the four winds. And many of the XV Legion perished in the sea crossing. We found many of their bodies flung onto the shore, driven by a sudden storm. The last I saw the auxiliaries and what legionnaires remained were trying to reform, but most of their heavy weapons and horses have been lost. And—" The man trailed off, unsure of his next words.

"Continue," Agricola said. "This Hibernia is a strange land, and I shall have no problem hearing anything you have to report."

"The seas raged, and men saw shapes in the water. When we stumbled ashore, some beast lumbered just behind the woods, it leered at us from between the trees, the head perched at a grotesque angle on its neck, one eye larger than the other. The thing laughed at us and retreated into the wood."

Agricola placed a comforting arm on Antonio's slight shoulder. "You have done well and are a credit to your legion. Can I expect any reinforcements from those in the north?"

"The commander survived as did many of his officers. Perhaps three thousand will come south. But they will not reach here for several days. Our scouts report large bands of warriors gathering inland. We don't know if they are friend or foe."

Agricola dismissed Antonio and signalled Valerius to follow him back into the camp. "I believe we have weathered the storm, so to speak."

Valerius cleared his throat. "What adjustments will you make to your plan? We have been reduced by two-thirds. Can we succeed with but a legion and a half?"

"Have courage, my friend. Once the tribes see the glory of Rome, we shall bring them to heel. Also, we have not met with Techtmar, and he will bring a good number of men to our banner. Tomorrow we make a grand tour of the hinterland tribes and meet with the survivors of the north. You will remember my original assessment called for but a single legion."

The wind returned with the night. Flashes of lightning illuminated the camp, and the air grew unseasonably warm. Horses stamped and tried to pull free of their lines. The wind died down to a low moan, replaced by singing, the mournful tones of a woman. Men emerged from tents and left cooking fires, enraptured by the pure lament. Though few understood the words, no one moved. Agricola stepped from his tent as his guards tried to shield their eyes from dust and debris from the gathering storm. Valerius, a cloth held over his mouth, his eyes red and watering, waved to Agricola.

"Who is singing? I've never heard anything so haunting," Agricola said.

Valerius nodded. "True, both chilling and spellbinding in equal measure. I should tell you, some of the sentries have reported figures moving toward the edge of the camp."

"Good. Perhaps these Hibernians have some iron, after all. I don't like night fighting, but it's better than waiting. I can't believe I am saying this, but I look forward to returning to Britannia."

Before Agricola's servants could finish strapping on his armour, the enemy struck. Large, lumbering shapes with uneven limbs and crooked backs smashed into the sentries, crossing the earthen ditch in but a single stride. The monstrosities, wielding tree-size clubs, maces, or greatswords, tore a bloody hole in the line, sending men pinwheeling through the air. An artillerist crew manning a large crossbow felled one of the attackers. The giant stumbled three paces before collapsing, the deep blue colour of its arm visible in the torchlight.

Screening cavalry fared little better, their mounts frightened by the scent of the nightmarish attackers. Some men urged the horses onward and hurled spears into the flanks and rear of the monsters. The brutish figures, some bleeding from great wounds, trampled tents, smashed men into pulp, and clubbed horses.

Valerius stammered, trying to find his voice. "The camp is under attack by the legions of the underworld. What manner of creatures are these?"

Agricola drew his gladius from its sheath. "We shall

have an answer when we examine their corpses."

Hulking shapes smashed through whole units of unarmed or unarmoured men. Roman discipline took hold. Centurions rallied their men into makeshift units and held the line along the main camp road. Ballista bolts sliced the air and impaled the giants. Agricola and Valerius stood beside the standard-bearer in the middle of the maelstrom.

"By the sword of Mars," Valerius called out to junior officers. "Reinforce the right flank. Get those men to their horses. Let's see how these brutes fare when men can thrust spears into their neck at eye height."

Thundering hooves, screaming horses, splintering spears, and inhuman curses reverberated throughout the camp. Agricola wielding sword and shield, waved his personal guard to follow. He staggered over bodies slick with blood and gore. A shadow engulfed him. Agricola glanced upward. A horse with the rider still in the saddle soared overhead. The shrieking beast and rider crashed with the splintering of bone. The horse lay on its side, legs kicking and flailing.

Agricola spotted one of the giants. Prying a javelin from a dead soldier's hand, he hurled the missile, skewering one of the creature's distended limbs. The monster whirled and stomped forward, one arm dragging along the ground. The enraged beast failed to notice the legionnaires who flanked it and hacked away at its legs and groin, it bellowed like a cow, falling under the assault. Legionaries cheered, swarming over the fallen giant, calling out praise to Mars, the god of war.

Chest heaving, Agricola took in the battle. Despite the initial surprise, the legion had rallied to the centre of the camp. A mix of slingers, archers, cavalry, and infantry held a shrinking ring. The giants, silhouetted by flashes of lightning against the broken walls of the camp, moved with inhuman speed, smashing and bludgeoning men with massive tree branches or bare fists.

Valerius, standard in hand, pounded toward him. "We have formed what remains of our cavalry in the south. In concert with the catapults and ballista, we might be able to drive these demons back into the night."

Agricola nodded. "Make ready then. Give me the standard, and I shall await the charge of these foul beasts."

The giants lumbered forward and brought the fight to the legion. But the average soldier, now supported by massed artillery, fought with the fury of cornered animals. Again and again, waves of enemies threw themselves against the Roman line and each time they broke against a wall of shields, spears, javelins, and swords.

Dawn caressed the land and drove back the night. The XX Legionnaires trudged through the carnage and surveyed the devastation. The giants had laid waste to half the area. The entire length of the north and west walls resembled a gaping wound, and the guard towers were now toppled piles of wood. Slaves and soldiers piled the dead and prepared to set the bodies alight.

Valerius, his head circled by a bandage, bowed to Agricola. "This expedition is at an end. We don't have the strength to impose our will. If the tribes attacked now, our armour would decorate some chieftain's hall."

Agricola clutched the eagle standard in shaking hands. "I don't know how I will live with this shame. I was there when we took Mona and slaughtered the druids, I marched into Caledonia and sailed around the northern tip of Britannia. What has happened? Why have the gods forsaken us?"

"We must make for the coast. There might be more of the giants."

Agricola swore as he smeared away hot tears born of frustration. "Any sign of the other two legions?"

"Our scouts are due back soon. I think it wise to march to them. We can then make a fighting retreat, if necessary, to the coast and sail for Caledonia. I don't want to land in Wales with our forces in such a condition. The Welsh tribes have long memories."

The XX Legion moved out, leaving clouds of greasy black smoke behind, each pall marking a funerary pyre for the fallen. Only the tramp of sandals against the grass broke the silence. Agricola rode near the head of the column. He took his mount off the road and watched the legionaries. A scowl marked his face—only yesterday he commanded a full legion, now only a shattered remnant trudged through the wilderness. By midday, scouts reported large numbers of Hibernians gathering on their flanks. The tribes sensed weakness and intended to turn a ruinous campaign into an outright slaughter.

Valerius, atop his magnificent steed, waited for Agricola at the base of a hill. "I have news which may hearten you."

"I would welcome good news. Have we linked hands with the northern legions?"

"Yes, we have. And even more promising, we have contact with Túathal Techtmar."

Straightening in his saddle, Agricola smiled. "The gods have tested us and now reward us. With the tribal allies, we can still conquer this island and bring it to

Rome's bosom."

At the confluence of two rivers, Túathal Techtmar, clad in a suit of chainmail and armed with a longsword and shield, awaited the Romans. The man stood at the head of a great host. The majority of the men sported shields and spears and wore patterned trousers and tunics.

Escorted by his personal guard, Agricola and Valerius rode over to greet their allies. Techtmar gave a curt nod. "You have finally arrived, Roman. But you appear to be heading in the wrong direction." He thrust the tip of his sword into the earth, making the blade wobble. "There is nothing but hostile tribes and wilderness to the north."

Agricola gestured at the legion. "We have met misfortune, but not defeat. In the dead of night, we were attacked by giants. Who are they?"

"Those are the Fomorians. They were the first peoples of this island. The land does not favour you nor Rome's rule."

"Never mind what those demons believe. How many warriors have you?"

"I can bring fifteen hundred spears and scores of charioteers."

"Excellent, the Hibernians are tempered for war. Two more legions are just a day's march away."

Techtmar sneered. "Who said we would help you? Look at the pitiful band behind you, and the others further up the road are no better. I wanted an ally, not a defeated army."

Valerius grasped the pommel of his sword, but before he could unsheathe the blade, a dozen warriors menaced him with spears. He released the weapon and waited.

Agricola sighed. "I shall remember this affront. Now all I want is to return to Britannia."

"I will not stop you." Techtmar waved to the north. "Next time, Roman, don't murder old men, and come with more legions."

The legionaries fought their way up the eastern coast, driving away waves of Hibernians by day and Fomorians at night. The three legions hacked a bloody path over the lush hills and verdant glens. On Agricola's express orders, all the horses and artillery were loaded aboard before the soldiers. This was a withdrawal, not a rout. At first light, the ships pulled away from the island and sailed across the narrow channel and back to the safety of southwest Caledonia.

Valerius debarked and fell to his knees, kissing the rich soil. Agricola shook his head. "It is a beautiful land, but I would not bow before it."

"I agree, but after Hibernia, even fighting alongside our noble dead on the Elysian Fields in the next life would seem like a paradise. I don't wish to distress you, but we need to have an official historical account of the invasion."

Agricola paced for several minutes, hands clasped behind his back. "When the historian arrives, make this account. We landed and were betrayed by peoples we thought our allies. The legions were overcome by both storm and treachery. I don't believe Rome wants to know the truth of the matter. Rome has marched to the end of the world, and we should go no further. Perhaps if we had conquered Caledonia first, we might have possessed the strength to take the wretched island."

"Do you think the emperor will allow you to retain your post? Some will say this is nearly as bad a disaster as the loss of the legions in the Teutoburg Forest."

Agricola gazed back at the sea which foamed and chopped against the shore. "I shall no doubt be recalled to Rome. In Germany, Rome only needed to contend with Arminius and his warriors, not deformed monstrosities."

Turning to Valerius, he forced a smile. "See to the immediate recruitment for the legions. The tribes of Britannia have never fully submitted to us, and they will make fine recruits. As for the Fomorians, they are another man's problem."

OWEN MORGAN writes science fiction, fantasy, and alternate history, and lives in the fishing port of Steveston, British Columbia.

Bibliography
Altered America, Martinus Publishing, 2014
2113: An Oral History of the Last God, Subtopian Press, 2014
Steamworld, Thirteen O'Clock Press, 2015
The Fall of Cthulhu, Horrified Press, 2015
Barbarian Crowns II, Rogue Plant Press, 2016
The Angel's Lamp, Rogue Plant Press, 2016
Attack of the Federation, Zimbell House Publishing, 2018
On Wings of Thunder, Cloakpress, 2018
Love, Black Hare Press, 2019
What If?, Black Hare Press, 2019
Apocalypse, Black Hare Press, 2019
Worlds, Black Hare Press, 2019

Connect
Blog: httpwwwkingauthor.wordpress.com
Twitter: @owen_morgan1066

THE TURF WALL

By Raven Corinn Carluk

Drusus and the Second Legion build the Emperor's wall block by block, day by day, while the Pictish warriors and witches watch and wait for their chance to bring it all tumbling down.

Drusus slammed the last block into place, completing the course, and stepped away with a groan. The Vallum Aelium had grown half a meter since he had started this morning. Only three and a half meters remained, then on the next section.

Same as it had been the day before, and the day before that, and every previous day for the last five years.

The legionnaire wiped sweat from his brow. It was never truly hot in the northern reaches of the Empire, but labouring beneath the unrelieved Britannian sun was nonetheless brutal. Drusus once more felt grateful that his cohort had not been assigned to the block fields. Laying the heavy pieces of turf was far better than cutting them free of the ground. It had a mindless monotony that he had become used to, had gotten good at.

"Hail, Drusus." Sergius approached, smiling too broadly, looking fresh although work had begun near dawn. He didn't care for the centurion's optio, but what was a mere fighter supposed to do about the second-in-command? Best to keep his head down, keep working, and take pride in his own work rather than worry about others.

"Hail," he replied brusquely, slowly reaching for his cart of turf blocks. Perhaps the smaller man would take the hint and leave. Drusus worked the first section of the vallum, just behind the team laying the foundation, because he was faster than any three men combined. Partly due to his size and stamina, but mostly because he didn't allow himself to become distracted.

"Perhaps some water, before you return to your labours." Sergius proffered a bulging water skin, his smile faltering only slightly.

The optio shunned manual labour like it was a diseased rat, so Sergius would only be this close to the construction if he wanted something. Drusus wouldn't allow personal distaste to outweigh the need for a drink, but he wouldn't indulge the man for longer than necessary. Grabbing the skin, the big man began gulping down cool water. He didn't stop even when he tasted the wine mixed in with it.

"If you continue to lay courses this fast, you may well finish this wall on your own. Emperor Aelius Hadrianus himself would honour you." Sergius glanced over his shoulder to watch Drusus empty the skin. "You would receive many laurels, even with your Germanian blood."

He capped the skin and glared down at the optio. Sergius was not a small man, lean and well-muscled, but Drusus towered over him. There were jokes that he was part bear, that he would go into hibernation once the great vallum was finished and there were no more Picts to fight.

"What might I do for you?" Drusus asked in a gravel tone. His Germanian blood prevented him from ever ascending rank, but his father's honour had given him a home in the Legio secundus Augusta. The Roman Empire ran on order, and the Nullpriests feared that men like Drusus could one day unleash barbarian magics, had most of them exiled or sent to the gladiator arenas. His fellow legionnaires accepted him as a fighting man. Pricks like Sergius enjoyed needling him about his mixed heritage.

"Yes, well," Sergius swallowed hard, not quite a gulp, and took the empty skin. "Several of the centurions have been talking about the Picts. The speculatores have given their reports, and I was sent to receive yours."

Drusus drew his brows together, his glare softening to a look of confusion. "What report?" He was no scout, hadn't known he was supposed to watch anything.

The optio gestured around the valley, taking in the under construction Fort Camboglanna, the recently finished milecastle, the block works, the River Irthing, and the group of Pictish warriors camped on the far bank. "Them. Have you anything to say about their activities?"

He turned his curiosity to the Picts. They'd been there since the legion laid the first foundations in the Cambeck Valley. A dozen warriors in furs and blue paint, one small fire, and a hide tent. Drusus was normally too engaged in his work to truly notice, but he'd yet to see them do anything but watch.

"There are more of them," Drusus said. He counted two dozen Picts, rangy men with a variety of weapons. Some of them might have even been women. Impossible to know for sure from here; they all favoured long hair and kilts, and most of them were too thin to have noticeable breasts. "When did they arrive?"

Sergius made a scoffing noise, shaking his head. "This is why the priests won't let your kind achieve ranks. Only good for manual labour, none of the positions that require true mental effort." Drusus swallowed a retort, as he'd learned to do in his youth, though it was harder with this optio. "I suppose during all this formidable wall building you've been doing, you haven't seen the other newcomers." Sergius pointed sharply at another camp farther to the northwest.

Drusus followed the direction of the gesture. He focused on whatever task he was assigned, putting the entirety of himself into it. If he was on guard duty, he would notice every leaf that fell and every blade of grass shifted by the wind.

But he was assigned to the wall, laying course after course of turf blocks, so all he noticed was how many blocks he had laid already and how many were left on the cart. He watched only his own work. Not even the work of the others.

He certainly hadn't noticed the encampment of light-haired warriors join the Picts.

Drusus straightened his spine, pulled his shoulders back, and glared at the newcomers, his focus shifting from the vallum to potential enemies. He took in as many details as possible from that distance, mentally preparing for attack.

Nearly two score of kilted warriors stood in silent ranks along the riverbank. No fires to be seen, their tents tucked into the shadows of the trees, horses grazing on the slope behind them. Most of them were sandy blond, but several had fiery red hair. Like embers amongst ash, or blood drops in snow, the bright red drew the attention of all viewers.

"Are those..." He started to ask their race, but Drusus noticed two women, standing just behind the ranks of fighters. Tall, statuesque, wearing long kilts and meagre breast coverings, a glint of gold at their throat and wrists. The one on the left held a white staff, black hair in a single braid hanging over her shoulder. The other woman carried an eagle on her left forearm, blood red hair dancing on the breeze. A sword hung at her hip, and the tone of her shoulders suggested she knew how to use it.

The cant of her head suggested she was looking directly at him.

"Hibernian? Yes, we believe so. They began to arrive three days ago, but those two witches appeared only this morning." Sergius made a sign to ward off wild magic.

Drusus took a step closer to Sergius, fists clenched but voice calm. "How did Hibernians cross the sea? Haven't we maintained a peace with Pictavia? Has there been any word from Oengus?" He tried to maintain at least a passing knowledge of potential enemies. The secundus Augusta was the first line of defence against barbarians that threatened the Empire.

The other man snorted. "As peaceful as their kind can ever be. An envoy was sent to their king, such as he is, but we have received no word back as of yet. Perhaps our party was attacked. Perhaps they are being kept at the Pictavian capital as hostages, and we have not received the ransom request yet." Sergius spat. "Perhaps they have eaten our men."

Distant rumbling reached his ears. There wasn't a cloud in the sky, making thunder impossible. Drusus searched and quickly confirmed his theory; the Primus Turma was on the move.

"Those stupid cunts." Sergius swore again. "They were supposed to wait for my return before sending the horses." He set his fists on his hips, planted his feet, and glared at the Pictish encampment. "We might as well enjoy the encounter."

Drusus clenched his fists, shifting from foot to foot. His weapons and armour were at the encampment, halfway back to the milecastle. He'd never felt so vulnerable, trusting in others to protect him and the rest of his cohort while they worked on the vallum. The legio vigesima Valeria had secured a peace with Pictavia before the Narrow Wall was finished, making the need for patrols cursory.

But watching thirty eques legionis approach the Pictish camp, Drusus longed for his gladius.

The Primus Turma forded the river, sunlight glinting on their harnesses and armour, moving at a steady trot, pennants snapping on the breeze. Evenly spaced, horse necks arched, they represented the ordered power of the Empire.

The Picts remained where they stood, loosely gathered on the upward bank of the river, not even touching their swords. Compared to the men of the Empire, they were tall and slim, pale with light hair, lacking armour. No one seemed bothered by the unit of horsemen closing in on them. Almost as if they were all old friends getting together.

Drusus looked to the Hibernians. The foreign warriors remained still, hands at their sides, watching the contingent of eques legionis. The two women had shifted, the black-haired one levelling her staff at the other camp. She gestured, and the hairs rose along his arms.

"Are those women—" He shuddered, swallowed, and started again. "Are they magic users? Wild magic?" Drusus gritted his teeth, making the sign against the barbarian power, just as the Nullpriests of the Empire had taught him.

Sergius spat and made the sign again. "We believe

so. Nullpriest Justinius has begun the rites to strengthen the wards. Keep their filth from crossing the border and polluting our works."

Drusus had been raised to understand the power of order, the same as every citizen of the Empire, and to hold true against the call of wild magic. Because of his Germanian blood, he'd received extra attention and lessons. Many in the priesthood worried he would revert to his barbarian nature, but the legionnaire could never see that happening.

Living on the border, he'd become intimately familiar with how the wild ways worked. So very destructive. Untamed. Like fire escaped a forge, burning everything in its path. He never wanted to be like that. Never wanted to harm the glory of the Empire.

The Primus Turma spread out in a semi-circle, confronting the Picts. Spears remained up in a non-threatening position, and the horses stood at attention, unmoving. The wind couldn't carry their voices this far, but Drusus imagined the decurion telling the barbarians to disperse back to their lands or face the consequences.

Pictish warriors laughed and jeered, making obscene gestures. A pair of them started a chant that was quickly picked up by the rest. The entire group was soon chanting, dancing, mocking the contingent before them.

The black-haired Hibernian woman lifted her staff,

and thunder rolled across the valley.

His mouth was filled with the taste of wildflowers and honey and lightning. Drusus took a step back, every nerve alight with inner fire. What in all the hells had she done?

The horses bucked and thrashed while their riders attempted to control them. Not just a little restless, the beasts appeared to go wild. The Picts jeered and laughed as the Primus Turma scattered, though no one attacked the helpless soldiers.

A legionnaire lost control of his spear. Drusus tensed as it flew, glinting in the sun before burying itself in the chest of a small Pictich warrior. There would be no maintaining order after this death, no matter how accidental. The day would only end bloody.

He hesitated. Should he run for his weapons? It would take time to reach his tent in the camp, and he would be turning his back on the battle. Should he charge and join them? The long-handled spade in the cart would work as a makeshift weapon until he could claim something off the battlefield. Most Picts used stolen legion weapons anyway, so he would simply be reclaiming a familiar blade.

The Pictish warriors stopped their hollering and stared at their fallen comrade. The Primus Turma continued to struggle with their mounts, and some had been thrown, their horses returning across the river. No one else attacked, though the barbarians began to stir and approach.

Drusus couldn't leave his fellow soldiers to fight alone. The taste of honey and lightning grew stronger as he grabbed the spade and ran toward the skirmish on the riverbank. He was only one man, but he could make enough of a difference until the riders dismounted. His instincts screamed at him that they would never get the horses under control, that the black-haired woman had everything to do with that.

Hairs rose along his arms as he ran. Drusus glanced at the Hibernian encampment and increased his speed.

The foreign warriors mounted their horses and trotted toward the Primus Turma. Even the two strange women mounted up, though they rode slightly behind their men. The redhead gave her eagle a kiss, then launched the bird into the air.

Behind him, Sergius shouted and began his own run. "To arms! A runner to the milecastle. To arms." His voice grew quieter as he made his way to the camp. Drusus wouldn't have to hold the Hibernians off for very long. If all things went well. He refused to think of anything going wrong.

Legion horses galloped past him, riderless, eyes wide with fear. For every one that passed, the sharp tang of lightning filled his mouth. The Nullpriests kept the legions protected, but the woman's wild magic was too strong, had clearly overwhelmed the wards laid on the bridles. Neither the horses nor their riders could prevent the arcane attack, and Drusus could think of only one way to stop her.

Death.

He was forced to slow his charge when he reached the river. The horses were able to ford the water easily, but Drusus struggled against the flow. Cold water battered his calves, then his knees. Halfway across, he was up to mid-thigh, the current and slick rocks attempting to rob him of his balance. Drusus growled beneath his breath, watching the Hibernians reach the Primus Turma. He needed to go faster but was unable to.

The Hibernians were at a full gallop when they crashed into the scattered cavalry. Hooves churned up turf and rocks, the thunder of their passage filling the air and rattling his chest. Horseflesh slammed into the soldiers, crushing them, trampling them into the ground.

The men that weren't felled by the horses were cut down by the swords of the Hibernian warriors. Blood splashed and legionnaires fell. Nearly half the Primus Turma were killed or wounded on the first pass.

Drusus surged out of the river and up the shore,

unleashing a mighty yell. He wore no armour, had only his significant skills to protect himself, but he didn't think about any of that. He was focused only on the fight, on killing the enemy, on being the best warrior he could be. Sharp tingles ran across his nerves and he joined the battle.

He flung the spade, sidearm, and it spiralled through the air. The head struck a Hibernian fighter in the throat and knocked him off his horse. The roan bucked as its rider fell, but continued running with the others.

Drusus raced to the fallen barbarian, scooped up his sword, and stomped on the man's neck. His enemy gurgled, eyes bulging, and reached for the legionnaire. Drusus finished him with a quick thrust, then faced the enemy mass as they wheeled their horses.

"On me," he bellowed, adjusting his grip on the sword. Eighteen Primus Turma men joined him, some with swords drawn, others with spears at the ready. Some of their wounded crawled toward the river, attempting to escape the next charge, but there was nothing to be done for them.

The Hibernians slowed to a canter for their turn, and quickly returned to a gallop as they charged once more.

"Sidestep and slash," Drusus bellowed. The legionnaire had faced very few charges during his years, but he knew how the Germanians had faced cavalry, how the Batavian detachment at Fort Camboglanna did it. He hoped the men beside him heard him, that their nerve held in the face of that much horseflesh.

The ground shook beneath the pounding hooves, rattling through his very bones, and Drusus tasted lightning on his tongue once more. He prepared to move, to cut the horse from beneath its rider, but his feet were suddenly too heavy, like he stood in sucking mud. That damn spellcaster must be working her wicked magics.

He roared, a sound of anger and frustration. It resonated from deep inside his chest, from his very soul. Drusus raised his sword, screaming into the face of his enemies, and took a step, swallowing down the sharp electric taste.

The other legionnaires moved and swung, most of them avoiding the charge. Seven horses screamed, stumbled, and threw their riders. Unwounded mounts raced past, then slowed for a third turn.

Drusus lunged, stabbing a fallen horse in the throat, then slashed its rider in the face. The Primus Turma did the same, killing as many as they could, creating hazardous conditions. Enough obstacles would prevent the third charge, would force the Hibernians to fight on the ground. Removing the horses would provide them an advantage, would give the remaining cohort time to arrive.

Pictish fighters engaged their flank, howling their eerie battle cries. Cavalrymen took wounds, but did not fall to the initial strike. They swung swords and thrust with spears, drawing the blood of the blue-painted barbarians. Several fell, but others took their place. Outnumbering them by only a handful of men, the Picts fought with wild ferocity, although without the skills of the Imperial legionnaires. They had never stood a chance in fair combat, despite their numbers.

Drusus let his brothers-in-arms deal with the Picts, giving the Hibernians his full attention. They were unknown, thus the greater danger.

The Hibernians halted, hanging back on their restless horses. Fallen mounts trumpeted in pain, men groaned in agony, but no one moved. Thirty-three foreign barbarians sheathed their swords and stared, waiting, changing the tempo of the battle.

He lunged forward, sword raised, and gave another battle cry. Drusus needed to keep them engaged, keep them from regrouping, but he couldn't charge them alone.

"We need to hold the ford," one of the Primus Turma said to him, breathing hard. "Keep them from crossing into the Empire."

Drusus's blood ran hot, nearly blinding him to all the strategy and training he'd received. The taste of honey filled his mouth, called to a wild place in his heart, and all he wanted to do was continue the fight. He wanted the lives of his enemies. He wanted to become an instrument of death until no one remained.

The women rode to the front of the line, and Drusus realized it was their wild magic attempting to drive him crazy. The redhead threw her head back and screamed in her native tongue while the black-haired woman levelled her staff at the remaining legionnaires.

Drusus lowered his sword, stunned by what had almost happened, and stepped back. For his entire life, he'd been warned of the dangers of his barbarian blood. Part Germanian might as well be full Germanian. Feral and dangerous, hungry for blood. All his restraint had fled at the faintest touch of wild magic, just as the Nullpriests had predicted.

"To the ford!" His voice rolled across the hillside, and the other legionnaires began to fall back. The Picts harried their flank but were unable to fell any of the cavalrymen. Half of them were dead by the time the Primus Turma reached the shore, further evening the odds.

"They're coming," a young man in the back cried. His voice rang with relief and panic, though mostly the latter. Too few of the men working at the vallum had faced actual combat. "The whole camp is coming."

Picts continued to throw themselves against the Primus Turma, losing another four of their number to take two of the legionnaires. Drusus shifted toward them, keeping his eyes on the Hibernian lines.

The black-haired woman shouted something, and the Picts fell back. "Leave them," Drusus commanded before any of their men followed. With his head cleared, he wanted to simply hold this position. Reinforcements would be here soon enough. If they remained patient, they need lose no one else.

Embers glowed at the end of the magic woman's staff. Faint, small, but swiftly growing in brightness and size. Drusus narrowed his eyes, watching as they began drifting to the ground, nestling into the grass.

Flames leapt to life, dark red, roaring as they licked at the surroundings.

The men around him gasped, murmured, and pulled back. Drusus held strong, though nervous sweat beaded along his spine. The flavours grew stronger, and he spat in attempt to clear them. Could they hold out until the others arrived? The Primus Turma wore Null-spelled armour, might survive whatever magic come at them.

But they hadn't been able to resist the spells that

drove the horses away.

The Hibernian warriors dismounted, eyes locked on Drusus and the Primus Turma. Horses tossed their heads before wandering back to camp as if they hadn't just been in battle. Their riders stepped over the fire, approaching the shore. Flames flared at their back, becoming an impenetrable wall.

Drusus knew there would be no avoiding further bloodshed. The most they could hope for was to take as many of the barbarians to the afterlife as possible.

The remaining Picts joined the Hibernians, marching closer as the fire raged behind them. One of the barbarians whooped, then another, and they all began jogging toward the beach.

"Hold," Drusus encouraged. "Steady." He shifted his grip on the sword, took a step forward, and locked eyes with the Hibernian in the centre of their line. "They will not pass us." He practically growled, pulse thundering in his ears.

Forty barbarians ran into the legion line, howling their war cries. Swords clashed when men came together. Blood flew, the dead fell, and the legionnaires sold their lives dearly. Superior training beat raw savagery and numbers.

Drusus fought with a fury almost as great as theirs. His sword seemed to be everywhere at once, blocking thrusts, batting blades aside, slicing unarmoured flesh. He killed one man, and two others took his place. It seemed they would never make a dent in the barbarian forces.

Flames raged behind the Hibernian line, taller than a house, hotter than a furnace. The heat scorched the air and nipped at their skin, drying the very breath in their lungs. Drusus took a step back with the other men, seeking relief from the unnatural attack. Water lapped at their heels as they entered the river.

Cool air suddenly filled the area. Not a breeze, but a stillness. The fire protested, flaring higher, burning almost black, but it could not compete against the supressing chill. The flames brightened, stilled, then shrank.

Drusus sighed in relief. His very eyes felt blistered, and he had nearly lost his grip on his sword. With the fire gone, he felt renewed. He thrust, driving his sword into a bright-eyed barbarian, then kicked the man out of his way. He dared glance over his shoulder to check on the reinforcements.

Seventy-five soldiers of the legion double-time marched toward them, composed of mixed centuries, swords bared and armour dull beneath the sunlight. Other lines moved out from the milecastle, and in the far distance, the Secundus Turma assembled their horses before the fort.

Sitting astride his horse three meters behind the reinforcements, Nullpriest Justinius gestured and chanted. He wove strands of anti-magic, smothering the power of the Hibernian witches. Order would be restored.

Drusus cheered, and several of the others lifted their voices with his. The barbarians could not withstand a Nullpriest of the Empire. He resumed the battle with renewed vigour.

Twenty Hibernians and seven Picts remained, not counting the two witches. Without their magical flames, and with more legionnaires arriving, they could only retreat. Keeping their swords up, the barbarians moved backward step by step.

Drusus had to press the advantage. Allowing the attackers to escape would set a bad precedent, would make the Empire look weak. He roared and charged, swinging at his enemies. The remainder of the Primus Turma followed him.

The Hibernians refused to engage, maintaining a gap between the lines. Smoke stained the air from the scorched grass, but the area remained cold and still. Drusus felt the Nullpriest's protection, and it was almost like wearing his warded armour. He felt neither wounds nor fear. Time to do the Empire proud.

He bounded forward with a fierce swing, caught the thigh of a retreating warrior. The man fell, but a flash of swords from his fellows kept Drusus from finishing him off. He countered their defence, cut another Hibernian across the bicep. A cavalry spear thrust lodged in the barbarian's throat, and the warrior fell.

The Hibernians put up a strong defence, though they mostly retreated. The fierceness displayed earlier seemed to have faded with the arrival of the Nullpriest. Everyone in the Empire was taught of barbarian cowardice, of how weak they were without the fake strength of their magic. Drusus killed another man and knew it to be true.

"Cowards!" Drusus lunged, swung, met nothing. The Hibernians retreated faster, though they had not turned to run yet. "Fight us," he challenged, his comrades close at his side. None of them seemed willing to let their enemies flee; too many fallen soldiers required vengeance for any quarter to be given.

They crossed the line of scorched grass, and the chill in the air immediately lifted. The Hibernian warriors all smiled, eyes sparkling, and parted around the two witches.

Drusus met the gaze of the redhead. Time came to a halt for him in a haze of honey and wildflower and lightning scent.

She was the same height as a man, but with all the curves and hollows a woman should possess. Emerald green eyes sparked with inner light, like gems in firelight. A smile spread across her milky face, and the scent of flowers grew stronger.

Her voice echoed inside his head, as clearly as if she spoke, though ten meters separated them.

You're not Roman.

Drusus never saw her lips move, knew nothing of how she put her words in his mind, but he managed to respond. *I am. I will kill you.* He tried to move, but the moment remained frozen. *What wicked magic do you work?*

I wouldn't be able to speak to you if you were Roman. Germanian, I'm guessing. You smell delightfully of their fearsome blood.

Get out of my head, witch! Anger pulsed in his veins, blurring his vision. Drusus blinked, and it seemed his hand moved a hair's breadth.

Don't you want to hear my offer? She continued when he didn't immediately rebuke her, *You needn't die with them. Our peoples, our cousins. You would be welcomed on our march against the Empire.*

He couldn't believe what she was saying. This raggedy group of barbarians thought they could take on the Roman Empire? None had been able to resist the might of mother Rome, let alone pose a credible threat. Gauls, Germanians, Keltoi, all had felt the crushing power of the Empire and her Nullpriests.

This rebellion of yours will fail, he told her. His arm noticeably moved, and he focused on his anger to drive her out. "You...will...die!" Drusus roared, breaking fully free of her spell.

Their conversation had lasted for less than the blink of an eye. The Hibernians were still lining up beside their magic users. The Primus Turma were still stepping forward and swinging their weapons.

The air still reeked of honey and lightning.

Flames roared to life behind them, hotter and higher than before. Men shrieked in agony as they were engulfed in magic fire. Some threw themselves to the ground, some ran, and a few attempted to lunge back into the Nullward.

Drusus's calves were scorched in the initial flare up, but he gave the pain no mind. He continued his battle cry and lunged forward, intent on the red witch. She smirked, but he saw nothing more than a throat that needed to be sliced.

Talons dug into his shoulders, wings slapped at his face. Drusus stumbled to a halt to swing at the eagle attacking him. Blood ran into his eyes as the beast tore at his scalp with its beak. His shoulders burned, and his right hand weakened on his sword. The reek of magic around it told him the foul woman was controlling the beast.

He managed to bat the eagle off, then swung his sword at it. The bird shrieked and flapped away, and Drusus took a moment to gather his breath. Wiping the blood from his eyes, he scanned the battlefield.

Most of the Primus Turma struggled with the flames. Their armour did little to prevent the fire from eating greedily at their flesh. Screams rent the air as they attempted to put themselves out, all thoughts of fighting lost in the frenzy of survival.

Across the river, the approaching reinforcements paused, a small wall of fire forming on that bank. Justinius gesticulated furiously, mouth agape, clearly attempting to nullify the barbarian magics.

From the forest behind him came pounding and bellows. Drusus turned, blood dripping into his eyes again. Even without the red drops blurring his vision, he wasn't sure that what he saw was real.

Three hundred Hibernian warriors rode forth, horses tossing their heads, swords drawn. Picts came as well, running for the river, moving too fast to be counted.

Alongside the warriors were bears and stags and wolves. Ravens cawed and circled, hawks and eagles soaring above them. Riderless horses joined the line, pawing at the ground and chomping their bits.

Drusus swallowed hard, straightening and drawing his shoulders back, ignoring the way his heart stumbled. He was alone on this side of the Rive Irthing, and there were only seventy-five soldiers on the other bank, but there was an entire cohort within a mile. Three more in the next two, and the rest of the Legio secundus Augusta not far. Several unattached battalions at the fort also waited for orders to attack.

Nothing the Hibernian witch could summon would survive the just wrath of the mighty Roman Empire.

He laughed, pointing his sword at the redhead, ignoring every other opponent on the field. Drusus held no hope for his own survival. He never had. The immortal Empire was all that mattered, and it would always shine. "You've failed. And now you will die."

The black-haired woman raised her staff. The wind gusted, driving the flames higher. Heat scorched Drusus, drying the sweat on his back, crusting the blood running from his wounds. She chanted, and her staff glowed with an icy nimbus.

Animals began the march from the tree line, forming a line in front of the men. The air reeked of magic, more lightning than honey, and it pressed against his skin like humidity. Warriors followed behind, lifting voices in an ululating chant. Up and down it went, matching the steps of the animals.

Drusus charged, intent on the red-haired woman. He could die satisfied if he slew her. The attempt itself would earn laurels for his name. The success would hearten the legion, would prove to the men that these barbarians were all show. Calling a few woodland creatures from the forest only looked impressive, but was not enough to stop the Empire.

She gestured, smiling, and several Hibernian warriors tackled Drusus mid-charge. He stabbed one of them, non-lethal, and struggled to cut himself free. They pummelled his joints, using their combined weight to bear him to the ground. Drusus growled, trapped, and glared up at the redhead as she rode closer.

"You had your chance." She lifted her arm, and her eagle landed. It gave its cry, staring at Drusus with one gold eye. "And now, you cheeky bastard, you get to watch as that wall of yours is torn down." She laughed.

The Hibernians forced him to turn, keeping him on his knees. Drusus trembled, using all his strength in an attempt to stand. Someone dug fingers into the talon wounds, and the pain blinded him, buckled his knees. Breathing hard, he bided his time and surveyed the scene.

Dark red flames consumed the bodies of the fallen,

dancing with the scented wind, throwing embers toward the sky. Justinius had kept the second fire from gaining a foothold, and the reinforcements threw sand at the fire, attempting to smother the remaining flames.

Lines of troops dotted the hill, pouring from the milecastle and worker encampment. Drusus gave a cheer at the sight of the Empire's glorious legion. There was no doubt in his mind how this day would end.

"Here they come." The witch's voice was pitched low, almost that of a lover.

The hands holding him relaxed, and Drusus surged to his feet. He could still kill the woman. He turned, swinging his sword, but all movement was arrested by sight of the newest opponents to take the field of battle.

Dragons soared overhead.

He counted three, then seven, then fifteen. Immense creatures, flying too high for him to properly judge their size. Covered in spikes and claws, they looked like death incarnate given wings. One roared, broke off, and dove toward their location.

What could stand up to such fearsome beasts? The Empire had weapons against barbarians, trolls, ogres, sea serpents, and magic users, but there were no dragons in any of their lands. No siege weapon could target one before it stuck, and foot soldiers were helpless against them.

The witch laughed. "Maybe you'll come with us to Rome. How would you like to watch it fall?" The diving dragon unleashed its fire upon the far bank, enveloping soldiers in flaming death. They burned too fast even to scream.

Drusus sank back to his knees, sword falling from numb fingers.

RAVEN CORINN CARLUK writes dark fantasy, paranormal romance, and anything else that catches her interest.

She has authored and self-published five novels and one novella, where she explores themes of love and acceptance. She has also self-published two collections of short stories, ranging from the lustful to the horrific, the darkly humorous to the tragic. Her shorter pieces, usually from her darker side, can be found in several Black Hare Press anthologies, at Detritus Online, with Fantasia Divinity, and through Alban Lake Publishers.

Bibliography
All Hallows Blood, RCC Tales, 2011
ANGELS, Black Hare Press, 2019
BEYOND, Black Hare Press, 2019
Coffins & Dragons, Dragon Soul Press, 2019
Deep Space, Black Hare Press, 2019
Handmaid, RCC Tales, 2012
Midsummer's Unveiling, RCC Tales, 2012
MONSTERS, Black Hare Press, 2019
Nomycha, RCC Tales, 2018
Saint Valentine's Clash, RCC Tales, 2011
stories with bite o,.,o, RCC Tales, 2010
stories with fang o,.,o, RCC Tales, 2011
UNRAVEL, Black Hare Press, 2019
WORLDS, Black Hare Press, 2019

Connect
Website: RavenCorinnCarluk.Com
Amazon: amazon.com/author/ravencorinncarluk
Smashwords: smashwords.com/profile/view/RavenCorinnCarluk
Twitter: @ravencorinn
Facebook: RavenCorinnCarluk

BLOODSONG

By Umair Mirxa

ALL SAINTS DAY - 1ST NOVEMBER, 866 CE
CITY OF YORK, KINGDOM OF NORTHUMBRIA

Brynhildr staggered as she struggled up to her feet and wiped the blood and sweat from her face. The searing pain in her left leg made her eyes water. Smoke from a dozen, scattered fires veiled the carnage which surrounded her. Slowly, she stood, and in the brief respite she had won, restored calm to her breathing. It took more effort than she had expected to withdraw her sword from the chest of the last warrior she had slain. He had been better skilled than most, and had earned a glorious death. A score of his companions lay dead around him, all of them felled by her sword.

"You should tend to the wound," said a voice in her head. She welcomed its gentle embrace, savouring its touch, drawing strength from it.

"It will heal presently, my lord," she thought in response. "I have suffered much worse in battle."

"It is never brave to act the fool. Take a moment. If you will not do it for yourself, then act as scout for me. There is much I cannot see from my vantage."

Her vision cleared, the sounds of battle struck up a crescendo, and the pain in her leg mellowed to a gentle cadence. She retrieved her helm from beneath the body of one of her victims, and found her ox horn still hanging from her belt. The note she blew upon it rang clear amidst the chaos and soon inspired a sight most welcome. She watched as her pegasus flew in ever lower circles before landing gently beside her. A brief moment later, she was flying high above it all, surveying the death and destruction below.

Mayhem reigned supreme on the battlefield. The winds howled, baiting the heavens into perilous challenge. Thunder roared in response, splitting the clouds asunder with a bolt of lightning, majestic with calamitous intent as it smote innocent Earth. Two score English warriors were burnt to a crisp where they stood, the roar upon their lips hushed before ever it was born. Shards of frost whistled through the sudden rain and shattered into sundry pieces a dozen Norse berserkers, their smiles forever frozen upon their faces.

Here, two English wyverns snapped and clawed at the wings of a Norse dragon. There, archers cut their fingers to the bone playing a melody of despair upon their bowstrings. Arrow upon arrow they shot at the dwarves, and yet in vain, for the shield wall was impenetrable, relentless in its unforgiving march. The fae fled before the elf, gentle enchantments frail and futile set against ancient dark magic. Earthen giants tore into the jötnar with bough and root, and were driven back savagely by spears of fire and frost.

The cavalries on both sides had been all but decimated. Dozens of enemy knights lay dead or dying among hundreds of foot soldiers. Berserkers and shield-maidens alike had fallen by the score, limbs entangled in final embrace. Death made no distinctions. Not for love or loyalties. Not for rank nor for wealth acquired in life. It cared but in equal measure for the wise and the fool, the poor and the rich, the strong and the weak. In the end, it came for them all.

Magic wielders in both ranks had wrought their own particular manner of havoc. Several among their number now lay dead, vanquished by powerful spells or by errant bolts when their wards had failed. Druid and monk, shaman and sorcerer. English and Norse. The archers had played their role, and suffered for it too. A scattered handful of them were yet alive, in either army, most with arrows spent and quivers empty. It mattered little, or not at all, in the moment, for no arrow could find its mark now. Fires burned in the rain, the earth was rent open, and smoke made it impossible to aim, whirled around by strong gusts of wind. The hum of magic yet lingered upon the air, and lent it hues both strange and marvellous.

Brynhildr laughed, nigh delirious with cruel ecstasy as she basked in the devastation before her eyes. Her sisters would be busy tonight, she thought. The ranks of Valhalla were going to swell with warriors, mighty and noble, their songs to be sung for ages to come. She sent a quick prayer to Odin, hoping such would be true of her own song.

There were a hundred ways to die, thought Brynhildr, standing watch under the stars at night. She was destined to die in battle. Of that, she was certain. For years beyond count, in one war after another, in more battles than she could remember, she had sought eternal glory. On the fields outside York earlier in the day, she had wondered if, at long last, it would be her final adventure. The enemy, however, had been routed ere dusk, and the city had been taken before nightfall. Her fate, once again, had been denied to her.

"I bring a message, my lady," said a gruff voice. "From the Lords Ivar and Halfdan."

She turned to see a grizzled old warrior, deeply scarred and with fresh battle wounds, standing nervously behind her. All men were thus affected by her. The nobles and the slaves. The brave and the timid. On most occasions, she enjoyed it, and even took advantage of it, but such was not her mood tonight.

"Speak, then," she said.

"You have been invited to the main tent," he said, his voice and tone at odd contrast. "Th-there to share in a drink, celebrate our victory, and to take counsel for the morning."

"You think we could do it all in one night?" she said, chuckling to herself at his discomfort. "Go, tell them I shall be there presently."

She watched him leave, and let a long sigh escape her lips. One night of peace and quiet. Was it really too much to ask?

Brynhildr had watched thousands of men and women, elves, dwarves, and giants, fight and die at her side. Many more had fallen by her own sword. In quiet moments of contemplation, often as she lay alone in bed of a night, she had found herself envious of every one of them. A terror had taken hold of her heart on rare occasion. What if she lived to be old, frail, and wrinkled, only to then die and be condemned to Helheimr? It was a fate her kind were protected against but what if she were to displease Odin? The Wanderer was not known to forgive easily. Would he then strip her beauty, her youth and immortality away?

For all her desire of a glorious death in battle, Brynhildr did take immense pleasure in life, and in the living of it. A few weeks ago, she would readily confess, she had thought herself to be entirely happy. The memory of it came to her now, fresh and clear. She had woken early on a morning, and in particularly good spirits. There had been a song upon her lips as she indulged in a long, luxurious bath, followed by a scrumptious breakfast of sausages, eggs, mussels, and mead.

Nothing, she remembered thinking as she walked out of her house, nothing could ruin her mood that day. Her hair shone, and her armour, polished to a gleam, sat on her better than ever before. Men and women alike gawked at her, their eyes windows into lust, envy, and desire. She took a detour across town for a visit to the beer hall. There, she pulled the maiden she was presently in love with aside, and stole a quick kiss. The girl, in return, treated her with one of her tinkling laughs, and a flagon of fine mead. Brynhildr felt like a Queen.

She smiled at everyone on her way from the beer hall to the longhouse from where Björn Ironside ruled over his people, and arriving ten minutes too early, found she was late for the council. Her eyes met those of her lord, and she stood rooted as he chastised her without ever having uttered a word. No one else present perceived what had just occurred, and yet, she felt a profound sense of shame as she took her place at the table.

Her lord's displeasure at her tardiness proved to be but the beginning of a good day quickly gone sour. Not long thereafter, she had been summoned to war, and before her day had ended, her splendid early morning mood had been spectacularly ruined.

"My friends," said King Björn Ironside from the head of the table. "It is a good day today. A day of hope, and we must celebrate. Drink with me. Skol!"

"Skol."

The word rang around the table as all present raised flagons of mead and followed the king's example.

"You are aware, of course, that we have been searching for an item for a very long time now," said King Björn. "Its true nature has been kept from you, and must yet remain a secret. However, it is my pleasure to share with you the news of its discovery. We believe it is hidden in the English city of York."

"Glorious news, indeed, brother!" exclaimed Halfdan Ragnarsson. "We must prepare a raid immediately."

"No," said Ivar the Boneless, in his quiet, venomous manner. "Our usual raids will suffice no longer. We shall not raid York. We shall not loot it for plunder and spoils."

"Not even for the women, brother?" asked King Björn with a chuckle, raising loud guffaws from everyone at the table.

Even Brynhildr had to smile. She knew, from personal experience, some of those English women could be quite scrumptious. If they were indeed going to York, she for one would certainly look forward to the pleasures on offer.

"Of course, the women," said Ivar with a smile, joining in the merriment for but a moment. "Yet we must go now, not to raid but to conquer. First York, and then all of England."

The mood at the table changed quickly. Brynhildr watched her lord lean in and hurriedly exchange whispers with the king. The jarls traded murmurs, and Ivar smiled again, this time with true pleasure.

"Such is not our purpose, Ivar," said King Björn.

"Why is it not? Even if we find this mysterious item there, I say we make it our purpose to take York, and hold it. Use it as a stronghold where we can winter. A base from which we can conquer England."

From there, the only recourse left had been a vote, one which Ivar's proposition won unanimously. Brynhildr too reluctantly voted with the ayes, for even if she hadn't been hilariously outnumbered, the quiet nod by her lord left her with no other choice. The final straw which broke her day was her lord then pledging, on her behalf, her services to King Björn, and placing her under his command for as long as the war were to last.

"Why did you do it?" she hissed at her lord, having cornered him as the king, his brothers, and his jarls left the room. "I do not wish to serve him."

"Why not?" said her lord in a calm voice. "You have served others before him. In any case, it is of no great import. For ultimately, you serve me. Always. Do you truly wish to be relieved from your bond of service to me?"

Brynhildr felt her breath catch, and imagined herself gone as pale as the white cape hanging from her shoulders. Her lord turned and left without another word, even as she stood there quaking in her boots. It was as if her lord had pronounced a death sentence. To be released from service was the absolute least of her desires, the greatest shame for one of her kind. She cursed the war, and all the years it had now raged on, and hoped York would be the end of it.

For nearly eight decades she had fought, and thus far, it had all been in vain. She feared now it might so continue for another age to come.

Well did she recall how it had all begun, and everyone she had watched die in battle, at her side or by her sword. Some she remembered more fondly than others. The memory of one man, the first under whom she had served by her lord's command, brought a smile to her lips. She made her way back to the beer hall, the thought of him on her mind.

…

8TH JUNE, 793 CE - CHURCH OF SAINT CUTHBERT, HOLY ISLAND OF LINDISFARNE

Eirik, Jarl of Björkö, stood tall at the prow of his longship and grinned with savage pleasure at the sight before him. The jubilant blowing of horns, accompanied by boisterous cheers, from the two other longships made it clear his countrymen had espied the same vision.

"We made it!" the cries rang out. "Row! Row for the shore."

"It is nice to see a smile again upon your lips," said Brynhildr, moving up beside him, grinning herself from ear to ear. "My sword too aches for battle."

"I fear it may be all too brief."

"Yet glorious nonetheless."

"Indeed," he said. "Have we received word from Lord Sigurd?"

"No. My lord and your own yet trade whispers together, and we remain the strangers to their thoughts."

"We will hear something soon. Go now, and prepare."

Brynhildr turned from him with a scoff, and he stood watching her for a moment, appraising the delights of her form. In all his years of manhood, she was the only woman to deny him. Quite naturally, it made him desire her all the more, and she yet refused to share his bed. *One day soon,* he thought. A different note upon the horns drew his attention. Their ships were now within a spear's throw from land. He shook his head clear, and found his mind wandering down the same path upon which her thoughts had turned.

Lord Sigurd had indeed become more distant by the day since the arrival of his mysterious guest, a man known to Eirik only as Valdemar—the lord Brynhildr inexplicably served with such fierce loyalty. It had been the stranger who had set them on the course they found themselves on today. For years, they had done as he bid, even if the commands they followed were issued by their own king. Eirik, despite his misgivings, chose to trust in

Sigurd's wisdom, and hoped the matter, whatever it truly was, would soon come to a resolution.

For here, now, was the beginning of an end to their arduous quest. Here were the riches so long promised to them. Here was the fame, the eternal glory Eirik and his warriors had yearned for these past few years. Long and hard they had searched, with burning desires in their hearts, and yet seemingly in vain, for what now lay within their grasp. Six weeks they had been at sea, on a voyage not without its peril. Storms, one after another, had chased them down and thrown them off course. Rations had run low, and fatigue had taken its toll. Lord Sigurd, struck by a sudden sickness, even now lay recovering on his own longship.

In the moment, as the early morning fog lifted its veil and parted before his eyes, Eirik let forth from his lips a primal laugh. He begrudged it not. None of it. Not the toil of the past four years nor the travails of the journey. Not the secrets kept and maintained by their strange companion, and certainly not the increasingly fickle moods of his king. For here were the fruits of their labour. Here, at long last, were the shores of fabled England.

The locals, as Eirik understood it, believed it to be a place of miracles. They had buried a saint here, and made pilgrimages to the site. Offered treasure in exchange for protection. Eirik laughed again, gathered his shield, and jumped out of the longship into the shallow waters as it approached the beach. *Oh, I will show them miracles,* he thought, landing with a splash. He would show them the error of their ways, and in the bargain, take from them everything they had hoarded away.

Eirik drew his axe across the monk's throat, slitting it open, and let the man crumble before him. He looked around and espied Brynhildr slashing open with her daggers two other monks. She roared with pleasure as they fell, and the sound of her laughter rang across the monastery grounds.

The Jarl of Björkö felt himself stiffen with arousal as she walked over to him, blood splattered across her face and chest, a wide smile playing upon her lips. He had never before laid eyes upon such beauty. The bright gold of her hair, the shimmering blue of her eyes, and all the wondrous rhythms of her body, they made him ache with desire.

"Why won't you come to my bed?" he asked, oblivious in the moment to the cries of battle and the screaming of the monks around him.

"Prove yourself worthy, and maybe I shall," she replied, the sound of her chuckle drowned by the horns blowing upon their ships.

"We have been summoned," he said tersely. "Do not think it over. We shall revisit this conversation presently."

"Oh, I shall wait with bated breath," she said, teasing him as they made their way back to the longships.

Valdemar stood waiting on the beach as they approached, and discovered most of their fellow warriors, with monks to be sold as slaves in tow, making preparations to depart.

"It is not here. We shall have to try elsewhere," he said to Brynhildr before turning to Eirik. "Let loose the dragons before we leave. Burn it all down."

"I do not take orders from you," said Eirik with half a snarl.

"My words merely convey your own king's command. You may go to him and verify them if you so wish."

"I would rather hear from *you* why we are leaving here so soon. You promised us wealth and eternal fame. We have found naught but trinkets and a few worthless slaves. Why now should we listen to you?"

"All will be revealed in time. Do not forget what I told you the day we first met."

Eirik stood in the sand, fuming as the lord turned from him and took his place on King Sigurd's longship.

He watched him go, and thought of all the times over the years he had wanted to plunge his axe deep into Valdemar's chest. The dragons rose, released from their chains, and from aboard his own ship, he watched them unleash their fury upon Saint Cuthbert's church. His men rowed, pulling them away from shore, and for a long time he watched the king's ship, his thoughts turning to the day he had first met Sigurd's new friend.

…

12TH APRIL, 789 CE
TEMPLE AT UPPSALA, ÖSTRA AROS

Eirik drained the flagon of mead dry and deposited it into the arms of the young maiden passing him. He slapped and squeezed her buttocks, and chuckled drunkenly when she blushed and squealed.

"Find my chambers, and wait for me there," he whispered in her ear, planting a rough, wet kiss on her flushed cheek. *By Odin, she is pretty*, he thought as she nodded and turned even deeper shades of crimson.

The summons could not have come at a worse time, Eirik thought with a groan as he watched the girl scurry away. He wiped his mouth with a large hand, tugged his tunic straight, and stepped into the king's chambers, hoping his arousal was not obvious to the stray glance.

"Ah, Jarl Eirik," said King Sigurd with a wide smile. "Excellent. Come join us. The smoked goose is succulent, and the *bjórr* some of the finest I have ever tasted."

Eirik had the impression he had interrupted a deep conversation. He did not recognise the man at the table with his king. Even with the hood drawn forward so it obscured all but his beard, Eirik felt certain he would recognise one such as his king's mysterious guest. He knew the man had not been a companion on their journey to the temple, and wondered from where he had sprung. How had he gained admittance to the king's chambers? There was an aura to him Eirik was not entirely willing to trust. Not yet.

A woman stood in the far corner of the chambers, near sullen and entirely silent. Tall and golden-haired, voluptuous and strong. She had a dagger upon her belt, and a sword resting against her leg. The cape upon her back was as snow on the mountains in winter, and her eyes a bright, blue ocean on a gentle summer day. *Now her,* thought Eirik, *I could trust, with all I have, including my life.*

The stranger, for his part, had made no attempt at a greeting, no move to even acknowledge Eirik's presence. He sat a giant, a god carved as if in stone, alive only in the gentle fall and rise of his broad chest. The bowl before him lay clean, his flagon dry and turned on its head. He had partaken of neither food nor drink. A pipe, freshly used, sat next to the bowl, and the scent of *angelikarot* was yet strong in the room.

"Thank you, Lord," said Eirik, moving forward to take the proffered chair. "I have had my fill of food tonight. The *bjórr*, however, I will gladly accept. If I may light my own pipe?"

"Of course, of course," said the king pleasantly, raising his own flagon in salute. "Skol!"

"Skol. My King, I was told you had urgent need of my counsel."

"Indeed. Eirik, my friend here, you may call him Valdemar. He has come to us tonight in dire circumstance, and he seeks our help. I must, in turn, ask it of you. Will you lend us your support?"

"If you ask it, of course I will, Lord. Who, if I may…"

"Ah. His true identity, I fear, must remain a secret. Yes, even to you, Eirik. Now, does your answer remain the same or must I look for help elsewhere?"

"No, Lord. I serve at your command. What is it we must do?"

"There is an item, Jarl Eirik," said the king's mysterious guest, leaning forward and speaking for the first time. "One of great import. We have been content, believing it to be safe, but it can no longer remain where it presently lies hidden."

"What item? Who is we?" asked Eirik, then let out a frustrated growl, realising his questions would not receive any response. "Alright. Where is it hidden?"

"We do not know," said Valdemar, speaking quickly past Eirik's exclamation. "It has been lost to us for years."

"So why go looking for it now?"

"There have been alarming rumours of late. News of grave concern. Given the circumstance, we believe it is imperative this item be retrieved before it falls into the wrong hands."

"I ask again. What is it we must do? What do you expect of us?"

"Why, help us find it, of course. I need warriors. Strong men and women I can trust. I need longships, for I do not yet know where this quest might take us. Provisions, too."

"So, let me see if I understand you correct," said Eirik with half a snarl. "There is an item you have lost but we do not... *I* cannot, know what it is, and you do not know where it is hidden."

"Yes."

"You will not tell me why you need it nor who you are, but you expect my trust, my help. You want me to place my warriors and my ships at your disposal?"

"It is exactly what I want you to do. I shall pay for it

all, of course, in gold and silver. Unless I am much mistaken, there will be plenty of loot and plunder too along the way. More than you and your people can spend in three lifetimes."

"How do I know I can trust *you*?"

"It is not him you have to trust, old friend," said King Sigurd. "The choice before you now is to trust me...or not. You are under no obligation here. I shall go, and I hope you will join us. I will, of course, understand if you choose otherwise."

"You ask a lot of questions, Jarl Eirik," said Valdemar. "All I can tell you now is if you do decide to come, you shall win eternal fame, and glory such as none before you have known. I must take my leave. Whatever your decision, make it soon, and let it be known to Brynhildr here. She will stay and help you prepare."

7th November, 866 CE - City of York, Kingdom of Northumbria

Deep inside a crypt, a hundred feet below the blood-stained, cobblestone streets of York, they stood before the item they had sought for nigh on a century. Brynhildr looked around the chamber, at her own lord, and all the kings and jarls, the warriors and shield-maidens there present. The search, the quest, the war. It was, at long last, all over. She could rest now. They could all, if they so willed it, return to their homes, and rest. By Odin, they had earned it, and paid for it handsomely in sweat and tears and blood.

She looked at Björn Ironside. Solemn and strong, magnificent. A man she had come to admire as a true king. Would he learn, as his father had known, of her lord's true identity, and of what he sought?

Eirik, the Jarl of Björkö, had died in old age, still asking questions, the answers to which he would never receive.

She glanced at Halfdan Ragnarsson, tall and proud, arrogant yet noble. A fierce warrior, worthy of Valhalla. Ivar the Boneless sulked to one side, contemptuous as ever of all and everything before him. *Hel will claim him*, thought Brynhildr. She winked at Freydis, the shield-maiden she had taken for consort these past few days. To Eirik, the berserker they had shared together in bed, she gave a quick smile. Last, her eyes turned to her lord, cloaked and hooded as he ever was in company. He gave no sign of joy or satisfaction in victory. No pleasure nor delight in finding successfully what he had sought for so long. He but stood in silence with his head bowed, his arms folded across his chest, and his feet planted firmly apart.

"Clear the room, please," he said now, so quietly at first almost nobody heard him. "I need everyone except Brynhildr to leave."

"What do you mean?" asked Björn Ironside, looking up in surprise.

"You know it well, Björn," said Valdemar, pointing to the tomb in the centre of the chamber. "What lies within is not for your eyes. It is for mine, and mine alone. No one else."

"I do not know what lies inside but I have come, *we* have come, too far and sacrificed far too much to turn away now."

"We are not going anywhere," said Ivar with a sneer, even as Halfdan nodded in agreement to his words. "You would not have it without us, without our help."

"Open the tomb before our eyes or not at all," said Halfdan, his hand straying to the hilt of his sword.

"Very well," said Valdemar slowly, searching each of their eyes. "The three of you may stay. No one else. They must go."

King Björn nodded his consent, and with dismay, much grumbling, and plenty of whispered complaints, everyone else filed out of the crypt. Brynhildr watched them go, and sealed the gate shut behind them.

"If you had not been the sons of Ragnar Lothbrok," said Valdemar with a quiet vehemence. "If I did not owe your father a great debt of gratitude, your insolence would at this very moment be severely punished."

Four swords were drawn in the next heartbeat. Three of them now pointed at Valdemar's throat, the fourth aimed at Ivar's chest.

"Drop your sword, Boneless," said Brynhildr. "Or feel the wrath of mine."

"You dare threaten us?" roared Halfdan.

"If our father had not charged us with your care," said Björn. "You would have been dead long before now."

It began quietly, with a chuckle so light even Brynhildr could not tell its source. Slowly, the sound grew, until Valdemar was roaring with laughter. The sons of Ragnar, their eyes wide with surprise, were so shaken by it they lowered their swords, and stood staring at the cloaked and hooded figure.

"So, quite often in our time together," said Valdemar as he calmed down, yet still sniggering to himself. "You have, each of you, made attempts to discover my true identity. Let me reveal it to you now. Brynhildr, if you would open the tomb."

"My lord, are you certain?"

"Quite so, dear one. I believe they have earned the right."

The three brothers stepped forward and looked down into the tomb even as Brynhildr pushed aside its lid. Valdemar chuckled again, as one after the other, they gasped at the sight before them. In that moment, he chose to remove his cloak and push away the hood from his face. A light shone forth from it, illuminating the entire crypt, brighter than a thousand candles.

Brynhildr smiled to herself as the sons of Ragnar dropped to their knees as one and bowed their heads in reverence. It warmed her own heart to once again gaze upon the cherished face of her lord.

"Lord Balder," said King Björn. "Forgive us, I beg of you. Had we known…"

"Stand now, Björn," said Balder, God of Light, and son of Odin. "You two, as well. There is nothing to forgive. You have acted, all of you, only as I would expect from any son of Ragnar. He looks down upon you now from Valhalla and is proud."

"Thank you, my lord," they murmured.

"Lord, is it truly…"

"Yes, Ivar," said Balder with a smile. "It is truly as you suspect. Mjölnir, the hammer of Thor, my brother. Now, I will be able to wake him from his slumber. For Ragnarök is upon us, and we shall have sore need of his help ere the end."

"Ragnarök is near, my lord?" said Björn.

"Yes, Björn. For you, there are yet ages to pass before it. The grandchildren of your grandchildren will be long dead ere it comes. For the Aesir and the Vanir, however, it is as tomorrow."

"Do you know, lord," asked Halfdan. "Or can you tell us if we might fight in Odin's army on the day?"

Balder smiled gently and looked at each of the brothers in turn for a long moment.

"This I will tell you before I go. For all you have done to help me recover Mjölnir, the songs of your names will be sung throughout history even unto its last day. When the Twilight of the Gods approaches, you shall stand and fight once again at your father's side before the world is submerged."

"Thank you, Lord," said the brothers in chorus again, Balder's own light reflected upon their ecstatic faces.

"I must bid you farewell now. Brynhildr shall accompany me, for even I cannot pass the gates of Valhalla absent a Valkyrie at my side."

UMAIR MIRXA lives and writes in Karachi, Pakistan. His first published story, 'Awareness', appeared on Spillwords Press. He has since had stories accepted for publication in anthologies from Zombie Pirate Publishing, Blood Song Books, Black Hare Press, Iron Faerie Publishing, Clarendon House Publications, and Fantasia Divinity Magazine & Publishing.

He is a massive J.R.R. Tolkien fan, loves everything to do with mythology, fantasy, and history, and wishes with all his heart that dragons were real. When he's not writing, he enjoys reading novels and comic books, playing video games, listening to music, and watching movies, TV shows, and football as an Arsenal FC fan.

Bibliography

ANGELS, Black Hare Press, 2019
APOCALYPSE, Black Hare Press, 2019
BEYOND, Black Hare Press, 2019
Blaze, Clarendon House Publications, 2019
Curses & Cauldrons, Blood Song Books, 2019
DEEP SPACE, Black Hare Press, 2019
Divinity, Iron Faerie Publishing
FLASH FICTION ADDICTION, Zombie Pirate Publishing, 2019
Galactic Goddesses, Fantasia Divinity Magazine & Publishing, 2019
MONSTERS, Black Hare Press, 2019
Of Kami & Yokai, Fantasia Divinity Magazine & Publishing
Poetica, Clarendon House, 2019
Summer's Splash, Fantasia Divinity Magazine & Publishing
Tempest, Clarendon House Publications, 2019
UNRAVEL, Black Hare Press, 2019
Waters of Destruction, Fantasia Divinity Magazine & Publishing, 2019
Winds of Despair, Fantasia Divinity Magazine & Publishing, 2019
WORLDS, Black Hare Press, 2019

SON OF THE DEVIL

By Zoey Xolton

Traded to the enemy in exchange for a tenuous peace, the young prince Vlad grows to become a killer of great renown—but he is so much more. A close brush with death, and a chance encounter with a beautiful, dark witch, changes not only him, but the fate of Wallachia forever.

Time is an illusion, it is said, the creation of man existent only to give meaning to the endless procession of days and nights through which we must march ever onward. Time, or more precisely, the lack of it, makes human life precious—our short years, the fragility of our form. From the cradle to the grave, the life of one man is measured in memories. Love, family, the fruits of his labours; these moments are treasured, etched in the mind, until the day that we breathe our last.

But…what if your last breath never came? What if the welcome embrace of death eluded you? What if you couldn't be killed? What if you were truly immortal? What of time? What of the burden of memory? I speak from experience when I say that the pain of loss only amplifies with time. I have heard philosophers and doctors of the mind say that it fades, leaving naught but a scar, a mere reminder of something that once was. However, I have found the opposite to be true. Perhaps it is an easy thing to say, when one does not have to endure more than a single, solitary lifetime?

Through all my long years, through the centuries I have lived—if lived is what you would call it—the traumas of the past remain fresh and raw in my mind. Like festering wounds, they taint my thoughts and colour my view of the world around me. The demons of eras gone by haunt me, forever reminding me of the mistakes I have made and what they have cost, not just me, but those I once loved.

Time has been no salve on my wounds, nor a balm for my heart. Time is all I have, and he is a cruel master. With each day that I exist, he continues to fuel my sorrow, and the rage that I have carried for more lifetimes than any one man could ever dream.

I am Vlad Drăculea, once called Vlad the Third, son

of Vlad Dracul the Dragon, and perhaps most infamously, I have been known as Vlad the Impaler. But most recently as simply Dracula. I am what man calls a vampire. Once feared, a living nightmare in the shadows, a beast, and monster, a warrior on the field of battle…now, no more than a ghost. To the world, I do not exist. At best, I am a memory, a snapshot in the annals of time, a Voivode of ancient Wallachia; a man, some say a hero, who lived and died; a mortal man.

What I truly am has passed into myth and legend, alongside the werewolf and baba yaga; and yet here I am. Ever present, ever watching, as man marches to the steady, relentless beat of the drum. The world is more connected, and more populated than it has ever been. The barriers of land, sea, and language? A thing of the past from which I was born…and still, I am more alone than I have ever been.

I miss my wife, my son, my country and speaking my native tongue. I miss water and wine, warm meals, and the comforting sounds of a land still wild and untamed, not yet industrialised and deforested. My pain could swallow me whole, plunging my soul into eternal despair, were I to dwell on such things. Perhaps, if I were to share with you these memories, my story—of who I was, and how I came to be—the weight of my burden would be alleviated, even if only for a short time.

Let me take you back to old Wallachia, to the ancient Kingdom of Hungary, when I was but a boy, and entirely mortal, when I knew not what bitter plans fate had in store for me.

"I am afraid, Father," I say, small fists clenched by my sides as the emissaries of the Ottoman sultan, Murad the Second, await me. My father, Voivode of Wallachia, holds my shoulders tight as he kneels before me, his heavy brows furrowed.

"Fear is for the weak, son. Do not be afraid. The people of Wallachia need a strong leader, they need the dragon heart that burns within you. You are a son of princes, descended from conquerors blessed by God himself. You will come to no harm under Murad," he assures me. "You are a token of my loyalty, and that shall never waver."

I feel hot tears well in my eyes, but by sheer force of will, I do not permit them to spill. I breathe deep, and nod. "I will be brave, Father. I will make our family proud."

Vlad the Second allows his stern-lipped expression to soften just a little, just for me. "I know you will, my son." With that, he rises to his feet and, standing beside my mother, a grim mask upon his face, allows the

Ottoman envoys to escort me away. I look back just once, as I am led towards what will become my new life, and see the pain in my father's eyes. They say more than words ever could. I meet his troubled gaze with all the courage I can muster.

Swallowing my fear, I leave the lands of my forefathers and begin my journey to foreign lands ruled by war, strange Eastern traditions, and an altogether different god.

I am Vlad the Third, Son of the Dragon. I will be brave.

Wiping the sweat from my brow, I ground my stance, long spear at the ready. My sparring partner, Murad's own son and heir, Mehmed the Second, stands several paces away, his kilij sabre in hand. We are the same age, he and I, and I know him as well as I know myself. Raised in his father's house, he is more akin to a blood brother than the son of my father's enemy.

Mehmed dances forward, his movements flowing like water. He is an adept swordsman, and easily my equal in combat, yet I am his opposite. Where he flows—smooth, elegant and lethal, his command over his kilij as beautiful as a poet's command of the written word—I stab and strike, brutal and fast, like the cobra.

"Are you ready, Prince?" he asks as he twirls, the silver of his sabre glinting in the morning sunlight.

"Always," I retort, a wry smile stretching my lips.

It begins.

Mehmed is fast, his kilij slicing through the air, aimed at my neck. I raise my spear, deflecting what would have been a killing blow. Having trained with them myself, I know all too well the keen sting of Ottoman steel. Turn for turn, we engage and parry, neither one of us willing to concede ground or admit fatigue. War burns in our blood as bright as pride, and we fight until the high orb of the sun marks noon.

The Agha of the Janissaries, the commander of the sixty-one regiments of the sultan's extensive army, and our personal combat tutor, signals the end of our match for the day. I obey immediately, returning my spear to right, bowing to our senior as is military custom. Not seconds later, as I straighten, I feel the all too familiar kiss of the kilij against my throat. I turn to my brother in arms, my hand straying to my neck. When I pull it away, a trickle of blood stains my fingers.

"Do not drop your guard, brother," he warns, a broad, wicked smile upon his face.

The Agha does not discipline the prince for his transgression.

"You have drawn First Blood," I say. "It will be my

destiny to draw the Last." I will never forget the moment his ill-gotten smirk of triumph turned to something more alike to cold disdain.

With the lands of my people a distant memory, my time spent with the Ottoman's continues. As each year passes, I become more certain that I will never see my father and family again. I feel lost, though no one would know it. I keep my despair and inner turmoil to myself. To display emotion is a sign of weakness, and I will not give the sultan the pleasure of my anguish.

In my own right, I have become a soldier of great renown. I fight side by side with Mehmed, and despite his great swordsmanship and his mastery of the tactics of war, it is my name that summons fear in the hearts of the sultan's enemies. For my brutal strength, and my penchant for running my enemies through with my weapon of choice, impaling them upon the field of battle, I am given the ominous cognomen: The Impaler.

When the Janissaries march, death flies upon swift wings. I am Murad's Angel of Death. At night, when I retire to my decorated barracks, I wonder if my father, The Dragon, has received word of my many exploits, and whether or not he is proud of the man I have become.

The year is 1447, and I am nineteen years old.

Before first light, the Agha announces himself. Rising, I rub the sleep from my eyes in the pre-dawn hours. "Come in," I call in fluent Arabic.

The Agha appears drawn, worry lines etch deep grooves into the corners of his eyes and his temple.

When did he get so old? I find myself wondering. "What is it, Agha?"

The Agha holds his head high, though for the first time in all the years since I was taken hostage by the sultan, I see unmistakable fear in his eyes. I feel the hairs on the back of my neck rise. Something is not right, I can sense it in my bones.

The Agha clears his throat. "News has reached us that your father is dead."

All colour drains from the world around me—all but red. "How?" I demand as evenly as my voice will allow.

"Your cousin, Vladislav the Second, is an ally of Hungary, and a traitor to your family. In exchange for the throne, he assisted the Hungarian, John Hunyadi, in laying siege to the Court of Târgoviște last night. It has been said that your father died fighting in the Bălteni marshes as he attempted to save your elder brother, Mircea.

I turn my back on the Agha, pain and rage rising like a tide within me.

"The sultan offers you his condolences, Impaler, and would have you reclaim your ancestral throne as Voivode of Wallachia, in your father's place. You would have Murad's personal blessing in this."

If the Agha continues to speak, I am not aware of it. My father is dead. Those four words repeat over and over in my mind, a debauched mantra. The Agha must recognise my spiralling descent, because he exits my tent, silent as a ghost. My world begins to spin, and I feel as if I have no control. The rage must be released, the fire extinguished. I throw my head back like a beast and howl out my pain.

I upend the furniture; tables fly, my cot upturned. I hurl anything and everything I can get my hands on. The encampment beyond is silent. The soldiers know better than to come near me. Grabbing my spear and kilij, I storm out of my tent and into the cool air. I feel every bit the dragon of my ancestry, my breathing heavy and hot. The darkness seems to envelope me, embracing me like a mother.

Mounting my horse in a single bound, I spur the elegant Arabian beast into flight. We tear through the camp and out into the wilderness beyond the fire light. Dismounting, I tie my steed's reigns to a gnarled tree and leave her to graze in peace. I need to be alone with the world that has forsaken me. Slashing at verdant brush as I go, I disappear into the ancient shadowed forests of the Carpathians.

The moon high overhead, I push through the dark hours of the morning, and deeper into the heart of the primeval beech forest. Finding a clearing, I stand tall in the gloom, and scream to the heavens. "Why? Why God have you forsaken my great family? We have served you without question! We have been your devoted subjects…and this is our due? Answer me!" The silence of the forest is deafening, and the fire within me burns like an inferno, desperate for release. I hack at several trees in rage, frustration and despair, blunting my blade.

Having spent some of my fury, I drop to my knees, emotionally exhausted. A soldier forged in the heat of battle, beaten into submission, I can go days without sleep. I can march on command, and fight until every muscle in my body weeps for reprieve; yet for survival, I have repressed all emotion for the better part of ten years. It feels cathartic, yet draining, to let the torrent of my inner demons free.

Amongst the shifting shadows, beneath the stars and the rustling canopy of the forest, I feel bereft. A lone, mournful howl breaks the night, and my pitiful reverie. My spine stiffens as I raise my head. In my blind fury, I failed to notice the beast's approach. Ahead of me, just hidden by the creeping fog that swirls by the tree line, a pair of golden eyes gleam back at me. Several more pairs reveal themselves, one after the other.

Every fibre of my being is suddenly alert and primed for battle. In the space of a single heartbeat, I am at the killing edge. My years of training have not failed me. Slowly, my fingers creep through the fallen leaves and mist to wrap around the hilt of my kilij. I draw it to me with a death-like calm, so as not to provoke them before I am ready. The alpha of the pack steps from the darkness and into the moonlight, and I find myself in awe.

This is no ordinary wolf. The wolves of the Carpathian Mountains are some of the largest anywhere, one alone would easily overpower most men; but I am not most men. This magnificent creature is twice as large as any I have ever seen. Its build is thicker, more muscular, and on all fours, it stands almost as tall as my horse. On its hind legs, it would dwarf me.

Rising to my feet, weapons at the ready, I consider my options. Fighting men is infinitely different to fighting beasts. I can deflect four incoming swords, but half a dozen or more monstrous, fanged jaws, each likely to target a different area of weakness? The odds are not in my favour. What I know to be mere moments, hang in the air between us like an eternity. Any semblance of legitimate fear in me dies as my rage comes screaming back, rising like a demon. "What are you waiting for?" I shout in my native tongue.

As if the beasts understand, three wolves are given leave by their alpha to attack; one to each side, and one at my back. Their lunges are staggered, a fine battle tactic, each wolf giving the other the opportunity to make purchase before the next one launches. I spin, a whirlwind of blades. My aim is true, and my kilij slices through thick silver fur and soft belly flesh. The first goes down, dragging itself and a ghastly trail of blood into the shadows, whimpering as it goes. It will not survive.

As my blade follows its natural arc, it rends the throat of the second wolf, dropping the beast at my feet, before it loses momentum. I follow through with my spear. Spinning on my knee, I brace myself as I drive it through the chest of the beast just as its leap reaches its climax. I use its momentum and my own strength to loose my weapon from its rib cage, and it crashes to the ground, swallowed by the mist with a mournful howl.

My face splattered with warm blood, my breathing ragged, I turn to face the remaining pack. The alpha pads forward, and the other glittering eyes in the darkness fade away as they slink back into the black or night. "It's just you and me, now," I say as I catch my breath. "Let's end this."

The alpha circles me and I pivot with him, never exposing my back. He is bigger than his betas, and no doubt, several times as strong. Man versus beast, a tale for the ages. The wolf launches himself, I twirl—as is the way to fight with the curved Arabic sword—and to my shock, my swipe is too soon; I over extend. The alpha latches onto my upper arm, his finger-long teeth finding their mark. I roar as they sink in, before he swings his mighty head, thrashing me from side to side by my bloody limb.

With seemingly little effort he swings and releases, I hurtle through the darkness, slamming into an ancient beech. I hit the ground hard, dazed. I rise with difficulty, using the tree for support. My injured arm is covered in blood, from my shoulder to my fingertips. The holes are deep, and the pain is raw. Blades sting, slice and stab, but the tearing puncture wounds are something else entirely. I'm going to lose my arm, I think in horror. I clutch at my arm in a vain attempt to stem the bleeding.

Blinking back stars, it dawns upon me that I am without my weapons. My kilij lies discarded at the centre of the clearing, and my spear is several feet in the opposite direction. The wolf watches me intently. If I didn't know better, I'd think that he was waiting, studying me—taking my measure. Wincing, I crunch to my left, carefully pulling a concealed dagger from my boot. In the style of the Janissaries, I wield the dagger, the crook of my elbow outward, the hilt of the dagger enclosed in a fist-grip, the blade outward, the pommel toward my chest; a defensive stance, a last resort.

In the battle-worn fog of my mind, I wonder if this is truly to be my end. The second son of the Dragon, the Impaler, Vlad Dracula himself, mauled to death by a wolf. Master of War, Angel of Death to the sultan of the Empire…brought down by a beast of the forest. Were the creature before me not so immense, I would feel shame. With the white fur around his jaws stained with my dark essence, his yellow eyes ablaze, he is the very embodiment of horror. He is the perfect natural-born killer, more perfect even than I.

Darkness teases at the periphery of my vision, and I feel faint. Glancing down, I see that I am standing in a pool of my own blood. I am done for. There will be no justice for Wallachia. I will never see the lands of my home, again. What a fool!

The alpha paws at the earth, growling, he bares his fangs. Pageantry aside, he pounds forward before flying through the dark, a nightmare in flight. With my fast draining clarity, I tell myself to hold. Hold. Hold. Now! Committed to his direction, the alpha's jaws spread wide as he prepares to lock his maw around my throat. At the last second, I twist around the beech, and the alpha makes impact with the tree, instead of me. I swivel back around to the front of the tree and I stab. I stab for all I am worth, I land a frenzy of blows, again and again, striking like a cobra. I drive it in, hilt deep—into his flank, belly, shoulder, neck, wherever I can while eluding his flesh-rending teeth.

The alpha falls sideways as I land hit after hit. He scrambles away, snarling. I drop to my knees, the last of my energy exhausted. I have lost too much blood. Not even the best doctors in the Empire could save me now. I look the beast in eye as he charges. He will have me, even if it's the last thing he ever does. As a fellow hunter of my own kind, I understand. I would do the same, given half the chance. There is no room for mercy in war.

I ready myself for the monstrous impact and the pain that will signal my end. He will tear out my throat, and I will lose consciousness instantly, dying several moments later. I close my eyes as he reaches the height of his jump—

"No!"

Am I hearing things—my mother's voice? I wonder. Am I so close to death, already? The impact never comes, and my tired eyes struggle open as I sway on my knees. A woman, a goddess, stands on the opposite side of the clearing, arm upraised, palm outward, an expression of determination and power painted upon her beautiful face. My eyes follow hers, and I fall back on my elbows at the sight that greets me.

The alpha hangs, suspended in time, jaws frozen open, primal hatred tensing every muscle in its being. I hear a sickening crack, and the wolf falls; a broken beast, eyes blank. I allow myself to collapse to my back. Sprawled upon the earth, mist swirling around me, dancing stars fill my vision.

"You are he, the Impaler, the Prince of Wallachia," says the woman as her face swims into view. She is kneeling beside me, looking down upon me intently. Pale, white-blonde hair, tangled with fronds of bracken and braided with seasonal blossoms, spills over her shoulders. Upon her brow, she wears a painted, or carved star, I can't be sure, as she begins to fade in and out of focus.

"I am," I manage.

"Do you wish to live, Prince? Do you wish to protect your lands from the traitors and the foreign invaders?"

I try to swallow, my mouth dry. "It is over," I whisper.

"It is not over," she responds. "This is your beginning, Lord Dracula."

The ethereal woman draws a short blade from her boot and I don't even have the strength to flinch. I want to ask 'What are you doing?' but I cannot. I feel dreadfully cold, starting at my extremities, like a living entity, it slides through my veins, spreading throughout my body until I understand the phrase 'as cold as the grave' intrinsically.

"I am Astrid, and I am going to save you," says my unlikely champion. Taking the dagger, she slices her palm, licks the blade, and begins to chant. Her words are foreign to my ear, though I recognise it as being one of the Northern tongues. Her voice rises and falls as she holds her hands above me, her eyes closed in concentration.

She is a witch! I realise. A heathen, working blood magic. Having been raised in the Light of God, I know witchcraft to be unforgivable sin. What is she doing to me? Will my soul be damned? Her palms begin to glow a turgid red, and the swirling mist that envelopes us reflects the dark light. I feel a stab of burning ice in my chest and I gasp, my body violently shuddering in response.

Astrid's voice changes, her feminine tone gone, as if someone, or something—ancient and timeless—speaks through her. With all my failing strength I will my eyes to remain open. Her head turns, cocking to the side to look me dead in the eye, an unmistakably inhuman movement. Her eyes are pools of black, gateways into the great Void beyond our world.

"Drink!" she commands in a deep, demonic voice. "Drink of the blood of the Dark One and live eternal! Seal your covenant, and each soul you take shall be mine!"

My eyes roll back in my head and I blink repeatedly to stay conscious. Warmth spills into my mouth, the tang of iron strong. I cough, my entire body screams with pain.

"Drink!" The voice is that of the Devil.

I swallow, my throat flexing as I try to save myself from choking—from drowning on the blood that is being forced upon me. I feel the blood burn as my body accepts the dark offering.

"Astrid," I whisper with what must be my last breath.

Her eyes are ice-blue once more, and with a stern, but comforting smile, she clutches my hand. "I am here, Prince. Sleep now, I will be here when you awaken."

Awaken? I'm dying…

I sit upon the throne of Wallachia, the rightful Voivode, my beautiful wife—the Doamna Astrid—by my side; the crimson, gold and sapphire banners of House Drăculeşti proudly on display. Musicians and entertainers fill my halls, and Bran Castle resounds with joy. Today marks our son's tenth birthday. Mihnea cel

Rău is the apple of my eye. Dark of hair, like me, but gifted with ice-blue Nordic eyes of his mother.

Mihnea sits upon the steps of the dais, opening gifts presented to him by the Boyars, the nobles, of Wallachia, and Moldavia. Wine flows freely and it seems that despite the terrors of my past, all is well.

"Father, father!" says my son, as he comes to my side. "Look! My very own throwing axe. It even has my name inscribed! Can we go hunting soon, please father? I long to try my crossbow, too!"

I smile at my dear boy's enthusiasm, and I am taken back to my own childhood. "We shall go hunting in the spring, when the deer are plentiful, their numbers renewed after the long winter."

"Thank you, father! I can't wait!"

I kiss my son on the head as he leans into me affectionately. "Go now, play with your friends. It's not every day you turn ten."

Mihnea goes to move when the ancient oak doors of my feasting hall burst open. I catch my son's wrist instinctively. A contingent of twenty four soldiers, a half dozen banner men, and two emissaries, bearing the crest of the Ottoman empire march in; brazen and bold, fearless. I feel Astrid stiffen beside me, and her hand seeks my forearm in comfort, and unity.

My men's hands rest upon the hilts of their swords,

but they remain still, put to ease momentarily with a look.

"Would you have peace, brothers?" I ask evenly as the emissaries come to a halt at the foot of the stairs. I recognise them all. The one called Ekrem inclines his head, meeting my eye.

"We would have peace, wherever possible," he replies.

"It seems a strange way to keep the peace, and ill-mannered, Ekrem, to march in on a birthday celebration, unannounced, and uninvited."

"You have my personal apologies, master Drăculea. As you well know, I go where I am told."

I know why they are here, and every bone in my immortal body fills with rage.

The emissary continues. "We are here on behalf of His Excellence, the blessed sultan Mehmed, and son of Murad. Ten years have come and gone since you defected from his father's army, and by way of forgiveness, and to keep the peace, he would ask the first born sons of Wallachia, including your own, brother," he says.

My hall is silent, as if every last man woman and child are holding their breath. All eyes are upon me, hanging on the silence that precedes what I will say next.

"In the name of peace?" I ask. "Of course." I rise

from my throne, and my eyes turn black. "Wallachia is no vassal state to the Empire, and we will pay no such tribute."

Ekrem's eyes are wide as he notices the non-too-subtle change. "You are a demon!" he accuses. "Blessed, Allah! Mehmed will have his price, whether it is paid willingly, or paid in blood."

I feel a deep, sadistic grin stretch across my face, and I take a step down from my throne. "If the sultan wishes blood, he shall pay with his own," I say. "Now go, bring word to your master that Wallachia will not bow."

"You are mad!" says Ekrem. "You know the might of the Janissaries, and we have only grown. There will be no Wallachia by the end of this!"

"We shall see," I say, my voice dripping with dark promise.

I watch as they turn and leave, my eyes returning to their usual dark green.

"You're letting them go, Prince?" one of my most loyal knights asks.

I sit back down and signal the entertainers to task. "I am, I will not spill blood this day."

He nods and resumes his place.

"Father, will they take me, like they took you?" Mihnea asks, his eyes full of concern. "I know what they did to you—"

"Quiet, my son. No one is going anywhere, least of all you. The sons of Wallachia will be safe, I promise. Do not let the foreigners spoil your celebration. Go now, make merry, and think no more on it. I will take care of everything."

"Yes, father," he says, and the Bran Castle resumes its festivities.

"My love?" whispers Astrid. "You have just started a war with the Turks."

I take hold of her hand and kiss it. "I am ending a war that started long ago, my lady," I respond. "Do I not have your trust?"

Astrid's pale beauty overwhelms me, even now, ten years from the night that she called upon the Dark Lord to spare my life.

"You have my trust," she assures me, "and my heart. Always."

I lean in, as does she, and our temples touch, eyes closed. "I will save our son," I promise her.

"I know," she whispers back, before she crushes her lips into mine, and for just a few precious moments, my world makes sense again.

The sun sets, and the stretching shadows of the evening melt into the complete, all-encompassing darkness of the night. My keen vampire eyes see as clearly as if it were day. From the balcony of the master chambers of Castle Târgovişte, I wait. The Ottomans are marching. I can hear them, their footfalls like the rolling of thunder through the valley.

Astrid appears silently by my side. "You will be victorious, my love, I have foreseen it," she says.

"I have no doubt of it," I respond. "The Dark Lord has given me more strength, and greater powers than God ever did. I will slaughter them all, and never again will the Ottomans dare challenge Wallachia."

My beautiful wife is quiet. Something is amiss.

"Speak to me, Astrid. You are a witch, and High Priestess; what troubles your thoughts?"

She hesitates before she speaks, and I know she is lying.

"Do not worry for me, my love," she begins. "There is no matter on my mind but your safety, and that of our son." She reaches out and touches my hand-wrought red armour, emblazoned with the likeness of demons and the scales of dragons. "The Dark Lord has assured me that the enchantments I have woven into your armour will protect you."

"Astrid."

She stands on the tips of her toes and silences me with a kiss. "I love you," she whispers.

When our lips part, I meet her eye and she smiles.

"I love you, Astrid. I might never have said it before, but thank you—for the gift of this second chance, to protect my family and our home. I'll never forget the moment I first laid eyes upon you. You were so strong, so powerful. I thought you a goddess."

"We were fated to find one another," she says simply. "We will always find one another."

Trailing her hand out of my own, she looks back just once, before she takes her leave, her emerald gown billowing in her wake.

I do not know what it is that she is withholding from me, but I have to trust that it is nothing of relevance to the impending battle. If it was important, she would have shared it with me, I assure myself. Turning back to the darkness below, I see the torches of war funnelling through the pass and into the valley beneath Târgovişte. I can hear the steady beat of almost thirty thousand men's hearts. They seem almost to march in unison, following their feet, and their sultan's pleasure.

"I am coming for you, Mehmed," I say to the wind as it howls by, swirling into the pass, and through the black forests of Wallachia.

The castle is fortified, no one is permitted in—and no one allowed out. Even my most trusted harbour fear in their hearts. They will not say it, but they believe I have entombed them, given them no means of escape, should the siege reach the gates. My people, at least, those within my court, know the nature of the beast that I am. I have never kept it a secret; but I have never displayed the extent of my power, either. I have never wanted to rule with fear, to me, trust and loyalty have always been paramount. I would never use my darkness against Wallachia.

Tonight, however, the world will know of the insatiable violence contained within my damned soul. I will unleash the devil, and blood will flow in rivers. I will create such a spectacle of the Ottoman Janissary army as to be remembered throughout all of history.

Thousands of torches light the night. The Janissaries are within the valley, and the only way up to Târgovişte is a long, narrow and solitary winding road up the mountain. In the distance, an almighty rumble shatters the silence. Despite their discipline, the rear of the army turns as one. A great landslide is triggered, and the way is shut; filled with thousands of tonnes of earth and rock. I smile. They are trapped. My men did their job well.

I hear the change in rhythm of the hearts of the men. They are used to being in a position of power, unstoppable. Now, they are at my mercy, and I will give them no quarter. Spreading my arms like wings, I launch myself into the inky night, plummeting some two hundred feet before I channel my gift of flight. I draw level, just a foot from the ground, and smash thousands of unsuspecting soldiers off their feet.

Panic rises among the ranks as bodies fly, yet in the dark, the source of the attack cannot be seen. I plough through their ranks, like a warm knife through fresh butter. Screams rend the gloom. The sound of breaking bones and spilled blood thrills me, fuelling my drive to destroy them. Kilij clash and arrows fly, directionless, and pointless. Most of them killing their brothers in arms. I laugh, amplifying my own voice with dark magic, and it echoes through the valley, bouncing off the hills and back at the now terrified Janissaries.

I break them all, hundreds at a time, casting them aside like piles of discarded dolls. I could cut them down, slicing them in half. It would only be too easy…but I have something in mind, an homage to my reputation, and I need most of them whole; still in once piece.

Inside of an hour, almost thirty thousand men are dead, strewn across the valley. Floating above the battlefield, or perhaps, the field of the massacre, is the better description, I allow almost seven thousand men fleeing for their lives to scramble away. They will return to their sultan and their families, and word will spread of my terror. No one will ever dare challenge Wallachia again, and that suits my purpose. Ultimately, they will all be put to the sword. The sultan does not abide deserters. It is the very reason why he has come against me with such irreverent force.

The morning is still several hours away, which permits me more than enough time to orchestrate my greatest artwork of atrocity to date. It is likely another such scene will never be viewed with mortal eyes, again. Through the dark hours I work, and by first light, I stand before the gates of Târgoviște, revelling in the beauty of my masterpiece.

Word will spread like wildfire of my macabre spectacle, my Forest of the Dead. I smile. Twenty-three thousand, eight-hundred and forty-four Janissaries impaled. I have ensured that Vlad the Impaler will never be forgotten.

As my court begins to spill out of the castle, eyes wide, and hands to mouths as they drink in the horror in the valley, I head back inside. "Astrid! Mihnea!" I call. I stop one of my men as he moves to go past. "Have you seen my wife, and son?"

"No, my lord. The lady barricaded herself in the Chindia Tower, the last I heard. She said she must not be disturbed."

The hairs on the back of my neck rise, and I feel my stomach drop. I run up the several flights of stairs that lead to the tower, a blur, or a trick of the light, to anyone watching. I reach the solid, iron reinforced door and knock, my heart thundering in my chest. "Astrid? Astrid, open the door." I wait but a few moments, before I put my knee through the door and toss it aside. The sight awaiting me shatters my very soul in the space of a single breath.

"No! My love!" The words escape me without thought. I break the circle of blood, salt and candles. Dropping to my knees I lift her, cradling her in my arms. "Astrid, Astrid, wake up! Please, open your eyes!" Her beautiful face is pale, and I can hear no heartbeat. "No!" I sob, over and over into her white-blonde hair. "What have you done? Why?"

"She did it to save me," says a quiet, familiar voice, wracked with guilt. "You were protecting all of Wallachia…she did what she had to do."

"Mihnea," I gasp, tears carving a clean path down my blood-stained cheeks. "I don't understand. What happened here?" Then I notice the blood stain on his shirt.

Standing, he comes to kneel down before me in the broken circle. From behind his back, he reveals a bloodied arrow, then placing it in his lap, he opens his shirt, and there, directly over his heart, is an ugly, puckered red scar.

I reach out and trail my fingers across it, and my lips quiver at the terror of it.

"How?" I stress again. "You were safe, you were inside! I barred the doors."

Mihnea tilts his head, gesturing to the far corner of the room. "No one needed to enter father, they were already inside."

I follow his gaze and find my most loyal knight, Ștefan, slumped on the floor, dead. All of a sudden, the circle of blood makes sense.

"He told us that a separate contingent of Turks were scaling the mountain and would breach the castle. Then he raised his crossbow…and he shot me. I heard mother scream, I saw a flash of light, and then, there was nothing but darkness. I think I died, father. I do not know for how long I was gone, but when I awoke, mother was dying. She told me not to break the circle. She said that she loved me, and that only life could pay for a life, and that the Dark Lord was calling her home. And then she—" Mihnea wipes the tears from his face with the back of his bloodied sleeve. "Father, she gave her life for me."

"Come here, son," I say, drawing him nearer. Together, temple to temple, we comfort one another, and mourn the light of our lives; my beautiful Astrid, my wife, my priestess, the mother of my only child, and the very reason I'm alive. She saved us both, I realise. She saved us both.

A funeral is held for the lady of Wallachia, the only loss of life from the night siege on Târgovişte, aside from that of the traitor. How long had he been in bed with Mehmed? I couldn't know, but it sickens me to dwell on it. In the way of her people, Astrid is burned on a mighty pyre, the embers of her mortal beauty soar into the dying dusk. I cannot believe that she is truly gone. My heart breaks with each breath I draw, and I suspect it will, forever.

Then I remember her last words to me: We were fated to find one another. We will always find one another, and a small smile tugs at the edge of my lips. If anyone knew the secrets of life and death, it was my precious Astrid. I realise that she was trying to tell me that we would find each other again. I don't understand how, or when, but there was a time I did not believe in the dark entities of the night, so I know better than to question her arcane promise.

In the weeks that followed, I hunted down Mehmed with the passion and deranged fury of a madman. To his credit, despite all that he had heard of what I had become, and what I had done, he faced me like a man. I toyed with him, gifting him the slightest of hopes as we duelled; as we once had, back in our youth. No matter how I threatened him, he would not repent for the murder of my wife. With defiance in his eyes, he swore to fight me until his last breath. My patience wearied, I tore out his throat, draining the monster until he was naught more than a husk. I mounted his corpse on a spear, as I had so many before him—a final warning to the Janissaries. No one was safe from my reach, not even the sultan, himself.

What remained of the Ottoman armies retreated to the East, leaderless, and fearing the wrath of the Devil himself. I stayed in Wallachia until my Mihnea was a grown man, and I passed on the title of Voivode to him so that he might lead our people into an age of prosperity and joy, free of the tyranny of the line of sultans. Our son became a good man, his mother would have been proud. Though he was aggrieved to see me leave, I felt it was time to explore the world, and gift Mihnea the opportunity to forge his own legacy, one outside the reign of blood that I had left in my wake.

With my enemies dead, and my vengeance

wrought, I felt no less broken, but finally, I felt free. I had kept my promises all, and in my heart, I found a measure of peace. Though it was not to last…

In the year 1510, when my son was just fifty years old, he was deposed by the Boyars of Wallachia. In secret, they had forged alliances with the Ottomans. The Ottomans wanted Mihnea dead in revenge for my atrocities. With the promise of wealth, the Boyars gave up the independence I had fought so hard for. Wallachia once more became a vassal state, and my son sought refuge in neighbouring Transylvania. Then, on the steps of the Sibiu Cathedral, he was assassinated, and I was not there to protect him.

The Ottomans had ultimately succeeded, and I fell into a deep despair. A despair so black and deep, that I could not distinguish it from the burning hate in my cold heart. I travelled to the Middle East, and for a hundred years, I stalked, butchered and drank of its people. A punishment; for all that they had inflicted upon me, and my great family. I was never found, and never stopped. I was a demon and there was no escaping my wrath.

I ended the line of sultans, and with the aid of the Western influences, the lands of sand and sun were thrown into chaos, never to truly recover.

And now, dear friend, I am here. A shadow among the realms of the living, I travel from city to city, country to country. My Wallachia of old is no more, it is a once kingdom, now a part of modern Romania. My legend and legacy can be found in textbooks the world over, and my mythology endures, despite the death of superstition among mortal men in these eras.

I have sat in theatres, and watched television shows of vampires, and not one, perhaps outside of Bram Stoker's Dracula, has managed to convey the true loneliness of an immortal life. In my search for hope, over the course of my long years, I have learned of all the religions and philosophies of the world, and most of them offer nothing more, or less, than eternal servitude, or damnation.

Yet, the Buddhists of Tibet offer the concept of reincarnation, of the energy of one's soul living countless lives, learning, growing and dying, only to be reborn again. This theory of belief offers me hope. Perhaps this is to what my beautiful Astrid had referred to when she said that we would find each other again? Perhaps, despite the hole in my heart, and the despair in my soul, I need only be more patient.

What if my beautiful wife is somewhere out there,

just waiting to be discovered? It was she who found me, fighting for my life that night in the ancient forest of the Carpathian Mountains. What if this time, it is my turn to find her?

Dear reader, I thank you for sharing in my tale, for allowing me to recapture what I had lost. For so long, I have tried to elude the demons of my past, when perhaps all along, I should have been embracing them. It seems that none of us can escape who we truly are, and it may be this very realisation that is our salvation.

I am Vlad the Third, Dracula, the Son of the Devil, and I have all the time in the world. My story continues from here, with hope.

ZOEY XOLTON is an internationally Best Selling Australian Speculative Fiction Author, and Award Winning Poet, with a penchant for the Dark Fantasy, Paranormal Romance, and Horror genres. Her works have appeared in dozens of themed anthologies, with many more due for publication.

She is especially fond of short fiction, and is working on future story collections, as well.

Bibliography
ANGELS, Black Hare Press, 2019
BEYOND, Black Hare Press, 2019
Coffins & Dragons, Dragon Soul Press, 2019
Curses & Cauldrons, Blood Song Books, 2019
Deep Space, Black Hare Press, 2019
Divinity, Iron Faerie Publishing, 2019
Fable, Iron Faerie Publishing, 2019
First Love, Dragon Soul Press, 2019
Forest of Fear -v1, Blood Song Books, 2019
Galactic Goddesses, Fantasia Divinity Publishing, 2019
MONSTERS, Black Hare Press, 2019
Organic Ink - v1, Dragon Soul Press, 2019
Organic Ink - v2, Dragon Soul Press, 2019
Sea of Secrets, Dragon Soul Press, 2019
Spring's Blessing, Fantasia Divinity Publishing, 2019
Storming Area 51, Black Hare Press, 2019
Summer's Splash, Fantasia Divinity Publishing, 2019
UNRAVEL, Black Hare Press, 2019
What If?, Black Hare Press, 2019
WORLDS, Black Hare Press, 2019

Connect
Website: www.zoeyxolton.com
Amazon: www.amazon.com/author/zoeyxolton

POWERS OF EARTH AND HELL

By Matthew M. Montelione

Four gifted anthropomorphic long-tailed weasels journey through New York on their quest to defeat Pan, a cunning villain who sparked the American Revolution.

PROLOGUE

Long ago, Thayer was a benevolent spirit who worked alongside his kin to build a spectacular world on planet Rancientia. He was renowned for his cunning and intellect, rivalled only by his Queen, Dalasia. Eventually, the spirits met a race of magical beings called the Magi. The spirits and Magi peacefully coexisted on Rancientia for many years, until a dangerous sect of dark magicians used black magic against them. Thayer was intrigued by their spells and learned them in secret. He tried to take over the kingdom but was defeated by the Queen. He fled to Earth, where he possessed the body of a British general in New York and dubbed himself Pan. In his new body, he grew physically and mentally stronger than the average man. He used magic to control the minds of humans and manipulate spatial dimensions.

Queen Dalasia long brooded over Thayer's betrayal. She saw visions of him ruling over a burning planet and was revolted by the fact that he walked freely on Earth, destroying life. She enacted the Spirit Guild Initiative, which sent lesser spirits to Earth where they usurped animals as hosts and manifested unique powers to combat Pan. Rancientians were divided on Dalasia's decree, because it was unknown—even to her—what happened to the spirits when their hosts died. Still, the Spirit Guild Initiative was their only chance of bringing Thayer to justice.

...

CHAPTER ONE

On a crisp winter night in March 1770, Pan walked through an agitated mob that gathered in front of the Boston Custom House in Massachusetts Bay Colony. The well-dressed man weaved in and out of the crowd unnoticed, like an unseen predator in turbulent waters. He smirked, knowing that he had orchestrated it all. All of the anger, all of the hatred. He had complete control over the lesser humans who stood before him.

The mob, armed with clubs and farming tools, screamed insults and hurled ice balls and rocks at the British soldiers who stood in front of the Custom House. The redcoats anxiously loaded their Brown Bess muskets, unsure of whether or not they should open fire on the hostile crowd.

Pan waved his hand towards the redcoats. "Ah," he said with a smile, "now I have you."

The redcoats aimed their muskets at the colonists. Their fingers nervously shook and hovered near their triggers. One of the privates bled from a gash across his head. The ruthless mob moved closer, taunting the soldiers, daring them to shoot.

Finally, Pan stopped. He closed his eyes and focused on all of the minds under his dominion. Their energies surged through him, he felt lifted like a great hawk gliding on strong winds.

A shot rang out.

A man fell, his white shirt stained red.

"Murderers!" the crowd yelled as they charged the soldiers.

More shots blasted through the cold night.

Four more people fell to the ground. Screams echoed throughout the street. "Tyrants! Devils!" the crowd screamed. Women wailed over their fallen husbands, their dresses soaked with fresh blood.

Pan watched it all in delight. His plan to excite revolution in the colonies had finally come to fruition. In reality, it was all a form of entertainment for him. He had no stake in the orchestrated war, indeed, he could kill all the weak humans before him in a matter of minutes if he wished. What was the fun in that? Since usurping his human host, Pan had his fill of debauchery and grew bored of Earth. He needed something to keep him occupied while he figured out how to return to Rancientia.

...

CHAPTER TWO

Western Long Island, New York. 27 August 1776.

Long-tailed weasels Blaken, Marston, Rowen, and Seddus walked through the thick woods towards their first major battle. It was a hot and humid day; the sun streamed through the tops of tall oaks and pines and soaked the ground in gold.

Blaken breathed in deep and wiped the sweat off

his brow. His anxiety was great, but the yellow sun reminded him of his home planet, Rancientia, somewhere out there in the vast recesses of space. It had a sun just like that. The thought of home allowed him a moment of mental peace, but his thoughts were interrupted by Marston's gruff voice.

"War is close, brothers!" Marston's fists were shaking. The tallest weasel could hardly contain his giddiness.

"British soldiers have swarmed across Long Island, that much is plain," Blaken started, "but although Pan wears a redcoat, he employs humans from all walks of life. Patriots, too, do his bidding. He carves symbols into their foreheads, so that they're easily identified. What is less apparent is how evil they truly are. I may be able to save some of the more noble belligerents…those who were taken by the villain against their better wills. We have to approach those particular souls with caution."

Marston was not one for complicating matters. He was a fiery soul who often acted first and thought later, if he thought about his actions at all. "Caution?" Marston retorted. "Our plan was set before us by Queen Dalasia. We're to wipe this planet clean of Pan's trace. That includes killing his minions. If they work for him, then they were vulnerable to begin with, and so cannot be that well-natured. Whatever colours they wear, we need to kill them. Simple enough."

Blaken was sensitive and empathetic; he realised the severity of their quest but did not believe in Marston's kill-first philosophy. "It's anything but simple, brother," he argued. "If I can save some of them, I shall do it. You forget, I have gifts here that you do not." Blaken straightened his yellow vest and tightly grasped it by its golden buttons in a dignified fashion.

Marston scoffed.

Blaken's golden eyes widened. "Blood also flows in our earthly bodies now," he said. "Would you take kindly to others saying that they would readily spill yours? Pan plays with the lives of men, women, and children, solely for sport!" Blaken laid his head in his paw, as if he had a headache from Marston's war-mongering. His face became tense.

Seddus, usually of a cheery disposition, tried to ease the tension between his brothers. "Come, Marston! Human insides shan't be particularly pleasing to behold. I will stun, along with Blaken."

Marston chuckled. "Oh, settle thyselves, kinsmen! Bloodshed cannot be that hard on the eyes. It's a wonder the Queen even chose you peace-lovers for this mission. And where do you stand in our debate, Rowen?"

Rowen stared solemnly at the ground as he walked.

He was not a talkative soul; he preferred to ponder rather than debate. He often felt that speaking unnecessarily drained him of energies that he would need to utilise. Rowen sighed, annoyed at the conversation without having been a part of it. "We should be thinking about our individual tactics in this war."

Marston flashed him an unsatisfied look, but Rowen's lethargic reply silenced the aggressive weasel. Much to the latter's delight, the weasels continued west through the dense forest in quiet. Blaken's anxieties started to subside.

Seddus could not stay silent for long. "Tracking is quite easy in weasel form, is it not? These hosts possess heightened senses; an innate ability to stalk others with grace! In this respect, we are stronger than on Rancientia."

"Indeed," Blaken replied. "Still, be on your guard. We are dealing with lost souls."

At that very moment, the weasels stopped in their tracks and cocked their ears.

Cries. Gunfire. Then a chorus of blood-curdling screams cascaded through the woodland.

The weasels ran to the forest's edge and observed the carnage before them.

The British and their Patriot enemies were in the

heat of battle, sticking one another with bayonets. Another round of musket fire clanged through the air.

"What a lot of filth," Marston said. "Look at them, slaughtering one another like cattle."

"I pity them," Blaken said. "This is all Pan's doing. His hold over these men is strong, but I'd wager some may be saved. If you see me working on it, do not obstruct me, Marston."

"I'll keep him in line," Seddus said with a smile as he nudged Marston.

Rowen charged his fur with hot electricity and unsheathed his sabre. In weasel form, he had manifested the power to naturally conduct electricity at will. His blade was his chosen conduit. He stared at the battle before him, his body jumping with sparks.

Blaken grew determined. "For over a year, we have prepared for this moment. Now, let our strengths be tested!"

He looked at his brothers. They tensely nodded, ready.

Marston fingered the fletchings of his arrow. His body quivered with pent-up energy.

"For Rancientia!" they cried out in unison.

The weasels sprung from the woods and leapt towards their unsuspecting enemies. Minions on both sides turned towards them in alarm.

Marston let loose an arrow from his bow. It found its mark in the chest of an out-of-control minion. The villain fell dead.

"God save us!" they cried.

"Run!"

They tried to flee, but were far too slow. The uncanny speed of the weasels overtook them like a storm.

Blaken's right paw was encircled by a golden orb. As he usurped his victim's mental energy, he struck him down with a numbing punch to the gut. The minion lay on the ground in a fetal position, yelling in pain. Blaken continued to attack while fishing out redeemable minions. The nasty cuts and scars on their foreheads made him shudder.

Rowen jumped onto the back of a Patriot and thrust his blade into his back, right below his neck. The man let out a tortured scream and fell dead. The smell of burned flesh permeated the area.

"Quick, Percy, to the forest!" a redcoat screamed as he and his stocky friend ran towards the woods.

Marston smiled. "Aye, to the forest, indeed!" As soon as the soldier set foot in the woods, Marston slammed his palms on the ground. His dark green cloak shimmered in the sunlight as tree roots burst up through the undergrowth, completely entangling the minion. Soon he was lost under thick roots.

With deadly speed and accuracy, Seddus threw a dagger at Percy, who had stopped in his tracks after his companion was consumed by the earth. The projectile embedded itself in the redcoat's left leg.

"Oopf!" Percy cried as he fell to the ground with a thud.

Seddus stared in wonder at the blood pouring down Percy's leg. "I knew it. Not too pleasing."

"Fear not, I'll end his misery," Marston said. He reached for an arrow.

"No, Marston!" Blaken cried, rushing over to him. "I can save this one. He's not wholly evil."

"Fine," Marston said, lowering his arm. "I'll find another to overtake." He looked around. The field was strewn with bodies. Some writhed on the ground, others fled west. Marston let out a disappointed sigh.

The weasels walked over to Percy, who cowered and held his hands up in defence.

"Please…spare me! Mercy!"

"Oh, relax," Marston said. "You're one of the lucky ones."

Seddus pulled out his dagger from Percy's leg. The minion screamed in pain. "Well, let's free him."

Blaken raised his illuminated paws close to Percy's face. "I've never done this before. But I feel in my heart that it will work. See me, human," he said.

Percy grew quiet and wide-eyed. Golden light danced on his face.

"I think it's working," Seddus whispered.

Blaken closed his eyes and concentrated hard. "You are free," he said. "Turn and walk away from this place. Forget about your master's errand, and live in peace, if you can."

Percy stood up and hobbled away into the forest. He never looked back.

"Wow," Seddus said. "Impressive, brother."

Blaken was proud of himself. He released a few other minions in like fashion, as the others gathered supplies from their foes. After a half hour, they reconvened.

"A waste of time, I'd say, brother," Marston said to Blaken. "My plan would have been faster. And, dare I say, Rowen's plan as well."

Rowen grinned. "I felt only anger towards them. You win, Marston."

Blaken shook his head and sighed. "Well, there is one thing that we can agree on: Pan is not here. And perhaps it's for the better as I doubt we could defeat him after one sole foray."

"How do you know he's not hiding out somewhere, observing us?" Rowen asked.

"I do not sense him here. Besides, that is not his way," Blaken replied. "The demon is vain. He's murdered many of our kin here, and easily, too, if the rumours are true. If he was here and wanted to kill us, he would have done it already."

"Yet, the fact remains that he's the most cunning of our forefathers. Would he not shield himself from others of like skill? He possessed a human, Blaken! His powers here are unchecked. I doubt even the Queen saw that coming. I do not wish to be equally surprised."

Blaken got defensive. "Pan has never encountered another psychic who can control human minds, as I can. If any spirit can find Pan—he who has taken human form—it is me."

Marston interjected. "Let us find shelter, in any case," he said. "I grow uncomfortable without the cover of trees."

"Alright, but we need more intelligence before scouting Pan," Blaken said.

Seddus grinned from ear to ear. "A tavern is the best place to hear news. I'd imagine the cider is particularly tasty at the inn."

...

CHAPTER THREE

York Island. Early September 1776.

Pan relaxed on his comfortable throne, flocked by half-naked women. His redcoat lay on the floor, his shirt untied at the throat. One woman stood near him, holding a silver pitcher of water, another caressed his shoulders. He paid the most attention to the voluptuous brunette who rubbed his leg that hung over the arm of the throne. Her long fingers moved up to his torso. Pan gently touched her soft chin, pulled her in, and kissed her. She moaned.

The giant wooden doors to his keep creaked and opened.

Pan's eyes widened in anger at the disruptive visitor.

Chief War Commander Weling stepped in. The bobcat's clothing, made from tattered pieces of British uniforms, was stained with blood. Weling cleared his throat. "I apologise for my intrusion, King."

Pan bristled and leaned towards his soldier. "As you should be, Commander! Can you not see that I am being entertained?"

"This news could not wait."

"What is it, then? Make it quick!" Pan snapped.

"Dalasia has sent another spirit guild for you to destroy," Weling said.

Pan's glare turned into a grin. "Has she indeed? I must

admit, I often pondered when she would try her hand again. How did you learn of this?"

"I saw them myself, at the Battle of Long Island. Four long-tailed weasels, no more than four feet tall. Yet, they decimated our forces. Their powers were…different from others. Stronger. One was some sort of psychic, another wielded heat from the sky. I called off the battle and withdrew our redcoats. I left the Patriots to be slaughtered."

"Did these…weasels…see you?" Pan asked.

"No, my Lord. They were oblivious to my presence, wrapped up in their first taste of blood. It was quite obvious they were young and unseasoned warriors."

Pan waved his hand in dismissive fashion. "They will make for better sport, then. We have more important matters to address. Soon I ride north to Valcour Island. It's time to make more minions." At this he grew somewhat giddy. The women around him smiled and swooned. His favourite brunette nuzzled her head into his chest. "Yes, Sarah," Pan cooed as he petted her head, "my powers will grow…my riches will grow."

Pan's gaze reluctantly gravitated back to Weling. "Once I arrive at Valcour Island, I plan to orchestrate a splendid naval battle as a test of minion strength. You will be left in charge on York Island. Defend my borders against all who would dare oppose me."

Sarah's hand reached below Pan's waist. His eyes widened in delight.

"Leave us!" he yelled.

"Yes, my King," Weling said as he bowed low and exited.

...

CHAPTER FOUR

The weasels came to the Red Lion Inn on a starry evening. The old tavern was situated at the junction of three country roads and was the most frequented inn west of the Hempstead Plains. The spirit guild planned to covertly stay there and find out where Pan was by spying on his visiting soldiers.

The weasels paused before the tall door. A large wooden sign swung above them, blowing back and forth with the breeze; a red lion was painted above an emblem of King George III. The tavern was abnormally quiet.

"Since the British occupation, only redcoats and their allies come here. That works better for us. They are Pan's favoured soldiers," Blaken said.

"It's perfect," Seddus cheerily said. "Lots of ale to have in the meantime." He licked his lips.

"Indeed," Marston said with a chuckle. "It'll make the ears sharper."

"Mind yourselves, brothers," Blaken said. "I've got a plan."

He knocked on the door.

Nobody answered.

He knocked again, firmer.

After a few moments, heavy footsteps approached the door. It opened; candlelight streamed out from within. A round-faced innkeeper stood before them. His face was jovial and kind, his long brown hair neatly tied back. No bloody marks scarred his forehead.

"Welcome, soldiers of the Crown, to the Red Lion Inn! Name's William Wickham, innkeeper here," the man said.

Blaken grinned. The other three weasels stared at Wickham in confusion.

"Thank you, Mr. Wickham," Blaken said. "We wish to stay at the inn."

"Of course, of course! Welcome! Come in! Our Majesty's troops are treated well at my tavern. Loyal maids come and go to clean and press your uniforms as well."

Blaken turned to the others. "He sees us in human form, complete with scarlet coats and tricorn hats," he said as he chuckled.

They all let out a laugh as they went inside.

"I knew you were up to some sort of hijinks,"

Marston said with a grin.

"This is too good," Seddus added.

"What will it be, lads?" Wickham asked, "I'd wager you're mighty parched from your trials!"

"Indeed. A round of ciders will do," Blaken said.

"Yes, yes! An excellent choice!" Wickham yelled as he ran off to fill four mugs with cider. The weasels soon heard him humming to himself.

They sat down at a table. They had the tavern all to themselves.

"Perhaps everyone has retired for the night," Marston guessed.

"Or Pan's war has really taken its toll on our land," Blaken said.

"Whatever the case, we're lucky," Seddus said. "No thirsty villagers to compete with!"

Wickham returned and placed the mugs down. Seddus and Marston started gulping theirs down. "And how about some roast chicken?" Wickham asked.

Blaken's ears perked up. His mouth watered. He was not much into alcohol like the others, but he was certainly into food. "My stomach rumbles," he lamented, "we have not fed since before the battle. Yes, yes indeed, do fetch us a feast of roast chicken, post haste."

"So much for the information," Rowen said as he swigged his cider.

"We'll be of no use against Pan if we wither away to naught but our bones," Blaken said as he licked his lips.

The wait felt like hours to Blaken. Wickham finally returned with delicious-smelling chickens. The weasels immediately dug in. Wickham fetched more cider.

"Please," Blaken said with a mouth full of chicken, "sit down with us for a moment."

Wickham plopped himself down on a chair next to them. He looked like a happy puppy waiting for another request.

"We were separated from our regiment. We need to know their whereabouts."

"Thousands of British and Hessian soldiers are camped throughout New York, Sir. Soon, they'll be moving towards Fort Washington, no doubt. That's the rebels' last serious stronghold on northern York Island, and mighty strong it is, atop a great hill. The King's men will claim it, make no mistake. Those hasty rebels will have no choice but to flee!" He slammed his fist on the table.

Marston drained the last of his second cider and knocked on the table in approval. "Hear, hear!" he yelled. Seddus happily joined in.

"What do you know of our general?" Blaken asked Wickham. "Does his cruel reputation precede him?"

Wickham's eyes widened. That question seemed to

set something off in him, something that he had suppressed before being mind-probed by Blaken. The innkeeper looked scared. "General White? I've...I've seen him once, but I shan't like to recall the time. I mean no treason, Sir, but he was rather...peculiar, if you follow me."

"I don't," Blaken said. His eyes sharpened. "Do explain. General White is what he calls himself, I take it?"

"Yes, Sir, of course. General White is a fearsome warrior, tall, blond, and very regal. Kingly, even, in his own right. But his eyes...begging your pardon, but they were red like hellfire. Made me shiver, they did. More so than that, I saw him go...he...he went through...he..." Wickham started trailing off, getting lost in his own thoughts.

"Speak directly!" Blaken demanded.

"It's going to sound quite queer. But I could have sworn I spotted him cut through the very sky. In the blink of an eye, he was gone, as if he was never there. None of his army noticed. Unholy it seemed."

There was a deep silence among the group.

At length, Seddus stirred. "Very good, Mr. Wickham. Now, more cider!"

Blaken sat back as Wickham sprang to his feet and went off to pour another round of ciders.

"This is most unsettling," Blaken started, "that Pan

travels through the very fabric of the planet. To disappear and reappear wherever he wishes. His skill has grown."

"Our mission is more hopeless than I thought. It is a fool's errand," Rowen said. "How do we fight an enemy we cannot pinpoint or even see?" His golden eyes drifted to his mug, he fell back into his chair and retreated into his own thoughts.

"If the British are heading to Fort Washington, it stands to reason that Pan will be there. Perhaps it's the sight of a new amusement," Seddus noted. "The ultimate test for his minions, to prove who can serve him best, no doubt. Yet," he started with a gleam in his eyes, "there's no way for him to know that we know of his plans. We have the element of surprise on our side, brothers. Perhaps he shan't have time to retreat anywhere, if we catch him unawares at the fort." Seddus was notoriously optimistic, but it was a valid point. Even Rowen glanced up at him, contemplating his words.

"For all of your cider, you still have wisdom," Blaken said. "Ambushing the villain at Fort Washington may be our only chance of a surprise attack. York Island is no short distance. If we are to go there, we must procure canoes to ferry us across the bay."

"I'll go at first light," Rowen volunteered, snapping out of his pensive state. "I don't think the bay is too far from here. Surely, I can find us vessels on a wharf."

"Two should go. It would be dangerous to travel alone. I, at least, must stay here to keep Wickham under my control," Blaken said. "Who shall go with you?" He looked at Marston and Seddus.

The two drunken weasels looked at each other, neither one wanted to leave the tavern.

Wickham placed another four mugs full of cider on the table.

Marston gave Seddus a stone-cold stare.

Seddus groaned in dissatisfaction. "Fine," he said, "I'll do it. But I'm taking some cider with me."

"Regardless of how quickly you secure the boats, we must linger here to hear what travellers have to say. Hopefully Wickham's words are true. I can make him see us as humans, but I have no way of knowing if his information is accurate. Allegiances shift like wildfire in these parts. Pan's mind games have everyone confused."

"How much cider can fit in a canteen?" Seddus asked.

"You silly rascal," Marston said, "you'd consume all the spirits if I wasn't here to help lighten the burden!"

Rowen smirked.

"It's going to be a long night," Blaken said. He finally swigged his cider.

...

CHAPTER FIVE

Pan and Weling sat at a long table in a library full of old tomes. Bottles of wine and open books were strewn around them. Pan was fully dressed in his freshly-pressed British uniform. His scarlet coat had silver buttons and was lined with silver stitching; his golden gorget reflected the bouncy firelight from the candelabras. He looked up from a book of ancient spells. "A tiny mind-reader is of no concern to me, Commander. For every minion he unmakes, one hundred more shall take his place. The weasels will be crushed in due time." His eyes gravitated downwards and he continued reading.

"I have no doubt of it," Weling said, "but Company Stillheart still poses a risk. They are constantly nipping at our heels, especially in the north. They've already slaughtered our regiments in Massachusetts and Connecticut. Borr is a capable leader."

Pan laughed as he carefully turned old pages. "I've kept the wolf and his company around for the same reason I've kept the humans around…for sport. How utterly boring it would be without the blood of beasts to soak the stillness of the ground. My arrival up north will keep Company Stillheart's attention. Perhaps I will kill one or two of them along the way."

"That reminds me, Lord. Excuse my ignorance," Weling started.

Pan's eyes glared at the bobcat.

Weling gulped. "Is this trip to the north…this sea battle you are orchestrating at Valcour Island…pertinent to our cause? After all, it shall take at least a month to draw enough of our forces there. And, although you'll sail with the redcoats, doubtless they will be killed too, in the heat of battle. You are spreading us thin. I believe our British troops, at least, should be spared from most of your northern games."

Pan's eyes widened in anger. "You dare question my plans? Have you not enjoyed great glory in my service, bobcat? Leading the mindless humans to battle at my beck and call?"

"I have, my King, but—"

"Do you wish to be King, in my stead?" Pan stared at Weling, his face tense.

"No, never," Weling replied, "you misunderstand me. I merely wanted to point out that we will need the manpower of the British army and navy to vanquish all of the threats posed on this planet, beyond the spirits of Rancientia. Our plan is to rule over Earth, is it not? At your discretion, I was named Commander of the redcoats, and I see their worth. Yes, humans are weak, but some among them have proven stronger than we had guessed. The hard-hearted Iroquois have so far resisted your sway. They've opened diplomacy with

Company Stillheart."

Pan slammed the book shut and stood up, proud and tall. Weling shrank back, Pan's towering figure stirring untapped fear within him.

"Then I shall tear them apart, limb by limb, starting with those who cause me the most grief!" Pan yelled.

There was a moment of tense silence which felt like hours to Weling. He realised he spoke out of turn and used his own silver tongue to defuse his master's anger. "My sincerest apologies, my Lord," he said as he jumped from the chair and bowed low. "I shall not question your judgement again, for you have never led us astray. I spoke in haste and ignorance. Forgive me."

Pan drained the remaining wine in his goblet and took a deep breath. "You test my patience, Commander," he said as he wiped his lips. "Do not let it happen again. I trust you know your role in my absence. I leave for Valcour Island at dawn and will be travelling on horseback as the inferiors do. More minions must be made. They shall follow me north, and when I deem it, the battle will commence."

...

CHAPTER SIX

Almost four weeks passed at the Red Lion Inn.

Blaken and Marston eavesdropped on many redcoats who came in and out of the tavern. They learned that Pan and his army would arrive at Fort Washington sometime in early November.

Blaken was mentally drained from probing Wickham's mind. Marston grew weary of being idle. At dawn, while Wickham snored, the two weasels convened downstairs.

"Rowen and Seddus have been gone for weeks. What's taking them so long?" Marston asked. "My bones grow sluggish."

Blaken shrugged. "Perhaps it took them a while to find the right vessels for our journey. Once found, they had to conceal them somewhere, too. That's not an easy task if minions patrol the waters."

"Sure," Marston started, "but four weeks? It's nearly October. Seddus must be out of cider by now."

Blaken let out a lethargic chuckle. He was tired.

"If they don't come back tonight, we should leave and catch up to them. We've attained enough information here. Besides, I miss the fun of hunting for our own food instead of having it served to me. I want to sink my claws into fresh chickens again."

"The fun of hunting?" Blaken asked with a frown. "I loathe the nasty business. Bless Mr. Wickham for being so stocked full of dead meat," he said. Blaken hated taking lives, even if it was to satisfy his stomach, which, out of all four weasels, was the roundest and most needy. Blaken was well known for catching the least amount of prey during hunts on eastern Long Island, yet, he would be the first to indulge once the meat was cooked.

Marston rolled his eyes. "Aye, you'd rather I do all the hunting and serve it to you cooked on a nice shiny platter."

Blaken grinned. "Well, sure. You enjoy it, do you not?"

Marston laughed. "What do you say to my plan, then? Let us find the furry rascals if they do not return tonight."

A worried look suddenly passed over Blaken's face. "Alright."

Marston was Blaken's best friend, he knew what he was thinking.

"Rowen and Seddus are fine, brother. I just want to leave this place and get on with our mission. We're constantly in Wickham's shadow, hiding like thieves in this human den. And, truth be told, my heart yearns for more than the hunt. I want to be in the forest again. I'm naught but an archer without living wood to manipulate."

"You heard the soldiers. Western Long Island

consists mostly of plains, unlike the wooded east, where we grew up. I fear you must wait until we arrive on York Island to see a forest again."

Marston sighed. "Right. I think I'll have another cider," he said as he made his way over to the barrels.

"You may as well get me one, if you don't mind," Blaken said.

After they both enjoyed a drink, they slept soundly and woke up to the sound of roaring thunder as night fell. Rain poured down, smashing against the roof. They waited until midnight, but Rowen and Seddus did not return. Blaken ordered Wickham to provide them with cloaks and supplies.

Blaken turned to the innkeeper. "Thank you for your hospitality, Mr. Wickham. The royal army shall never want for comforts with such a man as yourself at the helm. Goodbye," he said as he fastened his new brown cloak around his neck.

"Aye, thank you indeed," Marston added, putting on his new black cloak. "Especially for the spirits."

"Come back soon, Sirs! God save the King!"

They drew their hoods over their heads as they stepped outside into the pouring rain, leaving the Red Lion Inn behind them.

Blaken breathed a sigh of relief as he let go of Wickham's mind. "Forgive me, Marston, but I'm afraid

I will provide no conversation for some time. I'm exhausted."

"Worry not, brother," Marston said. "I shall lead us west to the wharf. Surely, we will intercept our wet companions."

For hours, the two weasels travelled in quiet across the muddy plains on all fours, being careful not to attract any attention. They did not pass a soul, but the rain was relentless. Thunder cracked and lightning flashed to the west. They were soaked and miserable.

Finally, as dawn approached, orange rays of sunshine pierced through the thick clouds, and the downpour turned into a drizzle. Warmth started to return to their bones. At mid-day, they reached the wharf.

"The canoes!" Blaken yelled. They ran over to the vessels, tied to two stakes in the sand, gently bobbing in the water. In them were the packs of Rowen and Seddus.

"Oh no," Blaken said.

Marston was wide-eyed. "No…" he muttered.

Blood stained the sides of the canoes. As the weasels examined the scene more closely, they noticed many footprints in the sand. Some were those of the weasels, of this they were sure, but two other prints were made by unidentifiable animals. They sniffed the ground near the unfamiliar footprints; the weasels were clueless as to what had made them.

"We've left the inn too late," Blaken said. "It's all my fault."

"It's *our* fault, brother," Marston said. "We've underestimated our enemies." His sadness turned to anger. "But look, these strange footprints were made by other beasts, not humans. There's no indication that Pan—or any human for that matter—has been here. If that was the case, I think our chances of finding them would be bleak. But there is still hope. We're going to find our brothers. Alive. And then we shall kill whoever has taken them."

Blaken looked miserable. He remained quiet, breathing heavily. At length, he spoke. "This is proof of what we had feared, that surviving members of past spirit guilds have defected to Pan. I wonder who they are?"

"Well, once we find out, I shall give them no chance to explain themselves. They will die traitors of Queen Dalasia," Marston said.

"There's no time to lose now," Blaken said. "Let's get to York Island and find our brothers."

The weasels untied one of the canoes, jumped in, grabbed the paddles, and rowed. Determined, they started crossing the brownish waters of the East River.

Their original plan was to wait until nightfall, but with the disappearance of Rowen and Seddus, they threw caution to the wind. If they were spotted, they would somehow deal with it.

After a half hour of rowing, the winds howled and grew stronger, rocking the canoe back and forth as the waters grew much rougher. Blaken started getting seasick. "Ugh," he said, grabbing his stomach. "This motion does not agree with me. I do not feel well, brother." He stopped rowing and lay down, groaning.

"I, too, hate this foul river," Marston said, "devoid of trees, out in the open. But at least it does not wield its evil upon me in the same fashion. I shall endeavour to ferry us across, brother."

Blaken, in pain, half-heartedly raised his paw to salute Marston's valiance. But then his eyes widened, his face grew more tense. He sprang up and hung his head over the canoe, vomit streaming from him.

"That's rather unpleasant. Do try to control yourself," Marston said with a chuckle as he rowed.

The winds howled.

Blaken continued to vomit over the side of the canoe. This went on for some time, until the water calmed down. Blaken sank back down and curled into a foetal position. "Agony, misery," was all he muttered, over and over again, interrupted by intermittent vomiting.

"Fear not, brother!" Marston yelled, rowing aggressively and embracing his role as a sea captain. "Just keep dreaming of land, we'll be there soon!"

After what seemed like forever to Blaken but was, in reality, about five hours with Marston taking brief rests, the weasels made it to York Island. Blaken breathed a sigh of relief as the canoe stopped in the sand.

"Told you we'd make it. With no help from you, brother. It's a wonder you didn't throw up your organs," Marston said, grinning.

Blaken wiped his mouth and breathed the fresh air. Slowly, the feeling of nausea left him. He was woozy, but happily stood up and got out of the canoe. "Thank you, brother. I wish I could have been of more help, but pray that you never experience such misery."

"Just think of the trip back," Marston said.

Blaken said nothing.

...

CHAPTER SEVEN

The weasels travelled north. They had landed near the southernmost tip of the island due to the winds and had many miles to go before reaching Fort Washington, which was positioned to the far north of the island.

They had not walked long when they spotted a dense forest. Marston smiled. "At last!" he yelled as he ran towards the trees.

Blaken was exhausted from the trip over the river. "Let's rest here, until nightfall," he said. Marston did not disagree.

They found a secluded spot in a thicket and lay down, using their packs as pillows. The ground was wet from the recent storm, but they did not care. Marston touched the dirt and pulled thick tree roots from it. He arched the roots as they creaked and grew, fashioning them into a dome over the weary travellers to shield them from unwanted eyes. They fell into a deep, dreamless sleep.

Blaken awoke to Marston shaking him. It was a hasty sort of rattling; Marston was not one for grace and finesse. Blaken slowly opened his eyes. It was bright outside, sunlight shone through the cracks of the small dome. What time of the day it was he could not tell, but it was hot for late September. He smelled the fragrant scent of cooked meat.

"Wake up, brother," Marston said, "it's near one o'clock in the afternoon, you've slept the morning away. I hunted a fat turkey. And yes, you'll be pleased to know that I cooked it."

Blaken smiled as he sat up. Marston had been known to, at times, feast on his raw kill, unlike the other three weasels who preferred cooked meat.

Marston handed Blaken some turkey.

Blaken quickly consumed it. He was hungry, and the warm meat hit the spot. After the weasels feasted and licked the bones of the turkey clean, they drank from a nearby stream. Refreshed, they continued through the woods. Blaken felt well rested, and Marston thrived in the dense, leafy kingdom. They travelled in silence for about an hour.

Blaken looked over at Marston. "Are you thinking about them, too?" he asked.

"I am," Marston said as he looked downwards.

"I hope we get there in time… I hope we—"

Marston cut him off. "We will, brother. We have to believe that we will save them."

At that moment, the weasels realised they had reached the abrupt end of the forest. An open field was before them. The stench of rot permeated the air.

"Human filth," Marston said. "They must have cleared the wood for their dwellings."

Blaken squinted his eyes to see better into the distance. "This is no community. This is a tomb," he said.

Marston realised it now, too.

The field was strewn with hundreds of dead bodies. Corpses with symbols carved into their foreheads; corpses of both sides completely equal in death. Equal in their sacrifice for Pan's pleasure.

It was a sad sight. Marston finally felt the weight of their entire situation.

"I suppose we should look for any supplies we can carry," Blaken said at length, "for our road ahead is long."

The two weasels carefully scouted the field of the dead for anything useful.

Blaken peered over at a fallen Native American. He had colourful markings on his dark skin, partially covered in blood. "So, the demon has started breaking down the walls of the more valiant ones, too," Blaken said with a sigh. He picked up a tomahawk that lay next to the dead man and studied it. It had a sturdy and slender handle about ten inches in length, painted red, with a triangle-shaped metal blade attached to the top. Blaken smiled, satisfied with the weapon, and placed it in his belt. "I shall use it well," he vowed to the deceased warrior.

Marston found a few usable arrows and filled his quiver.

After a while, the weasels reconvened. "Are you ready to move on from this field of blood?" Blaken asked.

"Aye," Marston said, "and, perhaps, I see now that too much bloodshed is not a pleasant thing to behold." He fell silent.

For weeks, the weasels travelled north towards Fort Washington. They kept to the forests as best as they could. Their natural abilities helped them avoid humans who were not under Pan's sway, although Blaken very much wished to converse with some of them. Marston was strongly against the idea, and so Blaken withheld his desire. They came across only one stray pair of minions, separated from their regiment as it marched north to the fort ahead of them.

Fed up with the barbarity of the minions, and anxious about the state of his brothers, Blaken did not hold back his anger when they engaged them. He clawed his victim almost to death, and would have, if Marston had not driven a thick branch into the vagabond's chest first. "Save it for those who have our brothers," Marston had told him.

At last, in mid-October, they reached the lower woodlands that surrounded Fort Washington. It was dusk; the westering sun's last rays glistened on the fort. The impressive structure loomed overhead, a few hundred feet above them, at the very top of the tallest hill on York Island. They looked upon it in wonder. It stood atop a fortress of solid bedrock, great abatis and other earthworks encircled the seemingly impenetrable fortress. Beyond, many feet below, the Hudson River flowed.

"Impressive," Blaken muttered.

"Wickham said this is the last Patriot stronghold in New York," Marston said.

"Well, yes, but we know that all these players, Patriot and redcoat alike, are just game pieces to Pan. He has set these Patriot pawns atop the hill so his favoured redcoats can knock them off it."

"He's testing their power…and their wills," Marston added.

"Indeed," Blaken said. "And, as a result, he tests our strengths as well."

After a brief silence, Marston spoke. "So, what's the plan?"

Blaken held his head. "My skull aches with all of this minion presence. They're all around us, marching to and from the fort. Everywhere. Let us ascend the great hill and search for our brothers. They could be anywhere; around the premises or in the fortress itself."

Marston was determined. "Lead the way!"

The weasels climbed the steep hill as night fell. They were careful to avoid minions, many of whom marched past them on a number of occasions but failed to notice them. It was not time for battle; not until they found their brothers.

They climbed for an hour, making their way over thick roots and around tremendous boulders before arriving within twenty feet of the abatis. They crouched in a thicket, carefully spying on the soldiers as they came and went. Still, there was no sign of Rowen and Seddus. Blaken's head pounded from all the human activity, but he knew that Pan was not there yet: his presence would be impossible to ignore.

At the southern side of the fort, the weasels spotted two strange figures standing atop the wall, looking out into the night. They could not make out details in the pale firelight, but they knew they looked upon fellow Rancientians. One figure was slender and on all fours; the other was stocky and hunched over, it had a long, rat-like tail. But that was all they could see.

"They must be the ones who attacked them," Blaken angrily said.

Marston's paws clenched in a tight fist.

Blaken could tell Marston wanted to bolt towards the fort and find entry, regardless of the repercussions if he was stopped along the way.

"I know what you're thinking, brother, but we need a plan to get into the fort. We'll be no use to Rowen and Seddus if we're caught, or worse, dead," Blaken said.

Marston relaxed. "I suppose you're right. Let's navigate around the base of the fortress. Find a point of least resistance."

"My thoughts exactly," Blaken said with a grin.

All that night, the weasels searched for an easy way into the fort. But every path was well guarded by hundreds of troops; it would be a suicide mission to storm it this way. Dawn approached and the weasels sighed, defeated.

For three long weeks, the weasels lingered around Fort Washington, stalking the minions and debating the right course of action. Scores of troops poured into the fort daily. Still, they learned no news of their brothers.

On the cold afternoon of 6 November, the weasels spotted a regiment of Patriot minions as they trudged up the hill and halted in a clearing near a precipice, midway to the fort. The brothers saw nothing out of the ordinary until the last soldier came up from the rear, dragging a struggling animal by its neck with a rope.

It was Rowen.

Blaken and Marston sprang up out of the bushes they were concealed in.

"Why does he not fight back?!" Marston asked.

"Perhaps they did something to him," Blaken guessed. "He looks hurt."

The weasels noticed Rowen's condition as the troops made ready for camp. He was badly beaten; his attire was ripped and filthy. Blood stained his light brown fur, especially around his neck where the rope had dug its threads deep into his skin. But he was alive. The soldier who dragged him threw him down to the ground and laughed.

Rowen did not bother to get up.

The weasels quickly looked around, scanning the area for other enemies. Only the Patriots were nearby. It was the perfect time to strike. They looked at each other and nodded. They ran towards the soldiers, angry, weary, and full of anxiety. Their limbs shook with anticipation. They had to save Rowen.

Marston reached for an arrow as he ran, and set it to his bow. He aimed, and it twanged before finding its mark in the neck of one of the soldiers.

The rest of the minions turned, their faces red with rage.

These minions do not fear us, Blaken thought to

himself, moments before they clashed. But it was too late to ponder. It was too late for a plan. *They are stronger than the others. None will be saved.*

The Patriots started loading their muskets.

Blaken jumped on the shoulders of the one closest to him. "What is it with humans and firearms?!" he yelled. Large orbs emitted from Blaken's paws, and soon the minion's head was engulfed in gold as Blaken scrambled his mind.

The minion screamed, his face turning from confusion to panic. Ghostly white, he fell to the floor, convulsing. Blaken took his tomahawk and lodged it into the struggling man's back. The minion stopped moving; Blaken had made his first kill. Anger took him as he pounced towards another enemy.

Marston's furious eyes were full of scorn as he ripped roots from the ground and curled them tightly around one minion's neck until it snapped. Many more rallied towards him, but one by one they were impaled by wooden spikes that rose from the ground at Marston's call. His bow sang as he sent many arrows towards his charging enemies.

Blaken absorbed as much mental energy as he could handle, his fists illuminated as he struck down the minions who crashed upon him. All of them fell to the ground and writhed in anguish, screaming and holding their heads. He could feel his power growing stronger. Just as he turned to find his next victim, he saw Marston drill the last minion with an arrow to the chest.

Blaken and Marston stood side by side, victorious among a pile of bodies. Their dark brown fur was soaked with blood, but it was not their own. They only suffered minor cuts and bruises.

They turned to Rowen.

Their hearts sank.

He was not there; his bonds were cut and lay frayed on the ground.

"Where is he?!" Marston yelled.

"Rowen!" Blaken called out.

Suddenly Blaken's ears cocked up. "Oh no. Marston, Pan is—"

Before he could finish his sentence, Pan ripped through the forest and onto the field in a blur of red. Blaken had no chance to react. He felt the general's strong hands grip his neck. Pan smashed him against a thick tree that bordered the field.

Blaken cried out in pain, pinned to the tree, unable to move.

"You lowly form, you dare have the audacity to enter my domain?" Pan screamed at him.

Blaken could not reply, Pan's grip was strong.

Pan grinned. He was enjoying watching Blaken

struggle. "Ah, little psychic, you are trying to enter my head. Alas for you, you see now, that I am far too aware for that."

Pan lifted Blaken by his neck and threw him to the ground.

"Ugh!" Blaken yelled as his body smashed upon the hard dirt. He held his throat in pain.

"You were overly foolish to seek me out, weasel," Pan said as he circled around him like a predator to its prey.

Blaken spat. "You…will burn…in the Houses of Fire!" he yelled.

"You speak of the eternal fire, but all I hear is the sound of running water."

Blaken wearily glared at the villain.

Pan bent down and grabbed Blaken by the nape of his neck. He started walking towards the precipice.

"I could simply run my sword through you, but what is the fun in that? You're a psychic, after all, the first true psychic that Dalasia has sent to die. You deserve a proper send-off," Pan said. He pulled Blaken close to his face. "But I cannot say the same for your brother Marston. He will die by the sword."

With all his might, Blaken swiped at Pan's face, drawing blood across his soft cheek.

"Enough play, then!" Pan yelled as he slammed

Blaken down on the ground again. He picked him back up and walked to the edge of the cliff.

Pan dangled Blaken over the Hudson River, hundreds of feet below them. The weasel squirmed, but could not break free.

"Perhaps you have learned that I can travel through the voids of Earth to get to where I want to go, faster than any mortal can. But did you know," Pan squinted his eyes in pleasure, "that I can also climb the sky?"

Blaken's eyes widened as Pan stepped off the cliff as if he had ascended an invisible staircase in the sky. He took another step. And another. Before Blaken knew it, he was at least twenty feet above the cliff, directly over the river.

"It is a shame, Blaken, that this is to be your fate. We have much in common in the way of mind games, you and I. I may have used you for my cause." Pan pulled Blaken's face close to his. "But Rowen proved to be smarter than you, when he accepted my offer."

Blaken's heart dropped. Had Rowen betrayed them? He was helpless, unable to get away, unable to make sense of any of it.

"And now, alas," Pan said with a sigh, "our fun is over."

Pan released him.

"Nooo!!!" Blaken yelled as he fell hundreds of feet

down towards the swift river.

An osprey called out in the distance. "Feeding time," Pan said to himself and smiled.

Marston looked on in horror as Pan overtook Blaken. Before Marston could react, a dagger found its mark just below his shoulder. Marston cried out in pain. He looked ahead at his attacker.

It was Seddus. But it was not the Seddus he knew; his eyes were blackened, his sharp teeth were exposed in rage. Seddus said nothing and launched another dagger at Marston.

Marston barely dodged it but quickly tied Seddus up with winding thick roots. He tightened them just enough to keep Seddus in place as he squirmed in anger, unable to break free.

Seddus was not alone. The two animals Marston and Blaken had spotted atop the fort came out of the woods. Behind them was Rowen, unbound and walking freely with the evildoers. Marston did not know how to react, he was so confused. What was going on with his brothers?

"You never really know some spirits, weasel. Not even your own kin," a scarlet-clad bobcat said. Weling released a large shadow from his body that charged towards Marston.

Marston raised wooden spikes, but they passed

right through the shadow.

"Oh no," Marston said, tightening his fists.

The shadow punched him across the face, and Marston stumbled before it lifted him and slammed him onto the ground. His arrows splintered everywhere. The shadow pummelled him; his face was bloodied. He started losing consciousness.

Weling called the shadow back into his body.

Marston rolled over and spat out blood. He braced himself as he saw a shadow peer over him. Someone removed the dagger from his shoulder, and Marston cried out in pain.

"Brother," Rowen whispered as he stooped near him, holding his paw to Marston's wound. "I'm so sorry. But you must trust me."

Marston could barely see, blood trickled down into his eyes. A stocky opossum scurried over to Rowen's side.

"Such a sweet family reunion, is it not?" he asked as he grabbed Marston by his cloak and pulled him in. "Your brother chose the winning side. But you," he said, as he viciously swiped Marston across the face with his long, sharp claws, "you chose death!" He swiped him again. Blood dripped from his claws.

Marston was on the verge of blacking out.

"Enough, Brune!" Rowen yelled.

Brune angrily looked up. "Impeding my duties, newcomer? Or are you having second thoughts?"

"We should wait for Pan to decide what to do with him."

"Very wise of you, to think of your Master first," Pan said from behind them.

"My Lord," Brune said.

They bowed.

Pan looked at Marston with a disgusted face. "He's practically dead. Finish him off, I have no use for him."

Rowen flashed a nervous look at Weling.

Weling looked away.

"My pleasure," Brune said. He lifted his paw to strike Marston again, this time to kill. "I'll cut him at the throat."

"No," Pan said calmly. "I think, to prove his ultimate worth, Rowen should do it. What do you say, weasel? Unsheath your sabre and finish it."

Brune grinned from ear to ear.

"But, I—" Rowen stammered.

"Now!" Pan demanded. His voice bellowed over the field, deep and terrible.

Rowen was sweating. He slowly unsheathed his sabre. He looked at Marston, bloodied and defeated, then glanced again at Weling.

Weling nodded.

Rowen charged his blade with electricity and moved towards Marston. Suddenly, in one swift motion, Rowen turned and thrust his sabre into Pan's mid-section.

Pan yelled in pain and pulled the sabre out.

Brune quickly stuck his claws in Rowen's side.

Pan pushed Brune aside and pinned Rowen down. He put the sabre to Rowen's neck and smiled as he cut across the weasel's throat.

Rowen gasped as blood poured from the wound. His eyes rolled back.

At that moment, a wolf howled.

Pan turned and saw Company Stillheart, led by the grey wolf Borr, dashing towards him.

Weling jumped at Brune and quickly stuck his sword through his gut.

"Huh?!" Brune gasped and turned.

Weling spat on him and thrust the blade deeper.

The opossum fell dead.

All at once, Weling and Company Stillheart attacked Pan.

Weling released his shadow.

A skunk warrior released a stream of fire from his paws, torching Pan and setting his coat ablaze. Pan ripped it off as he tried to ward off Weling's shadow which landed several punches.

A great horned owl flew overhead and dropped a potion over Pan. His body immediately weakened, and he fell to his knees.

"Fools!" Pan yelled. "I will kill you all!"

"No, you will not!" Blaken yelled. He jumped from the back of his saviour, the osprey Hera, who had caught him before he fell into the Hudson River. He landed on the ground, bright golden orbs encircling his paws. "You will not harm another soul. *I* have you now. You cannot escape through the voids, even if you tried." Blaken squinted. "It seems I have caught you…unawares."

Pan's eyes widened. He ground his teeth in anger. "You—"

"Now, Borr!" Weling yelled.

Borr leapt onto Pan and sunk his ice-cold teeth into his neck. Blood squirted everywhere. Borr vigorously and repeatedly shook him back and forth; Pan looked like a ragdoll.

The wolf tossed him down.

Pan's limp body lay in a gathering pool of his own blood. His eyes were open, his face blue. Suddenly, his body started to crumble, and in a matter of seconds, all that was left of him was a blob of skin and clothes. A black mist rose from his body and was blown away by a gust of wind.

Weling stood tall, his shoulders back. "At last, his reign is over."

In tears, Blaken ran over to his brothers. He took Marston in his arms. "Please!" he yelled. "Please, someone save them!"

Company Stillheart gathered around the fallen weasels.

"Dell is a healer," Borr said. "She may be able to help."

The great horned owl looked closely at them. "Marston may live, if I tend to him straight away. And you have wounds that need healing, too. But alas," she said as she glanced at Rowen. "Rowen the Brave is dead."

"Rowen was a hero," Weling said. "He knew the risks—pledging fealty to Pan, baiting you and Marston in order to convince the villain of his loyalty. But our plan worked, thanks to his bravery. Seddus also played a part, until Pan used black magic to brainwash him and ensure obedience."

Blaken looked up, a gleam of hope in his watery eyes. "Seddus is alive?"

"He took to the woods after Marston's roots loosened. He is still under the evil spell and will commit more violence in the name of Pan. We will find him, and Dell will do her best to undo the demon's hold, but that day is not today. For years, I have worked with the Company to kill the tyrant. Never did I think I would see the day. Rowen gave his life so that the rest of us—including the humans—may live in a free world."

Blaken drew Marston and Rowen close, and wept.

In the weeks that followed, Dell tended to the weasels. They recovered well, although they carried scars and aches for the rest of their days. They grieved for Rowen, but luckily found Seddus in late 1777. Dell reversed the spell over him, and eventually, the surviving weasels returned to their home on eastern Long Island.

It was there that Blaken set this tale to paper.

Pan's lasting legacy was the American Revolution, started by the villain for his own pleasure. However, the war continued after 6 November 1776 without his interference, and was decided by human agency.

MATTHEW M. MONTELIONE writes horror fiction and American history. He lives with his wife in New York.

Bibliography
ANGELS, Black Hare Press, 2019
BEYOND, Black Hare Press, 2019
COLP: Solitude, Gypsum Sound Tales, 2019
Eerie Christmas, Black Hare Press, 2019
Gravely Unusual Magazine (Issue 1), 2018
It Came Out on a Wednesday (Issue 4), Alterna Comics, 2019
"Maintaining Normalcy in British-Occupied Brookhaven, Eastern Long Island, New York," *Journal of the American Revolution*, 2018
MONSTERS, Black Hare Press, 2019
Organic Ink (Volume 1), Dragon Soul Press, 2019
"Patriots Against Loyalists on Eastern Long Island, 1775-1776," *Journal of the American Revolution*, 2018
Quoth the Raven: A Contemporary Reimagining of the works of Edgar Allan Poe, Camden Park Press, 2018
"Richard Floyd IV: Long Island Loyalist," *Long Island History Journal*, 2015
Summer's Splash, Fantasia Divinity, 2019
Thuggish Itch: Devilish, Gypsum Sound Tales, 2018
Thuggish Itch: Hospitality, Gypsum Sound Tales, 2019
Winds of Despair, Fantasia Divinity, 2019
WORLDS, Black Hare Press, 2019

Connect
Website: maybeevils.com
Amazon: amazon.com/author/maybeevils
Twitter: @maybeevils
Facebook: maybeevils

MY FATHER'S DAUGHTER

By Cindar Harrell

Rochelle Flamel wakes to find herself in a far different time than she remembers, however she has a mission: to protect her father's legacy. She swore an oath. The Philosopher's Stone must not be found, no matter the costs, or the reason.

FRANCE, DECEMBER 1795

The forgotten girl didn't know how long she had been a prisoner. Her family was gone, and she was left alone with her thoughts for far too long. She owned nothing now, save for a small jewel-like stone that her mother had given her.

"Save it for when you really need it. When you are desperate and all hope seems lost," she had said. Well, hope was certainly lost, but she didn't know how the tiny red gem was supposed to help her.

She fingered it absently.

Eventually, a noise at the door made her look up. When someone entered, she offered the stone to him in exchange for freedom. However, the stone had other ideas. She gained her freedom, the man obeying her every command, a crimson glow dominating his eyes.

Whatever the stone was, it was powerful. Powerful enough to control the minds of men. Maybe even powerful enough to bring a country to its knees and grant her revenge.

The forgotten girl smiled.

She needed to find another one.

...

A FEW MONTHS LATER

There were papers littering the floor and cascading through the air in a strange dance. The smell of sulphur, oil, and hot metal permeated the area. Shouting and gunfire rose up from the streets outside. Blood entered the concoction of smells, a lot of it.

Men were dying. No, not men, boys.

I was splayed out, face down on an uneven, rocky surface, the contours of the environment matching the aches in my body.

Opening my eyes, I scanned the rubble that used to be my father's study. Centuries old dust was now covered with new debris and fallen mortar. I wasn't sure how long I had been asleep, but I knew that the war raging outside had nothing to do with why I had been awoken. Something else triggered the complex mechanism of my resting place.

When the men draped in shadow, came for my father—some after his research, others simply afraid of his knowledge and power—he sealed me away, giving me an elixir.

"Rochelle," he had said, "drink this. I don't know what will happen to me, but I am doing this for your protection and the protection of our family's secrets. I am truly sorry, but you will have to pay for my sins. You belong to God now."

"Of course, Father, I will guard the stone and elixir with my life," I had replied.

He smiled. "I wish I could tell you to guard yourself first, but...well, should there ever come a time when someone returns seeking riches and immortality for ill, you will be restored. You know me well, daughter, follow the clues and make sure you get there first." Banging outside had made him turn for a second before looking back at me. "Your mother's sorcery combined with my technology and alchemy made this chamber. You will be safe until God calls upon you."

Then he was gone and I was placed in a strange sleeping stasis by the Elixir of Life.

The elixir was made from the stone of immortality; the Philosopher's Stone. It had been my father's obsession, something that could cure any diseases, grant immortality, and transmute anything without being bound by the laws of nature.

My boots crunched on the debris as I walked around, looking for any signs of who might have been here. When I found nothing, I went to the crumbling back wall and felt for a hidden enclave. Inside was everything I needed. The equipment and outfit I had hidden away before the men came knocking down our door weren't exactly lady-like and not at all acceptable in my time, and most likely not in the new one I found myself, but it was certainly more sensible. I pulled on the pants and blouse quickly. Lacing the corset took a little longer, but at least it wasn't as bad as some of the others I had been forced to wear in the past. Gloves, scarf, belt, goggles, boots, and long coat followed.

Now for my gear.

I pulled out several small machines and gadgets my father had invented. All were way ahead of their time. My favourite was a golden hand canon, pistol he had called it, run by cogs and compressed steam. Different from the powder I smelled coming from outside. I oiled up the gears and smiled as they whirled to life in a huff of steam.

"Thanks, Papa." I smiled. "Now, time to get to work."

My father said that I knew him well, and indeed I did, but I knew this still wouldn't be easy. For one, I had no idea how long I had been in my slumber and therefore didn't know if the places I would think to go would even still exist. I decided it would be best to get my bearings on the current time and events. Leaving the now dilapidated building, I turned towards where the library used to be and prayed that it was still there.

The streets of Paris ran with blood flowing from crudely constructed barricades. Night had fallen and all seemed quiet now, but I still stayed alert.

I saw ghostly shades in hazy crimson screaming in terror, reenacting the moment of their deaths. Memories from the tragic events bleeding out of their proper time.

It didn't take me long to find the library and sneak in. The first thing I needed to know was what time I was in and what had happened during my extended slumber.

From what I could tell, I had been asleep for nearly

400 years. My father's achievements had been recorded with growing speculation and sensationalised. Not all accounts were accurate, however. Apparently, many believed my parents still live, although he was recorded as having died. There were no details, no cause of death or burial place, only a date, which seemed to lead credence to the claims. I smiled.

A lot can change in 400 years, even a city as timeless as Paris. The world was not the same, and some of my father's ideas had finally caught up to the world around him. Some, but not all. It appeared that monarchies all over Europe were falling. Mistrust in the abilities of a single man to rule thousands was spreading. I couldn't help but laugh. It was about time the general populace learned to think for themselves. Although, from what I could tell, it didn't appear the revolution was going well. The king and queen had been executed and yet the aristocrats still fought to restore the monarchy, refusing to let their way of life be cut as easily as their monarch's heads with their new execution device.

Now that I had some of my bearings, I went back to the streets and headed towards the one place my father would entrust his most prized documents; his church. Whatever history now said of Nicolas and Perenelle Flamel, my father had been a good Catholic man. He had a grand church built and he called it his greatest invention, next to me.

I used the small steam and sorcery powered engines on my boots to aid in my travel, allowing me to jump further and higher than my body could on its own. I made my way to the cross streets named for my parents and saw what remained of my father's hard work. Only the towering spire remained of his beautiful cathedral, decimated in the war, no doubt. With a heavy heart, I approached the entrance of the spire. The carved panel above the door that featured my parents' kneeling forms lay broken and discarded on the street corner like trash. I knelt and ran my hands over their cracked stone faces, the only image I had of them.

"I'm sorry I was too late to save your church, father, but I will save the rest of your legacy."

Taking a deep breath to compose myself, I carefully entered the ruin. In the space under the standing spire, I found some books surprisingly intact. It wasn't much, but it was all I had. One of them was in my father's hand. I looked at the dates.

1416… 1417… these are all from before I was sealed. April 1418… Wait!

April 1418. A month after the recorded death of my father.

This has to be it!

25 Avril 1418

They have cornered me. Even though I am dead and buried to the world they still do not cease. I am not safe here even in my own sanctuary, I need to seek out another. I can only think of one that can save me. I pray to God that this trial will pass and that I have done the right thing. The world is not ready for my creations. I beg His forgiveness for trying to get too close to His glory. It was never my intention. I wanted to help mankind, but instead I may have doomed it. Man is not ready for this power. It should be left in His hands alone. I will seek refuge in the great lady, only her walls are strong enough to protect the stone.

"The great lady?" I smiled. There was only one place I could think of that matched that description, *Notre Dame de Paris*, Our Lady of Paris.

My breath caught in my throat as I touched down on the bank of the Seine and stared up at the imposing facade of Notre Dame. The war didn't even leave this sanctuary untouched, the most holy and mystical place in the city, the world, to me. Anger flared inside my chest at the insolent youths playing at war and revolution who would dare take their struggles out on such a place, but I knew I didn't have time to spare them any further thought.

I walked to the front, my boots clicking on the crumbled stone, and gently ran my fingers across the painstakingly carved figures around the door. I leaned my forehead against the structure, closing my eyes in a silent prayer. A prayer for safe passage, a prayer for my mission, a prayer for the safety of those I once loved now lost in time.

I entered.

An ethereal wind greeted me, coming from deep within the bowels of the structure. An energy echoed within this place even back then and I was glad to see that it had not been lost due to the damage. I opened my eyes and watched as the lights danced, painting the darkness with shadows across the huge vaulted ceilings. I remember coming here with a friend. I had mentioned the presence here—the wind, the lights—but my friend had just looked at me in confusion. She could not see it. She did not understand. To her it was simply a building like any other. To me, it was a sanctuary, in its most pure, truest form. If I failed my mission, my spirit would rest knowing I fought to my last and was granted one last look inside this angelic place.

Everyone always said that the cathedrals were the houses of God. I never believed it until Notre Dame. He may visit the others, but to me, it seemed like this is where He actually dwelled.

As I passed by the rose window, the filtered moonlight casting patterns of colour across the marble floor, I couldn't help but stare up at it and allow a silent tear to fall. This place always gave me pause, but I knew I couldn't linger. The dread that had filled me before was erased by a sense of warmth and peace, and I said a silent thank you to Notre Dame herself.

I walked all the way to the back where I knew a secret crypt lay hidden. I begged forgiveness and pried the stone away. Stale air greeted me, and I climbed through the cob-web lined hole.

Notre Dame was a mistress of great beauty, and great secrets. Her hallowed halls were guardians to truths long forgotten by the world. Beneath the crypt of Notre Dame were ruins more ancient than even I knew. Paris was known for its vast system of catacombs nesting just below the surface, and these ruins contained one of the many entrances into the complex system. However, it was my belief, as well as my father's, that whatever purpose the catacombs were first created for stemmed from the ruins resting beneath Notre Dame. They held a dark secret. My father had believed that a great evil was attempted there and that many died, later to be scattered in the catacombs. In recompense, Notre Dame had been built over it. A great force of good to counterbalance the darkness. That's why this place was so powerful. It was a nexus for spiritual energy, the oldest site in France of the fight against good and evil, maybe one of the oldest in the world, I didn't know. But I could feel it. I always could. I was sensitive to its energy, the life force of Notre Dame, suppressing the devil within its depths. God's great warrior, our lady of Paris, ever watching over us.

It made sense that if my father had to move the stone, then he would have hidden it here. If Notre Dame could protect Paris from the ancient evil in its crypts, it could protect the stone. But Paris was under attack now, and not even Notre Dame was being spared. The sanctuary of the church was no longer sacred. It had to be moved. It had to be protected.

I grabbed a torch from the wall, lighting it with a small contraption my father had rigged to emit fire at will. No more need for flint. I smiled. He truly was a genius.

The crypt was filled with ruins on top of ruins, like a burial ground for forgotten civilizations and relics long past recognition. Everything had a matching layer of dust, with one exception, the only thing in the room that didn't look like it belonged.

At the very back was a door made of a shining metal, dulled only by the centuries of grime, however, there was a long swipe where the dust had been disturbed recently.

I held up my hand and ran my fingers over the cleaned surface, it was like someone had rubbed the metal with a dusty cloth, trying to better discern what was beneath.

I was right, someone is after the stone.

The door didn't look like it had been moved, but even if they couldn't figure out the mechanism's entrance, I knew they wouldn't be deterred for long and would be back, better informed, better prepared.

I needed to get the stone before them and move it to a new location.

I lowered my goggles and withdrew my gun, ready for whatever awaited beyond the door. My father had told me the stone would be guarded, but he did not tell me in what manner, and I wasn't sure if there were safeguards in place for me to pass.

I pulled a large lever to the side of the door and listened carefully as the ancient gears ground against the rust.

Torch in one hand and gun readied in the other, I entered the darkness. The passage led beneath the surface, deep into the catacombs of the city. There was a canal that led off into multiple directions, but I knew they were false leads. My father wouldn't have left the stone so open and vulnerable as to let the passage connect to outside channels. This was a diversion, an illusion of openness that he had created, wanting unsuspecting marauders to think that this was just another section of the labyrinthine system of catacombs and tunnels beneath the city.

So three lead to dead ends and most likely fatal traps…only one leads to the stone. But which one? There should be a clue somewhere.

Carefully, I walked to the corners of each tunnel, studying the walls for any markers. Barely visible beneath the grime, I found small etchings. There was a different one at each entrance.

Pick the right image and it will lead me to the stone.

One depicted a pile of gold, one a cross, and the final a stone radiating light.

I smiled and took the path of the cross. It was a trap set for the ignorant and greedy.

Soon enough, the tunnel opened up into what appeared to be an ancient tomb. Skulls lined every crevice of the wall, and a large marble structure sat at the edge of the channel's waters. Whether it was meant as an altar or a coffin, I wasn't sure.

The back half looked as if it had been smashed in. A large piece of debris the obvious culprit. I looked up and saw that part of one of the columns was broken off, either during the war or perhaps some other time over the past few centuries as it had grown weak. I sifted through the marble debris until I saw a lever resting at the bottom. I pulled it.

The mechanism whined as a platform tried to rise from the rubble, but the large stones were too heavy for the centuries old technology.

Damn.

Before I could begin uncovering the lift, pain filled my head and I was thrown to the side. Large hands grasped my arms as I struggled to regain my blackened vision.

Finally, it cleared enough for me to see two men digging out the hidden plate. Another two had me pinned down. Four in all.

It didn't take long for the weight to ease enough for the gears to lift their buried treasure. A cylindrical container appeared, glowing red and saffron in turns.

The stone!

"Mistress, we found it," one of the men said, gently lifting it from its pedestal.

"Wonderful. I should thank you. I wouldn't have known which path to take if not for you. I'm glad now that we waited," a voice came from the darkness, soft but arrogant.

"Who are you? Reveal yourself!" I called out,

struggling against my captors.

"I don't see why it matters; you won't know me. No one does, not anymore." A woman stepped from the shadows, more like a girl playing at womanhood. Reverently, she took the container from the man. "My mother was sacrificed for this revolution going on outside. I was imprisoned for crimes I neither knew nor committed. I had no power. But with this…" She held up the stone, "I can have the power, the *life*, that I deserve, that my mother deserved. The power that is my birthright. I will not be sacrificed on the altar of the revolution like them!" There was a madness in her eyes as she focused on the glimmering stone.

"I don't know who you are, but no one deserves power like that."

"I am Marie-Therese Charlotte, eldest daughter of King Louis XVI and Marie Antoinette and lone survivor of the royal family of France. And I know who you are, Rochelle Flamel. You are just as much a victim as I am. You should understand my sorrow, my plight, as you are a tool of your parents' failures and desires like me!" She turned her crazed eyes to look at me. "Your father entombed you! Doomed you to sleep until you were of use! Just like me! I was imprisoned with my family, I watched, as one by one, they were pulled away from me, their fates unknown until, years after spending all my days in solitude, I was finally liberated and told they were all murdered! They call it execution, justice for crimes they committed just like my imprisonment, but it was murder all the same."

"I am sorry you were put through that, but that doesn't change anything," I said softly. I could see the sorrow lining her fair face and knew the pain she must have felt.

"But it does! Don't you understand? We can both be free now!"

"And what do you know of me? Why do you assume I am enslaved? That I need to be free?"

"I know you… This may be our first meeting, but I know you. I know the look in your eyes, you are haunted." She began to walk, slowly, her skirts billowing around her. I noticed then that although they were made of fine materials, the fabric was worn and threadbare. They were the garments of a noblewoman, but a true noble would have discarded them long before they reached such a state. "I grew up in a palace, you know. The grandest in the world: Versailles. There were grand parties there all the time, and I was surrounded by luxury and elegance. Now I am only surrounded by death." She looked to the skulls encased in the walls around us before continuing. "I returned there, once I was liberated from my solitude. It was stripped bare of everything. The paintings I knew so well, the sculptures, even the mirrors were not spared. I remember standing in its once opulent halls feeling as empty as it was. I don't know how long I stayed there, wandering like a ghost haunting its old home, longing for the living, longing for the dead to be returned. But then, I made a discovery. In the old library, I found some papers that had been left, soiled and forgotten on the floor."

"And what were these papers?"

"They were letters and journal entries dating back 200 years. Diane de Poitiers, yes, that was her name. She was the king's mistress at the time from what I could discern. It was before Versailles was built, but the papers must have been stowed in a book that was moved with the rest when the palace was built. My mother gifted me a tiny stone, my guess is she found it among these papers."

"Would you get on with it? As fascinating as your life story is, I can think of much better ways to spend eternity," I growled.

She glared at me, but finally continued. "Diane de Poitiers wrote about a tincture she took to stay young and beautiful, a mixture that was provided to her by an alchemist. She mentioned that she had to keep his identity a secret for he wasn't supposed to still be alive, but within the confines of her private journal pages she revealed his name: Nicolas Flamel. She wrote of the stone and its power, how it could make you live forever. That its ability was beyond measure. She said it was heavily guarded, that he entrusted his own daughter as its keeper." She smiled. "I knew then, that is what I needed. If I am to take back France, take back what is mine and avenge my parents, then I will need the greatest power on Earth. I will need the power of immortality. No blade shall sever my head!" She raised the cylinder and opened the front panel. A crimson blast shot toward me, hitting me square in the chest and releasing me from the men's grasp.

Thanks for that...

I recovered quickly and rolled into a crouch. I aimed my gun and raised my scarf to cover my nose and mouth to protect against the hot steam I knew would pour from the weapon when it was fired. I shot at her head, but she evaded and ducked behind a pillar.

"You can't win, Rochelle, not when I have the stone."

"Do you honestly think that my father didn't create a failsafe for something like this?"

I could sense her hesitation. "What?"

"My father was a genius, a scribe, an alchemist, and inventor. He devoted himself to God, and God blessed him with knowledge. He planned for everything. Every situation, every possible outcome. He created the stone. He knew its power. Once it had a form of its own, he had the knowledge of the ages. He felt cursed by it and knew he had failed in his duty to serve God. that is why he sealed it away. Do you really think he would leave something like that to chance? Think about it, Princess." I paused, my eyes tracking her every movement, her every breath, watching. "Why would he leave such power to chance? That is why he left me as its keeper. Do you really think he would have left me powerless against it?"

"What are you saying?"

"I'm saying, you cannot kill me with the stone. While it is true that the stone can take life as quickly as it can give it, mine is not one it can take. You see, my life already belongs to the stone."

She peered around the pillar and I knew from her expression that she saw the crimson glow in my eyes.

"My father did not leave me powerless. Why do you think I was able to sleep agelessly for so many years? My father was an inventor, and some would say that I am his greatest invention."

"You aren't human?"

"I suppose that depends on how you define humanity. Was I born? Yes. Will I die a mortal death? Too early to tell." I smiled. "My father gave me the Elixir of Life, but he also infused my blood with that of the stone. In addition, he used my blood to fuel the stone. We are linked, me and it. Two sisters born of the same father. My father gave my life to God as recompense for creating the stone. I was the price for his knowledge, my life is not my own any longer. My sole purpose is to ensure that humanity never uses the stone."

"Why create such a thing if not to be used?" she asked, her voice shaking.

"Just like Eve in the Garden, knowledge was placed before him and his hunger for it consumed him. But we are not meant to have such knowledge. We are not meant to have immortality in this world. Only the will of God determines our fate. I have God's will on my side, what do you have on yours?"

"How are you so certain that you do His will? My family has reigned for centuries! My line is pure! I was born to rule, if not France, then another country!"

"From what I see, your family drove this country into the ground! The people have spoken, the time of the royals is at an end!"

"Never! I won't let it! I will have what was promised me. It will live on forever, just as I will!" The glow from the cylinder pushed out and engulfed her four henchmen. Their eyes glowed like that of the devil himself and they rushed towards me, all power and madness.

I shot the first two quickly and they went down. The third I dodged while I charged the fourth, picking up a large piece of rubble and bashing in his head, stopping him in his tracks. I turned on my heel to face the third man, recovering from my evade. I threw the rock at his face as means for a distraction as I reloaded my pistol and aimed. I fired.

All four men lay on the ground broken and bleeding. I said a silent prayer for them before turning back to face Marie-Therese.

"I am the only daughter of Nicolas and Perenelle Flamel, my life given solely to God." I shot the stone from her hands, making her cry out and regard me with terror-filled eyes. "The history books will not remember me, but I am my father's daughter. I am his greatest invention and I will do God's will and make him proud. Tonight, the Philosopher's Stone will be no more. You have a choice; do you wish to be destroyed with it?"

She hesitated, looking to her lifeless bodyguards.

"I…I don't want to die…" she stammered.

"Few do." I sighed. Before me was a lost girl, raised in privilege and broken by tragedy. In the end, she was right about one thing, we were both slaves to our parents. They shaped us and then left us to clean up their messes. "Many have died seeking immortality, and even more have died in the name of vengeance. Do you wish to be one of those or do you want to make the best of the life that you have? It may not be the one you were raised in, or the one you feel that you deserve…you may never be the Queen of France, but you can still have a life. A good one, better than many others in this country." I saw the tears flowing from her eyes and my heart ached for her.

"I just wanted to make them pay for what they did to my family. I…I just wanted to make them proud."

"You still can, but not if you're dead. Leave this country. There are those who will grant you asylum until the trials here have passed. See what you can do for France and those around you with the power you have. That's all anyone can ask of you."

She nodded and turned to leave. She looked back to me and seemed as though she wanted to say something else. Deciding against it, she smiled and left.

I picked up the stone, left forgotten on the ground.

Now…to do what my father should have done.

The only option was to destroy it. There would always be those who would seek out the stone, to seek immortality or the power to do as they please with no regard for the consequences. There was no place for such temptation in the realm of man. It had to be destroyed. I released it from the cage that contained its full power and regarded its glowing light. It truly was beautiful.

I let its power flow from my hands, using its ability to transmute to my advantage, rebuilding the structures around me and solidifying them. I would make my own tomb. I used the carbon in the rubble to harden the entrance and walls so that it was the consistency and durability of diamond. My father's alchemy lessons were not in vain.

The result of my efforts was an impenetrable room, strong enough to withstand both time and man.

Now, for the stone itself.

Me and the stone were linked, like two sisters, I wasn't lying when I told her that. It had the power of life, me of death. The only way I knew to destroy the stone was to use its own power against it, to channel its energy through my blood and back into itself, causing a destructive reaction. This was what I was created for. Maybe not at first, but it was the destiny I was shaped to fulfil.

Closing my eyes, I started the process of transmutation. I felt the power course through me, building until my body was being torn apart.

I screamed and collapsed, pain racing through me like every particle of my being was on fire.

Something exploded around me, but I was paralyzed and couldn't tell what. The stone, still clutched in my hand, felt more fragile now, and I looked to it.

As I lay there, staring at the stone as its light dimmed, my blood flowing around me like a blooming flower, my thoughts drifted. Marie-Therese's words came back to me; *"I just wanted to make them proud."* I understood how she felt. My mind wandered back to my own mother and father. I was given to God as payment for my father's sins, and at last they were paid in full. I served my purpose.

"Are you proud of me, Papa?" I muttered into the silence.

As my eyes closed, I heard a quiet, "Yes."

CINDAR HARRELL loves fairy tales, especially ones with a dark twist. Her writing is often fairy tale inspired, but she also loves mystery and horror. Her stories can be found in various anthologies from publishers such as Black Hare Press, Iron Faerie Publishing, Dragon Soul Press, Blood Song Books, Soteira Press, Fantasia Divinity and more. Traveling is a passion for her as it inspires her imagination to run wild, especially in places that have a mystic presence in the air. She regularly moonlights as another human, but no matter who she is, she is always writing. Her novella inspired by The Snow Queen is set to release in 2020 as well as her debut novel, Lithium, and short story collection, Perchance to Dream.

Bibliography
100 Word Horrors vol. 3, KJK Publishing, 2019
Beneath Yggdrasil's Shadow, Fantasia Divinity, 2018
Coffins and Dragons, Dragon Soul Press, 2019
Curses & Cauldrons, Blood Song Books, 2019
Dark Drabbles vol. 4: Beyond, Black Hare Press, 2019
Dark Drabbles vol. 5: Unravel, Black Hare Press, 2019
Dark Drabbles vol. 6: Apocalypse, Black Hare Press 2019
Divinity, Iron Faerie Publishing, 2019
Ever Dream of Me, Fantasia Divinity, 2016
Fable, Iron Faerie Publishing, 2019
Forest of Fear vol. 1, Blood Song Books, 2019
Galactic Goddesses, Fantasia Divinity, 2019
Halloween Frights & Autumn Delights, Fantasia Divinity, 2019
Midnight Masquerade, Fantasia Divinity, 2018
Spring's Blessing, Fantasia Divinity, 2019
Storming Area 51, Black Hare Press, 2019
Stuff of Nightmares, BMR Promotions
Summer's Splash, Fantasia Divinity, 2019

Connect
Amazon: amazon.com/Cindar-Harrell/e/B07W8W3CV7
Facebook: CindarHarrell

OF DESPERATE MEASURES AND VICTORY

By Jo Seysener

Lord Horatio Nelson despises the new weapons forced on him to turn the tide of war, but when Julian Herrington's pet scientist pushes the issue outside of parliament, Nelson fears the outcome of the impending Battle of Trafalgar may be out of his strategic control.

Giant moths flexed their wings lazily in the haze of the pre-dawn fog illuminated by the gaslight they clung to. Lord Julian Herrington tossed a coin to the sleepy boy rocking on his heels beneath them. The boy caught it with surprising dexterity, slipping it into his pocket and reaching for the nearest moth.

"It's alright. I've got this one," Julian told the boy,

detangling a moth's legs from the lamp post higher up. The boy flashed him a dimpled grin, tipped his cap down his face, and resumed his snooze.

Letting the moth wrap its thin legs about his arm, Julian flicked the beast so its wings opened at the first page and began to read the morning's early edition of the broadsheets.

His tiger brushed moth dust from his jacket, fussing about his ankles.

"Yer valet won't be pleased, you reading those things."

"You should learn to read, Sam. It broadens the mind." Julian tapped the boy's head. "No point fussing. We'll be home soon, and Wick can whine about it all he likes."

"It not just yer clothes he'll be whingin' about," Sam muttered, gathering the reins of the matched pair, "it's the company yer keep too. Him."

A shudder ran through the boy, twitching his tiny body as though he was possessed. The young lord laughed.

"You've been listening to kitchen gossip again, haven't you? That old bag will have you on a snipe hunt next. Though I believe she's making Flaune Almayne tonight—no need to rush, there are plenty of pears in the orchard. Pick a few when you get home and perhaps she'll serve you an over-large piece with custard." A wide grin settled over the young lord's face as his thoughts returned to his protege. "Some of his techniques are…unusual, I must admit. But it's only science. Working those brain cells never hurt anyone, did it now?"

Sam shrugged, urging the qirin into a trot. The Chinese chimera arched their backs, stretching. Muscles rippled beneath dragon-like scales that gleamed damply in the morning fog.

"If yer say so, Sir."

"I won't use those bloody things, Hardy. I'll fight this war the way I know best." Lord Horatio Nelson pounded the table with a display of passion not unknown of the naval genius. He turned to the captain with a barely restrained grimace. "Make sure that doesn't make it to the broadsheets, would you? I have a staid reputation to maintain. King, country, and all. Let's not leave my dirty laundry flapping all over England."

"Desperate affairs require desperate measures, right, Sir?"

Nelson sent him a sour look at having his own words thrown back in his face.

"Never that desperate. Unpredictable. Uncontrollable. God didn't give us those beasts for such a purpose, certainly when I don't recognise the name of the engineer on the bloody papers. No. I won't use them, Captain!"

Hardy opened his mouth then closed it, not bothering to reply. What was the point? Half the ship had heard the admiral's diatribe, but by the time they got back to England bad press would be the least of the admiral's worries. If they returned at all. Hardy doubted they would last the morning.

"Fresh paint, new sick bay…just beautiful. We're a sight to be feared, eh?"

Like a fat bumblebee sailing into the throes battle against an unforgiving enemy.

Hardy didn't voice his misgivings. He understood Nelson's pride—nearly two years it had taken for the ship's upgrades. Fresh everything—sails, sleeping quarters, medical bay, scullery, adornments—including those black and yellow stripes that dominated the ship's visage. The Victory would stand out during combat indeed.

The coming battle brewed heavily in the sultry air of the Strait of Gibraltar. They'd passed Cape Trafalgar, the arse end of Spain, earlier. Nelson muttered to himself as he jotted the day's intent in his journal.

A storm was coming, so the admiral said. It wasn't unusual for a clear day to turn sour come evening. Hell and high water. Hardy had seen his fair share of cloud bursts over the seas but he wasn't convinced there was one coming today.

Hardy sent a prayer heavenward. He knew the master tactician preferred his own methods, but to deny them the advantage in war... He shrugged, epaulettes rattling upon his shoulders. Well, therein lay Nelson's genius. He just hoped they wouldn't wait until it was too late to turn the tide of battle.

"Annihilation. That is how we shall win this infernal war. Give the Empire supreme rule over the oceans. All of them. Here."

The admiral unrolled a sheaf of papers, flicking through until he found the right one. Hardy studied the diagram Neslon had placed on the small table of the Captain's quarters. Two long columns lay down the centre of the page, representing their ships, surrounded by the land that bordered the Strait. The enemy ships should sail right between their ranks.

Villeneuve's ship would approach head on, if it all went to plan, leaving their lead ships open to broadsides. But if they trapped the enemy flagship first... Nelson interrupted his train of thought.

"Time is everything, dear fellow. My band of brothers will ensure the win of the day, eh? Well trained, those captains are. Trained for the stresses of war. Five minutes will make the difference between Victory and defeat."

Nelson chuckled at his own joke while Hardy stared at the page, hoping desperately that the admiral was right.

Smoke filled the small attic when Julian opened the door, dumping its contents into the hall. He grimaced, knowing his father's housekeeper was already less than pleased with the arrangements. Julian waved at the billowing clouds, trying to stuff them back into the small space.

Giving it up as a bad job, he stooped under the doorframe, hoping the mess would dissipate before it caused him any grief. Julian shut the door and wandered through the smoky interior noting, with a small amount of alarm, the growing collection of specimen jars populating the sparely furnished room.

"Cotswold. Where are you doing, dear fellow?"

"Over here…ahem, here. I am. Here." Benedict Cotswold emerged from the smoke clutching a long specimen that brushed the dirty floor, leaving long trails in the dirt. Julian made a mental note to ensure the housekeeper cleaned Cotswold's rooms, regardless how much he had to pay her.

"Is that a tentacle?"

The curiosity was thrust at his face. Julian did his best not to recoil, taking a minute step backward to avoid the blasted thing touching his skin. The smell of ammonia permeated the room.

Long and slippery looking, the appendage was covered in large suckers that drooped woefully outside a fluid environment. Compared to the tiny octopi floating in their jars around the room, this specimen qualified as giant.

"What's it from?"

Julian didn't really want to know the answer but felt compelled to ask. He leaned down to study the suckers. In the centre of each was a very thin, curved hook. He put his finger to it and drew back with an oath, squeezing his fist tight as blood dripped from the cut.

"Ah, yes. Well, that can sometimes happen."

Cotswold disappeared back into the haze, reappearing with a cloth. Julian wrapped his finger up, resuming his observations from a safe distance, and repeated his question.

"A species of giant cuttlefish. For the war effort."

Julian's eyebrows slid up his forehead.

"Indeed. And…what are we going to use them for?"

"The underwater vessels, of course! It was in the notes I gave you last…ah." Cotswold peered at him for an uncomfortable moment. The tiny scientist harrumphed, fixing a pair of rose-tinted spectacles to his nose. "Though you would think a patron would read the work of someone he sponsors...but never you mind. There are more important things in life than a broad education and understanding. However, this," he drew Julian deeper into the haze, "this is my design. You see the shape, to draw speed in deep water? And here, these are handles. The cuttlefish hold on, propelling the craft at great speed. With fins operated from within the craft, a two-man crew can steer her quite effectively."

"Amazing!"

"Thank you. I call it the waterborn."

Julian looked confused for a moment. The little man bounced on his feet, ripe with enthusiasm.

"For William Bourne, of course! Fabulous, fabulous man. Made working plans for a submarine in 1578! What a modern time we live in, eh? And here we are, putting something similar in the water. Though my genius is naught compared to his."

Cotswold bobbed on the balls of his feet for a moment more. Julian marvelled at the diagram. It was an amazing feat of engineering, if it truly worked. He'd heard of horrible fates of the men who tested such contraptions. Brave souls. But if they could transport troops, weapons, in this manner with speed to Nelson's fleet...he traced faint lines decorating the sides of the vessel.

"What are these?"

"Pressurised tubes. We load them with ballistic projectiles, surrounded with a refined gunpower." Cotswold made a whooshing noise, flinging his hands forward of the picture and dropping the tentacle on the floor where it broke into two pieces.

"Kaboom!"

Cotswold smiled, apparently expecting him to cheer.

"Kaboom," Julian responded faintly, hoping he wouldn't be responsible for blowing the whole fleet to hell and do the enemy's job for them. He frowned, looking around the room—the parts he could see.

"And the smoke?"

"I've found the best way to preserve my specimens," the little man collected both sections of dusty tentacle, "is to smoke them. I don't have a jar large enough for these." He sent Julian an apologetic glance.

Julian frowned, recognising the thundering of the housekeeper's shoes. Nobody could miss the caterwauling that came next. He wondered if they shouldn't be sending her to the front instead.

"Turn the smoking down, old chap. Or perhaps open a window."

The men stood in rank, tall and sharp, as Hardy

strode the deck beside Nelson. The admiral had given a rousing speech. Hardy wondered if he would ever be as glib in the face of certain destruction—and yet the men had cheered. Truth be told, he had felt the same way. Any man who could approach battle in such form was formidable indeed. Nelson spoke gravely.

"You have trained for war. Our enemy is almost upon us. England expects every man to do his duty." Emphasis was placed on the last three words. Nelson cleared his throat, making eye contact with every sailor on the deck, regardless of rank. He was talented in that way. "That includes me."

The admiral gave a rare smile.

"Send the signal."

Hardy nodded to the seaman, who waved his flags energetically. A new cheer rose from the men gathered in a tight knot. As the signal passed down the line of twenty-seven ships, shouts filled the vast waters of the Strait.

This would be a battle to remember.

"Tell me again what you told the vice admiral."

Julian held the whiskey glass to his forehead, hoping it would take away the thudding migraine that threatened his consciousness.

Cotswold gabbled on for a moment and Julian let him

go until he got to the part he wanted to hear again.

"Stop. Say that again."

"I told him it would be an easy fix, bring the squid alongside the vessel, offer it some food, and presto! It's attached."

"No, not that bit—wait, will the squid eat the waterborns?"

"Cuttlefish. And no, they won't."

"What a relief. Now, the vice admiral said what about the cuttlefish? And the waterborns?"

"They're already in use. I sent in the plans a while back and they had them made up. My creations, off to war."

Cotswold's cheeks were so cherry red he looked like he might pop. Julian had no such reaction. He sank lower in his seat as hope drained out of him, certain the blasted things would explode in the middle of the fleet. Or worse. He scrubbed his bristled face with one hand.

"Why didn't you tell me you had sent the plans off? I'd planned to present them in session…damnit."

Julian cursed as his whiskey slopped on his riding breeches, staining the fabric. Warm liqueur turned to cold fingers dribbling down his inner thigh. Russet liquid pooled on the seat around his leg. Wick would not be pleased.

"Ah, but then it would have been a game of politics

in parliament—this is a game I know how to play!” He patted Julian’s shoulder and waddled off, presumably to make more dangerous contraptions.

Julian groaned. Those damned rules were there for a reason. And it wasn’t all class based, though perhaps he shouldn’t challenge those boundaries quite as often. Likely the scientist had accosted the vice admiral during his morning tea, rattling off ideas and adventures with passion…it was how Julian had gotten involved with him in the first place.

Hopefully he wouldn’t be reading about the demise of the English fleet at their own hands any time soon.

“Villeneuve has thirty-three ships, out numbering us by five, Sir. Ships, that is. Five ships. Your plan…I’m not sure it will—” Hardy silenced the officer’s drivel with a stern glare, motioning for him to vacate the quarterdeck while he still had his dignity—and rank—intact.

The silly boy, barely one and twenty, opened his mouth to continue. Hardy didn’t need to stop him this time.

“It is daunting, seeing the enemy lined before us, ready. Waiting. The plans are strong, boy, though it will be warm work. But we must give Villeneuve a chance, befitting his rank before we take it away, eh? We shouldn’t decimate the enemy before he has had an opportunity to retain his dignity. Something must be left to chance; nothing is sure in a sea fight, after all."

The lieutenants stood frozen as though he couldn't believe Nelson had spoken directly to him. Hardy recalled the boy's silent countenance over dinner the night prior and had put it down to the angst of the eve before a battle. Such times did funny things to a man's wame.

Now he wondered if it hadn't been about the battle at all. He placed a weatherworn hand on the boy's shoulder, gently guiding him off the quarterdeck with instructions to be passed to the men.

The ship rocked violently, sloshing about sloppily in the water. Nelson cursed and they both ducked instinctively, expecting cannon fire or some other barrage from the enemy flagship. Hardy uncovered his head after a moment, wondering at the sudden silence. Nelson leaned over the railing, red-faced, shaking a fist at the waters below.

Crewmen craned over the port side railing, exclaiming. Some crossed themselves. Others reached out, as though they could touch the sea despite their height above it. Hardy leaped over the crouching officer, peering into the depths.

At first nothing changed about the waters; they were as they had always been. Ripples disturbed the surface, and a sleek shadow passed beneath the boat. The crew rushed to the other side, calling out as they saw the thing reappear. Hardy marvelled at how long it took; the submersible must have been twenty feet long.

The ship rocked again and reports flew up the deck of two more on the starboard side.

"Impressive, what?" he commented to the admiral who had appeared by the helm. Nelson grunted, watching the shadow slink by.

Hardy gave Nelson a sideways glance. Though he believed in the genius of the man, he couldn't help but be reassured by the presence of the behemoths. Perhaps this war would be won through annihilation, after all.

"Oh, yes. Brilliant contraptions. Lovely, er, creatures." The vice admiral of the Royal Navy sent Julian a watery grin. Or a tipsy one. Julian had finally located the aged politician at Whites. The man had downed three whiskeys in the time it had taken Julian to order a single glass of port. Apparently, wealth and speed of service went hand in hand. Julian swished the liquid in his glass, reflecting garnet tones across this lap.

"My…colleague didn't bother you in any way, did he?" He avoided the word 'pester' whenever he could, reminiscent of his childhood. A deep chuckle drew Julian out of his reverie.

"Oh, no." The vice waved a chubby hand, chuckling, "Nothing of the sort! Good to see new up-and-comers. Give Horatio a run, this will!"

Julian stared. Surely this wasn't all a joke to the naval commander? The success of the war hung on this battle—any man with half a brain could see that in Nelson's relentless pursuit of Villeneuve, drawing him across the strait. The vice admiral's jovial attitude sat poorly with the young lord who wondered when he had last seen him in session.

"At least we will hear the news straight away," Julian commented.

They were damned lucky to have such direct communications with the fleet, else it would be months before they heard anything. How archaic a society that would make.

"The waterborns…I'm concerned they could be a detriment in battle."

Or a calamity.

Julian didn't add the last. Fat fingers stuffed a reddened face with tiny cakes.

"Not at all, dear boy. Not at all! They are a show of industry, progress! It will make us a great nation, an empire worthy of controlling the seas…" He trailed off, spitting crumbs as he spoke, "Besides, if Nelson can't wield them, perhaps he should have stayed at home, eh?"

The pieces finally fell into place. Nelson's recent appointment as 'First Naval Lord' clearly wasn't sitting well with his present company. It must be difficult to be passed over by a younger man of such genius compared to the mountain of a man seated before him, languishing in indulgence.

Cotswold had chosen his target well, Julian admitted ruefully. Perhaps he should be the one standing up for policy in the House of Lords.

"Nelson does have sound strategy," Julian tried again, "His theories have won many battles in the last few years alone, and his ideas on annihilation…"

He broke off as the vice admiral swelled, a flush reaching out of his collar to encompass his entire face. Julian watched with fascination.

"No such thing, boy. Those skirmishes are luck, that is all! Not a real warrior, just one who hasn't outlived his usefulness yet."

"Don't be daft, sir. Bonaparte keeps a bust of Nelson in his quarters."

The words tumbled from Julian's lips without any pre-emptive thought. The vice admiral's eyes narrowed, focussing on Julian wholly for the first time, halfway through lighting a cigar.

"My boy, those waterborns will win us the war, and

I hold their leash! Their success will be mine, and mine alone. Of course, should this venture fail, the entire fault will lay on your young shoulders. Keep your tame scientist close to home, won't you?"

The cigar lit up, obscuring Julian's vision. The vice admiral's voice drifted from within the cloud.

"I don't want state secrets running about the streets until it suits me."

Julian extracted himself from the table, pressing coins into the waiter's gloved hand as he passed, praying fervently the vice admiral would never hold the reins of the Royal Navy.

"Fifty men killed or wounded, Sir, and the Victory has yet to open fire!"

Hardy puffed a small breath between his cheeks, letting them out slowly so he didn't blow up like a great pair of bellows. He kept pace with Nelson as they strode the quarterdeck, calling encouragement to the men, his second lieutenant trotting to catch up.

The Victory was positioned at the head of one of the columns strung out in the water. Villeneuve had taken pause, surely, when he saw them waiting for him. Nelson had predicted his every move and now the enemy was trapped, his flagship making a run directly at them.

"Thank you," Hardy curtly dismissed the lieutenant who disappeared amidst a bombardment of debris as cannon fire hit the helm, blowing it to bits. He peered through the rain of splinters, glad to see the young officer scramble to his feet and dash off to assist the men.

We must turn soon. Broadside the bastard.

Nelson turned to him, a glimmer in his eye.

"Soon," he murmured. "You there, stand tall for England! You wear her colours, nary a wrinkle in sight, eh?" He turned back to Hardy, speaking out of the corner of his mouth, "I could not tread these perilous paths in safety if I did not keep a saving sense of humour."

Hardy grinned, opening his mouth for some witty retort he hadn't thought of yet, when another explosion rocked the ship. An enormous splinter shot past him and he ducked. Nelson smiled, his eyes bright with anticipation as he pointed down to Hardy's shoe. The leather was torn apart where the buckle had been ripped clean off. He found it embedded in the deck, impaled by a long sliver of wood.

"This is too warm work to last for long." Neslon signalled the lieutenant. "Ready fire."

The call echoed below decks, the noise of the well-practiced war machine a comfort. Waiting was death to a sailor; action his only recourse. Fire was lit in the men. Hardy could see it in the way they straightened, readied their firearms on deck.

Villeneuve was closer now, bearing down on them.

Any time now. Turn. Turn!

Hardy kept up the regular pace along the quarterdeck in the shadow of the greatest naval commander in history. His nails bit into his hands as another barrage struck the Victory. Splinters showered the men but still they waited for the signal.

Nelson stared out at the approaching ship, hand half raised. Hardy frowned, wondering if Nelson had finally frozen under pressure. The admiral's other hand raised slowly, pointing at the oncoming vessel.

Hardy squinted, shielding his eyes against the glare of sunlight glancing off the water. Two dark shapes trailed through the water ahead of them. He lurched as the ship rocked, two more dark shadows streamlining out from beneath the Victory's bow.

No gasps sounded this time; the men, battle-ready, didn't move. Hardy admired their strength, their respect for the man who led the fleet. Nelson stood frozen, watching the behemoths shoot toward Villeneuve's flagship, his mouth a thin line.

Hardy couldn't work out if he was pleased with the new weapons or not. Then it hit him—Nelson hadn't given orders for the waterborns to be used. If he wasn't controlling the damned things, who was?

He expected the ship to sink slowly, slammed by projectiles the submersibles carried. Instead, the waters on either side of Villeneuve's ship swelled, great crests that met the tops of the masts, showering the men beneath with seawater. Cries of alarm filtered across the ocean.

Through the clear water of the twin waves, Hardy could see the submersibles, as long as the ship they towered over. Tentacles swirled around the machines, living hybrids.

A puff of smoke blasted from the flagship—a last-ditch effort of attack or a shot at the death that overshadowed them, perhaps.

In that moment there was silence, then the waterborns came crashing down. The ends of the Villeneuve's ship rose into the air, meeting in the middle over the cuttlefish and its cargo. Enormous slivers of wood tangled in ropes and sails. Debris hung in the air then rained destruction beneath.

The mess floated, stilled, tentacles slung across the wreckage. The nose of one of the waterborns protruded from the side of the mass. Then the ordnance caught, obliterating the whole thing in a show of lights and smoke.

The deck broke into cheers from the men. Hats were thrown. Hardy could barely hear himself think over the cacophony. Grinning so hard his cheeks ached, he waved and cheered alongside the crew.

"Well done, Sir! Your theory of annihilation…"

The words died in his throat. Nelson lay upon the quarterdeck, a trickle of blood decorating his salt-worn face, the timber stained a red to match his coat. A round hole cut through the deck behind him.

The last shot. Those bastards actually hit him.

Hardy yelled to the medic waiting below who waved to him, continuing to cheer with the rest of the crew. Smoke and ash drifted over them as the seas stilled, air heavy with the oncoming storm.

"Help me!" Hardy yelled, pounding the railing, "Get him below!"

Not a soul stirred from their celebrations, the noise was so great. Hardy tore at his coat, pressing it to the admiral's side where blood pooled around him, thick and gluggy.

"Sir. Sir!"

Hardy knew better than to shake the admiral. He had seen many men rise from a seemingly innocent knock to fall only minutes later from some damage inside their bodies a mortal eye could not see.

Hardy passed a hand across Nelson's mouth. No breath moistened the toughened skin. Barely able to draw breathe, he leaned in to listen to the man's chest.

Waited.

Tears spilled over his cheeks, coursing through layers

of salt and grime of the day. Forehead pressed to the rough material of Nelson's coat, a hand gripped his shoulder, drawing him back. He stayed kneeling beside his mentor, turning his face to look up at the men gathered around. Faces blurred, but it didn't matter. None of it did.

"He's gone."

The captains of the fleet did as Nelson had bid, easily annihilating the enemy ships as they were forced to sail between the columns Nelson had arranged. Broadsides battered them until there was little left but debris floating on the surface. The wreckage of Villeneuve's flagship drifted away, separate from the rest of his broken armada.

Hardy sat in Nelson's quarters, head in his hands. They had lost the most significant figure in naval history. That the admiral wouldn't see the Empire establish naval supremacy—his dream—tore at his heart.

His second lieutenant entered the cabin, roles of parchment strung under both arms.

"Sir, I have the sheets ready to stamp, but I need one of the boys to run up the mast to collect the moths. The damned things have flown up there to be near the moon, we think. Won't come down. Who should I send…"

The lieutenant trailed off. Hardy didn't bother to move.

"Pick one."

"But, sir—"

"Pick one. Any damned one! Just choose."

"Aye, sir."

The lieutenant left the cabin hurriedly, his footfalls fading away.

Hardy wasn't sure when they had arrived, but judging by the amount of noise, there were quite a few of them.

"You can't use that one. The bloody stripes make it look like the Victory is being smashed to smithereens!"

"You're the one who suggested we show Villeneue's ship from that angle."

"But not like that! Here, we can fix it…"

There was a tearing sound followed by cursing. Hardy smiled into his hands. Then his heart clenched again, face warming, or perhaps it was his hands.

"If you can't keep the peace while you're here, feel free to get out."

The noise above him ceased and he breathed.

"Sir, we really do need to ask you what you want done. With the body. And there are the broadsheets to approve, too. We would like to send them across to the channel as fast as possible. We need to log the account and—"

The voice was cut short by a muffled cough. One of his officers had sense. That was a relief. Perhaps he could run the ship for a while.

"Yes, but we need to reappoint an admiral, sir. For the fleet, now that Nelson—" The voice halted abruptly, Hardy's breath along with it. He prayed the man would stop there. Unfortunately, today seemed to have only one miracle in it.

"It's you, sir. You're admiral of the fleet now Lord Nelson is gone."

Thomas Hardy raised his head, looking the complement of officers in the face, sure his eyes were as bleak as his heart.

"The world is a smaller place without him already."

Moth dust covered Julian's fingers. The lad beneath the gaslight had given a convincing spiel, giving a grateful jerk of his head as he pocketed the coin Julian had tossed his way, keen for news. An extra late edition meant some progress in the war. He just hoped the waterborns hadn't damaged their chances of winning the war. The moth's wings flicked, opening to the front page. He didn't have to look far before the headline hit him.

VILLENEUVE DEFEATED, NELSON KILLED IN

BATTLE

A picture beneath showed the enormous waterborns destroying a ship, its distinctive stripes crushed beneath the weight of the machine and its monster.

"Oh, my god."

Julian's face was numb, though he was certain it wasn't from the cold. His moth shook as he read the words printed on its enormous wings again and again. His eyes closed, fingers loosening just enough for the moth to slip free. It reattached itself to the lamppost, vying for warmth amongst its kin. Julian's qirin stamped, restless in the twilight.

They'd won but lost.

The young lord stood in the centre of London, oblivious of the gigs and people swarming around him, reality blurring his senses.

"Ah, these bloody fools, look what they've done! Now everyone will think—"

"Yeah, yeah, 'cause you know what's going on out there, right?"

"Better than you. When was the last time you saw the channel?"

"It's not even bein' fought in the English Channel, you halfwit!"

Chatter surrounded him but none of it made any sense, floating somewhere above him. He stared at the moths clinging to the lamp post, wings swishing in lazy motions. The glow of the gaslight overwhelmed him and he stood, wandering through traffic toward it.

Muck from the side drain of the cobblestone road drenched him, reality rushing back in a clamour of sounds and movement. He leaped out of the way of the next vehicle that barrelled at him, its driver cursing as he weaved his way across the road, trying to get his gig under control.

"Oh, my god." Stuck on that phrase, his mind jammed. None of it mattered to Julian. He stepped back, letting the world pass him by.

"I've killed Horatio Nelson."

JO SEYSENER is a mum of three crazies living with her husband in rural South-East Queensland. Jo writes speculative fiction for adults and picture books for children for Library for All, a not for profit Brisbane based enterprise who aim to increase literacy in third world countries. She is dabbling in romance and next year will release her first middle grade series. Jo adores alpacas.

Bibliography
Angels, Black Hare Press, 2019
Being Clean Keeps Me Healthy, Library for All, 2019
Beyond, Black Hare Press, 2019
Elemental, SWG, 2019
Feeding Shari, Library for All, 2019
Greg and the Egg, Library for All, 2018
Hawthorn and Ash, Iron Faerie Press, 2019
In my Family, Library for All, 2019
In My Village, Library for All, 2019
It's Beginning to Look a Lot Like Christmas, Share Your Story, 2018
Monsters, Black Hare Press, 2019
Play with Me, Library for All, 2019
Return, SWG, 2017
Sea of Secrets, Dragon Soul Press, 2019
Shari's Busy day, Library for All, 2019
Sideshow Alley, Little Quail Press, 2019
Storming Area 51, Black Hare Press, 2019
Unravel, Black Hare Press, 2019
When the Ground Shakes, Library for All, 2019

Connect
Website: www.joseysener.com
Amazon: Amazon.com/author/Joseysener
Twitter: @JSeysener
Facebook: joseysener
Instagram: @fancynancyer

THE RED, GREY, BLACK, AND WHITE

By Gabriella Balcom

Geronimo and his small band of Apaches race across the prairie, desperately trying to evade the United States Army--hundreds strong. The braves' situation is grim indeed. What follows takes everyone by surprise, and the United States will never be the same.

APRIL, 1862
PELONCILLO MOUNTAINS,
ARIZONA TERRITORY

Leaning forward, the Apaches—a band of fifty-eight Chiricahua braves—used their moccasined heels to kick their horses' flanks, urging them to go faster. Some turned to look at their pursuers, whooping and screaming in defiance, shaking their spears and tomahawks as they galloped across the prairie.

Despite the white man forcing them off their ancestral lands and into a reservation—a form of imprisonment, since they were used to being free—they'd escaped several times, the last being a few months earlier. Their anger was an eternal fire burning in their guts, driving them to raid settlements, military encampments, and wagon trains.

The whites hadn't been satisfied with merely encroaching on the Native Americans' homes, hunting grounds and sacred burial grounds. They'd claimed to want a peaceful coexistence, but they'd lusted after the lands that weren't theirs and claimed them, burned down villages, killed the buffalo, and massacred thousands of Native Americans. And no matter how many so-called peace treaties they'd made, the white man had broken all of them.

Last year on the reservation, the Apaches had realised the rations the whites promised weren't coming—at least, not in sufficient quantities to feed their people—and the lack of food had brought them to the very brink of starvation. Their resentment and fury had steadily risen, more each time they'd heard how other Native Americans had been treated. Some had gone to what were supposed to be peaceful talks, but they'd been murdered instead.

Now the Apaches raced toward Guadalupe Canyon about a hundred horse-lengths ahead. They knew it well, so they hoped to have the advantage over their enemies there.

The United States Army chased them, several hundred strong. Soldiers occasionally fired from horseback, picking off targets.

Glancing over his shoulder, Geronimo frowned. "The white men smile," he called out to the braves. "Something is wrong. Remain alert."

As they charged through the narrow entrance to the canyon, soldiers appeared on top of a cliff to their right and raised their rifles.

"It's a trap!" Geronimo yelled, but two of his men fell to the ground. "Get to the boulders ahead as quick as you can. Don't sacrifice your life needlessly."

"We should fight, not run like scared children," Nantan argued. Quick-tempered and prone to act before thinking, his rage and thirst for revenge had increased since the white man had captured, tortured, and hung some of his relatives. "The rest of our people who've escaped the reservation need to know the army is here."

"A dead man can fight no one," Geronimo stressed. He understood the pain of loss, since his wife and three little children had been murdered. "To save others, we must first save ourselves. And our people may hear the guns."

After they reached the jagged line of rocks, the Native Americans concealed themselves and their horses as best they could. They studied the now-halted army, which grew as dozens of men poured into the canyon. Their numbers weren't surprising, considering how much they wanted to catch Geronimo and his men.

"Look," Taza said. The brave stood and pointed toward the cliff.

The soldiers pushed out a large gun on wheels, moved it into position, and turned the hand-crank.

"Stay down," Geronimo snapped. "Remember, that weapon shoots many times."

Even as he spoke, shots rang out and Taza crumpled, blood gushing from his head. Nantan screamed and landed on his back. Ignoring the danger to himself, Geronimo raced to his men. Taza was dead. Nantan had been shot in his shoulder. Geronimo dragged him to safety and used a knife to dig the bullet from the injured man's flesh. He pulled a pouch from his waist, retrieved some herbs from it, and used them to pack the wound, staunching the flow of blood.

The army advanced again.

Glancing from his remaining men to the soldiers,

Geronimo murmured a quick prayer to Ussen—the main creator in which he and his people believed—and the ga'ns, who were lesser gods and protective mountain spirits. He felt the hair rising on the back of his neck and arms as he prayed but didn't know why. Heart pounding, he glanced upward and frowned.

Above the canyon, the sky darkened and the clouds churned. Something appeared in the midst of them and rapidly descended. The military didn't seem to realise anything was happening. By the time they did notice the silver, saucer-shaped object, it was only a few hundred yards from the ground. The soldiers fired at the mysterious thing, but their bullets did no damage and bounced off harmlessly. A green ray of light shot from the unknown object, struck a soldier, and he fell down face-first.

The Native Americans looked at one another, some pale and wide-eyed, others glaring.

"Quick," Geronimo commanded. "We go." Whistling, he beckoned his stallion, leapt onto the horse's back, and pulled Nantan up in front of him.

His people followed his lead, mounting their own steeds. Taking advantage of the situation, they hurried from their current position to further up the canyon.

Behind them, the army fired upon the silver thing, now floating motionless a couple hundred feet above them. Dozens of beams came from the object, reducing men to piles of ash. The army panicked and scattered. But even as men ran or rode away, the lights followed. One soldier after another dropped, burned where he stood, or exploded into pieces.

Several men rode in the direction where the Native Americans now hid, reaching them within seconds. But when the braves emerged from hiding to fight, more shafts of light shot from the unknown something, and reduced all but two of their enemies to fragments.

"We need to leave," a brave whispered.

Geronimo stood, widened his stance, and aimed his tomahawk. He threw it with deadly accuracy, lodging it in the forehead of one of the remaining soldiers.

The last soldier stood only a few feet away now. He raised his rifle, aimed at the Apache leader, and fired. A clanging noise sounded throughout the canyon, and the bullet fell to the ground just inches from Geronimo. Then, a green ray hit the shooter in the back, incinerating him.

"Do not flee," Geronimo told his men, most of whom had prepared to do exactly that. He stared intensely at the silver thing in the air. "This is a sign from the gods. Someone must be inside *that*. He could have killed us but didn't. He *helped* us." Geronimo scanned his surroundings and the dead soldiers. "The enemy of my enemy is my friend," he said quietly.

His braves lowered their eyes, showing respect. His people considered him a great warrior and skilled medicine man, but they also admired him for his wisdom.

The unknown object lowered to the ground. It was larger than the braves had expected. A door on the side opened, and beings wearing short-sleeved black uniforms exited. Their heads and bodies were elongated as compared to the Native Americans' and they stood about two feet taller. As they approached, it became obvious their skin was grey.

They spoke amongst themselves in an unknown language. The one in the front glanced at a small device on its left wrist, before turning to the Apache leader, raising one three-fingered hand—palm outward—and saying, "How."

Geronimo raised an eyebrow and exchanged glances with his men. Some tribes used that greeting—a word which sounded similar to it, anyway. Whites often used it when they tried to communicate with Native Americans, but these creatures weren't white. They weren't Native Americans either. The chief was almost certain they were gods, come to save his people from their treacherous enemy—the white man.

"I thank you for what you have done." Geronimo

sank to his knees and bowed his head.

His braves followed his example.

After studying and tapping its wrist-device, the being spoke in fluent Apache. "That is not necessary. Please rise."

Geronimo and his band stood.

"We come in peace," the being said. "We have studied your world and are appalled. People enslaving or mistreating others because of their skin colour is *wrong*. It's unfair because all of you are the same inside. The way tyrants have treated your people and others like you—the theft of your lands, the pollution of the very Earth itself—these are grievous wrongs. We have come to offer our assistance."

"You saved my life and my people. You have our gratitude forever," Geronimo said. "We can never repay you, but please allow us to share what we have with you. We will have a feast in your honour."

The grey creature accepted his offer.

"I am Geronimo and I lead these braves. What is your name?"

"Ooloon. I also lead my people."

That evening, they sat around a fire in the Apaches' camp hidden deep in the Peloncillo Mountains. Geronimo smoked the peace pipe before passing it to Ooloon. After some direction, he inhaled deeply and handed it to another grey man.

After they had all shared the peace pipe, Ooloon stood. "I wish to bestow a gift upon you, Geronimo." He placed his hands on the chieftain's head and they glowed brightly.

Geronimo felt warmth moving from his head throughout his body, and felt energised and alert. In fact, he felt more alive than he had in years. He wasn't sure what the grey man had done, but knew it was done with good intentions.

"You will be able to discern the thoughts and true intentions of others now," Ooloon explained.

"Thank you." Geronimo wore a thong around his neck with a small leather pouch. It was his most prized possession and contained sacred herbs and objects. It also contained locks of hair from his dead loved ones. Removing the thong now, Geronimo placed it around Ooloon's neck. "And I gift you this. I consider you my brother."

The Native Americans provided venison and buffalo to their guests, along with wild potatoes, maize, sweet bread, and berries. As everyone feasted, Geronimo shared his people's beliefs about the gods, preserving the earth, and much more. Neither he nor the newcomers were surprised to learn they agreed on a great number of things.

...

AUGUST 1862
CHARLESTON, SOUTH CAROLINA

"You speak of this *technology* as if it is all-important or a god to be worshipped, but we do not agree," Geronimo told Governor Henry Clarke and the officials with whom he and his grey brethren were meeting.

Other chieftains had joined their alliance after hearing about their plans. Cochise, who led another band of Apaches, Crazy Horse of the Sioux, and Sitting Bull of the Lakota had chosen to attend the meeting, too. They'd been reluctant to travel through the air in the strange thing called a *spaceship*, but once they'd agreed, they were amazed by how fast they'd travelled from one place to another.

"Progress is bad if we destroy Mother Earth," Cochise stated firmly.

Crazy Horse asked the whites, "Where will you live if the land is dead?"

"You will die without food and water," Sitting Bull added.

"Our beliefs are different," Governor Clarke said, clearing his throat. "But we'll do what we think best with the land. We own it."

"No, you do not," Crazy Horse retorted. "You talk

of ownership but our people have been here for generations. We have respected and preserved the land. You are killing it."

General Burnside snorted. "The land is fine." He murmured to the governor, "I'm glad I insisted on being here." He'd brought at least forty armed soldiers and they were positioned around the room. "Governor Clarke," he added, "I know you're trying to be patient with these...uh... But this is ridiculous. We're fighting a war and can't afford to waste time on nonsense like this."

"We came to you because this is important," Geronimo stated calmly.

"In the past, we could not stop your destruction," Cochise rasped, his voice cold and threatening. "But this is a new day. And your thoughts are not hidden from us." Geronimo had shared his special gift with Cochise and the other chieftains.

Crazy Horse nodded. "You will not be allowed to harm the land anymore."

"No, you will not," Sitting Bull said, frowning at the governor and general.

Burnside glared at him. "You are a murderer who's killed innocent men and women." He looked around at each of the Native Americans. "All of you are murderers who've killed innocent people." As he spoke, the governor glanced away.

No one responded to the accusations, although there were some cold stares.

"Some of my bronze brothers lost their wives," Ooloon said, his voice devoid of inflection. "Many lost their children, brothers, sisters...parents." After getting no response, he added, "You haven't asked *how* they lost their loved ones, but I'll tell you. They were killed."

Clarke paused before saying, "Many Americans were killed, too."

Burnside abruptly changed the subject. "We heard your threats to destroy our factories. But you need to know we won't sit and do nothing while you try."

"To *try* is one thing," Geronimo said. "But we didn't say we would try. We said we would *do*."

"We mean what we say," Cochise said.

"How do you not comprehend our concerns and the consequences of your actions?" Ootoon asked, his English fluent and ringing with conviction. "You have petroleum refineries, sawmills, textile mills, steel plants, and many other factories. Poison runs from them into the rivers and seas. It seeps into the ground. Already plants and trees in the affected areas have stopped growing and withered. People are getting sick, and dead fish float on the water. *You* have done this with your technology. I know all about technology and the harm it can cause because the unrestricted use of it destroyed my planet."

"*Planet?*" Burnside exchanged a glance with Governor Clarke. "I admit your height and body shape are unusual, but I've seen traveling circuses that feature abnormal people. And I could easily use paint to change my skin colour. Saying you're from another planet is preposterous."

"He speaks the truth, even if you don't believe it," Geronimo stated. "You and your men have the right to think as you wish. But on the matter of this Earth, we bronze men are in agreement with our brethren, the grey men. We will not let you do further damage."

"Pah!" Burnside stood and walked away. He turned before going out the door and uttered a warning. "We do not tolerate threats and will take immediate action if anyone tries to damage our industries." Turning to his soldiers, he commanded, "Arrest them."

Geronimo, Ooloon, Crazy Horse, Cochise, and Sitting Bull spoke quietly amongst themselves before facing the white men once more.

"We asked you to shut down your factories until you find a safe way to dispose of the waste and byproducts, but you refused," Ooloon stated. "We asked you to consider how you've damaged the Earth in the past—how you *are* damaging it—but you refused. We asked you to work with us to preserve the land and achieve peace between all peoples, but you refused. You have made your choice clear."

"Choices have consequences," Sitting Bull stated.

Crazy Horse's lips curved, but his gaze remained icy.

"Now see the result of your choice," Geronimo said. Beside him, Cochise merely nodded.

The Native Americans and grey men stood and prepared to leave. As they did, the soldiers reached for their revolvers and rifles, but froze with their arms at awkward angles. From their panicked expressions, twitches, and jerks, they'd obviously found themselves unable to move.

Once the visitors went out the door, Ooloon tapped his wrist and his ship appeared in the sky.

The government officials and military men, now released from their immobility, rushed outside, instantly bursting into startled chatter. As they took aim at the ship in the sky, green beams emanated from it, striking a factory with tall smokestacks across town.

The army rallied, firing on the ship, but nothing they did made a difference. In rapid succession, the spaceship blew other factories to smithereens.

...

OCTOBER 1862
ATLANTA, GEORGIA

Geronimo, Ootoon, and the Sioux and Lakota leaders approached Atlanta, accompanied by a number of Pawnee, Iroquoi, and Cherokee. Thousands had joined them; their numbers increased every day.

Soldiers had constructed barriers to block the roads, and fired as soon as the group was within range. They used rifles. They used cannons and howitzers. In fact, they used every weapon in their arsenal, but none of their projectiles hit their targets. Rather, an invisible barrier stopped the bullets and missiles, and they fell to the ground.

Then Ootoon blew up an Atlanta factory.

...

APRIL 1863
DAKOTA TERRITORY

"It is important to treat captives fairly," Sitting Bull stressed, addressing two braves he'd caught torturing white prisoners. "What you have done is not honourable."

"*White* men have no honour," the torturers argued.

"They murder our people and do not deserve to be treated well. Remember the Dakota." They referred to the mass execution of Dakota warriors the previous year.

Cochise said nothing, but his eyes glittered.

Listening from where he sat, Geronimo frowned. He glanced at Ootoon, whose eyes were troubled. Unspoken communication passed between them.

Ootoon looked at his men, and they took away the two torturers.

"We cannot blame those men for their hatred," Crazy Horse commented. "I *hate* the white man, but the braves should have obeyed orders."

"I agree with you," Sitting Bull said. "And I hate whites, too."

Geronimo nodded. "I also have reason to hate them. But the disobedience of two—even one—could lead others to act the same way and our word must mean more than the white's word."

"Not all of them are bad," Ooloon said. "Many have joined us, and some are quite kind and good."

"Some of our kind are not good," Sitting Bull offered.

Ooloon sighed. "Every race has good people and bad people, but everyone is equal and should be treated fairly. And our goal is peace."

He and the Native Americans had formed the

United League of Nations, with their own government. Despite the United States deciding not to join the alliance—probably due to their energies being focused on their civil war—many white men and women joined the League on their own, appearing to have good intentions. But the same couldn't be said for all. Some whites were in an uproar because the U.S. government had decided not to retaliate for the destruction of the factories, and they'd made their hatred of the bronze and grey men clear, continuing to fight. As a result, the allies had set aside a prison camp for the most violent individuals—the camp they came to inspect that day.

In addition, they'd moved several groups of non-allied whites off Native American lands and into reservations for their own good. There, volunteers were teaching them how to respect living creatures and the earth. Reservation officials had outlawed and confiscated guns and weapons. They'd banned firewater and strong spirits, too, because white men tended to overimbibe and act irrationally.

...

JULY 2, 1863
GETTYSBURG, PENNSYLVANIA

Thousands of bodies lay on the ground, the hot sun

beating down on them. Some of the dead wore blue uniforms. Others wore grey. Slain horses lay here and there, and the stench of death filled the air. Even so, the battle raged on.

But the Union and Confederate forces stopped fighting when the silver spaceship appeared in the sky, and watched it slowly descend, landing on the battlefield. No one spoke when Ooloon stepped out, followed by the United League of Nations' governing council, and several other grey and bronze men.

"Your war is over," Ooloon announced, his voice ringing clearly. "Tens of thousands have died, and for what?" He surveyed the combatants to his left, then the ones to his right.

A shot rang out as someone fired at him, but he ignored it as the bullet struck an invisible barrier.

"Is life of so little value to you?" he demanded.

"We know you don't value the *bronze* man," Geronimo yelled. "But do you not value each other? Are you and your sons and brothers not worth more than this?"

"Our fight isn't your business," a man called out.

"It is everyone's business," Ooloon said.

"What are you?" another man asked.

"A living being like you," Ooloon replied loudly. "Just like my bronze brothers. Our skin may be different colours, but we're the same in the ways that matter. The black men some of you use as slaves are just like us, too. They are *people*, not property. This war is over."

...

AUGUST 12, 1863
GETTYSBURG, PENNSYLVANIA

"Four score and seven years ago," President Lincoln said from the podium, "our fathers brought forth..."

Journalists had said this gathering would be the largest, most memorable one in United States' history. And they'd been right. Not only were American citizens in attendance, including men who'd fought on both sides of the Civil War, but also many Native Americas, Negros, and the visitors from another planet.

While Geronimo and Ooloon listened to the speech, they looked at one another and the other chiefs with them. Lincoln had joined their alliance the day the Civil War ended. So had Frederick Douglas, who'd done so on behalf of the Free Negro Men and Women of America. He'd been chosen as the first president of the newly-formed organisation. Afterward, the United League of Nations had added "and Free Peoples" to their name.

"I don't know whether to smile or cry," Douglass commented, his eyes shining. "I dreamed of my people being free for so long, but at the same time I worried it might never happen."

"When we were fighting the whites and they were forcing us into the reservation, I had the same fears," Geronimo admitted. "And the same dreams."

"I did, too," Cochise said. "My anger at the white man gave me strength to keep fighting but ate away at me."

"We were always meant to be free, but I grew tired of fighting," Sitting Bull said. "I longed to live the remainder of my life in peace and quiet."

Crazy Horse stated, "My life was nothing but war. I thought my children and grandchildren would never know anything but that and the same hatred I felt."

"You saved our lives and changed our future," Geronimo told Ooloon. "If you and your people hadn't come when you did..."

"But we did," Ooloon replied. "And we've helped you, but the dreams were mainly yours. Together, we've already achieved important things, but there's much more to do." He told Douglass, "You told us you believe education is vital for the Negro people—for all people— and we agree."

"I believe all Negros need to learn how to read and write," Douglass said. "They need the same opportunities as white people have had all along. And women are just as intelligent as men; they need better treatment also."

"We want you to write that and make it a law," Geronimo told him.

Ooloon nodded. "You could call it Equal Education for All or whatever you want." He lowered his eyes for a moment. "And I want to say something to all of you that I should have said long ago. I apologise for not coming earlier. We knew your world had problems, but our focus was on our own planet. We were trying to save it from the mistakes of earlier generations, but couldn't. Now we know that wasn't meant to be. But you endured horrors in the meantime, and I am sorry for that. If only we'd—"

"You have nothing to be sorry for," Geronimo replied. "You saved me. You saved my people."

"And mine," Cochise said. "If you hadn't come, we'd still be fighting."

Sitting Bull nodded gravely. "I could have died by now."

"Death rode after me and I believe I may have sought it," Crazy Horse admitted.

"We cannot change the past." Frederick Douglass spoke softly. "All we can do is work toward a better tomorrow."

...

JULY 2, 2019
PORTAL, ARIZONA
BY CHIRICAHUA NATIONAL FOREST

Children chased each other through the wildflowers, their laughter carrying as they played. White skin almost seemed to blend with bronze, grey, and black skin as they rolled on the ground in a brief tussle. Then they dashed toward the Apache River and jumped in. Giggles rang out and droplets flew back and forth from the water they threw on each other.

Two solar-powered air-buses soared overhead, landing on bus pads. Dozens of people disembarked, ready to enjoy the festivities. Individuals had been arriving all day, some travelling by hover-car or air-bus, others choosing to stay on the ground and drive crosscountry.

The public considered flying solar vehicles one of the best innovations of the twenty-first century. The United League had rejected designs for petroleum-powered vehicles throughout the years. They'd only approved vehicles after inventors, scientists, and environmentalists had worked together a long time, finally devising a way to convert potentially harmful emissions into energy and harmless by-products. They had eventually eliminated the need for petroleum altogether.

Aatoor, descendant of founding father Ooloon, smiled indulgently as he watched the children—two of whom were his—play in the river. He sat on the grass with his arm around his wife Ebony's waist; she was a many-times-granddaughter of Frederick Douglass. Nearby, Aatoor saw his brother Uumool smiling at his wife Kushala, who descended from an Apache father and white mother.

Past treaties had abolished discrimination long ago, but every administration since 1863 had firmly believed in keeping history alive. In Aatoor's position in the government, he represented both the Grey People—the name the original alien arrivals had adopted—and the Apaches, and they'd enacted a law requiring history books to cover reality. They believed knowing the truth about the past was important, served as a reminder of what hate and greed could do, and honoured those who'd gone before—those who'd lived through harder times.

Today's Peace Day festivities were all about the past. The national holiday celebrated the cessation of a war which had divided their nation and resulted in heavy casualties, and the freeing of the Negro people. It also celebrated multiple leaders agreeing to work together.

Aatoor considered the colours of the League flag flapping in the breeze—each one significant to their nation. The red and white stripes represented not only purity and valour, but the blood of all men, regardless of their colour. A block of black lay alongside them—signifying strength and their Negro brothers and sisters—and was dotted by dozens and dozens of stars, one for each of the allied Native American nations. A grey border surrounded the entire rectangle, standing for balance and equality. It also honoured the Grey People who'd come to save a society threatened with utter extinction, and who'd helped to unite and hold together the entire nation.

Aatoor felt a surge of pride in his great homeland. His forefathers on his alien line had come from a distant planet, but *his* home had always been Earth—here in southeastern Arizona. Chiricahua National Forest was one among hundreds of protected forests. Neither man nor industry had molested thousands and thousands of acres. They'd been safe since the end of the Civil War, and they'd remain safe because laws protected them, along with the animals, plants, and trees within them.

Many years ago, the founding fathers and industrialists had exchanged hot words over the matter of trees. People had cut down forests in the name of progress, but the founding fathers had put a quick stop to the cutting. Tens of thousands of whites and blacks had taken to living in tents on the ground alongside their Native American brethren. Scientists and innovators had considered possibilities, and after a great deal of work and time, they'd learned how to replicate trees. This had allowed for the use of artificial, mass-produced ones rather than those which were "real."

The founding fathers' reasoning and determination to save living things hadn't just been applied to forests. It had been applied to all types of industry. The League hadn't given the industrial giants of the latter 1860s and later years a say in the matter. They couldn't have done much in the way of argument anyway, since their factories had already been reduced to rubble. "Progress" might have been slowed—*had* been slowed—and The League had kept those chomping at the bit chomping longer, but everything had been worth it in the end.

Scientists had finally devised ways of converting harmful, poisonous waste products into clean energy. But getting to that point had required creative thinking. Top factory and plant owners had refused to cooperative at first, so the founding fathers had forced them to drink and bathe in water polluted by waste, and live on poisoned grounds. As the industrialists and their families had suffered ill-effects, they'd experienced a rapid change of heart. Well-motivated at that point, they'd poured all their efforts into what the founding fathers had demanded in the first place. And, as a popular saying went, the rest was history.

Thinking about the past and the stories he'd heard first-hand from his long-lived great-grandfather, Ooloon, Aatoor smiled. His home in Portal was less than an hour from the very spot where Ooloon had saved Geronimo's Apache band.

Aatoor's children ran by, as full of energy as ever, and he chuckled, hoping they'd always be as contented as they were now.

Staring into the distance, he noticed a large herd of buffalo racing across a far-off meadow. Dozens of antelope ran with them. Wolves loped behind but weren't giving chase yet. A band of Apache and Grey People appeared, chasing the herd. Aatoor knew they'd kill only what they needed. It was the way of their people.

"How," a deep voice said behind him.

Aatoor turned to see Denali smirking at him. "Idiot," Aatoor responded, grinning.

"Is that any way to greet your leader?" Denali quipped before pulling Aatoor into a tight hug.

Denali was an Apache, chieftain of the Chiricahua nation living in the Peloncillo Mountains which ranged from the southeast border of Arizona into New Mexico.

He had an offbeat sense of humour and he *was* Aatoor's leader, since Aatoor was part-Apache.

"You haven't changed yet," Denali commented, all seriousness now. "Surely you of all people haven't decided to sit this one out."

"What?" Glancing at his watch, Aatoor realised the time. He dropped a quick kiss on Ebony's lips and hurried to remove his jeans, t-shirt, and boots, leaving him in just his loin cloth. He donned a short-sleeved black uniform next. Every year, he took part in the reenactment of Ooloon's historic appearance to Geronimo. He and his brother always took turns playing the part of Ooloon, and Denali was usually Geronimo for the event. Their white brethren acted out the parts of the U.S. Army chasing after them, or painted their skin bronze and portrayed Apaches.

Today's activities would continue through the night and all day tomorrow, with more attendees staging re-enactments. Then, on the Fourth of July, the focus would switch over to when their nation gained an earlier independence from Great Britain.

Denali and Aatoor mounted stallions and rode toward the enactment site.

"You know how I love science fiction and fantasy?" Denali asked.

"Of course," Aatoor replied. "Why?"

"Do you ever imagine an alternate reality?"

"What do you mean?"

"What if he hadn't come—Ooloon, I mean? I think our lives might not be what they are now."

"I haven't thought about it," Aatoor admitted. "This life is all I know. I can't imagine anything altered from what it is." He frowned briefly, then smiled at Denali. "I mean—things wouldn't have been *that* different, right?"

GABRIELLA BALCOM lives in Texas with her family, loves reading and writing, and thinks she was born with a book in her hands. She writes fantasy, horror/thriller, romance, children's stories, sci-fi, and more.

She likes travelling, music, good shows, photography, history, interesting tales, and animals. Gabriella says she's a sucker for a great story and loves forests, mountains, and back roads which might lead who knows where. She has a weakness for lasagna, garlic bread, tacos, cheese, and chocolate, but not necessarily in that order.

Bibliography
ANGELS, Black Hare Press, 2019
APOCALYPSE, Black Hare Press, 2019
BEYOND, Black Hare Press, 2019
Curses & Cauldrons, Blood Song Books, 2019
Eerie Christmas, Black Hare Press, 2019
Gold, Clarendon House Publications, 2019
Horror USA: California, Soteira Press, 2019
Magical Reality, Pixie Forest Publishing, 2019
Miracle, Clarendon House Publications, 2018
MONSTERS, Black Hare Press, 2019
Phuket Tattoo, Zombie Pirate Publishing, 2018
Storming Area 51, Black Hare Press, 2019
Summer's Splash, Fantasia Divinity Publishing, 2019
Tempest, Clarendon House Publications, 2019
What If?, Black Hare Press, 2019
Wishes of Illusion, Fantasia Divinity Publishing, 2019

Connect
Facebook: @GabriellaBalcom.lonestarauthor

BLOOD RITUAL

By Simon Clarke

Hiding behind the cataclysm of World War One, powerful cultists plan a vile ritual to enhance their power. A small group has uncovered their plan, but time is running out...

A clock was ticking in Room 40, the oldest part of the Admiralty Building. The only other sound was the riffling of papers as Admiral Sir Reginald Hall read through the reports presented to him twenty minutes previously.

"What do you make of this, John?"

The officer opposite him took some moments to answer. "I don't know, sir. Or rather, I know what the report suggests, but I struggle to believe it. It's just fantastic."

"What about the author, this Flight-Lieutenant

Jackson, do you know him?"

"Yes, sir. My nephew. He's a good sort. Head firmly screwed on. Certainly not the type to imagine such things, or make them up."

"OK, John, let's get him in."

Flight-Lieutenant Charles Jackson was deep in thought. Sitting in the ward room, winding his pocket watch, he was thinking through recent events as he tried to make sense of what he had seen last week. The RNAS had been a new venture for him, one that promised to get him into the war as soon as possible. He was a good pilot, having flown regularly before the war at the Royal Aero Club. He was pleased the Navy had taken the need for an air service seriously and was impressed by the way they had extended the organisation to include tanks and armoured cars for supporting the fighting inland. Flying patrols to provide cover for these forces was the reason he was now waiting to be summoned to London.

He had been flying back from high altitude observation duties when a stray anti-aircraft shell exploded below him. A piece of shrapnel flew into his engine, causing it to fail, and he tried to land the plane rather than bail out and let it crash. It was late afternoon, the sun was low, and a mist had been starting to rise up from the meadows as he brought the plane down safely with hardly a sound. The only sign of his passing being the swirls of mist curling round his wing tips as he trundled to a halt on the grass.

He clambered down from the plane and looked around without concern; this was allied territory after all. Yet, he was aware of a level of tension within him, his heart beating faster than usual. Something wasn't right. Across the meadow, half a mile away, stood a large farmhouse. He headed towards it in the hope that there was someone there who could help him make contact with the airfield. The mist grew thicker as he walked, but as he reached the perimeter fence, he could just make out a faint light from a ground floor window.

To rid himself of his feelings of unease, he had decided to stride to the front door and knock loudly. However, hearing a seemingly meaningless guttural chanting coming from the house, he stopped half way across the yard to listen. He crept closer to the lit window and peered between cracks in the shutters. A group of robed figures stood in a half circle around a large table, their eyes closed, repeating the same chant over and over again. On the table lay a large sheet of what seemed to be thick paper, perhaps even leather. Jackson could just make out hieroglyphic symbols around its edge, but it was the diagram in the centre that caught his attention. It was a representation of the battlefield around Verdun he had just been flying over. Oddly, an area of the recently constructed defensive trench system had been coloured red.

The chanting was getting louder and faster. Suddenly, the map moved. The group stepped back, still shouting, and the sheet began undulating and thrashing about on the table. Just as suddenly, it became still, and Jackson heard a shrill noise rising as if from far away, not just from the room, but all around him. It had grown louder, and the map started to levitate above the table. The noise was unbearable. He pressed his hands to his ears, staggering away from the window and into the bushes by the fence where he collapsed.

He thought he'd lost consciousness for a while, because when he came to, the group were outside the house, preparing to leave. It was then Jackson saw the thing that terrified him the most. Not some hideous manifestation, but the sight of senior British and German army officers mingling and laughing together. Without warning, a hand came from behind and clamped over his mouth. A voice hissed into his ear.

"Ssh."

Jackson made to grasp the hand and squirm round, but a knife appeared in front of him and was held close to his cheek.

"*Dummkopf,* quiet."

Jackson stopped struggling.

"Wait here. Stay." The hand and knife were removed, and Jackson had turned to face the German.

The German soldier held a finger to his lips, winked, and then quickly disappeared into the mist. As he did so, Jackson heard voices calling out from the group of officers who had just left the building, their shapes just shadows in the mist. He watched the soldier he had just met move towards them, and then an English voice had called out, "Oberleutnant Hoffman."

"Ja, mein Herr."

"Did you see anyone?"

"Nein, Herr Oberst... Colonel Macmillan."

"Right, let's get cleared up and back to our posts. Oberleutnant Hoffman, make sure the room is empty."

"Ja, mein Herr. I will see to it we have taken all with us, even, as you say, the kitchen sink."

Jackson noticed the German spoke in a louder voice as he had said this. Jackson stayed where he was until he could no longer hear the sound of the staff cars in the distance. He entered the farm house, and then the main room where the ritual had taken place. A strange cloying odour lingered. He quickly left the room, found the kitchen, and walked over to the large sink. Using his lighter, he began searching, soon finding a packet wrapped in oilskin stuffed behind the sink. Wanting to show as little light as possible, he stuck the packet inside his shirt. He then explored the outbuildings, hoping to find some way of getting back to the airfield. Inside one of the barns, he discovered a bicycle. He knew roughly where he was in relation to his base and set off through the mist.

Jackson's reverie was interrupted by a Petty Officer approaching him.

"Flight-Lieutenant Jackson, sir."

"Yes, Smith. What is it?"

"A telegram from the Admiralty, sir."

Jackson took it and began to read.

Petty Officer Dick Smith was in his early thirties. Always ready for new experiences, he had jumped at the chance of joining the Royal Naval Air Service. He revelled in keeping fit, as evidenced by his broad shoulders and narrow waist. Jackson knew he was a good man to have with him in a fight. Aware that Smith had not moved, Jackson looked up.

"What is it, Smith?"

"I've made the Albatross ready for us, sir…took the liberty. It seemed urgent."

"Did it now?"

"Just following orders, sir."

"My orders, I suppose."

"Yes, sir."

Jackson stood and grasped Smith by the shoulder.

"Good man, let's go."

Charles Jackson revelled in flying. He felt at home, at peace even. The flight from their Royal Naval Air Service base near Dover took little time, and less than an hour later, they were coming in to land at RNAS Hendon Aerodrome, North London where a car was waiting to take him to the Admiralty. Smith stayed with the plane, not trusting anyone else with its maintenance, but also to check on the information Jackson had given him before he left.

Within the hour, Jackson had been shown through a doorway marked 'No Admittance' into the group of offices known as Room 40.

"You made good time, Flight-Lieutenant Jackson," said Admiral Hall

"Yes, Admiral, with some help."

Admiral Hall was a man of medium height, in his late forties. He spoke in a clipped manner that suggested he had no time for extraneous words. His eyes had an energetic glint that Jackson decided indicated a sharp mind; one that could see the best course of action in any situation.

"Quite so, Jackson. Let me introduce you."

Admiral Hall led him over to the oak table dominating the far end of his office. A tall middle-aged officer stood and approached Jackson.

"You know Commodore Harvey, of course."

"Yes, how are you, Uncle?"

They shook hands. His uncle's tanned face readily wrinkled into a warm smile. Jackson could recall always feeling at home when, as a young boy, he had spent time with his uncle. He had been a second father to him when his father had died and had paid for his flying instruction. *It's the future, young Jackson*, he used to say. In the service, he was known as a hard taskmaster. Jackson trusted him implicitly.

"Troubled, if you must know, my boy." Commodore Harvey returned to his seat.

There were just two other people at the table; they stood as he entered. One a tall bearded man with a weatherworn face and blue eyes. The other, a tall woman whom he reasoned was about his own age, in her mid- to late-twenties.

"I am Sub-Lieutenant Annabel Vine. Pleased to meet you, sir" said the woman. She had high cheek bones with, perhaps, too much powder applied. Her pale grey eyes easily held his. She wore a dark blue shirt with chest pockets that gave no indication of rank, and dark blue trousers. *She looks dressed for action*, thought Jackson.

As they shook hands, Jackson noticed her cheek had the beginnings of puffiness from some bruising under the face powder. She caught him eyeing her face, cocked an eyebrow and smiled. "Cut things a bit fine recently, you know how it is." Jackson wasn't sure he did. However, he did know that her smile was very attractive.

As the man skirted the table to shake hands, Jackson noticed he moved with an easy grace belied by his size. He noted the man's clothes: dark trousers, heavy white roll neck jumper and heavy short coat. *He's like someone off a fishing boat,* thought Jackson.

"Hello, Flight-Lieutenant. I am Captain Clarke."

His handshake was steady, his calloused fingers pressing firmly against Jackson's hand. His smile exuded a certain warmth, but Jackson had the sense that this could disappear very quickly. He would hate to get on his wrong side.

Once they had all taken a seat, Commodore Harvey spoke.

"We are the only people to know all the details of what we are going to discuss today. It must stay this way until we have a clear idea of who, and what, is involved. I fear time is running out, so we must act quickly. A lot of lives are at stake, and the consequences of what might happen are catastrophic. Even if we succeed in our endeavours, our lives, and the lives of many others, will never be the same. Make no mistake, if what we have discovered is true, an ancient evil has been discovered and brought back to life by a group of self-serving fools who imagine they will attain even greater power and influence. Captain Clarke?"

"I can't explain everything, but can speculate. Sub-Lieutenant Vine and I have just returned from an incident in the north. Disturbing news had reached us of the disappearance of a shooting party in the Highlands. Some senior members of our armed forces were present. The party was the cover for a secret gathering to plan our strategy to end the war. All we had was a garbled message picked up by a Destroyer patrolling just off the coast where the meeting was taking place. Fortunately, we were nearby, looking into seismic disturbances, when the call came. I led a shore party to investigate. We found mutilated bodies, no one alive. Exploration of the castle revealed a turreted room with a stairway that seemed to descend well below ground level to an enormous cavern dotted with ancient cyclopean buildings. Attempts to investigate further were halted by the distant sound of inhuman guttural chanting. We retreated to the turret, laying explosives as we went in order to seal off the cavern forever. Further investigation revealed that something profane had happened in that place hundreds of years ago, connected with attempts to bring to life an ancient blasphemous power that had lain dormant for millennia. I have here, a facsimile of some of the carvings we were able to see on buildings in the cavern."

He paused, looked around at the group, then continued.

"Since the Great War started, there have been more manifestations of such evil than ever before. It is something we have been studying for many years. I and my crew have been tasked by His Majesty to react to any incident which threatens the safety of anyone under Great Britain's protection."

"Thank you, Captain," said Commodore Harvey. "Perhaps you can now see, Flight Lieutenant, why your report proved so very interesting. It promises to add a further level of information to that which we already know. Please tell us your observations."

The Commodore passed over the thick file Jackson had sent to the Admiralty several days previously. Jackson reached for the file and paused. He had felt his heart pounding when Captain Clarke showed the drawings. They looked familiar—and he was sure they were identical to the markings he had seen on the vellum map in the farmhouse—yet these were not the representations of arcane carvings, but designs for the new trench system to defend Verdun. Flying through enemy fire and being under attack from other fighting planes was nothing compared to how he felt trying to absorb the implications of what he had just learnt. His uncle was looking at him with some concern. The others, he felt, were just staring at him, waiting. He shifted in his chair.

"When we recovered my aircraft, it became clear that it wasn't an anti-aircraft shell that had damaged the engine. We found a high-powered hunting rifle bullet in the casing. I am sure this was fired from the farmhouse to stop me flying over. There are two details I didn't put in my report. One was about the German officer who helped me: Oberleutnant Hoffman. He left me information suggesting he was going to England. I have asked Petty Officer Smith to make contact with him. I think we need to understand just what he knows about all this. The other detail is one of the names I overheard—that of Brigadier MacMillan." Jackson paused, aware that this name appeared to mean something to the senior officers.

"This Oberleutnant Hoffman is not known to us, is he Admiral?" said Vice-Admiral Harvey. The Admiral held his gaze for a few seconds before replying.

"Need to know, John…even for you."

"Of course, Admiral."

"However, we do know about MacMillan. He is well connected, is he not, John?"

"Yes, Admiral. We have a file of radio intercepts. He is suspected of being a German sympathiser. This puts things in a new light. The latest reports have him hosting a soiree at Lynchwood Manor at the end of this week, after a strategy meeting. I was planning to send a junior liaison team," he looked at Jackson and Vine, "but I think we have just the people here. What do you think, you two?"

Jackson glanced at Annabel Vine and raised his eyebrows a fraction. He had been inactive for over a week and was keen to start doing something—anything—to feel back in control. She held his gaze and spoke, "I am happy to go, Admiral. Since our action in Scotland, I'm ready to take the fight to them."

"Ah, yes, Sub-lieutenant," said Admiral Hall, "I understand you are Captain Clarke's explosives expert."

"Yes sir, you can blame my father." She looked over to Jackson, enjoying the surprised look on his face.

"But surely we need to get over to the Front as soon as possible, sir?" said Jackson. The Admiral looked over to Captain Clarke, who stood up and distributed several photographs as he spoke.

"These pictures have been taken over the past 18 months. They show dead and dying whales, porpoises, and dolphins that have stranded themselves. We know whales do this sometimes, but it's never been observed in other species. Here you can see dozens of porpoises and dolphins have either been driven out of the depths, or, as we believe, chose to die rather than stay at sea." He paused whilst everyone studied the photographs. "All the incidents have been on the coastlines of Norway, Denmark, and even the Highlands. All of which border the North Sea." He reached under the table and picked up a large canvas holdall, placing it on the table. He opened it and grasped something from inside. "This was caught up in a British trawler's nets recently. They were fishing between Dogger Bank and Jutland."

Captain Clarke heaved the large heavy object out onto the table. It was a slab of stone, carved with markings that matched those they had already seen.

"Twenty thousand years ago, that area was dry land," he continued. "These carvings were made long before then. We believe something is down there, and it is becoming active. I can only surmise that the rituals we encountered in the Highlands, as well those reported by Flight Lieutenant Jackson, are focused on communicating with something that used to be worshipped millennia ago. I agree we must get back to the Front, Lieutenant Jackson, but I fear what you uncovered is just the trigger for something far more dangerous."

"What do you suggest we do, Captain?" said Admiral Hall.

"We must consider sending the Grand Fleet into the

area, Admiral. We must be prepared in case all other efforts fail. These rituals will be leading to the final ceremony at Verdun. Incredible as it may sound, these madmen are determined to recreate a blood sacrifice. Looking at the drawings that Flight Lieutenant Jackson has produced, I can see they have recreated the occult maze on a massive scale. Their plan will be to ensure that channels of the maze, now a section of the Allied trenches, will be filled with human blood when the Germans attack at Verdun. They are willing to sacrifice hundreds of thousands of men to feed their maniacal obsession with worshipping an ancient evil. In their madness, I fear they do not understand what they will unleash. The trenches need to be destroyed."

"If we send our ships towards Jutland, the German High Seas Fleet would have to come out and challenge us," said Admiral Hall. "We could end up fighting two enemies at once. Even if we are successful, there could be great loss. In addition, destroying the trenches will put the army at greater risk."

"What choice do we have?" asked Captain Clarke. The room was quiet, the clock steadfastly ticking away the minutes.

Eventually, the Admiral said, "We have a lot to do and need to finalise our plans. John, your priority is to get me a meeting with Admiral Jellicoe and Vice-Admiral

Beatty."

The Admiralty car containing Jackson, Vine, and Clarke stopped at the dockside. The HMS *John Dee* was moored in front of them, its curious stubby five-faceted tower at the forecastle framed by Tower Bridge.

As they walked towards the destroyer, Jackson asked, "What is that structure for, Captain?"

"Experimental, Jackson. It has a search function."

As they drew nearer, Jackson noticed a strange machine attached to a platform to the rear of the vessel. Captain Clarke noticed the look.

"That is also experimental. It has the capability to lift-off vertically and land the same way. It is very innovative. Now, let's get on board so you can both set off. I need to get to sea as soon as possible to support the Fleet."

Jackson wondered at this turn of phrase. How on earth could one destroyer be enough to support the Grand Fleet? They descended to the lower decks and were led to a large copper bulkhead with a combination lock. Annabel Vine seemed very at home on board and quickly turned the dials to open the door. Jackson followed them in and found himself in a long room of polished steel with an arrangement of electronic devices down one side. Several men were busy manipulating the confusing array of dials and switches. At the far end was an old oak door, guarded by two armed Marines.

Captain Clarke followed his gaze. "Not everything we have here is new," he said. "We have to use artefacts from another era sometimes. In there could be our salvation."

Jackson saw a familiar person waiting for him.

"Smithson."

"Hello, sir."

"So," said Jackson to the group, "what now?"

"Now," said Captain Clarke, "we get some kit together for your assignments. Sub-Lieutenant Vine, I think you know what is needed from your point of view."

"Yes, Captain." Turning to Jackson she said, "I'll meet you on deck shortly."

Jackson watched her go. *Remarkable*, he thought, *I've never met anyone like her.*

"Come with me, Flight Lieutenant," said Captain Clarke, "Let's get cracking. First, we need to organise weapons, then communications equipment."

An hour and a half later, Jackson and Smith met Vine on the dock. A Vauxhall staff car was waiting for them. Vine and Jackson were to drive to Lynchwood House eighty miles away near Dover. Smith was tasked with arranging a lorry to transport the equipment to the aerodrome near Dover. He would then fly the Albatross back to base and make it ready to go to the Front.

U-3 sat waiting silently on the sea bed, one hundred and twenty feet below the surface of the North Sea. They were one of a number of German submarines stationed in a line, ready to ambush any Royal Naval warships making their way towards Jutland. The crew would be able to detect the sounds of approaching vessels long before they arrived. Just the normal creaks and taps echoed in the engine room. Unexpectedly, a loud bang reverberated throughout the ship. The crew, now alert, looked to the Captain. Another boom sounded and, unbelievably, they felt the whole vessel scrape along the sea bed, as though being pushed. The Captain grabbed the radio. They were being attacked, but how? By what?

"Secure for depth charges," he ordered, thinking it might be an attack from above. He then ordered the U Boat to surface.

"Negative venting," came the reply. Something was stopping the tanks from emptying.

By now, the submarine was being pummelled from outside and pushed further along the sea floor. With growing horror, the Captain realised what was happening. They had positioned themselves near the edge of Dogger Bank, in the relatively shallow water, well within their dive maximum of two hundred and fifty feet. If they were pushed off the bank, they would sink to the furthest depths of the North Sea, over two thousand feet. They had to get away.

"All ahead, one third," ordered the captain. The ship shuddered but didn't move. "All ahead, full." Still no shift in position.

In the forward torpedo compartment, the crew could see the sides buckling and distorting as though some incredible force was being applied to the bow. Abruptly, a crack appeared in the side and water started rushing in. The submariners died screaming, never knowing they were the first humans in over fifty thousand years to come into contact with an ancient abomination that had lain dormant since the last Ice Age.

Jackson and Vine crunched to a halt in the Vauxhall on the wide gravel area in front of Lynchwood Manor. The sun was setting, and lights were being lit in the grand house's windows. *Can all this be real?* thought Jackson. He suspected his companion was much less shocked at today's revelations and events than he had been. They made their way to the front door, which opened before them. A butler stood in attendance.

"Lieutenant Jackson and Sub-Lieutenant Vine of the

Royal Naval Air Service," Jackson said. "We're here as Conference liaison."

"Very good, sir. Please come this way, the Conference will be starting soon. We have made available some guest quarters, as I understand you to be staying for a few days, sir?"

"Yes, indeed."

"I'll show you to your rooms."

Later, the house was bustling with activity and, as no-one came forward to greet them, they took the opportunity to explore further. Along from their quarters was a turret room. Vine stopped to look inside. After knocking, they went in. It seemed empty. She started moving quickly around the room.

"What is it?" he said.

"This room is very like the one we came across in the Highlands. It led us into the cavern. It can't be a coincidence, surely."

A voice startled them. "It certainly isn't."

They turned around to see an army officer emerging from where a section of the wall had move inwards, revealing a stone stairway. Jackson recognised the voice.

"Brigadier MacMillan."

MacMillan's eyes were wide and staring. He blinked slowly like a reptile, as if he had all the time in the world. He was a big man, but stocky and sweating from his climb up the tower. His voice slithered out between spittle-flecked lips.

"Indeed. You're just in time for the penultimate ritual and we need some living blood. Are either of you virgins?" He smiled, licking his thin lips. "Forgive me, my little joke. This isn't some penny dreadful, you know." His grin faded. "This is deadly serious. There will be no help, by the way. Of course, we know all your plans." He turned directly to Jackson, "I very much regret that all your equipment disappeared along with the lorry when it crashed into a river on the way south. A tragic accident. As for Captain Clarke…one little destroyer? What good is that? Our followers will make sure the Fleet never goes to sea over such a ridiculous story. Now, get down these stairs."

As they began to descend, Jackson thought he heard a familiar sound reverberating in the distance. It disappeared as they continued down, the stairs continuing well below ground level, the air becoming dank and cloying. Jackson glanced at Vine . Her expression gave nothing away. The stone staircase ended in an archway which opened into an unlit cavern. Macmillan pushed them forward. Jackson sensed he was in an extremely large hollow space, his stumbling steps seeming to echo away into the stygian distance. A cold sweat formed on his face and neck, and he felt nauseous. Suddenly, a few pin pricks of light appeared far away in the darkness. They appeared to be moving towards them with incredible speed. The three had now entered the cavern, the dull glow from the weak electric lights hanging in the stairway barely lighting a few yards of the space in front of them. Jackson looked back at MacMillan. His face was contorted by an insane look of rapture as he began mouthing wordless sounds. Vine was surreptitiously reaching into a leather pouch on her belt and pulled out a small slim cylinder about six inches long. She turned the bottom half, which sprang open a few inches. Jackson could hear the sound of wings clearly now and could dimly make out a pair of large creatures coming ever closer.

"Close your eyes," whispered Vine as she took the cylinder and smashed it into the stonework behind her. The gun shot was immediately followed by a blinding flash as the Mini-Very pistol discharged its flare, lighting up the surroundings with a brilliant light. The winged creatures screamed and veered away blindly, careering back through the cavern. Jackson turned and launched himself at Macmillan, punching him to the ground where he lay still.

"There must be others in the house. We need to be quick," said Jackson.

"And others down here," said Vine. "Listen…" They paused briefly, hearing noises in the distance, then started up the stairs. Halfway up, they could hear a commotion above them; voices shouting and sporadic gunfire. They stopped, both breathing hard. Then a package rolled and bumped its way down the stairwell towards them.

"Look out," a voice called from above, "something for you, Sub-Lieutenant." Glancing at each other, they grabbed the package to stop it falling further down the stairs. Annabel asked, "Was that a German accent?"

"I believe it was," said Jackson. This was confirmed a few seconds later. "Pleased to see you again, Oberleutnant Hoffman."

Vine quickly got to work opening the bulky canvas bag. She prepared the detonators and positioned groups of explosives on the stairs, trailing the connecting fuse wire behind them. They reached the top of the stairs and cautiously entered the turret room. There were several dead bodies by the entrance. Smith was standing by the doorway to the corridor, weapon at the ready.

"Hurry," said Hoffman, "we don't have much time."

Jackson could hear scrabbling, grunting noises in the stairwell. He watched as Annabel lit the bundle of fuses she was holding, dropped them onto the first stone step and hurriedly crossed the room, urging the others to get into the corridor. A few seconds later came the first, muffled, explosion, followed in quick succession by a series of ever louder blasts. The final one, near the top of the stairwell, shot dust and stone into the room. As they ran through the house to the outside, they need not have worried about being seen. The tower had begun to collapse, taking with it a good proportion of the right wing of the mansion. People were screaming in panic. The four hurried to the cars. Hoffman spoke to Jackson.

"You and Sub-Lieutenant Vine need to get to France as soon as possible," Hoffman said. "Smith flew us here in the Albatross." He indicated the plane in the next field.

"But what about all the equipment we've lost?" said Jackson.

"All safe, sir," said Smith. "It was never on the lorry. Too obvious, sir. I called in some favours at Covent Garden and hid it all in lorries delivering veg to the Navy at Dover."

Jackson grinned at the Petty Officer and shook his hand before sprinting with Vine towards their plane.

Captain Clarke stood in the bridge of his destroyer as it sliced its way north through the cold black swell. Bad weather was forecast, and he could see the slate grey anvil of the storm looming over the horizon ahead. The last communication with Admiral Hall had not been good. He could imagine the objections: *"Fantasy, magic, balderdash. Not things His Majesty's Navy should listen*

to." The Fleet was anchored in the far north at Scapa Flow, closer to Jutland than the *John Dee*, but now unlikely to be part of the action. It was time.

"You have the Bridge, Number One."

"Aye-Aye, sir." Commander Frederick Beeston had been on many missions with him. As had most of the crew.

"Remember there's no shame in abandoning the ship, Fred."

"No, sir." The commander maintained his gaze out to sea.

"This boat has the potential to win, even as it seems lost."

"Yes, sir." There was nothing more to be said.

Captain Clarke made his way through the control deck to the oak door. The two marines saluted and stood aside. Captain Clarke stood still for a few minutes, breathing deeply. Placing his hands on the door, he began muttering a series of repetitive sounds. The door creaked and seemed to shift in its frame. Captain Clarke gently pushed the door, which floated forward into the chamber beyond.

"As you were, Marines. Good Luck."

"Good luck to you, sir," said one of them. They stood back to attention as Captain Clarke entered the chamber. The door floated back into its frame and became whole once more.

The Battle of Verdun had begun. The arcane trench system formed part of the defences to the left of the citadel. Jackson and Vine's task was to destroy the central trenches, the heart of the magic. They had to get the troops out and set the powerful munitions supplied by Captain Clarke to destroy the maze. The destruction of Lynchwood Manor had helped delay any German offensive. All the cultists had died as the mansion collapsed and sealed off the cavern. Their negative influence on strategy and supply of Allied plans to the enemy had died with them. However, the ritual would take place automatically. It was just a matter of time before the battle changed.

It was impossible to move all their equipment to the Front without being stopped. Difficult also because of the terrain, poor roads, the everlasting mud. Once there, they had to persuade several hundred men to move.

Captain William Clarke stood in the centre of the copper- and wood-lined room in the bow of his ship, listening, feeling the thrum of the ships passage through worsening seas as its powerful engines drove forward. He had opened the hatch that connected the room with the five-faceted tower that protruded from the deck. The tower was hollow, apart from the platform attached to the wall inside the sphere at the top of the tower. There was another feeling also—a sense of heaviness —in the atmosphere, as though some immense power was building. He set about preparing for what was to come, doubting that even the sophisticated fire power available within his ship would be enough. He had to channel far older forces, ones that had been in existence from time immemorial. He had to fight fire with fire. As he began focusing his mind on the objects carefully placed around the room, he felt the pressure lessen. His spell was working, so far.

"Are you sure this is the only way?" Vine asked Jackson as they stood by the ambulance she would drive to the trenches. Smith had joined them the previous day and was sitting in the ambulance. She had grown fond of Jackson over the days they had been travelling and getting ready. His energy seemed unfailing.

"This was always going to be what needed to be done."

"But you won't be able to land in no-man's-land."

"Then I'll crash. It's the only place to release the fake

gas so it drifts over the trenches. You won't be noticed as you go forward to find casualties."

"But will I find *you*?" She reached up and touched the roughness of his cheek. Touched by this simple intimate act, Jackson put his arms around her and pulled her close.

"Everything will be alright, I promise. You know we must do this."

"Yes, Charles, I know."

Annabel turned away and climbed into the ambulance. Jackson hurried to his plane, started the engine, and taxied to the end of the field. He took off and circled above the rear supply area. He could see Annabel's ambulance jerk its way along the rutted roads. Gas canisters had been strapped to his wings and the fuselage. If he released the gas whilst flying, it would never appear to threaten troops on the ground. He decided to fly a few miles parallel to the trenches in order to turn towards no-man's-land and make a fast run between the opposing defences to land in the right place. From his vantage point, he could see German troops amassing on the ridge leading down to the trench maze where shells were already landing on the troops. Blood was flowing. He accelerated in a dive and flew so as to provide a target too fast to be hit—he hoped—and to prevent the barbed wire fouling the fuselage and stopping him before he was in position. He made a final adjustment to the joystick and ploughed into no-man's-land just as the German troops started their attack. He didn't need to release the gas. The violence of the landing tore the fuselage and the canisters apart. The last thing Jackson saw were the rolling clouds of gas spilling across no-man's-land in both directions.

The trenches echoed with cries of "Gas! Gas!" as Vine reached close enough to unload the ambulance. Vine and Smith put on gas masks and went to the back of the vehicle. The powerful explosives were strapped to a stretcher and covered with blankets. They hauled it out and made their way as fast as they could to the centre of the trench network. It took much longer than expected. The reality of living and manoeuvring in the trenches could only be understood by those who had to endure it. Eventually they found their objective and proceeded, under Vine's instruction, to mine the trenches. The gas was clearing quickly, and the attack would restart very soon. As she climbed to the parapet to place more charges, she spotted the familiar silhouette of Jackson's plane through the fading smoke.

"Petty Officer Smith," she called, "I can see his plane."

Smith peered over the parapet. It seemed too far to get to him in time, before the cover dissipated.

"I'll see if he's there," he said.

"Let me help."

"No, Sub-Lieutenant, you have to finish the job here. I've done all I can. It's up to you now."

Before she could reply, Smith ripped off his gas mask, leapt out of the trench and started making his way to no-man's-land. She knew he was right and hurriedly continued to set the charges on her way back to the main detonator. The smoke was still lingering in the hollows in front of her as she charged up the detonator. Despite being a long way back, she put the gas mask back on and a helmet that was lying nearby. These explosives were experimental, after all. She charged the detonator and pushed the plunger. The explosion blew her to the ground, sucking the air from her lungs, mud and detritus raining down on her and the surrounding area. Near where she lay stretched a crater over 100 feet deep and 400 feet across. Sub Lieutenant Annabel Vine had succeeded in obliterating the heart of the blood ritual.

The storm was in full force as HMS *John Dee* ploughed into the centre of the maelstrom. The sea was churning, and not just from the storm winds. The water was heaving and boiling, as if some monstrous being was struggling to break free of its constraints. Captain Clarke, now strapped into the tower on his ship, attempted to focus all his and the ship's power through the Astral Projector in the turret in order to contain the entity. A mass began to emerge from the waves and bear rapidly down on the ship.

Commodore Beeston gave the order to set detonators in the ship's armoury. He was about give the order to increase to ramming speed when several gaping holes appeared in the undulating flesh towering over them. The powerful guns of the Royal Navy Grand Fleet had opened fire. Shells pounded relentlessly into the creature, followed by innumerable torpedoes. The thing continued to attempt to rise, but abruptly crumpled, started to disintegrate, and then slid beneath the waves.

In the tower, Captain Clarke had collapsed. The two marines were surprised when the door floated open, seemingly by itself. They rushed in and carried him to the Sick Bay. Commander Beeston hailed the flagship and was given permission to return home. The second Battle of Jutland was about to start.

EPILOGUE

The Great War continued for two more years. During the four years of war, there were many brave and selfless actions undertaken by men and women for their nations. The highest order that could be awarded in Great Britain was the Victoria Cross. Fifty-one were officially awarded to the Royal Navy and Marines. However, closer inspection of the original records, now buried deep in a dusty archive, would indicate that fifty-five had been awarded. These other four names have been redacted. None were awarded posthumously.

SIMON CLARKE lives and writes in Norfolk, United Kingdom. His first published story, 'Loss', appeared on Black Hare Press. He enjoys writing fiction and poetry and has been published by Hedgehog Press, Black Hare Press and Fifty Word Stories. He regularly submits to UK and international publications as well as reading short pieces and poetry at open mic events. He is currently working on his first novel.

The main influences for his writing reflect the authors he enjoyed reading as a young teenager: J.R.R. Tolkien, Ian Fleming, Peter O'Donnell, H.P. Lovecraft, Raymond Chandler, Arthur Conan Doyle. He loves gothic literature and poetry and all things mystical and mysterious and has a collection of arcane artefacts he has found on his travels.

Bibliography
Hedgehog Poetry Press, 2018
Fifty Word Story, 2019
ANGELS, Black Hare Press, 2019
APOCALYPSE, Black Hare Press, 2019
MONSTERS, Black Hare Press, 2019
UNRAVEL, Black Hare Press, 2019

Connect
Facebook: sclarkenp

PRISONER OF WAR NUMBER ONE

By J. Motoki

On the eve of Japan's attack on Pearl Harbor, a young officer of the Imperial Japanese Navy is promoted to be the rider of a powerful but untrained war dragon.

"My steps were these: all-out attack, failure, capture, a sense of dilemma, mental struggle, attempts at suicide, failure again, self-contempt, deep disillusionment, despair and melancholy, reflections, desire to learn and yearning for truth, meditation, rediscovering myself, self-encouragement, discovery of a new duty, freedom through love, a desire for reconstruction."

Kazuo Sakamaki
I Attacked Pearl Harbor, 1945

14 November 1941
Kure Naval District, Hiroshima, Japan
0810 Hours

Everywhere, that hazy blue. The tingle of the depths, held back by a waning spell. Kazuo urged his dragon to the USS *Arizona* and braced himself for shockwaves. A16 opened his jaws and released a water torpedo, a cyclonic swirl that rushed underwater in a roar of foams and jets, crashing into the flank of the target. The USS *Arizona* screeched and thrashed. It sent a water cyclone spinning towards them which A16 slithered around in graceful loops. Kazuo hunched over the mottled green hide of his mount. This was it—the final drill. If they failed to destroy the target, they would have no more time to practise. They would have to endure the wrath of commanders, the disappointment of their families.

The target was a life-sized replica of the USS *Arizona*. Fifty metres in length—far larger and heavier than any war-dragon in the Imperial Japanese Navy—the animatronic beast took several years to construct and a team of Japan's best Mages working day and night to enchant. The results were flawless: the foreign red dragon moved and roared so realistically that Kazuo dug his hands into his harness, and repeated the incantation to fortify their defence shield. A16 was a Type A Kō-hyōteki-class—the smallest breed used in the navy. Each A-dragon had two torpedo attacks before they became exhausted. A16 had only one shot left in him, and Kazuo knew that they looked like a gnat darting around a bear. He wasn't frightened though—his consciousness was melded to A16's in full battle unification, and what his dragon felt was *excitement*. Battle lust. A readiness to fight and die for the hunt.

A16 dodged another attack and released the contents of his second lung. The final torpedo in his arsenal. This time it launched into the target's chest. From the corner of his eye, Kazuo saw A18 approach the target from behind. Although he couldn't see him, Kazuo knew that Hitaro was urgently commanding his mount to silence as they moved into their flank attack. Then the *Arizona* was surrounded. The rest of Kazuo's unit appeared on their mounts—A20, A22, and A24—each dragon holding in their breaths, ready to release bolts of water. The riders were armed with limited spells as well—basic defences. It would have to be enough to take down the deadliest weapon in the United States Navy.

A volley of charges launched from all sides. The *Arizona* disappeared behind a frothy whirlpool, its roars choked by mechanical rasps. With a last explosive surge, the animatronic dragon tore apart and sank. Although he was safely encased in his bubble, Kazuo shivered at the last deafening shriek and the violent pull of its sinking body.

The ensigns and their mounts surfaced to rounds of applause from surrounding light armoured cruisers. The flags of the Imperial Japanese Navy flapped in the wind, the red circle and the rays of the rising sun vivid against the white fabric. Captain Hankyu greeted them with a rare smile.

"Twenty minutes," he shouted at their unit, all five of them bobbing in the waves with their dragons. "Twenty damn minutes! Well done, all of you."

Kazuo, still tuned into his dragon, felt composed. Unmoved by their enthusiasm. He felt annoyed with the noise and fanfare. Ready to eat. Look at all those tasty fish flitting about. Kazuo gently pulled his mind away from his mount and patted the base of his neck. Sharp spines poked along the dragon's back to a cluster between his horns. A16 shook his head of water, his whiskers whipping through the air.

"You did well today," Kazuo said.

When can we eat? A16 grumbled. A-dragons, as a rule, cared little for banter or tactical strategies. Conversing with A16 was fascinating if one were interested only in hunting, mating, and sleeping. Kazuo stroked his mount's scaly hide, rubbing in half-circles in the way he knew that A16 liked, and watched as his mount blinked slowly, heavy eyelids closing in reluctant contentment.

In the distance, a wall of water rushed to meet the sky. The C-dragons appeared in gleaming scales of jade and sapphire. Kazuo watched the shapes dive below the surface. Their size and speed always knocked the breath from him. Type C Kō-hyōteki-class dragons were difficult to breed, and notoriously selective about their riders. More than twice as long as the A-dragons at twenty-six metres from head to tail-tip, they were manned only by high-ranking and decorated naval commanders. The Japanese Imperial Navy had five adult C-dragons that were battle-ready, compared to the hundreds of A-dragons in training. Altogether, the ten riders and mounts from A-class and C-class teams made up the Special Attack Unit.

As Kazuo watched, one of the C-dragons lunged at another. He gasped. At his sudden surge of alarm, A16 whipped around, scanning the horizon for danger. Even from this distance, they could hear the agonized roars from the attacked beast, as deep and reverberating as rounds of thunder. Captain Hankyu stopped his talking in mid-sentence, and the unit fell silent.

Something had gone wrong. Every dragon in the Special Attack Unit had been carefully trained since they were hatchlings, brought over to the southern military bases from the breeding grounds of Maizuru Naval District. Left to their own devices in the rare moments when they were not in training, the dragons engaged in playful nips and chases, or an affectionate head-butt. But never violence. Not like this. And never during a training session. It was an offense severe enough to get both the mount and the rider Mage-tortured for lack of restraint.

Another roar. The fighting dragons disappeared under a wall of foaming water. The A-dragons began to bare their fangs in response. A growl rumbled throughout A16's body, and Kazuo patted him reassuringly.

Not in front of the captain. Kazuo's reprimand quieted A16, although the dragon's long body remained tense. There was no coming back from this error. The rider of the attacking C-dragon would be severely punished indeed, decorated or not. It was rare to punish a mount and its rider—the naval dragons were too precious to the nation—but it had been known to happen. Kazuo's unit had been forced to watch Hitaro, who shouted an incorrect command during practice that left the entire unit vulnerable, get shocked by a Mage. Hitaro was forced to keep his mindlink with his dragon, A18, who roared again and again with each burst of electrical shock.

A16 caught this flash of memory from their mindlink and began to writhe. Kazuo forced himself to calm, to steady his breath and heartbeat, and managed to bring himself and his mount under control once more.

What are they doing? Could it be part of their training? Even as he projected the thought, Kazuo knew it was foolish speculation. War-dragons did not practice attacks on each other. They were controlled in every movement and manoeuvre, and the C-dragon training was even more rigorous than that of the A-units.

A16 snorted, his nostrils flaring. *No. Those are defence calls. Can't you hear it?*

The sea was rising as if from an incoming storm. Already emergency cruisers were dispatched, with Imperial Mages at the helm readying themselves to face the implausible C-dragon confrontation.

A white flash. Both Kazuo and A16 shared a moment of alarm as a seagull dove from the sky. The bird landed on Captain's Hankyu's outstretched arm and whispered into his ear. The captain quickly straightened and addressed his men.

"Everyone return to the base. Immediately. There has been a situation, but the Mages are taking care of it as we speak. No need for alarm."

The riders saluted him. The celebratory mood had vanished entirely.

"Don't let this unusual circumstance diminish our victory today," Captain Hankyu called over the waves. "You did well. You are a testament to the might and power of our glorious country and our Emperor is very pleased with our progress. May his reign continue for a thousand generations."

They would succeed. And when they did, none of the A-dragons or their riders would return to the naval base.

Long live our nation. Long live our Emperor.

As A16 snapped at flying fish, Kazuo repeated the praise with his squadron.

The naval superiors knew their men well—there was no better way to erase rising tension than with warm food and bottles of sake. The mess deck resounded with loud voices and laughter. The men celebrated with rice wine fresh from the country, which were expensive and hard to come by as a result of the rationing and rice shortages. They were presented with bowls of rice-barley, pickled radish, and tender bits of squid. And for dessert—a special treat—red bean cakes. From the portholes, they could see their dragon feasting in frenzied circles.

Hitaro toasted Kazuo and they threw back their

drinks. Even the other three ensigns of their unit had succumbed to the festivities, flushed with drink and laughing over their victory that morning. All five of them had been selected from thousands of applicants for the Kure Naval Academy, a training program so rigorous it had caused some cadets to drop and others to commit suicide. More often than not, the cadet chose to die by his own hand rather than face ostracism from family and friends. Kazuo was glad for Hitaro's companionship—the other three ensigns had little to say beyond the topics of their training, on manoeuvres and mindlink guidance and precise spell commands. Kazuo did not blame them. They had all lost comrades to the intensities of the Naval Academy. It was far simpler to focus on the goal of the mission, to distance oneself from friendship and maintain a professional relationship with your squad.

"Sakamaki."

Startled from his thoughts, Kazuo looked up from his food. A steward stood in the doorway. He looked around the mess hall.

"Kazuo Sakamaki. You are summoned to the Wardroom."

An instant hush. Hitaro gaped, glass frozen in mid-air. The dread was back, sinking into each of them like a talon through the gut. Kazuo felt feverish under the gaze of so many eyes. Ensigns were not summoned to the

Wardroom. Ever. The Wardroom was a room reserved for commissioned officers only. Remotely, as if another person were controlling his body, Kazuo stood and pushed his chair from the table. The mess was silent and watchful as he exited.

The steward motioned him forward. Kazuo swallowed, his dry throat clicking. Then, straightening his shoulders, he stepped through the door that the steward held for him and into a room with the highest-ranking officers in the Japanese Imperial Navy. The room was severe and undecorated. Admiral Mitsumi sat at the head of a table and next to him, the Vice-Admiral of the First Dragon Division. Kazuo's collar felt uncomfortably tight against his throat. He recognised some of the faces around the table, although he had never exchanged a word with the majority of them. Captain Hankyu was there, as well as the captain in charge of the C-units.

But most surprising were the five C-unit riders staring grimly at him. They did not interact with the A-units often, but every lower-level officer knew who they were. The five commanders of the C-dragons: Red Bird, Black Turtle, Green Dragon, White Tiger, and Yellow Snake.

Kazuo bowed low. He wanted to sink through the

floorboards, straight into the ocean. Kazuo looked to the admiral for an explanation and was surprised when Captain Hankyu spoke first.

"Ensign Sakamaki. You impressed us today with your courage, your ability to anticipate attacks, and the bond you share with your mount. As you know, the C-dragon riders were selected with utmost care. They were one of three hundred chosen out of thousands of applicants for our elite Kure Naval Academy. The five, chosen from the entire Imperial Japanese Navy, had these common attributes: bodily strength and physical energy, as well as determination and fighting spirit. They had to be unmarried, and from large families. You are one of eight sons, correct?"

Kazuo bowed his head. "Yes, sir. I am the second eldest. We had only three in the family old enough to enlist." He thought of his hardworking parents, working the rice fields in the mountains of Tateyama, in Toyama Prefecture. Their country home had been a happy one until his father became ill from the smoke from a nearby factory. Kazuo was on his way to Tokyo University, a mind-boggling three hundred kilometres away, when the war was announced. When every physically fit man and woman were called to arms to serve the country. The government awarded each household a stipend for their service, and the ones who died in combat were memorialised forever in shrines and celebrated as heroes.

"Good," the captain said. "Your family will have sons enough to continue its name. The Emperor was emphatic about choosing only the best for our Special Attack forces, and only those from large families. He will not have it said that Japan does not protect its own, nor ignore the familial duties of its courageous people."

"We are all ready to give our lives for the war," Kazuo said, reciting the words drilled into him from the academy. "To protect our nation and families. To keep our boundaries from the defilement of foreign invaders."

Captain Hankyu smiled at him.

"Excellent response, Sakamaki. You were always ahead of your class in terms of intelligence and courage. We consider you to be the finest of our ensigns, and we have auspicious news for you today." He glanced at the admiral, who nodded once.

"A recent discovery was made today," the captain continued. "An…unexpected oversight. During the drills, one of the C-dragons was discovered to be pregnant. Red Bird. She was aggressive and injured another dragon who swam too near her. We will be sending her back to Maizuru Naval District. It is unfortunate timing but, as you know, dragons are slow to brood and it is essential to increase our supply. We have far fewer than the combined Allies, and our breeds are much smaller in size. We do have plans set for enhanced breeding programs with breeds from Italy, but they have not yet been put in place."

Kazuo nodded, but he was screaming inside. Breeding with foreign dragons? After all of the propaganda pamphlets distributed to keep pure bloodlines, both in people and in dragons. And the words drilled into the naval cadets at the academy that he had just recited—now meaningless and called into question. *Our nation must be desperate to plan for such a thing.*

"In the meantime," the captain continued. "We need a replacement for Red Bird in our Hawaii Operation. To uphold the ten assault forces as ordered by the Emperor. You understand why this number is imperative."

One of the C-unit commanders made an almost imperceptible movement, his face twisted in fury. He looked as if he was ready to fly out of his seat and throttle Kazuo where he stood. Of course—that was Red Bird's former rider.

Kazuo nodded his understanding, his head spinning with this new information. Ten was the number of success, of good fortune. You could not send such an unlucky number as four or nine into battle—the very characters of the words contained death and pain. And how unexpected! Red Bird, the dragon of keen eyesight and accomplished tactics, who was subjected to anti-fertilization treatments and prevented from moon-rut, now pregnant with a clutch. After a brief silence, the commander spoke again.

"Ensign Sakamaki, we would like you to become the fifth addition to the C-unit."

Kazuo stood before them, the solemn faces of decorated officers, and it took every measure of his military training to suppress his shock. He, a mere ensign, training alongside the C-dragons and their captains! But the Hawaii Operation was too soon. They were due to launch to their enforcement location off the island of Hawaii in just two weeks. And, now that Red Bird was not capable of battle, that left only four. Who would replace the fifth dragon?

The captain's stern gaze held Kazuo's shocked one.

"This is truly unprecedented, Ensign. And a most auspicious opportunity for you."

"Yes, Captain," Kazuo said. "Thank you for the honour. Thank you all." He bowed low again and held the position for a long time, grateful for the opportunity to control himself and think. When he rose to face them again, he had summoned enough courage to ask the burning question in his heart.

"Would I still train with my A16, sir?"

There was a stirring among the people in the room,

like a breeze agitating long grasses. The captain's face turned bright red.

"Of course not!" The captain snapped. "The idea of an A-dragon training with the C-unit. No—absolutely not. The council has appointed another ensign to your mount."

Kazuo's mouth fell open. The reality of the situation struck him like a fist to the gut, robbing him of breath. To part a living rider from his mount? Such a thing had never occurred before in Japan's naval history, outside of illness or death.

"Then—there is another C-dragon available?" Kazuo kept his eyes locked on the captain's. The people in the room shifted, someone coughed. The C-unit commander looked even more furious. Kazuo flushed. He wished he hadn't said anything. Obviously, they wouldn't allow A16 to join the C-unit. Immediately, he felt a pang. He had been riding A16 for two years, and they had become closely attuned to each other's battle sequences. A16 was brutish and whining, but in training he remained unsurpassed in their unit. They had been the best. Kazuo thought of the relaxed and trusting way A16 closed his eyes as Kazuo cleaned his teeth and scales with a bristle-brush, the way the dragon gently nudged his shoulder for treats. Now A16 would die without his original rider, under the command of a stranger.

"Very good, sir," Kazuo said, his voice faint. A thought occurred to him. "Forgive me, Commander, what of Red Bird's rider? He would know the techniques and manoeuvres of the C-dragons better than I."

He was careful not to look in the direction of the C-unit commanders as he spoke.

"It is a complicated matter," the admiral said suddenly. It was the first time that he had spoken. The way everyone in the room immediately straightened and snapped to attention reminded Kazuo that he was a small fish in an unfathomable sea. The admiral smiled.

"It would be best to show you."

"His name is Ryūjin," the admiral said as he led the group. His Mage flanked him, dressed in the long black robes that bore the golden Chrysanthemum Seal of the Emperor. Kazuo bit back a grin. The Mage looked like a little dog trying to keep abreast of its master. The admiral was tall, stocky, with a moustache modelled after the great commander across the sea. "Named for the sea god, yes. Even as a hatchling, his caretakers determined his fierceness was beyond any dragon they had ever seen. This one is destined for great battles."

Ryūjin, the sea god—god of all dragons. Said to be able to change at will to a man. The sea god lived in a palace of coral under the sea where he controlled the storms and tides with magical jewels. This dragon must be something exceptional to have such a namesake. Kazuo's head spun with questions. What were they doing with him? He was just an ensign, accustomed to his small A-dragon. Why were they not using Red Bird's former ride—a captain whose military experience far exceeded his own? How could he, Sakamaki Kazuo, the son of farmers, ride with one of the giant ones—and one named after a sea god, at that?

The admiral led them to a massive water-filled container at the side of the ship. A dark shape swam within in lazy spirals.

His colour was different from the others, luminous and swirling throughout with a thunderstorm of greys, greens, blues. His limbs with three-claws scratched the sides of the container. What struck Kazuo the most, however, was his size. Ryūjin was small. Larger than his A16, but minuscule compared to the other C-dragons. He had to be eighteen metres to their twenty-six, and sinewy where their middles bulged with muscles.

Ryūjin noticed the men above him and stopped abruptly in his circling. For a second, the men caught the dark glimmer of the dragon's eyes. Then a roar of water rose from the container and onto them, drenching them completely. A few officers yelled and jumped back, their uniforms now pulled wet and taut against their bodies. In the sudden rush, Kazuo realised that Ryūjin had spat water at them. *At the admiral himself.* In spite of himself, Kazuo felt admiration for such a fearless act.

They heard the dragon chuckling, a deep sound that resonated from the walls of his container. At a signal from the vice admiral, the Imperial Mage brought his hands together and froze the dragon where he swam. Ryūjin was then levitated from the water into the air, up to the top of the container. Water cascaded from his body. The dragon floated before them, limp and helpless, his eyes glaring at them in outright and baleful fury. Not at all the image of the proud, benevolent dragon of myth and legend, beautiful beyond measure, immortalised on paper scrolls and screens and ancient tomes.

"You will show respect to your commanders," the Mage ordered and began to chant in an unintelligible tongue. Ryūjin's heavy eyelids wavered, closed.

"He is but a fledgling," the admiral said, calmly. He waved a hand over them and they were dry once more. Kazuo gasped outright. The magical abilities of the head officers were kept secret from the people.

"This is Ryūjin's first year of training and he has never bonded with a rider. We don't send dragons to battle until they are fully grown, as you know, at about forty years of age. He is hardly half that. What we need you to do, Ensign Sakamaki, is to bond with him within two weeks. He has taken a...particular dislike to Commander Hara."

The commander in question stood apart from the group, his fists clenched at his sides. A shockingly emotional display from an officer of his rank—bordering on disrespectful. But the more Kazuo studied him, the way he scanned the ocean that he had ridden with his Red Bird just hours before, whispering commands through their shared bond, the more Kazuo felt pity for the man who struggled so openly with his emotions. It was a rare thing to part a rider from his mount. The admiral's words echoed his thoughts, once again, as if he were reading his mind.

"Of course, this is not standard protocol," he said. "We do not have the time or the resources to make other arrangements. No one in the Imperial Navy is happy about separating an experienced dragon-rider partnership. However, the Emperor demanded ten, and ten is how many we shall launch into battle. The eve of the attack draws near."

In the air, Ryūjin began to struggle against his stupor. His long-spiked tail sliced towards them again and again, as if searching for a target.

"He is young," the admiral said thoughtfully, as if to himself.

"As are most recruits in the Academy, sir," Kazuo said, and straightened proudly. He had, himself, been one of the youngest recruits of the program in generations. The admiral's lips thinned, and Kazuo was fearful that he had misspoken. He averted his gaze.

"Yes," the admiral said. "They are blossoms scattered on the fighting field. They learn quickly. Our youngest recruits know what the wisest commoner does not—that one man's life or death is a matter of no importance."

Admiral Mitsumi turned to face the sea.

To die for Emperor and Nation is the highest hope of a military man. The oft-repeated mantra of the Academy rose unbidden to Kazuo's lips.

"Your mission is to protect Ryūjin," the admiral said, his professional tone returned. "Assist the other C-Units in their mission, be the lookout and vanguard. But no full-on attacks—Ryūjin isn't ready. He won't be ready. We just need you both as reinforcement. Remember that he is invaluable to the Japanese Imperial Army. And he is—well, he is very young, as I believe I've mentioned. In truth, we thought your youth would appeal to him more than our older and experienced officers."

As if to contradict these words, Ryūjin roared. It was a terrible sound throbbing with spit-fury. His sharp teeth gleamed in the sun, the size of *kama*, the harvesting scythes Kazuo's family used in the fields. The fledgling's jaws were large enough to swallow two men.

The admiral noted Kazuo's unrestrained horror. "We ask much of you, Ensign," he said. "But we would not have appointed you this task if we didn't think you could manage it. Remember—all of this is for the good of the country. We are a small nation in a sea of warring hostilities, many of whom can easily swallow us in one gulp if we do not fight back. Our boundaries are threatened at every moment."

Kazuo wanted to scream. He wanted to run to A16 and return to their daily training exercises as if nothing had happened. He wanted to ask the man before him, plead with him, to choose another. If he failed, not only would he be executed and erased as if he had never been, his entire family would be ostracised and persecuted as punishment. He could not do this impossible task. Instead, he bowed.

"I will do my best, sir."

The admiral nodded once.

"Good. Your training begins now, Ensign Sakamaki. You will have Ryūjin ready in two weeks."

...

25 November 1941
0215 Hours

The Special Attack Unit assembled under the cover of darkness, with the waves lapping sluggishly over the mothership. They were to begin their journey, along with the Dive Bombers, to meet at the launching point some five hours away from the island. There, they would refuel and recharge and ready themselves for the early attack that would catch the American forces by complete surprise.

Kazuo waited on the deck of the mothership as the Imperial Mages lit the area with soft glowing lights. They whispered incantations of strength and good fortune. The spells broke through Kazuo's growing unease and filled his mind and body with strength.

Commander Inagaki called to Kazuo over the wind and the waves. Her black hair was drawn and tied severely from her face. Her mount was White Tiger, the largest of the dragons. He rose like a dark mountain from the waves, his eyes tracking Kazuo's every move.

"Ensign Sakamaki. Where is your mount?"

"He was not at the anchoring place, Commander," Kazuo said and bowed his head in embarrassment. "I thought he would join the fleet here."

"Find him," she said. "Get the Mages if you must.

Quickly. We depart in ten minutes."

He turned to leave, and stopped when she spoke again.

"And Sakamaki," Inagaki said. Her voice was cold. "You are new to our unit, and haven't had much time to learn our tactics. But if you or your mount fail in your duties, in what little instruction I had been able to impart on you these last two weeks, then I will personally make sure you retire in disgrace. Any defections endanger the entire mission. Is that understood?"

Kazuo glanced at her serene face, pale as the moon, and looked away quickly, his heartbeat erratic. He bowed low and held the position as he heard her commanding the other officers into position. His hands dug into the sides of his legs. Despite the Mages fortifying incantations, his uniform stuck to his body in a cold sweat.

The C-unit bobbed in the waves, forming a half circle around the mothership. Each of the riders and their mounts seemed to look at Kazuo with reproach and judgement. Kazuo retreated into the darkness and began to walk along the sides of the ship. His anxiety was coming back. Imagine the young dragon disappearing on the eve of departure—the shame of it. It could only end with his sudden retirement and a public demand for him to commit ritual suicide—the dishonourable end of any military personnel who fails in his duties.

The A-dragons breached the surface, slipping across the roiling waves. They stayed a respectful distance away from the C-dragons. Kazuo strained to find A16 among the dragons but could not distinguish them from the other serpents. Shadows flitted over the water. Kazuo looked up. Dive Bombers were flapping overhead, headed towards the island. They sounded like a hush of bats.

Kazuo stood alone on the deck and looked into the waters. He called his family members by name, and those bound by the stone shrines on his family lands. He prayed.

...

7 December 1941
19 km from Pearl Harbor
Oahu Island, Hawaii, USA
0330 Hours

The Special Attack Unit were in position, waiting in the black stretch of sea. Even in his air pocket, Kazuo felt the freeze of the Pacific piercing his skin. Ryūjin looked miniscule compared to the grown dragons next to them. The young dragon's feral hunger clouded their mind-link, and Kazuo gripped the harness to suppress the urge to follow the hunting call. He mentally went over the plan, in the hopes of reminding the dragon of his duties to the nation, and felt a cold wall of indifference from his mount. Ryūjin was wickedly smart, far more intelligent than A16, and decidedly more unpredictable. Even after two weeks of continuous training with the rest of the C-unit, Kazuo felt as if he hardly understood the dragon. He felt uncomfortable in his harness.

In the distance, the black silhouettes of the A-unit writhing like current-stroked seagrass. Hitaro turned to look at him and they exchanged nods. His old unit had stopped talking to him after his promotion, after he moved quarters. Kazuo missed the easy banter of his comrades, the mess hall conversations, manoeuvring A16 alongside Hitaro's A18 in practiced serpentine rotations.

A16 also twisted his head to look at Kazuo. Although the dragon lacked human emotion, it seemed to Kazuo that an accusation gleamed in his shiny black eyes. His replacement rider, an ensign that Kazuo disliked, a small and smug man named Aki, yanked on his reins. A16 turned away immediately and Kazuo gritted his teeth. Slowly, he became aware of Ryūjin's head tilted backwards to study him. The dragon must have felt the sudden emotions transmitted through their bond, the pulses of anger and regret and sadness.

Kazuo tried to pull himself together. He cursed himself for his weakness, for being such a poor example of duty to the new war-dragon in training. He projected a new thought through their mindlink.

To die for Emperor and Nation is the highest hope of a military man.

On their journey to their station near Hawaii, all those hours of swimming and sudden attacks by sharks and deep-sea creatures with searching tentacles and bioluminescent flesh, Kazuo attempted to make conversation with Ryūjin. Interpersonal connections were highly encouraged between rider and mount, although Kazuo knew of those who perceived the dragons as mere beasts and refused to address them as anything else.

The last two weeks had been extraordinarily difficult. Ryūjin was silent and stubborn. The immeasurable power of the young dragon frightened Kazuo, and he worried that it showed through his commands. Ryūjin abandoned formation to follow prey, and ignored Kazuo's entreaties to remain with the unit as he devoured dolphins, whales, and giant squids. Kazuo felt the sea creatures' screams of agony in his bones, alongside the dragon's savage satisfaction over flesh and entrails. On one occasion, Officer Inagaki appeared before him in a flash, White Tiger roaring in their faces.

White Tiger slapped his serpentine tail along the spiky sides of Ryūjin's spine, rocking Kazuo nearly out of his harness. Ryūjin shrieked, his pain flooding through Kazuo who cried out as well. It had become increasingly clear the other dragons disliked the new addition to the C-Unit squadron, with his immaturity and inability to follow directions.

"You waste time, both of you," Officer Inagaki yelled, her voice muffled by her air pocket. "Sakamaki, Ryūjin, you will follow the fleet or be punished in equal measure."

Now Ryūjin stilled his body and drifted farther from the others, who undulated in place against the currents that fought against their bodies. Even now, after all the training and corrections by the Imperial Mages, his resistance was obvious. Kazuo spoke to him, hoping one last time that they could connect before the final signal into battle.

"Ryūjin," he said. "Are you ready?"

The young dragon ignored him, but Kazuo felt his contempt. These dragons were more than reptiles brought to harness, despite what some people thought. Kazuo always felt that they were beings who lived closer to the spirit realm than any other living thing on the earth.

"I think we made incredible progress these last two

weeks. We had little time to achieve what the others have had years to prepare. And you grew several metres! You'll soon dwarf the others in a few years, and then be able to slap them back with your tail."

The dragon turned around to stare at him again. Cold eyes, betraying nothing. Even their bond was distant and cold, like the deep and unexplored abysses of the sea.

"I—" Kazuo began and was startled by a sudden stirring by all the dragons in the water. A school of silver fish appeared from the dark, moving as one.

They stopped in front of the dragons and spoke in many shrill voices.

Niitakayama nobore.

Climb Mt. Niitaka. The code signal. Far away, from the Battle Cruiser, the Imperial Mages strained to control and speak through the voices of the sea creatures.

It was time.

In the distance, they heard explosions. The ocean, torn apart by missiles, rocked and set waves leaping into the sky. The water around them came alive with turmoil. Spurred into action, the A-dragons moved as one. Kazuo watched as A16 swam fluidly, gracefully, toward the entrance of Pearl Harbor. Dark shadows in black water—impossible to detect. A16 didn't look back. It would be the last time Kazuo would see his old dragon alive. If all went to plan.

An instant later, Black Turtle, Green Dragon, and Yellow Snake disappeared through the port. Ryūjin and White Tiger, as ordered, settled into position to guard the entrance to the harbour. Their mission was to rescue or assist any of the other three, although the dangers were not expected to be too extreme. They were not to go back to help the A-unit. They had one mission only: take down the *Arizona*, and die doing it. Honour drove them—and fear. Those who returned from suicide missions were severely punished—their names stricken from government records, their families ostracised for life. Once chosen, there was no coming back.

The United States Navy had the USS *Arizona*, the largest war-dragon in the Allied forces, and smaller dragons surrounding the naval base. Without the distraction of the aviation dragons, any hope of entering Pearl Harbor was impossible. The port was a narrow twenty-meter-deep channel. The channel was closely guarded by two sentinel water dragons, one on each side, and between them a force-net ten metres deep.

The sentinels on either side of the net were trained to disable the force-net to allow Allied personnel through. To further protect their naval base, American destroyers prowled in an eight-kilometre radius around the harbour entrance, assisted by watchful US scrybirds and patrol dragons.

The plan was for the Special Attack Unit to lay low until the aerial attack sowed chaos throughout the harbour, at which point they would unleash their torpedoes at any American battleships or dragons that survived the initial bombing. Afterwards, the C-unit would slip away undetected to Lanai Island, several kilometres away.

Kazuo could see some of Officer Inagaki's mask slipping. She did not enjoy the prospect of being backup any more than he did. Most, if not all, of the assault would be achieved by other dragons in the unit. She was restless, and influenced by their bond, White Tiger began to move in jerky movements. Meanwhile, Ryūjin did not mimic the anxiety of his rider. The young dragon was placid. Inscrutable.

The port sentinels had been dispatched by the first wave of attacks. They were small brown dragons, six metres in length, the colour of earth. They lay floating on the surface, blackened by fire from the surprise air force from the sky, in clouds of blood. They had not had time to shriek.

Through his periscope, Kazuo could see the A-dragons ripple through the shallow waters, the larger C-dragons keeping close to the edges of the harbour to dispatch smaller warships. Although fire and missiles rained down on the ocean, the dragons were protected by human-controlled shields. The enormous red body of the USS *Arizona* flailed in a cloud of froth and blood, rider-less and disoriented, as turbine after turbine shot at her diamond-hard scales. Above her, an aerial attack tossed missiles at her back. Kazuo thought about the A-unit manoeuvres, the order of assault fire. The mission was too easy—the enemy forces ridiculously unprepared.

Kazuo leaped in his harness as Officer Inagaki let out a wavering cry and a stream of curses. Shocked, he turned to her. Her typically stern features were twisted. She yelled at him through her air pocket.

"Sakamaki! Stay here!" White Tiger raced through the port entrance, faster than any war-dragon Kazuo had ever seen. He stared after the flurry of bubbles with his mouth open, stunned by the swiftness of their departure and by Inagaki's distress. Ryūjin sounded interested for the first time Kazuo had known him.

It's Yellow Snake. Look!

Kazuo, with shaking hands, lifted the periscope again. And there, in the distance, lay the limp and unmoving body of the great dragon. His rider drifted beside him. Another missile shuddered the dragon's body, made the rider's body bob up and down like driftwood. White Tiger spat turbine fire again and again at the battle ships above them, as Officer Inagaki skilfully deflected shots. Kazuo recognised the destroyer USS *Ward*, a hideous dragon with distended belly and ragged black hide.

Kazuo gripped his harness until it cut into his skin. Sweat broke out on his forehead and rolled down his face, and he found air pressed in all around him as if he were being suffocated within his shield. He began to breathe fast. The C-dragons were supposed to be safe at the edges of the harbour.

"How could this happen? Ryūjin, how could this—"

We need to go to them. Kazuo felt Ryūjin's heat and fierceness. The dragon's battle calm washed over him. Ryūjin moved through the port without his rider's command. Kazuo didn't try to stop him. He watched Inagaki in her bubble, with her hands raised to issue incantations, her mouth moving soundlessly above the writhing body of her mount.

A glowing blue missile hurled over their heads, barely missing them, spiralling down into the bottom of the harbour. Kazuo collected himself. He needed to be more alert. He needed to protect his mount.

They stormed Pearl Harbor, the rising sun turning the water into fire and blood. In his haste, Ryūjin's underside scraped the bottom of the harbour and he released a pained roar. Another roar answered his, louder and more agonized. The USS *Arizona* still fought, her movements slower, and three of the five A-dragons and their riders lay in pieces around her. The sea was thick with blood and torn flesh and entrails. Hitaro on A18 and Aki on A16 were all that were left, weaving around the USS *Arizona* like leaves falling from a massive tree. A wickedly long curved claw whipped out from the frenzy and A16 screamed in pain.

Kazuo felt himself crying out helplessly and reaching for them. Ryūjin sped towards White Tiger and Officer Inagaki. Adrenaline coursed through them. Heat. Hunger. Rage. Kazuo gathered all the power of his years of training and turned his mount away from that direction, and toward the A-unit. Towards the USS *Arizona*. Ryūjin roared.

What are you doing!

"We need to help them," Kazuo said. He tried to explain through his bond with the young dragon. "My mount—my former mount is back there. They are losing and we need to help them."

It was full light. Ryūjin struggled against him and howled as they headed nearer to the storm.

Our orders—

"And when did you begin to obey orders?" Kazuo asked him.

Ryūjin growled, his sinewy body heaving wildly.

"Officer Inagaki is strong—look how she wields her spells! She is worth twenty allied attackers. We need to destroy the *Arizona*. The A-dragons are almost done."

Ryūjin didn't answer him, but shot a turbine into the frenzy, blinding the USS *Arizona* in one eye. The water resounded with screeches, with pain. In her agony, the *Arizona* lashed out a claw—four claws to the Japanese dragon's three, like the Chinese dragons, Kazuo observed hysterically—and cut A16 cleanly in half. Screaming, Kazuo deflected a spinning missile and watched as his former dragon writhed in a dying roll, the two pieces of his body spinning away from each other.

"Kill her!" Kazuo screamed to Ryūjin. "Kill that bitch!"

Ryūjin, woefully small before the great dragon, took out her other eye. Another turbine to her throat, and another that ripped a hole clean through her skull. The USS *Arizona* was dying at last, her final howls and breaths and explosions creating a maelstrom that surrounded her completely, a powerful blast of lung fire that wiped out Aki and Hitaro and A18 into nothingness. From the *Arizona*'s body poured blood and a viscous black liquid, tar-like, that rose in large droplets to the surface.

Like tears, Kazuo thought distantly. The force of

the dying dragon dragged them down to the blackness of the harbour, a full sixteen metres from the surface. Kazuo rocked in his harness and put his hand to the scales of his dragon, caressing the smooth surface. He couldn't speak. He poured all of his remaining strength into their mindlink.

I'm sorry, Ryūjin—I'm so sorry.

...

1 January 1942
Quarantine Island Detention Camp
Honolulu, Hawaii, USA
0600 Hours

The morning began as usual.

The armed American guard tapped on the cell and slid a plate of food under the door. And, as usual, Kazuo begged for the soldier to kill him. He knew bits of English from his military training and the coarse words fumbled from his mouth, foreign and foul-tasting.

Kill me, I cannot remain alive, kill me, my comrades are crying over my failure and I am ashamed. Dishonoured. Kill me. And if you will not, allow me to kill myself. Let me apologize to the spirits of my comrades, to Japan's heroes—the ones who died honourably. Let me join them in death. Let me die.

The guard ignored him. Kazuo had been surprised, then furious, at the polite treatment he was subjected to in his imprisonment. The soldiers were aloof and suspicious, but not cruel. The food was, if not the best quality, plentiful. Strange. He was allowed books and an American tutor was beginning to teach him English. He was even allowed walks under close supervision, up and down the beach shore.

Kazuo wondered at the exercise. He eventually came to the conclusion that the Americans were preparing him for labour camps.

I will die alone, nameless, in the hands of foreigners.

The morning continued. Two large guards came for him. And it was on his beach walk when he discovered that his link to Ryūjin had returned.

He heard Ryūjin's voice on the beach, as he passed the chain-linked fence that bordered the detention camp. The two large guards flanked him closely. Theirs was a rapid-fire defence magic, inescapable, that could take a man down in seconds and paralyze him for hours. Kazuo experienced this in the first couple days, when he struggled and screamed and pleaded with them to finish him. He raged, beating his hands bloody against the bars, the walls of his prison. He took the cigarettes the soldiers gave him and burned the flesh from his arms and legs. He seared his eyelids trying to burn the eyes from his head. And still the pain did nothing to take away his agony. The whispers of the dead would not leave him. The images of his fallen comrades filled his mind until he saw nothing else, and he refused all food and water in the hopes of making them disappear forever.

The American medics were summoned, and the process of forcing food intravenously into him was so uncomfortable he complied with all their demands thereafter. Their best-behaved prisoner of war, compliant and disgraced, the first Japanese POW. The first Japanese soldier taken alive by the Americans in a hundred years of war.

Ryūjin's voice in his head:

Sakamaki.

Kazuo stopped so abruptly the soldiers raised their rifles. He apologized, bowing several times. They moved on. Ryūjin's voice stayed in his head all down the beach.

Sakamaki. Beware the foreigners. They have a monster greater than any of the dragons in Japan. It flies.

It comes for me?

It flies for Japan. You are safe here. But do not go back.

What happened after the battle? After I was knocked unconscious?

The Special Attack Unit was obliterated, Ryūjin told him. Nine dragons, nine riders, dead. The remaining rider had washed ashore and been taken by the enemy. His conduct was dishonourable. After all, he was still alive. The remaining dragon disappeared—his body never recovered. This, at least, was what Ryūjin had learned from listening to the distant thoughts of the Imperial Navy.

The remaining dragon? Kazuo thought. *Then— you deserted our nation?*

The water dragon whispered as Kazuo was led back to the camp:

I have no nation. I have no one.

Kazuo felt his eyes burn. He too had no nation— had no one who would call him friend. The realization made his body sag until the soldiers surrounded him, making worried calls in a language he barely knew. Kazuo didn't care. He wanted nothing more than to run to sea, calling for his dragon, urging him to take Kazuo from this place of ghosts.

Sakamaki. The dragon's words snaked through his thoughts.

You have come to say goodbye, Kazuo whispered back. Tears blurred the sand, the green spray of grass at the end of the beach.

And then Ryūjin opened his mind to Kazuo, let him see that ocean deep where the dragon slid along cold currents, eyes flashing for fish. In his mind was a hunger for freedom—a desire always embedded there, from the first cracks of his egg to the long hours of training to today, when the serpent's last tether to the surface was to be cut.

The young dragon of C-unit yearned to dive down to distant lands, to see those great castles and wilds of the deep. He wished to meet others of his kind, free from harness and incomprehensible rules. There, the dragon would know total freedom; gift from himself to his own soul. He would find his coral palace, find a mate wilder than storms and tides.

Who knows what the soldiers thought of Kazuo smiling through his tears? In their final mind-link, as a parting gift, Kazuo felt a fierce joy flood his body. A wild exhilaration of soaring through blue waters without restraint. Of filling his mouth on squirming sea creatures, of leaping over bending waves.

Sakamaki. The last words Kazuo ever heard from his mount. *You are not as despicable as your kind.*

Kazuo restrained himself from looking at the beach—he knew he would not glimpse the dragon. The sun shone on his face, the beach stretched before him, the sky and sea merged into an indistinguishable blue.

Things stirred across the sea. Thousands of kilometres away, a looming shadow stretched over America, larger than the horizon—a black and unimaginably vast dragon with red eyes, with fire breath that was cultivated to wipe out cities—and its sights were set on Hiroshima.

J. MOTOKI is a speculative writer who lives in Colorado with her husband and two belligerent cats. She is the Short Story Editor of Coffin Bell Journal, the Strange Editor of Rune Bear, and a shushing library clerk at a high school. She received her BA in literature from the College of Creative Studies at the University of California, Santa Barbara, and her works have been published in The Other Stories Podcast (Hawk & Cleaver), Enchanted Conversation Magazine, Blood Song Books, Coffin Bell Journal, and others.

Bibliography

Apocalypse, Black Hare Press, 2019

Curses & Cauldrons, Blood Song Books, 2019

Daily Tally, Rue Scribe, 2018

Dark Moments, Black Hare Press, 2019

Directions After Death, Coffin Bell, 2018 (Nominated for The Best Small Fictions 2019)

Fever of the Wendigo, Haunted MTL/Czykmate Productions, 2019

Gods of Rags, The Other Stories Podcast/Hawk & Cleaver, 2019

Hydra, Rune Bear, 2018

Like Flies, Like Lights, Nowhere.Ink, 2018

Peterel and the Terrible Head, Enchanted Conversation Magazine, 2019

What If?, Black Hare Press, 2019

Connect

Website: www.jumotki.com

Instagram: instagram.com/jumotki/

Goodreads: goodreads.com/jmotoki

Twitter: @J_Motoki

THE NIGHT WITCH

By Blake Jessop

At the desperate height of the battle of Stalingrad, an idealistic Russian bomber pilot finds herself at the mercy of a force far older and darker than war. Can she outwit the legendary Baba Yaga and stave off inevitable defeat at the same time?

"We've been up too long, sunrise is coming," Panna yells into the wind. "The boys have their food, forget the bombs!"

Zhenya pretends that the sewing machine rattle of the Polikarpov's engine has drowned her navigator out.

The ruined city stretches away below the biplane, and the two Russian girls fly low. It's like flying through the corpse of a giant whose body has concrete ribs. Stone flesh and veins made of rail siding flash beneath their canvas wings. It's hard not to see Stalingrad as a dead place. It's hard to see it at all at night when it's lit only by the fires set by rockets and artillery shells, but dawn is threatening the horizon.

"There's always time," Zhenya says to herself, craning her neck to see anything on the ground that might be a target. It pains Zhenya to return to the airfield with any bombs on board. Panna taps her shoulder from the rear seat and points. New trench lines spread outward from the Barrikady Tractor Factory like a sickness under the skin. Zhenya slides the biplane toward them and switches off her engine. The Polikarpov goes silent except for the eerie whistling of wind through the struts.

They pass so low over the German trenches that they can actually hear men yell in alarm. They'd loaded their bomb racks with food and ammunition for their own side tonight, so Panna starts dropping hand grenades over the side as they whoosh past the Wehrmacht lines, leaving blood and chaos in their wake. In the moment before Zhenya switches her engine back on to climb away, she hears a word screamed into the darkness. Indistinct, but she knows what the Germans call them. *Nachthexen*. Night Witches.

The Polikarpov feels wonderfully light as Zhenya flees the sudden crack of rifles and steers for home.

"I knew we had time," she yells back exultantly, "Nice work back there!"

Panna, a demure little mouse who is braver than anyone Zhenya has ever met, stays silent. *Fine, let her sulk.*

They buzz low through the ruined city, down toward the river, and are almost past the boat landings when Panna lets out a shrill cry. It's indistinct, but another German word Zhenya knows very well.

"Messerschmitts!" Panna screams, and Zhenya discovers she didn't have any time left, after all.

In a forest on the eastern bank of the Volga, a very old woman hears the distant thunder of guns from across the river.

The noise keeps her up at all hours, and she curses the constant thumps and bangs. She is in the midst of sweeping her cabin, an ancient thing that sits on rickety stilts. Her little homestead is a humble one; skeletal fence posts surround a small garden, a few pear trees ripe with autumn fruit, and a little pond for fishing. Dawn has broken high over the trees and brought with it the distant roar of artillery.

"Be quiet, damn you!" she cries, and her voice rattles the leaves in the orchard. There's a moment of stillness, then the earth resumes its intermittent rumble, as if the sun was bursting from the horizon instead of rising. She wonders if it disturbs the fish in her pond.

"Probably the Tsar and his miserable cannons. I shall pay him a visit, if he is not careful."

The crone sniffs the air and tilts her head sharply. The necklace she wears rattles like a garland of dry bones. There's a new noise in the wind, like the clatter of a table loom, and the smell of something burning.

Zhenya Rudneva flies through the failing night like a comet. She wrestles with the controls, fighting to keep the biplane in the air.

"Panna!" she screams over her shoulder, "Panna, where are we? Panna, answer me!"

Panna points weakly, her hand gloved in leather and slick with blood, indicating a small clearing in the endless woods. It's better than hitting the trees. Zhenya rolls the burning Polikarpov toward it, and the glade rushes up to meet them.

The old woman watches the comet fall into her orchard. The thing glides in like an obese pelican. There's a giant crash as the landing gear collapses and the monstrous machine knocks over a pear tree and ploughs into her garden. She hustles to the wreckage on spindly legs. To her surprise, the occupants of the evil thing are little more than girls. She expected large and arrogant men, who are usually the ones responsible for explosions and fires and machines that produce too much smoke.

She beats at the burning canvas with a broom made of twigs. The machine smells like brazier coals and roasting meat.

"What have you foolish girls done?" she shrieks.

When she wakes, Zhenya feels like freshly killed game. Her flying suit is stiff with dried blood, and she has a terrible ache in her throat. She lies on a long chaise by a stone fireplace, though the pulsing coals do not make her feel any warmer. Some partisans must have found her if she went down on the German side of the river, or peasants if it was the East bank. She is well and truly lost.

"Panna?" Zhenya says softly, and her voice croaks. She reaches a hand to her neck. Someone has tied a ribbon or kerchief tightly around it to stop her bleeding. She tugs at it, trying to feel how bad the gash is.

"Do not fuss with that," a strange voice says. The voice of a very old woman, punctuated by the soft click of bones.

At a table opposite the fire is an old and exceptionally ugly *babushka*. She has a long nose and spidery fingers that clink with an abundance of rings. Around her neck is hung a broad necklace of what look like lustreless white pearls. She has her bony elbows on the table and is gnawing at a haunch. The meat looks tough and ill-cooked.

"You almost lost your head when your machine crashed in my orchard. If I hadn't tied that ribbon around your neck you would have bled to death like a lamb at Easter."

"Thank you," Zhenya says, "where is my navigator?"

"Your what?" the old woman says.

"The girl in the other seat. Did you help her too?"

"I helped myself to her," the old woman says.

"You… killed her?" Zhenya thinks, and realises both the fact of it and that she has said it out loud in the same moment. A wave of grief passes over her and washes away. All her history with the mousy girl from Leningrad. The smell of her hair and the grease on her hands.

"No, I ate her. That's different."

Zhenya is a modern Soviet woman. Before the Great Patriotic War, she was a member of the Moscow branch of the Astronomical-Geodisical Society. She doesn't believe in folk tales, though a folk tale sits across from her, chewing on gristly meat.

"I have dreamed about you since I was a child," Zhenya says in a tiny voice.

"You are still a child," the Baba Yaga says, "or should I say a lamb?"

Zhenya thinks that she has probably died. The old witch has eaten Panna, and soon they will walk together into darkness when the crone takes her hand. She closes her eyes to see if she's ready, and finds she is not.

"What I am is a Guards Senior Lieutenant in the 588th Night Bomber Regiment. I have flown more than two hundred missions against the fascist invaders. You will stay away from me."

The ancient witch stops chewing. Her eyes narrow suspiciously.

"Russia has been invaded?"

"Yes, by the fascists," Zhenya says, and some of the cabin's evil aura is displaced by confusion.

"What on earth are fascists?"

"The Germans," Zhenya says, "We have been invaded by the Germans."

"Well, I suppose that explains all the noise. What does the Tsar have to say about it?"

"We shot the Tsar. We have a worker's party, and Comrade Stalin is leading us as equals in the defence of the Motherland. How long have you been hiding in this forest?"

"Longer than you can imagine. Did you say you were in a regiment?"

"Yes. They give the men all the good machines, so we make do with obsolete Polikarpovs like the one I crashed into your garden. We have to fly at night or the Messerschmitts swat us like flies."

The witch settles back in her chair. Something, at least, seems to make sense to her.

"That is wise of you; women should only fly after dark. So you're saying that we have been invaded by Germans, that peasants have taken over the country, and that someone decided to let little girls fight for St. Petersburg."

"We call it Stalingrad." For a moment Zhenya does not look like a child. Her eyes are an angry, arctic blue. "We will all die before winter, but we will not give in. My girls and I are the most frightening monsters in the entire miserable war. The Germans have a name for us: *Nachthexen*."

"And what does that mean?" Baba Yaga asks, with a curious expression creasing her wrinkled face.

"Night Witches," Zhenya says. The crone seems to be pondering some deep question. Zhenya runs her fingers along the ribbon around her neck. "How badly was I hurt? What will happen if I fuss with this?"

"Your head will fall off, of course. I had planned to save you for tomorrow night, but that was before I learned you are a witch."

"I am nothing like you," Zhenya almost spits.

"That remains to be seen. I will make you a bargain, little witch. Make me a feast tonight, and perhaps I'll let you keep your head."

Zhenya, at the end of her endurance, nods her head. It hurts."And how am I meant to get back to my airfield?"

"I don't know what that is, but we will fly in my mortar and pestle, obviously. That is what witches do."

Like a sleepwalker, Zhenya staggers along a dusty runway. Artillery thumps in the distance, and the fetid smell of the river is on the air. Her barracks is the only shelter anywhere near the airfield, and the girls have draped it artistically with camouflage netting to avoid becoming a target for German dive bombers. She waves weakly at the netting, as if trying to brush away a spider's web. The first to see Zhenya is Yevdokia Bershanskaya, her squadron leader.

"Comrade Rudneva?" The lean Muscovite looks stunned. Zhenya realises she must look frightful. The Lieutenant Colonel usually has a snide remark ready for her, but she just stares. The words are loud enough to make everyone who isn't asleep look up from their meagre breakfast.

"We thought you were dead!" Nadya Litvinova cries. The rest of the girls wake up fast. For an instant, Zhenya forgets her sorrow; she is a popular girl, and she loves to be loved.

"What happened?" Yevdokia asks.

"A Messerschmitt caught us. Panna was hit," Zhenya says, "and the plane caught fire. I got lost and crashed in the woods."

"Is she alright?" Nadya asks, more quietly.

Silence.

"She's still in the woods," Zhenya says, and finally bursts into tears. The rest of the girls surround her. Some cry. Even Yevdokia sighs and runs a hand over her eyes. After a while, everyone returns sadly to what they were doing.

"You better get to the aid station for your neck," Yevdokia says, "but we still need you. Will you fly tonight, comrade?"

Zhenya knows this is more like an order. She wants to hate Yevdokia for it, until she realises that she will need to fly back to Baba Yaga anyway. The old hag left her at the edge of the road and fled in her mortar as soon as she saw her first American lend-lease truck. Thinking of the witch reminds her of closing her eyes and wondering if she was ready to die. Reminds her of her answer.

"I will, comrade Colonel. I am not finished yet," Zhenya says, and finds she means it.

Instead of hitching a lift to the aid station, Zhenya thumbs a ride from a staff car headed to the river crossing. In the pandemonium around the jetties, she hunts for the makings of a feast.

Her deal with Baba Yaga is simple; bring the witch dinner or the witch will find her and pull the ribbon from her neck. It doesn't feel real, and Zhenya has no idea how to make a supper for Baba Yaga, serve it, and somehow get back in time for her night's flying. When is she supposed to sleep? When is she supposed to grieve?

Worse, it becomes obvious that cooking a feast is going to be impossible. It's complete bedlam at the river crossing, and there's no meat to be stolen nor flour to be bartered for. All that crosses the Volga is vodka and bullets and men. Even fishing is out of the question; the surface of the water is foul with diesel and debris and a kind of blackened scum that smells like rotting meat. War is always terrible, but it's worse when you're losing.

In the end, all Zhenya manages to scrounge up is

some dried fish, bread as hard as a pane of glass, and a small sack of potato skins that might make a weak soup. This is actually a pretty good haul, but she knows it won't satisfy Baba Yaga. The witch asked for a feast, and that means borscht, blintzes, and fancy old wine.

Zhenya's neck hurts. She finds her way back to the airfield with a feeling of deep fatalism. She wishes she had a litre of vodka. That would ease her last few moments before the witch eats her in her sleep.

Thinking miserably about pouring spirits down her throat, Zhenya has an idea.

Baba Yaga watches Zhenya land her plane along the exact same glide path she did the night before. This Polikarpov isn't on fire, and the old witch reluctantly admits that the girl handles it well. Zhenya climbs from the open cockpit and pulls a small sack from the navigator's seat behind her.

"I have brought your feast, Baba Yaga," Zhenya says, "so let us hurry. I have bombing missions to fly tonight."

"I wouldn't worry about that if I were you," Baba Yaga says, "based on how small that sack is."

The sun is setting. In the dusk, Zhenya makes out that the ornaments topping the fence posts that surround the cottage are skulls. As she watches, their eye sockets start to glow gently, like the most modern electric lights in Moscow.

"I have a secret ingredient," Zhenya says, and pulls a bottle of crystal liquid from her bag.

Back at the barracks, Zhenya prepares to face death, weaving slightly. Yevdokia has already assigned Nadya as her new navigator. Pairing up survivors is normal, and Zhenya knows Nadya from flight school. The two of them load munitions unsteadily onto the Polikarpov's racks.

"Zhenya," Nadya hisses, "are you drunk?"

"It's not serious," Zhenya replies, "besides it's best not to bomb the Barrikady Tractor Factory if you're too tense. Now turn the prop and let's go."

For three days in a row, Baba Yaga gives Zhenya ridiculous errands and threatens to kill her. For three nights Zhenya tries to stave off both the Germans and the witch's cruel demands.

On the fourth day, something has changed. Rather than croak orders at her and send her on her way, Baba Yaga makes Zhenya tea in an ancient samovar. The tea is wonderful, and Zhenya finds her exhaustion wafting away in its steam.

"You are cleverer than I expected," Baba Yaga says.

Zhenya remains silent. She hates the dim cottage, and the wondrous tea is probably just a novel way to make sure she can keep the charade going. They sip in silence for a while until Baba Yaga speaks.

"Your trick with the vodka was clever," she admits, "and I haven't been able to stump you, yet."

Zhenya looks over the rim of her cup as though sighting a machine gun.

"You are very angry," Baba Yaga says.

"Either the Germans will kill me or this stupid bargain will. Am I meant to sing? Am I supposed to be happy my friends are dying and I'm losing this war while I serve you like a scullery maid?"

"That's not it," Baba Yaga says, "it was that girl I ate, wasn't it?"

Zhenya surges to her feet and dashes her teacup on the floor.

"You wouldn't understand!"

Unruffled, the old witch looks at the young pilot with calculation. Zhenya isn't sure what's changed, but something in the air is different. She slumps back into her creaking wooden chair, exhausted all over again.

"I fight all night and spend all day finding you stupid

and unimportant things," Zhenya says, putting her head in her hands, "And I have not even been able to bury my friend because you ate her and boiled her bones in a soup. The world has gone mad."

"That's true, but I'm a witch, what did you expect?" Baba Yaga says.

"You ate her," Zhenya says, "I can't stop thinking about it."

"That's not true. Lie to yourself, but don't lie to me; you don't feel like I killed her, you feel like you did."

Zhenya replies so softly that even the witch's sharp and pointed ears strain to hear her.

"I decided to stay out too long, and I crashed the plane," she whispers, "How am I meant to save the Motherland if I couldn't even save her?"

Baba Yaga reaches across the table and puts her leathery hands on Zhenya's. The girl sniffles and looks up. Reflected in her arctic blue eyes, Baba Yaga sees an ocean of grief and confusion. The crashing waves of youth and war. Then she sees Zhenya weeping in a shower, and the little mouse from Leningrad stepping under the water with her. Baba Yaga takes her hands away.

"Ah," the witch says while Zhenya blinks. "I see that you loved her. Well, know this: you did not kill Panna anymore than I did. We both did with her what came naturally. What happened to your friend is part of a chain, and you just happen to be the link that broke."

Zhenya tries to compose herself. "How did you know about us?"

"The same way you did. The same way you know your war is lost and that the tasks I gave you were pointless. This is not intuition, it is foresight. You are seeing the world as it is, and that is why you carry such heavy burdens."

"You mean that these terrible things are not fate. That there is something I can do about them."

Baba Yaga nods. Almost smiles.

"The world changed while I wasn't looking, and that perhaps it's time for me to change with it. I have been thinking about retiring and moving to a nice pine wood in Sochi. I might try being a kind witch."

"Even if you manage the kindness," Zhenya says, "who would take your place?"

"I thought you might."

"Me?" Zhenya chokes on her tea.

"I've been doing this too long. You're a modern sort of witch, and this little cabin isn't so bad."

Later, in quiet moments, Zhenya will feel shame for her answer. Not for its contents, but for how long she hesitated before giving it.

"No. I will not just run away to the woods so you

can go on vacation. This war is bigger than my sorrow, and if I have to die for it, I will."

Baba Yaga's face darkens, and without warning, she reaches across the table and grabs Zhenya by both ears. The witch pinches the tips and gives her a violent shake. Zhenya cringes away.

"How dare you preach to me? Do you understand what I'm offering you? Why can't you listen?"

The witch reaches for the ribbon at Zhenya's neck, and this time Zhenya doesn't flinch. Their eyes meet.

"How dare you refuse me?"

"It's not you I'm refusing," Zhenya says, "It's this life you've led. You have no idea what the war is really like. You ran back to this miserable little cabin before you could so much as smell it. You can kill me if you like, but I am finished being your errand girl."

"So be it," Baba Yaga says, tugging ever so gently at the knot. Zhenya doesn't move an inch, as still and unmoving as a caryatid. The old witch wavers.

"We made a bargain," Zhenya says, very quietly, "so you have every right to kill me, but before you do, why don't you fly with me and see the world before you give it up again?"

"Fly in that machine?" Baba Yaga says hesitantly, caught off guard.

"If you want to know why I am what I am,

understanding why I love is not enough. You have to understand why I hate. For that you will need to have the courage to see what happened to the Russia you abandoned. Will you do that before you undo the ribbon?"

There is a long pause and the air between them is heavy.

"Yes," says Baba Yaga, "show me this new war you need to win."

Zhenya dons her flying helmet and it chafes the tips of her ears. She helps the old witch into the navigator's seat, holding her breath against the smell of mildew. She taxis them nimbly around a pear tree and takes to the air with the Polikarpov's engine hammering like a giant sewing machine.

Zhenya flies high above the forest and puts the biplane through its paces, doing her best to make her passenger as nauseous as possible. Baba Yaga cackles as the wind pulls her wiry hair in every direction. After some more aerobatics, she leans forward to yell into Zhenya's ear.

"This is excellent, I must admit you really know how to fly. Now, take me to see the war."

Zhenya obeys. They fly along the Volga and look at

the opposite bank. It is a Golgotha, a city of the dead. Clouds of dust blast into the air at intervals, and the rattle of weapons is constant. Stalingrad looks like the lower jaw of a long dead giant. Zhenya flies low to avoid detection, and they both smell the evil muck in the river.

North of the city fields of golden wheat are almost intact, un-reaped. Zhenya is about to turn back when Baba Yaga cries in her ear and points. A squat Panzer tank is parked close to the river's glistening edge. The crew is splashing in the water. Zhenya laughs at the naked boys.

"Don't laugh, it's beneath you!" Baba Yaga yells. The rage in her voice is as naked as the German tankers. "How dare they caper like it's a summer holiday. What can we do? It's too far for spells."

"There's a *Papasha* at your feet," Zhenya calls back.

"What? Did you say my father is here? What is this thing?"

"A PPSh submachine gun. Pull the handle on the side, then point the end with the hole at the Germans. You fire it by depressing the little lever, there. It will rattle around a lot, so hold on tight."

The old witch leans dangerously out of the side of the biplane.

"Fly a little lower," she says. Zhenya does, and the cool air fills with the raking chatter of the gun and Baba Yaga's delighted cackling.

A pretty little fishpond is tucked away in the shade behind the orchard. Zhenya fishes patiently for a few minutes with Baba Yaga's antique rod.

Zhenya has always been utterly incapable of catching fish, even though she's from Berdyansk. She doubts Baba Yaga will kill her if she fails to reel in their supper but feels itchy about taking the chance.

She trots back to the biplane and rummages around the navigator's seat. It's full of spent cartridge casings and her memories of Panna. Before she can get depressed, Zhenya smiles at the image of the naked German boys fleeing like hares. She finds what she wants and returns to the pond.

Baba Yaga comes looking for her just as she makes it back.

"You useless little chit, you haven't caught anything," she says.

"Just wait," Zhenya says. She pulls the pin from the hand grenade and lobs it gently into the pond. It plops among the fat, startled fish like a rock. Smiling, Zhenya mimes putting fingers in her ears as the muted explosion blasts a fountain of spray into the air. Dead fish float to the surface.

"That is not fishing," Baba Yaga says.

"It is now," Zhenya replies, "you have to get with the times."

Baba Yaga contemplates Zhenya as she stands in front of the pool.

"If I told you that as Baba Yaga you could win a battle like the one you showed me, that you wouldn't have to stay in this cottage, would you reconsider my offer?"

Zhenya's eyes meet hers.

"I might."

Without warning Baba Yaga reaches out and grabs Zhenya by the cheek. The witch reaches greasy fingers into Zhenya's mouth and tugs at her teeth. Zhenya gives a muffled cry, though to her own ears the shriek sounds clear and musical.

"Try it out, and see what you think," Baba Yaga says.

Zhenya cleans the fat Caspian trout in a flash, something she did a thousand times as a child, but there isn't time to cook them before night falls. Baba Yaga suggests eating them raw.

"That's disgusting."

"Not to a witch, it isn't. Aren't you hungry?"

Zhenya takes a tentative bite, and finds that her

teeth slice through the fish, bones and all, like razors. The meat is irresistibly sweet. She forgets her trepidation and eats.

"Well," she says between mouthfuls, "How did you find the war?"

"Totally abominable, thank you," Baba Yaga replies, "but you were right; Russia has changed beyond my understanding. You killed so many fish we won't be able to eat them all. I'll give you a sack and you can feed your girls."

Zhenya nods her thanks and they eat in silence.

"I'm sorry I ate Panna," Baba Yaga says after a while. "Not because she wasn't delicious. She was. I'm sorry it hurt you."

Zhenya looks up at the witch, and her childish blue eyes meet the old woman's black, depthless gaze.

"Wait there a moment, Zhenya, I have something for you."

Zhenya sits in a trance. Baba Yaga returns with a round object wrapped in a thin stole and places it on the table. Zhenya reaches out to touch it. The silk is as smooth and immutable as a glacier.

"I miss her," Zhenya says.

"She can still be with you," Baba Yaga replies, "if you choose."

Feeling as though she is crossing a river even wider

and darker than the Volga, Zhenya pulls the silk away. The object on the table is a skull, small and feminine. Zhenya touches it and finds the bone smooth and cool under her fingertips. She takes her best friend back into her hands, and her tears tap softly on the tablecloth. She kisses Panna's skull very gently, and a warm light starts to glow in its eyes. Her tears stop as though someone had turned off a tap.

"Good," Baba Yaga says, "now go on little night witch, you have work to do and a choice to make."

The wet sack of fish mutes every question about where Zhenya has been. The girls skin them expertly and start a frying pan.

"They're lake trout," Nadya says delightedly, "tough but tasty."

"Like us," Yevdokia says in passing. It's so unexpected that no one laughs. The dour Lieutenant Colonel looks at them awkwardly, takes a piece, and returns to her maps.

They eat hurriedly and go out to check the planes. As Zhenya is about to put on her flying helmet, Yevdokia pulls her aside.

"Comrade Rudneva," Yevdokia says, "you missed the squadron briefing today. Where were you, and what's wrong with your ears?"

Zhenya touches one ear and finds it a little pointed. She tries to think of a lie.

"I have been experimenting with being a witch during the day, as well," she says, instead.

Yevdokia raises her eyebrows, but before she can respond, Zhenya cocks her head like a dog hearing a whistle.

"That sounds like Vanyushas," Zhenya says.

"Nonsense," Yevdokia says, "the Germans haven't taken the ridge above the landing. There's nowhere for them to spot from."

"They took something," Zhenya says, and the look on her face makes the Lieutenant Colonel blanch. Certainty. A few seconds later the rockets begin to fall on the airfield and teach Zhenya her last lesson about war.

The German rockets make a shrieking sound like a chorus of madly braying donkeys. They explode amongst the biplanes and the runways and the huts, throwing plumes of earth and debris and blood into the burning sky.

The barrage only lasts a minute, but it feels like the passing of an age, like everything that came before it has been flattened and consigned to history. Biplanes burn.

Some are reduced to matchsticks, others lean on broken wings. The girls run around, frantically trying to put out the fires and drag their comrades from the ruins.

When it's over, Zhenya sits on the grass next to one of the runways. All around her individual blades of grass smoulder. Her eyes ache, but no tears flow. She can't remember whether one of the tests for witchcraft is an inability to cry. She hears the crunch of flying boots behind her. Yevdokia comes to stand beside her.

"We might just get one runway clear enough to take off, and we still have a few planes that can fly."

"How can you even think of flying?" Zhenya moans. She puts her head in her hands and the long tips of her ears poke out between her fingers.

"We're not finished yet," Yevdokia says coldly. Zhenya shakes her head.

"Then go get Nina and fly across the river and see how much good you can do with a half dead squadron."

"My navigator," Yevdokia says, with a quaver in her voice, "is lying by the hut. Most of her, anyway."

Panna steps uninvited into the shower stall of Zhenya's mind and reminds her how her Colonel must feel. She starts to say something but Yevdokia waves her into silence.

"Forget her. Forget me. I am flying back to Stalingrad even if there isn't enough time. Even if I have to go alone."

Zhenya hears her perfectly. The older woman's voice carries something other than pain or arrogance. Yevdokia has not given up hope. Zhenya can't imagine why.

"Red Army command says Batyuk is taking his Siberians across the Volga to try saving the river landing. I'm sending every girl we have left to help."

"What about the artillery spotters? If they can hit us here, they'll tear those men to pieces before they take two steps off the boats," Zhenya says. Yevdokia squats down next to her and looks into the crimson distance.

"I've got that figured out, too," she says, "the only place they could spot us from is the top of the Univermag department store. Far behind enemy lines, now. It's suicide, obviously, so I'll go myself, but I don't have a pilot. I wonder if you would fly for me."

It's the only true question Zhenya has ever heard her ask. She glances over at the Colonel and realises how much courage it took for Yevdokia to approach her. How much rage and humility.

"I needed to hear that. I would be honoured to be your pilot."

Yevdokia stands and reaches out a hand. Zhenya takes it and rises to her feet.

"Thank you, Zhenya, we will certainly be killed

when we fly to the Univermag, but we won't let this insult pass."

"Certainly not," Zhenya says, "and it isn't us who are going to die."

Yevdokia sighs.

"This is not a fairy tale, Zhenya."

"We'll see about that. Come with me."

Zhenya finds her Polikarpov untouched, invincible. Nadya is nowhere to be found. She ushers Yevdokia into the navigator's seat. Before they take off, Zhenya removes the skull from the little sack where she keeps grenades and mounts it just ahead of her cockpit.

"Is that Panna?" Yevdokia asks.

"Yes," Zhenya says.

"I thought so," Yevdokia says, as if this confirms some long held suspicion. "Where are we going?"

"I have decided to switch careers," Zhenya says, "Pay close attention to our route, you may need to follow it again someday."

When they land in Baba Yaga's orchard they find the old witch tying up bags full of grain and trinkets and dumping them in the mortar. When Zhenya climbs down, she embraces the old woman, who gives her a kindly squeeze. Yevdokia watches the strange reunion with her arms crossed.

"Do you know who I am, young lady?" Baba Yaga asks, releasing Zhenya.

"Based on the length of my lieutenant's ears and the sharpness of her teeth, I have a pretty good idea," Yevdokia says coolly. Zhenya can't believe how calm she is.

"That's good," Baba Yaga says. "Zhenya tells me you are intelligent and cruel. That is correct for a witch."

"Babushka," Zhenya says, "the Germans have destroyed our planes and killed many of my sisters."

"I was afraid the war had one more lesson for you," Baba Yaga says, "What have you decided?"

"I accept your offer," Zhenya says, "so long as there is no limit to what I am allowed to do as Baba Yaga. If I want to interfere with the world, I will interfere with it."

"Agreed," Baba Yaga says simply.

"Good. Yevdokia and I have a score to settle across the river."

"There will be no going back," the old witch says, "for any of us."

"I know."

"You will not get Panna back."

"I know that, too," Zhenya says.

"Very well," Baba Yaga says, "bow your head."

The ancient witch lifts the necklace from around her

neck. Yevdokia takes a breath and holds it. Zhenya closes her eyes and bends forward. Baba Yaga raises the necklace of bird skulls carefully over the tips of Zhenya's ears and settles it around her slim neck. The little charms rattle and click against her flight suit.

"Nothing is beyond you, anymore," Baba Yaga says."Would you like me to get rid of that ribbon? You no longer need it."

"I'll figure it out myself. Besides, I rather like it."

The old witch claps her hands. "That's the spirit. Good luck, and remember that when men say 'witch,' they say it with fear."

"I will," Zhenya says, and they exchange excessively sharp smiles. "Enjoy Sochi."

It's almost dawn before the Night Witches finally fly over the river. Beneath them, Batyuk's Siberians charge off the ferries and fishing boats and straight up the hill towards the Germans with the traditional cry of *Urrraaaaaah!* The attack is suicidal, but for one thing. As German machine guns start to rattle, extinction rains abruptly from a silent sky.

Men desperately angle their guns skyward. Tracers and searchlights criss-cross the night. They find nothing but darkness, ghostly glimpses of planes, and bombs fall as if there were no end to them.

Dawn fails to come, like there is no more light at all in the world, and the Night Witches put their persecutors to the torch. They blast the Germans from the ridge in an orgy of sudden, explosive violence. As the Siberians secure the landing, Zhenya veers into the crumbling maze of Stalingrad. Yevdokia leans forward to yell into her ear.

"Due west! Turn!"

A hail of fire rises from the ground to meet them, and the biplane leaps like a ballerina through the air. Cruel light shines from Panna's eyes as they streak into the dying city.

Atop the Univermag department store, the stitching noise grows louder, and the soldiers crane their necks. The noise stops.

"Die Nachthexen," someone whispers, and they check their watches. Seconds do not pass.

The first explosion blasts half a dozen landsers off the roof to fall screaming into the dark. They hear a biplane's engine start again, far louder than it's ever been before.

"Look up!" their captain yells. "They're coming back!"

Bolts clatter and charging handles click back. The hammering of the engine surrounds them, a machine made to break the world. They are as ready as they can be, for all the difference it makes. They might as well be trying to stave off the turning of the planet.

When Zhenya banks above the Univermag Department store, she has no bombs left on her racks.

"Yevdokia, the gun!"

Panna's eyes illuminate the roof of the crumbling monolith. As they pass the department store, Zhenya side slips to slow down and tilts the Polikarpov's nose up. The engine screams. Yevdokia leans out of her seat and brings the PPSh to her shoulder. When she fires, the tearing muzzle flash is like a dragon breathing fire with a terrible roar.

Bullets crater the roof like a rain of meteors, and above the howling cacophony of the gun Zhenya hears Yevdokia's cries of triumph and joy. Zhenya banks and wheels, and her friend scours the roof until nothing is left alive and the fire of the gun is the only light in the world.

The Night Witches kill and kill and kill, and only when they turn for home does the sun dare to rise.

A cold October morning brings the 588th Night Bomber Regiment consolation, if not relief. Their attack succeeded, and Batyuk's Siberians hold the river bank. There's a nip in the air; the first sharp hint of the coming winter. The bite in the wind is greeted with optimism; Russians fight better in the cold, and when the Volga freezes they will be able to just walk men and supplies across the water like prophets carrying good tidings of vodka and bullets. At the airfield, the Night Witches are sombre in spite of their victory.

"This is the last time you'll see me, girls. But I'll always be there for you, in one way or another," Zhenya says, with the rest of the squadron gathered around her. She has loaded her Polikarpov with supplies and scavenged copper pipes she hopes to turn into a still for her new cottage. The girls embrace her in turn, but it takes too long so everyone crowds in at once. They don't seem to care about her ears or her teeth or the strange ribbon around her neck.

Yevdokia isn't part of the group. She stands by herself, aloof.

"What will we do without you, Zhenya?" cries plump, faithful Nadya, her head swathed in bandages.

"Yevdokia will lead you," Zhenya says, and the taciturn Muscovite meets her eyes evenly."This is her squadron, not mine. Remember that she is not here to be your friend, but your commander. If you follow her, you'll have no trouble."

They all look back at Lieutenant Colonel Yevdokia Bershanskaya. Her black hair whips in the morning wind. She is as beautiful and terrible as a Night Witch ought to be. She puts her hands on her hips.

"Girls," she says, "if you show me respect, I will repay you threefold. If you obey me, you will survive. And if you trust me, I will lead you all the way to Berlin."

She says this in a firm, clear voice, and the rest of the witches hear her perfectly. They finally understand that her flaws conceal virtues, like the shining opposite side of a coin. She is not just hard, but courageous. Not petty, but precise. And not just a rich girl from Moscow. She is a regentess among the witches who whisper in the night.

Before Zhenya leaves, someone breaks out a bottle of vodka. Their tin mugs clink and the bottle gurgles.

"Remember, all of you," Zhenya says, "that when your enemies say, 'witch,' they say it with fear."

"With fear!" they cry, and drink. There is a chorus of teary goodbyes. No one prolongs the farewell; things are sad enough, and war has taught them that the best way to see someone for the last time is quickly and sweetly. Yevdokia is the last to leave.

"Do you remember the way to the grove?" Zhenya asks.

"I do," she nods.

"Well, stop by whenever you're in the area."

The two women share a smile.

"Shall I turn your prop?" Yevdokia asks.

"Please, comrade," says the Baba Yaga.

BLAKE JESSOP is a Canadian author of science fiction, fantasy and horror stories with a master's degree in creative writing from the University of Adelaide. His work frequently delves into the ethical implications of new technology, personal deliverance, huge explosions, pizza, and epic heavy metal guitar solos.

Bibliography

Classics Remixed, Left Hand Publishers, 2019
DreamForge Magazine, Issue 2, 2019
Earth: Giants, Golems, & Gargoyles, Tyche Books, 2019
Glass & Gardens: Solarpunk Summers, World Weaver Press, 2018
Grimm, Grit, and Gasoline: Diesel and Decopunk Fairytales, World Weaver Press, 2019
I Didn't Break the Lamp: Historical Accounts of Imaginary Acquaintances, DefCon One, 2019
In the Air, Transmundane Press, 2019
Terra! Tara! Terror! Third Flatiron Anthologies, 2018
The Clarion Call, Volume 5, Agorist Writers Workshop, 2019
The Mad Scientist Journal, Winter Quarterly, DefCon One, 2019
The Razor's Edge, Zombies Needs Brains, 2018
Triangulation: Dark Skies, Parsec Ink, 2019
What If? History Rewritten, Black Hare Press, 2019
World War Four, Zombie Pirate Publishing, 2019

Connect
Amazon: amazon.com/author/blakejessop
Twitter: @everydayjisei

OROCHI

By Jonathan Inbody

As the second World War nears its end, two escaped American prisoners of war make a desperate journey to the city of Hiroshima, where a creature slumbering deep underground may be the only thing that could save it from destruction.

I: DESTROYER OF WORLDS

The morning of August 6th, 1945 started like any other; with the rising sun. The air raid sirens had stopped around seven in the morning, and now, as it approached eight, Kaito Tanaka walked quickly down the street towards the hospital. In his arms, he was holding his daughter, an inquisitive six-year old named Himari. She had twisted her ankle falling down the small staircase

429

into the basement where her father had been ushering her for safety, and once the sirens had stopped, Kaito knew they needed to find a doctor.

Himari's ankle was swollen, hanging limply next to her other leg as she was jostled back and forth in her father's arms. She was afraid of that morning's sirens for a reason she couldn't yet articulate; the kind of deep, helpless fear only known by children. She knew they were at war, that they had been at war for a long time, but not why.

The people lining the crowded street hustled this way and that, and as Himari was carried past them she took in all the different faces. There were the faces worn with worry, those sunken with exhaustion, and those with smiles and sad eyes. Those were the kind she was used to; the sad-eyed way her widowed father looked when he tucked her in at night, the silent struggle she saw every day as he got dressed for work. He was unhappy, but he worked very hard to keep his daughter from seeing the worst of it.

Kaito pushed through the hospital door with his shoulder, then approached the front desk. The attendant, a pleasant-looking woman in a nurse's uniform, handed him a clipboard and pen and told him to fill out some preliminary paperwork. After assurances that they would be with him shortly, Kaito put Himari down on the wooden seat beside his own and began to write.

This would have been so much easier when Akane was alive. She had been his whole world, his partner, the only one he felt truly understood him. But they had been unlucky. There was no getting around it; accidents happen, even to schoolteachers. The driver of the car hadn't seen her coming, and Kaito had been told she was dead before she had hit the ground. He hoped that wasn't just something they told people.

Himari stared through the glass of the large window in front of them, taking in the streaks of early morning sunset with an innocent smile. Kaito looked over at her for a long second, letting the start of a smile creep across his face. Where would he be without her?

Himari pointed at the sky. "What's that?"

Kaito looked out the window at an approaching dot, squinting in an attempt to make it out. "I think it's a plane."

Suddenly, the sky was engulfed in fire. The clouds burned, buildings rippled and fell. The glass window shattered inward, sending jagged shards of glass flying into and through Kaito's face. Beside him, Himari screamed as a wall of flame billowed through the broken glass and flash-fried her outstretched arm. The ceiling above them collapsed, burying their mutilated bodies under tons of newly formed debris. Screams echoed through the falling building all around them, drowned out by the sizzling of the gigantic fires consuming the only world Himari Tanaka had ever known.

Hell had come to the city of Hiroshima, and the Americans had brought it.

Charlie Kelleran bolted up in his rusted cot, throwing his thin blanket aside as he looked around in terror. Where was the fire? Where were the toppled buildings? Where were the desperate screams of the dying, and the grim silence of the dead? He looked down the row of cots at his fellow prisoners of war, all sleeping soundly, then reached up and wiped his sweat-covered brow. It had felt so *real*. But no weapon could cause the kind of desolation he had just dreamed of, at least none he knew about, and if there was one, why hadn't his country used it sooner? Had America abandoned him?

Now in its sixth year, the second World War had been winding down. Mussolini had been executed by partisans, and the Germans had been forced to surrender after Hitler ate a bullet. Victory in Europe had been assured and roundly celebrated, and all that was left was the quagmire of the Pacific theatre. All of this, however, was unknown to Charlie, and in the early morning hours of August 4th, he struggled to maintain hope. All he knew was that he had been a prisoner of the Japanese for almost a year now, and that the camp he was being held prisoner in was somewhere near Shimonoseki on the Japanese mainland. The odds of rescue were low, the rates of torture by his captors were high, and every day he grew closer to the edge of despair.

He rolled over and closed his eyes, trying to push the memories of his apocalyptic dreams out of his fear-addled mind. Maybe the stress was getting to him, or maybe he was losing his mind, but as he tossed and turned in the uncomfortable cot, he couldn't shake the feeling that what he had seen was not only true, but inevitable.

The next morning, Charlie took his usual walk around the inside edge of the camp, avoiding eye contact with the armed soldiers stationed every ten yards. As he finished and headed back to where his fellow prisoners were sitting in huddled circles in the dirt, his gaze caught the eye of a lone GI. The man, who Charlie knew conversationally as Sgt. Logan Copper, glowered at him with casual malice as he tapped his dog tags with one finger.

"You alright?" Charlie asked.

"No, Chuck," Sgt. Copper replied as he wiped sweat from his brow with the back of his hand. "I'm really not. I've got a fucking kid at home I've never seen."

"It's *Charlie*," Charlie corrected as he stopped in front of Copper. He looked at the dark bags under Copper's eyes, then down at his clammy hands. "I've been having some trouble sleeping. Looks like you have too."

Copper furrowed his brow and gave Charlie a long look, then patted the grass beside him. "You want to sit down?"

Charlie plopped down into the grass beside him. Copper ran a hand through his salt-and-pepper hair, then looked over at Charlie and flashed a faint smile.

"They make you sleep on the floor, Chuck?" Copper asked. "Or are you one of the lucky ones they want information from?"

"I'm in intelligence, if that's what you mean," Charlie replied.

"That *is* what I mean," Copper replied flatly. "Have you talked?"

"Talked? You mean given up information?" Charlie asked. "Of course not."

Copper glanced over at him with an untrusting look in his eyes, then shrugged. "Okay."

A few silent seconds passed. Charlie wasn't sure what to make of Sgt. Copper, or his strange blend of hostility and casual friendliness.

"So, what are you doing over here?" Charlie asked.

"Planning to escape," Copper replied flatly.

Charlie raised his eyebrows and glanced over to see if he was joking.

"I know how I'd do it, too," Copper added. "They get supply trucks every other day at three in the afternoon. It takes them five minutes for three of them to unload it, while one with a gun watches. They check the drivers, they check the storage space in the back…they don't check underneath."

Charlie took in the determined look on Copper's face. "Do you really think you could do it?"

"I don't know," Copper replied. "But I'm getting close to trying."

The two men sat in an extended silence, watching the armed guards standing along the fence surrounding the camp.

"So, what makes you so special that they give you a cot?" Copper asked.

"I'm a translator," Charlie replied. "And a cultural specialist."

"A cultur— What does that mean?" Copper replied.

Charlie chuckled in spite of himself. "It means that before the war I was a folklorist. My specialty was Japan, but I could tell you the common myths from most of the Asiatic continent."

Copper cast a sidelong glance at him. "You know

what I did before the war? I worked in a butcher shop. That's why I sleep on the floor and you get a cot, I guess."

"I guess," Charlie replied. He looked around quickly, unsure of whether or not he could trust Copper, then decided that it didn't matter. "Do you ever have bad dreams?"

Copper gave him another look. "No. I can't sleep."

"I had a dream last night," Charlie said. "But it didn't feel like a dream. It felt real."

"I had one of those once," Copper replied with a smile. "I dreamed about a French whorehouse. It was the first time I woke up happy in months."

"Mine wasn't one like that," Charlie said solemnly. "I dreamed about a bomb; a bomb that destroyed an entire city."

"A Jap city?" Copper asked.

"Yes," Charlie replied. "Hiroshima."

Copper smiled. "Then it was a good dream."

"It wasn't," Charlie replied. "There was this little girl and her father. She had twisted her ankle. Probably nothing serious, but they were going to the hospital, and there was this flash of white light in the sky…and after that everything was burning."

Copper turned and looked at Charlie, taking in the visible fear on his face. "It was that bad, huh?"

Charlie closed his eyes, then tried to push the images

out of his mind. "It was the worst thing I've ever seen."

"Just a dream, though," Copper offered.

"I'm not sure it was," Charlie replied.

"What else could it be?" Copper asked.

Charlie took a second to think, scanning through any minute detail he could remember from his dream. "What day is today?"

"Friday," Copper replied.

"I mean the date," Charlie said.

Copper tried to think. "Should be August. August 3rd, maybe? 4th?"

"In my dream it was Monday," Charlie said. "Monday, August the 6th."

"So what?" Copper asked sceptically. "You think you saw the future?"

"What if I did?" Charlie asked. He glanced over at the disbelieving Copper, then down at the brown grass in front of him.

Copper leaned back and smiled. "Well, if you did, we'll find out in a couple of days."

Charlie looked up at the wispy clouds gathering in the clear blue sky above them. "I suppose you're right."

That night, Charlie Kelleran had another dream.

Bunji Kanamori stepped down into the outlet

tunnel, then held his map up in the light and looked at it again. This had to be where the missing water was going; it was the only sewage outlet he hadn't checked already. How had the city lost track of hundreds of gallons of water anyway? It had to be somewhere.

Bunji ducked down and began to crouch-walk down the stone tunnel, hiking up his rubber boots to keep the raw sewage from dripping down his legs. He waved the beam of his flashlight back and forth along the walls, looking for the next turn. That would take him to the central chamber, and from there he would follow each of the inlets until he found the problem. By Bunji's estimation, it must have been a burst pipe somewhere, and he thought he'd have been done fixing it already if not for the air raid sirens that had kept him from getting an early start that morning.

He turned down the next tunnel, stepping over the floating corpse of a dead rat, then put a gloved hand against the stone wall and continued slowly walking. As he approached what he knew was the central chamber, waves of heat began to wash over him. Billows of warm air wafted past him in the cramped tunnel, and he held a hand up to keep his eyes from drying out. Where was it coming from?

Bunji emerged into the central chamber, and both of his questions were suddenly answered. Water was rushing down through the broken floor of the central chamber and pouring into a huge underground cavern where it was rising around a gigantic shape covered in shadows.

Bunji pointed his flashlight down into the massive cavern, running it along the surface of the huge shape. Golden light reflected back at him from lizard-like scales, sending a wave of colourful light dancing across the sewage chamber. The shape slowly expanded and contracted, like an unthinkably massive creature breathing in and out. With each exhaled breath, another wave of hot air flew up from the cavern and into the chamber, then pushed down the countless tunnels into the rest of the Hiroshima sewage system.

Bunji stared at the huge golden shape in stunned silence, slowly tracing its shape with his flashlight. He saw two gigantic wings folded around its arched back, four clawed feet with their huge talons dug into the bedrock at the bottom of the cavern, and a multi-pronged tail that wrapped all the way around the creature's giant body. But where was the head?

He ran the flashlight beam up the creature's protruding spine and down its bronze-scaled neck, where it split at the scrag into eight pieces. In the tangle of twisted anaconda-like necks, Bunji could see four heads, each with a horned crest and a mouth full of interlocking jagged teeth. Each time one head shifted, he could see the edges of another underneath it.

Bunji swore under his breath and took a step back from the edge of the collapsed central chamber. What was that thing? A childhood story tickled at the edges of his mind, a story about a being of chaos born of pure primordia. *Orochi.*

An ear-splitting rumble echoed through the sewers from above. Bunji fell backward into the water as the ceiling of the central chamber began to collapse, sending huge chunks of brick splashing down into the pitch-black chamber. Blinding light came blasting down from above, sending shock waves of flame billowing down. A wall of fire consumed Bunji, burning through his skin and sinew and almost instantly reducing him to bone.

The city of Hiroshima fell downward and inward, filling the sewers with pieces of collapsed buildings and half-smashed bodies. The gigantic shape in the cavern, what Bunji had called the Orochi, did not stir.

The next morning, Charlie Kelleran finished his morning walk without saying a word, then crossed the camp and sat down next to Sgt. Copper. The two exchanged a glance, then looked out at the fence surrounding them.

"I had another dream," Charlie said finally. "About the bomb dropping on Hiroshima."

Copper sighed and nodded his head. "Anything new this time?"

"Plenty," Charlie replied. "You really think you can escape this place?"

Copper shot him a look. "Why?"

"Because I think I can stop it."

...

II: THE GREAT MARCH OF THE YOKAI

It was a long wait until three in the afternoon. Charlie and Cooper went about their ordinary business, trying to avoid drawing suspicion while they closely watched the guards. Copper knew most of them by sight already and was fairly sure of which would be unloading the supply truck. As the last ten minutes before three o'clock crept by, the two men moved slowly around the edge of the camp towards their captor's barracks, taking care to only move when they were unobserved.

As they crouched silently against the wooden wall of the barracks, they could hear the supply truck approaching. An officer barked orders in Japanese and the gate was unlocked, clattering loudly as two soldiers pulled it open. The truck pulled into the camp and stopped. Copper leaned his head around the side of the building, watching as three men began to unload the supplies from inside the truck. Between them and the truck stood an armed guard, resting the barrel of his gun on his shoulder as he watched the others work.

"You speak Japanese, right?" Copper asked in a whisper.

Charlie nodded.

"Call him over," instructed Copper.

"I don't know his name," Charlie replied.

"Then call him 'soldier,'" Copper replied harshly. "Just get him away from the truck."

Charlie sidled over to the edge of the building, then said something in Japanese. The armed soldier turned, looking around to see who had called him, then started walking towards the barracks.

"What do we do?" Charlie asked quietly.

"Around the other side," Copper replied. "Quick."

The two men crept along the wall and to the back of the barracks, then slipped around to the other side and waited to see if anyone around the truck was looking in their direction. They wouldn't have long now, the armed guard would turn around as soon as he realised he had been drawn away, and the truck would soon be unloaded.

"*Now!*" Copper whispered.

Copper sprinted out into the open and dived forward, sliding underneath the truck. He quickly unbuckled his belt and looped it around part of the truck's undercarriage, tying his hands in place so he wouldn't lose his grip.

Charlie turned, hearing the approaching footsteps of the armed guard. It was now or never. He dived out into the open and army-crawled forward, quickly scrambling under the truck just as the guards finished unloading it. He reached down for his belt, but Copper grabbed his hand and held it still. Just inches away from Charlie's shoulder stood two booted feet; one of the workers had stopped.

The two Americans held their breath, frozen in fear of discovery as the worker kicked his heel against the side of the truck. The guard said something in Japanese, and the worker responded. Then he walked away from the side of the truck. Charlie let out a quiet sigh of relief, then quickly secured his belt around the truck's undercarriage.

The truck roared to life, and slowly pulled out of the camp and onto a side road where it began to accelerate. Underneath, Charlie smiled. He was on his way.

For the next hour or so, the trip was unexceptional. Charlie and Copper had to occasionally shift to avoid an upcoming rock in the road or flatten themselves against the undercarriage when the truck went over a hill, but otherwise their less-than-dramatic escape was proving effective.

The truck driver slowed down and stopped at a gas station as the evening sun blanched the hillside in orange light, then got out and stretched his legs. As the driver walked into the station to use the bathroom, Charlie and Copper quickly unfastened their belts from the truck's undercarriage.

"Are you sure about this?" Charlie asked.

"Absolutely," Copper replied. "They'll do a count at dinner, and it won't take them long to figure out how we got out."

Charlie slid his belt back into the loops on his pants. "We'll have to walk from here."

"Can't be too far," Copper replied as he slid out from under the truck.

The two soldiers got to their feet around the side of the truck, then quickly looked around. On one side was a forest-covered hill, and on the other was the ramshackle gas station. They crouched down and began to quickly shuffle towards the forest treeline, keeping a careful eye out for Japanese onlookers.

They reached the trees and broke into a full sprint, running up towards the top of the hill as they dodged around low-hanging tree branches and jumped over fallen logs. Copper reached the top first, then stopped and doubled over to catch his breath. Behind him, Charlie smiled as the wind rushed through his hair. He was free, really free, and although he knew it was fleeting, he was determined to enjoy it. He threw his hands over his head and stifled an energetic whoop as Copper shot him a glare.

"What is wrong with you?" Copper asked flatly.

"I'm happy," Charlie replied. "We *made* it."

"We're on an island surrounded by Japs, on our way to a Jap industrial centre because you had a nightmare," Copper replied. "Forgive me if I'm not thrilled."

"You were the one who wanted to escape," Charlie countered. "Now that we're out of the camp, you can go wherever you want."

"Without a translator?" Copper asked back. "No thanks. Besides, there's safety in numbers."

The two looked for shelter, food, and water as the sun sank in the sky. By sundown, they had found a relatively safe spot near a small creek, hidden in a grove of bamboo trees miles from the gas station. They could hear small animals moving through the brush as they leaned thick leaves against the trees to create a makeshift lean-to, but by the time they had settled into their shelter for the night, the forest was eerily silent.

Charlie took first watch, scanning the pitch-black

forest for signs of movement. The night was calm and clear, with hundreds of stars visible through the scattered trees above them. Japan really was beautiful, at least the rural parts, and despite the circumstances Charlie felt oddly at peace. There was something calming about this forest, tranquil in the way only something untouched by human hands can be.

A branch snapped somewhere behind Charlie and he froze. Then he could hear the scuffling of nearly silent feet, rapidly approaching. Charlie turned his head slowly to look, then went wide-eyed as a tall black figure ran past him and disappeared into the brush. Another figure bounded up on Charlie's other side, then leapt from the ground into a nearby tree and scrambled up it.

Charlie reached over and shook Copper's arm as more dark figures sprinted through the woods, running with the abandon of an Olympic sprinter and moving with the effortless grace of a ballerina. Copper sat up, clearing his throat as he gave Charlie a confused look. Charlie pointed ahead as another dark figure ran out of sight, then looked up as another rush of wind moved past his head. There were more of the humanoid figures now, bounding from tree to tree with the weightlessness of a feather as they passed over the heads of the two Americans.

One of the figures skidded to a stop on a taloned

foot, then turned its beaked head to look at Charlie. It was covered in jet black feathers, and its bright green eyes gleamed in the moonlight as it considered its observer for a tense second. Then, as quickly as it had stopped it was off again, running through the forest in a near-silent sprint until it vanished from view.

"*Tengu*," Charlie said quietly.

Copper gave him a look. "What?"

"Bird-men, monks of the forest," Charlie said as he stared out into the dark forest. "They're yokai, creatures from Japanese mythology. I didn't… I didn't think they could be real."

"Where were they going?" Copper asked as he looked around at the trails all around them from where the tengu had run.

"I don't know," Charlie replied.

Bright light shone down from above them, blinding the two men for a second as their eyes adjusted. Soaring through the sky was a gigantic heron, glowing bright blue as it weaved in between tall trees toward the small creek.

Copper stared up at the giant bird in silent awe, then turned to look at Charlie. "What about that one? Another yokai?"

Charlie nodded. "Aosaginohi."

Copper got to his feet and began to push forward

through the forest, following the strange creatures. Charlie followed closely behind, carefully looking around for tengu eyes in the dark surrounding them. They emerged from the bamboo forest onto the side of the small creek where the glowing heron was perched. It bobbed its head up and down, picking fish out of the water and gulping them down as it rested its folded wings.

"This thing; is it dangerous?" Copper asked as he stepped towards it.

"It isn't supposed to be," Charlie replied.

Copper walked cautiously over to the heron and extended a hand to touch it. The giant heron extended its luminous wings and lifted off, soaring up into the night sky and far from Copper's reach.

"This can't be real, right?" Copper asked. "We've got to be dreaming."

"I saw a thing like this in my dream," Charlie replied. "But it was bigger, sleeping beneath Hiroshima like a slumbering dragon waiting to be woken up."

"This is fucking crazy," Copper said as he turned back towards Charlie. "Stuff like this doesn't just happen; things like this don't just *exist*."

"Maybe they do," Charlie replied. "Maybe they're just good at staying out of sight."

"But where are they going?" Copper asked.

Charlie frowned. "Away from Hiroshima. They know the bomb's going to drop; they can *feel* it somehow. They're getting as far away as they can, like animals fleeing an earthquake."

Copper didn't respond, and for a second Charlie didn't notice. Then he looked over at where Copper had been. He was gone, and the creek beside him was still rippling from recent movement.

Charlie took a step towards the creek. "Copper?"

A webbed claw wrapped around Charlie's ankle, pulled him off his feet, then dragged him into the creek as he struggled to get his bearings. Two clawed feet dug into his boots as another webbed hand grabbed his hair, pulling him deeper under the surface of the black water as he thrashed. He opened his eyes, flailing his arms wildly at his attacker. The creature had the face of a turtle, with demonic red eyes and a caved-in forehead above a clacking beak and whip-sharp tongue that lashed back and forth across Charlie's face.

Charlie pulled a hand free and grabbed the creature's throat, tightening his grip to crush its windpipe as it slashed at his chest. Finally, it moved its hands to free its throat, and Charlie pulled his feet up between himself and the beast and kicked it away into the dark water. He sprang up to the water's surface, gasping for breath as he wondered what had become of

Copper. Kappa, as Charlie knew the creatures were called, were opportunistic predators that drowned children and small animals. These ones were desperate somehow, almost feral, and as Charlie ducked back under the water to look for Copper, he knew the danger hadn't passed.

Charlie swam forward, straining to look through the murky water as he reached out in front of him for his companion. His hand brushed the clammy skin of a kappa and he reeled back, then reached forward again with both hands and took hold of it. He pulled the creature off the thrashing Copper, grabbed Copper by the shirt, and pulled him up to the creek's surface.

Copper gasped, then coughed up lungfuls of water as Charlie dragged him to the riverbed. Nearby, Charlie could see the heads of the kappa, bobbing silently on the surface of the water as they watched their prey flee with malicious eyes. Charlie climbed out of the water and pulled Copper up beside him before reaching for a nearby shoot of bamboo to use as a weapon.

"What the hell are those things?" Copper asked as he spit out muddy water.

"More yokai," Charlie replied. "I think they thought we'd be an easy meal."

Copper pulled himself away from the creek bed and slumped over, still struggling to catch his breath. "We almost were."

Charlie watched as the kappa's heads sank beneath the surface of the water, then followed their glowing eyes as they swam downriver. "They're leaving. Just like the others."

"What about your dragon under Hiroshima?" Copper asked. "Is he leaving too?"

Charlie shook his head. "He's asleep."

"But he's like them? A yokai?"

"No," Charlie replied. "Yokai are like animals, the Orochi is like a god."

Copper shot him a look. "And you want to wake it up?"

Charlie nodded. "I think I'm *supposed* to."

"But if there is a bomb, won't it just kill it?"

"It took a god to kill the Orochi the first time."

Copper let out a frustrated sigh. "You're really going to try to do it, aren't you? Find that thing and wake it up, all just to keep something you dreamed about from happening?"

"What else am I supposed to do?" Charlie asked. "I have a chance here, a real chance to save thousands of lives."

"Jap lives," Copper replied.

"*Human* lives," Charlie corrected.

"And what if the bomb you're trying to stop is going

to end the war?"

"I don't care what it's for," Charlie said. "I don't have the *luxury* of caring. All I know is that an innocent little girl and her father die on Monday morning, along with a sewer inspector and a hundred thousand other non-combatants. It doesn't matter what side is doing it, or why; it matters that it's being *done*. If I can undo it…then I have to."

Copper rolled his eyes. "Bullshit. It's some Jap mind game to get you to give up secrets. We're probably drugged up to the gills in some pitch-black jail cell right now, babbling our brains out about monsters while the interrogators write everything down."

"It doesn't matter," Charlie reiterated. "Someday, people are going to look back on the war. It's going to be taught in history books, debated on the radio, written about in newspapers…they might never know our names, or know that we could have stopped it, but they'll know about the bomb. *We'll* know. Your boy, the one you haven't met yet, he's no different than that little girl I watched burn. When he asks what you did in the war, are you going to tell him you let children exactly like him die, just because they weren't yours?"

Copper turned and gave Charlie a long, angry look. Then, he sighed. Letting his shoulders slump, he put his head in his hands. "Fuck you."

"I know you can't just let it happen," Charlie continued. "Not any more than I can."

Copper looked up at the stars glittering in the night sky. "If you're wrong about this, Chuck... I'll kill you myself."

Charlie smiled. "If I'm wrong about this, I'll want you to."

...

III: EIGHT FIFTEEN

The next day passed uneventfully. They slept until sunrise then continued their trek through the forested hills towards the city in uncomfortable silence. Charlie still wasn't sure how Copper truly felt about him, or even how he felt about Copper. If not for Charlie's dreams, would they ever have even spoke? What did they really have in common, other than the flag they marched under?

They stopped at midday in an abandoned grove of apple trees, sitting down to regain their strength for an hour as they ate.

"What if we get there and your dragon doesn't exist?" Copper asked as he wiped sweat from his brow with his sleeve.

"We steal a vehicle, try to make it to a port, then

stowaway on a ship bound for anywhere but here," Charlie replied, chewing on a piece of green apple.

Copper chuckled. "Why don't we just do that, then?"

"You know why," Charlie replied firmly.

They filled their pockets with apples and continued through the forest, stopping only to relieve themselves or catch their breaths. In the late afternoon, they passed a road sign, emerging onto a paved road just as the sun sank in the western sky. They walked along the side of the road for hours, ducking into the nearby brush whenever they heard a car coming.

As the last trickles of red sunlight disappeared into the darkness, Copper pointed ahead to a distant flurry of lights. "Is that it?"

Charlie squinted at the distant city, then nodded. "Hiroshima. We're not far now."

"Good thing, too," Copper said. "Your bomb's supposed to drop tomorrow morning."

They walked through most of the night, ascending a lopsided roadside hill to keep from being spotted as they approached the city. That night, there were no stars.

They stopped a mile outside of Hiroshima and slept for an hour each, steeling themselves for the morning. While Copper slept, Charlie looked up at the cloud-filled sky through the treetops. He could see creatures dancing back and forth through the clouds, pulsing with iridescent light and swirling around each other like hungry dogs waiting for fresh meat. They were Shinigami, spirits of death and eaters of suffering, and they had come in anticipation of a feast.

Charlie lowered his eyes to the city. He wondered if any of them knew what was coming. Could any of them feel it in the air, the way he could? Were there more dreamers there, fleeing the city or trying to tell themselves that what they had seen would never come to pass?

A ripple of lightning shot across the sky, and in the flash of light, Charlie could see a gigantic shape rising in the clouds behind Hiroshima. A skeletal face stared down at the city with a rictus grin as its spike-fingered arms spread across the sky from one end of the city to the other. The flash of lightning passed, and the bony giant disappeared, sending a shiver down Charlie's spine. It was still there, looming invisibly over countless souls as it waited for the next morning, and if Charlie lived through the next day, he knew the image would be burned in his mind forever. He had seen what no human eyes were meant to; Gashadokuro, the god of the unburied dead, readying himself for the same feast that had drawn the Shinigami.

Charlie resolved to make the god go hungry.

As the sun crept up in the morning sky, Charlie and Copper slid down the forested hill towards the outskirts of the city. They moved quickly and quietly, slinking from building to building as they kept an eye out for the locals. The streets were far from empty, with mothers ushering their children to school and well-dressed businessmen talking near newspaper stands.

Copper and Charlie stopped in an alley between two buildings, watching the busy streets around them buzz with activity. Charlie could see the worry and fear on every face, and he suddenly felt as though he was surrounded by a city of ghosts. They'd all be dead soon, burning in an American-made Hell.

Deep guilt rose up in Charlie's chest and he pushed it back down. He knew the horror of war, and he knew the terror of the innocent in a world consumed by it. Japan wasn't innocent, anymore than Germany or Italy, but the citizens… People were just people, weren't they? Even if they were making the vehicles and weapons of war, the people of Hiroshima weren't responsible for the actions of their empire. But still, fair or not, they were going to be the ones to suffer.

"What do we do now?" Copper asked quietly, jarring Charlie out of his sombre thoughts. "They're going to see us."

An air raid siren rang out in the sky, echoing off

buildings and filling the streets with noise. An official sounding voice read a prepared statement over the loudspeakers and the people all around them quickly dispersed, emptying the streets in a matter of minutes as they took shelter.

"The siren; is that for the bomb?" Copper asked.

"No," Charlie replied. "It's a false alarm."

"How do you know?" Copper asked.

"The people in my dreams knew," Charlie said. "If the siren's already started, we're running out of time."

The two men began to run through the streets, weaving up and down alleyways towards the neighbourhood where Charlie knew Bunji Kanamori was going to be. They passed a school and an empty playground, dodged around empty bus stops and ducked under low-hanging canopies over the doorways of abandoned stores. The sound of the siren echoed down the empty streets all around them as they navigated towards the open sewer grate where Bunji would enter only minutes later.

They reached the entrance to the sewers and stopped, sitting on the ground to catch their breaths.

"Do you know the way from here?" Copper asked.

Charlie nodded. "Bunji knows it. He might catch up with us on the way."

"What do we do if he does?" Copper replied.

"Whatever it takes to keep moving," Charlie said firmly.

The air raid siren stopped, sending one last rippling echo through the city before the streets fell eerily silent.

"We have to go," Charlie said. "There's not much time left."

They stepped down through the sewer grate, then waded into the knee-high sewage and sloshed down the inlet corridor towards the central chamber. As they went, Copper looked ahead at the back of Charlie's head while he led them deeper into the darkness. Was the thing from his dreams really going to be there? And if it was, would waking it up be enough to stop the bomb? *Should* it be stopped? If it would end the war, did they have any right?

As they stopped temporarily to get their bearings at a fork in the sewers, Copper reached over and took hold of a loose brick on the wall. He pulled it free and weighed it in his hand for a long second before looking back at Charlie. If this was a trick, if Charlie was compromised or insane, Copper wouldn't be the one caught off guard.

A burst of warm air swept through the sewer corridor, sending ripples through the discoloured waste around them. They were close. The sound of rushing water rose from one of the open corridors and Charlie followed it, Copper walking closely behind.

They emerged into the central chamber where golden light danced across their faces as they stared down in awed silence. The collapsed floor in front of them stood above a gigantic cavern where a massive shape lay still as rushing water rose around it. The bulk of its gigantic body was covered by two sprawling wings, and through the rippling water around it, they could see the shadowed silhouettes of four clawed feet at the end of thick, golden-scaled legs. Atop the unthinkably massive creature sat a tangle of snake-like heads, coiling and weaving back and forth around each other as eight draconic heads peacefully slept.

Charlie stared down at the slumbering Orochi as a broad smile crept across his face. It was real, and more importantly, it was *here*. He felt a chill run down his spine as gooseflesh spread from the back of his neck down his arms. He could really do it. He could save them. He could save *all* of them.

Beside him, Logan Copper's mind reeled with abject horror. The creature beneath them was beyond reckoning, unbelievably huge and unthinkably dangerous. The warmth in the air licked at Copper's heels like the rising flames of Hell, and the golden light blinded him with waves of terrifying awe. It was Death given flesh, a muscular coil of pure destruction readying itself to burst free. The unthinkable beast was plainly unstoppable, and Copper feared that if it was awakened it could effortlessly cripple the world. America would be nothing but burning ash and falling cinders, reduced to flash-fried rubble by a thing beyond reason and time.

"It's beautiful," Charlie said vacantly as tears welled up in his eyes.

Copper looked over at his companion fearfully. "I don't know if I can do this."

"We have to," Charlie replied without looking.

"What if it's worse than the bomb?" Copper asked. "What if it destroys everything?"

"We don't have time for what-ifs," Charlie said firmly. "All I have is now. And it's worth the ri—"

CRACK! Charlie stumbled forward, grabbing the back of his head as pain radiated across it. His hand came back covered in sticky, deep red blood, and as Charlie sputtered incoherently, he turned to look at the bloody brick in Copper's hand.

"I'm sorry," Copper said flatly.

Charlie stumbled backwards to the edge of the collapsed floor, wobbling in pained disorientation, struggling to understand what Copper had done to him. At last, he fell back, plummeting down into the black abyss where the sleeping Orochi lay. He landed with a splash in the roiling water around the gigantic creature, then sank like a rock to the bottom. Blackness edged in at the corners of his eyes as he gasped for breath, and after a few gentle shakes, he stilled.

Charlie Kelleran's glassy eyes stared up blankly at the water's surface. The top of the water was bubbling now, and as thick blood streamed out from the back of Charlie's head, the water began to turn red. The red cloud spread and drifted towards the golden scales of the massive beast half-submerged in the flooded cavern. As it got closer, thin streams of blood swirled as if pulled by invisible gravity and then slipped through the gaps in the scales, disappearing.

Copper looked down at the bubbling water surrounding the sleeping creature and dropped the bloody brick. A ripple of red light spread across the golden creature, then pulsed brightly underneath the scale-covered skin and began to glow.

Somewhere in the maze of sewers under the city, Bunji Kanamori shivered. There was something in the air now; a sickly warm red glow that spread through the corridor as the sewage around Bunji's rubber boots began to boil.

Copper fell to his knees in the central chamber and wept, overcome with self-hatred and mortal fear. Beneath him, the Orochi pulsed brighter and brighter, sending rippling waves of fiery heat emanating through the surrounding sewers. It was beginning to hurt now, singing his clothes and burning away his hair as his eyes were bleached blind by the intense light.

"I hope you were right, Chuck," Copper said quietly as he began to burn. "God help us."

The central chamber collapsed, pulling the surrounding sewers down with it. Buildings collapsed inward as the huge creature began to move, flaring out its gigantic wings and reaching up with clawed feet. The Orochi's eight heads were coiling around each other rapidly now, tangling and untangling in a manic frenzy.

The huge wings plunged suddenly downward, pushing the colossal beast up from inside the collapsing sewers. It was rising now, thrusting upward towards daylight as it let out an ear-splitting bellow. It clawed at the sides of collapsed buildings, pressing towards the surface while the tangled heads wove in and out of each other's necks, letting out low thrums of animalistic glee.

The city street exploded outwards as the creature emerged, surrounded by fleeing people and burning buildings. The Orochi soared up through the city and into the blue sky, sending streaks of red and gold energy shooting in all directions around it like bolts of holy lightning. It was as if reality itself was warping around it, deformed and reshaped by the risen god's fell gravity.

Somewhere beneath it, a clock ticked 8:15.

Himari Tanaka sat on the wooden bench in the hospital waiting room, swinging her unswollen ankle and staring out the window at the blue morning sky. Beside her sat her father Kaito, hurriedly filling out the admittance paperwork.

A dot appeared in the distant sky. It was moving, growing larger by the second as it quickly approached. It looked almost like a bird, soaring through the air like a knife through warm butter. Himari furrowed her brow and pointed. "What's that?"

Kaito looked out the window and squinted at the sky. "I think it's a plane."

Bright white light consumed the sky.

On board the American plane above the city, the pilot removed his goggles and let his jaw drop open. "Oh my god."

The pilot's radio buzzed to life. "Tibbets, are you there? Did you drop the bomb? It is done?"

Tibbets shuddered, but found himself unable to respond. Out the plane's front windshield, he watched as the ancient god Orochi absorbed the brunt of the atomic blast, its golden skin rippling with waves of mystical energy as its gigantic wings pushed billowing smoke clouds out into the open blue sky all around it. Its eight heads writhed and intertwined like charged particles surrounding an atomic core, swirling rhythmically around a floating bulb of glowing, white-hot energy. It had tamed Death, the destroyer of worlds.

Beneath it, Hiroshima was still standing.

JONATHAN INBODY is an author, filmmaker, and podcaster from Buffalo, New York. While he mostly writes surrealist horror, he also dabbles in magical realism, scifi, fantasy, westerns, and pretty much anything else that can have monsters in it.

His flash fiction work has been featured in the Dark Drabbles series from Black Hare Press, his short film "Unearthed" recently screened as an official selection of the Buffalo Dreams Fantastic Film Festival, and he can be heard every other week on his improvisational movie pitch podcast X Meets Y.

He is always seeking creative collaborators.

Bibliography
ANGELS, Black Hare Press, 2019
BEYOND, Black Hare Press, 2019
Grievous Bodily Harm, Zombie Pirate Publishing, 2019
MONSTERS, Black Hare Press, 2019
UNRAVEL, Black Hare Press, 2019
WORLDS, Black Hare Press, 2019

Connect
Amazon: amazon.com/author/jonathaninbody
X Meets Y Podcast: xmeetsy.libsyn.com

MONSTERS IN VIETNAM

By R.J. Hunt

Private Thompson's squad of men and orcs have a routine mission in Vietnam, but they aren't the only monsters in these jungles.

It was the first time I'd ever seen a breather. It nearly filled the sky, blood red wings painted with white stripes, fifty white stars speckled across its head. If it was supposed to make us feel patriotic, it wasn't working. It just made me feel like a little boy, in a helmet that didn't fit, too scared to look down at the ground, wishing the chopper would land already. Thumping helicopter blades shook my entire chest, muffling out radio chatter. The American beast opened its terrible jaw and drowned the village below in flames.

Soon, all I could see was black smoke and endless,

rolling fire. And still it kept coming.

"Smell that?" shouted Buck, sitting opposite at the edge of the chopper. His hands rubbed nervously across his camouflaged thighs. When he smiled, his eyes didn't join in. "Barbequed Charlies."

Nobody laughed. Nobody spoke. I doubt anybody so much as curved their lips.

Even the orcs were silent as we watched the flames lick out, eating the small huts away, covering the ground with fire that couldn't be extinguished until it had run out of things to burn. We passed over rice fields and untamed jungles. The lush Vietnamese countryside looked like somebody's version of paradise, but we had all seen its dark, hidden heart. Within the canopies far below, the enemy waited.

The breather flexed its enormous wings and relented. As it finally stopped its molten barrage, it turned, revealing its mind-taming rider, barely visible in the saddle on its back.

"I tried to join the Dragon Corps, ya know?" said a voice at my side.

I turned to Deez and looked the scrawny kid from Nebraska up and down. "That right?"

"Yup," replied Deez easily. "Turned me down. Said I was too hot headed."

We watched each other for a few seconds, then he

cracked a toothy smile and the air burst out of me in a laugh that didn't quite want to be born. "That's a shit joke and you know it."

"If you know better jokes, you should be telling em," said Deez, taking his helmet off and adjusting the strap. From behind him, a green hand tentatively reached out and grabbed Deez's scalp. He flinched and whirled around, slapping the orc's hand away.

The orc barely reacted. He slowly withdrew his hand, turning to the other orc at his side. "Not hot," he grunted, as if they'd been discussing it.

The spell cast by the distant flames seemed to have faded from the rest of the soldiers, and attention turned to Deez, who was smoothing his hair over and sniffing his hand to see if the orc had left a smell.

"You can't tame dragons but you've got orcs covered," Simmons shouted from the opposite row of seats.

"No friend like a green friend, eh Deez?" asked Buck, throwing an arm around the orc at his side.

The orc shrugged the arm away and glared at Buck. "We wrestle on ground, not in sky."

"I ain't trying to wrestle, greenskin, I'm trying to be friendly-like." Buck tossed the opposite arm around Simmons, "Like this, see?"

Simmons tried to push away, but Buck grabbed

tighter and caught him in a headlock. Then he scraped his knuckles over Simmons head and made monkey noises, much to the delight of the other soldiers. The orc next to Buck just watched, seemingly fascinated.

"Look like wrestling to me," he grunted finally, scratching his protruding tusk with a claw.

At the front of the helicopter, Chief turned to face us and laughter died in our throats. "We're touching down soon," he barked, his infamous glare masked by aviators so that each of us feared it might be trained on us. "When boots hit the ground, you put your game faces on. And somebody wake up Frank."

Reluctantly, my eyes slid to the far end of the row of seats where the giant monster slept.

"Who's volunteering?" asked Chief.

I suppressed a shudder. That phrase was Chief's way of forcing misbehaviour to reveal itself. What he actually meant was 'who deserves this particular punishment right now?', and if the team didn't guess correctly, Chief would name them personally, at greater cost to all.

"I am, Chief," said Buck glumly.

"Correct, Buck," replied Chief with a grim smile, "since you like handling military property so much."

The rest of us didn't need anything else said, and Chief knew it. He turned back and motioned to the pilot. Voices kept silent and gazes drifted back outside. Back to the flames.

Helicopter skids hit the ground in a patchy landing. My helmet fell into my lap and Deez clutched at me to stop himself tumbling off his seat. The orcs barely jostled. Chief screamed out orders, and we leapt to our feet, touching down on lush overgrown grass. Humans took point as the orcs leapt forward, glaring deep into the distant tangle of trees and sniffing the air. It was hard to imagine they could smell anything other than ash and burning. Behind me, a surge of electricity made the hairs on my arms stand up. It was followed by a deep roar that rattled the bullets in my rifle.

Within the grove, I searched for eyes, faces, weapons. It was easy to get lost just looking into that jungle; with so many shades of green, you began to wonder if other colours existed. So many avenues of attack that your eyes couldn't quite pull away.

"Clear!" bellowed one of the orcs, before I'd finished my endless search.

The helicopter tipped as something stepped onto the rim; something so heavy it made the skid dig into the ground. I kept my eyes forward.

"Frank's up," said a weary Buck.

Something high above me grunted. I tried not to

look at the ground; at the enormous shadow swallowing my own. I failed, and as my eyes slipped downwards, I felt my muscles tense unwillingly.

"Frank, pick up and follow," said Chief, pointing to some supply crates.

"Gruuh," agreed Frank, immediately following orders and making the helicopter creak under his size 15 boots.

Chief gave the order and we moved up to the orcs who were already tugging at their uniform and eyeing the helicopter's spinning blades. They knew the rules; uniform had to stay on whilst anyone could see them, but once our unit was alone, they could go caveman. They were more camouflaged naked anyway.

"Itchy," muttered one, tugging at his collar.

Chief ignored him and gazed at the smoking village through binoculars. Some of the soldiers copied him, but I kept my eyes on the trees. Nothing was alive in that village. Nothing survives a breather.

The helicopter that had dropped us off, lifted into the sky. Orcs watched intently, and as it disappeared into the clouds, their gaze drifted eagerly to Chief, never tearing his eyes away from the binoculars.

"Fine," he said after a moment, never dropping the binoculars. "Orcs can debrief." He laughed at his own joke, then spat on the ground. Maybe he had seen something he didn't like. Maybe he remembered we were watching.

Whatever made him spit, the orcs didn't seem to care. All three of them were caught in a delicate ballet of removing their clothes as quickly as possible without wanting to tear them and have it docked from their rations. Me and Deez were caught in a dance of our own, wanting to look away but at the same time morbidly curious. Orcs weren't like men, not in the way that counts. We thought of them as 'he', but they weren't. Genderless, like those new action-dolls for the kids. Nothing between the legs, no pride, no weakness. It was gross…and fascinating.

"How you wear this?" asked one orc as he stuffed the clothing into his backpack. They kept the helmets on; Chief wouldn't let them take off anything made for protection. It was only when the orc's yellow eyes looked over that I realised he was talking to me.

"Uhh… Just used to it, I guess?"

"Better this way," said the orc, making a real mess of zipping up his bag and leaving a sleeve dangling out as he threw it over his back. He walked off before I could form a response.

"I'll get naked if you do," said Deez, nudging me with the butt of his rifle.

The walk to the village was long and silent. As we stepped over burnt ground, rising heat warmed my boots and legs. Smoke clung inside my nostrils like it was all I'd ever smell. Buck made no joke about 'Barbequed Charlies' now. Flames still flickered here and there, eating away whatever was left.

Chief ordered the orcs to establish a perimeter and got Frank to set down our supplies and start clearing debris. Our mission was to find evidence of VC tunnels or operations that were rumoured to exist in this village. Former village.

Towering over me, Frank grabbed burning timbers and pulled them loose as though they were bothersome twigs. The eight-foot-tall grey giant made quick work of the larger, more dangerous parts, which gave me and Deez room to shovel out the ash underneath. Soot swirled in the air around us, and we both pulled our shirts up over our mouths. It didn't stop the taste seeping in. My shovel hit something hard. At first I thought it was a stone, but when I struck again, it shattered completely. Some dim part of me knew it was a human skull, but I kept moving and forced myself to focus on the job. Clear the dirt. Prove that this was a Viet Cong base and not a village with mothers, fathers, and childr—

Just a Viet Cong base.

"...Thompson."

Just a Viet Cong base.

"...Private Thompson."

I kept digging, digging, digging.

"Mike," said Deez, grabbing my shoulder before lowering his voice. "Nothing here. Chief said to move to the next one."

I looked around and saw we were alone. Beneath my feet, there was no more ash to dig, and it was only then I realised I'd been carving my way through virgin soil. At the next hut, Frank was hefting a wooden beam that still glowed with embers and was surely burning his hands. Deez narrowed his eyes at me, kept his hand on my shoulder.

"You ok?" he asked.

"Yeah," I said quickly. "I just... Yeah."

"Come on," said Deez, motioning to the next hut, "before Chief makes you volunteer for something."

I nodded and rubbed at my shoulders. Tight knots of pain began to worm their way into my muscles, and I gulped down great lungfuls of burnt air. Me and Deez moved over to the next hut and began to shovel that one clear too. Then the next, then the next.

"Watch your footing," said Chief, "Mr Charlie digs his traps forty foot deep and fills them with poisoned spikes. Mr Charlie will blow off your legs and stick needles in your eyes. You don't wanna slip on one of Mr Charlie's surprises, believe that."

Whether Chief took off his shades and rubbed at his eye to prove a point, or whether he just had an itchy eye, I wasn't sure. I just made damn sure I watched where I was stepping. We'd all heard enough stories of the Viet Cong traps to be scared straight whenever they were mentioned. I wasn't sure I completely believed them, but it was a bit like ghosts—you can convince yourself there's no such thing all you like, but when you get up at midnight to take a piss and hear a creaking door, or see something in the shadows, your heart starts pounding pretty savage. Viet Cong were the same. I'd never even seen one alive. For all I knew, they were just an excuse to get us fighting this war. God knows, none of us knew the real reason. But we were scared enough of this latest boogie man—the Viet Cong, the VC, Mr Charlie—to keep our heads down and ask no questions.

After clearing the sixth hut and finding nothing, me and Deez stopped for a rest. He offered me a cigarette, but breathing in this air, I felt like I'd smoked a pack already. We were chatting amongst ourselves when one of the patrolling orcs walked past.

"Find things?" he asked in his gruff voice, as though he had to curl the words around his teeth.

It was the orc who'd spoken to me before, with the dangling sleeve. Rare for an orc to be this chatty. They weren't normally talkers. They weren't normally thinkers. They were just…orcs.

"Nah," I said, leaning on my shovel. Deez kept silent as the orc walked closer to us, watching him through a veil of smoke.

The orc lowered his rifle and sniffed at the air, his eyes slowly sweeping over the wreckage we were supposed to be digging.

"Smell something?" I asked.

The orc nodded gravely. "Bad. Bad things."

Before I could say anything else, Deez flicked his cigarette stub away and puffed himself up. "Are you the one who touched my head?" he demanded, jabbing the orc's chest with a finger.

The orc eyed the prodding finger, the set of his jaw twisting slightly with some emotion I didn't recognise. "No," he said, meeting Deez's gaze.

Deez relaxed a little. "Oh, OK then."

"What," shouted a voice from behind, "exactly are you boys doing?"

It was Chief. My head went down and my muscles set to digging. Deez had been caught without his shovel and tried to quickly grab it, but Chief got there first, snatching it up and running a thumb along the metal edge.

"Cos it sure don't look like digging to me," said Chief. He turned and weighed up the orc. "What you think, greenskin? You ever seen a man dig without a shovel before?"

The orc looked at each of us in turn, taking much more consideration in his response than I'd ever seen an orc take. "Human can't dig long. Arms too weak."

Chief barked a false, one syllable laugh. "That right? Well, with Private Deez here, you might just be on the money. I've seen water reeds with more definition." He threw the shovel at the orc who barely caught it as it bashed against his chest. "Show us how greenskins dig then, Twenty-Seven. Private Deez, you can do orc work, can't you?"

"Yes, sir," said Deez, quickly saluting.

"Good, off you patrol then," Chief said, motioning for him to move out. As Deez picked up his rifle and jogged past him, Chief followed the kid with his eyes. "You're in luck Private, you might actually be too thin to get shot. Bullets will just whizz right on past you. Hell, I might even fire off a couple myself, test the theory."

Chief stayed a moment, watching me and the orc silently dig. I couldn't say how long he stood there, but by the time I eventually dared risk looking, he was gone. The orc was indeed better at digging than me or Deez, and it wasn't long before he finished his patch of soot and began sharing mine. He struck something hard and scattered pebbles in front of my path. I didn't really notice until he stopped digging, then I realised they were teeth. Too small to be adult teeth. Too many to belong to just one mouth. My shovel dropped from my hands. I looked at the orc and his eyes met mine. I'd never really noticed before how small orcs eyes were, dwarfed by their large snout and mouth. I'd never looked at an orc before in any detail, really. This one's small, perfectly round eyes were watching me closely, perhaps in the same way I was measuring him. I picked up my shovel and spoke to end the silence.

"Why does Chief call you Twenty-Seven?"

The orc turned around and pointed a claw over his shoulder, gesturing to a scar on his back. There was a brand seared between his shoulder blades, blackened and ridged where his skin had swollen. Imprinted stars and stripes of the American flag. The number '018027'. The words 'Property of the US Government'. I wondered if all orcs had that. I'd never noticed.

"Who did that?" I asked quietly.

The orc shrugged. "Human." He rubbed at it self-consciously. "Uru was very young."

"Is that your real name?" I asked. "Uru?"

Uru nodded. "Uru Korok."

"Well," I said, offering out my hand, "It's nice to meet you, Uru."

Uru looked at my outstretched hand, and his eyes slid cautiously up to meet mine. Orcs rarely showed any expression on their faces, beyond surly miserableness or rage, but Uru seemed to soften. He took my hand and shook it lightly, seeming to take great care not to crush my knuckles in his grip.

"Is good to meet you, Mike Thompson."

I almost dropped my shovel again but played it out as a casual return to digging. He copied me. "You know my name?" I asked.

"Uru listen to human," he said, nodding to himself. "Want to learn."

I couldn't help but laugh a little as I dug. When Uru cocked his head at me, I explained. "Don't think you'll learn much from this bunch."

Standing to his full height, Uru checked over his shoulder before prodding a clawed finger to his chest. "Why John Deez do this?" He poked himself a few more times, seemingly mesmerised by his own finger.

"Aah, I wouldn't worry about that," I said. "You know John's name too, huh?

Uru shrugged. "Human all look same. Smell different though."

"Bet we stink of shit right now," I laughed, wiping

sweat off my forehead.

"Not shit," said Uru seriously. He sniffed at me and pointed to my armpits. "Mike Thompson."

Although he was a better digger, Uru turned out to be no luckier than me or Deez at uncovering VC traps or hiding spots. We'd searched the whole village and found nothing except burnt bones and a rotten feeling at the bottom of our stomachs. Chief radioed in our lack of discovery and we were given our next marching orders; coordinates to the location of an ambush that had happened yesterday and left some poor grunt dead. Ten klicks south of us, deep within the woodlands. I gripped my rifle so hard it hurt my hands.

Frank sat down in one of the huts and wriggled himself into the soot as we buried him. He'd do nothing but expose us in the forest, so we'd let him sleep and grab him on the way back. He didn't seem to mind.

We kept our voices low as we stepped over vines, between trees, and under dense bushes. Creatures chirped and chattered, fleeing from us as sticks snapped underfoot and leaves brushed against us. Two orcs took point, Chief close behind, the rest of us in pairs, with Uru alone at the rear; standard Greenback formation. We were as quiet as we could be, setting our ears to listening and our eyes to watching. I'd heard there were elephants in the Vietnam jungles, but if there were, they kept quieter than we did.

"Piece of shit plants," muttered Deez, shaking his foot to free himself from a snaking vine.

When it didn't come loose, I unsheathed my knife and cut it off his boots.

"Thanks, brother," said Deez, giving me a wink.

I smiled back and placed my knife back in its sheath. "Any time, brother."

Deez focused on the plants in front. As I weaved around a particularly knotted tree, there was a clawed tap at my shoulder.

"What is this word?" asked Uru, leaning in conspiratorially, "Brother?"

"We're not actually brothers," I said quietly, stepping over an outstretched root, "It means…uhh…closeness. We're so close, we're like brothers, you know?"

Uru watched me as though I were some great puzzle, the muscles in his green jaw twisting and tensing. "I do not know."

"Brother… It means," I paused, grasping at midair, struggling to define such a simple word, "if your mother had another son, he'd be your brother."

Uru's brow looked like it might crush his tiny yellow

eyes. He shook his head, showing he didn't understand.

"It means family," I whispered, "You know, brother, sister, someone who was born from the same person as you."

"Ah," he said in a low rumble, eyes lighting up, "Spawn."

"Yeah, I guess."

The orc scratched at his lips, weighing this up. We walked together in silence, the only sound was the crushing of leaves and grass underfoot. "Human and orc spawn different, I think," he said finally.

It dawned on me that I had no idea how orcs reproduced. "How do orcs spawn, Uru?"

The orc's mouth spread wide, revealing sharp brown fangs. It took me a moment to realise Uru was smiling. "I thought human know everything," he said with something resembling a grin. "It OK. Uru teach. When old orc die, new orc born. Many orcs born at same time. Spawn…very small," he made a pinching gesture with his clawed green hand. His smile slipped away and his brow sagged. "We fight, grow, fight, until only strongest is left. Until only Uru is left."

My feet stopped trudging forwards and Uru glanced around at the canopy, thinking I'd seen a threat. "You have to kill each other?" I asked.

"Orcs born fighting. Killing. Is all we are good for."

Uru's hand drifted to the base of his neck as his eyes stared pointedly ahead. His fingers rubbed across the raised skin, the brand seared into his flesh; the flag and his serial number.

I forced my eyes to watch the trees, saying nothing.

"Brother," said Uru slowly, tasting the sound of it on his thick tongue. "I like this word."

If there were any VC on the way to the ambush site, they never said hello. It took twice as long to walk ten klicks than it would in the open, and felt twice as long again. 'Running on Jungle Time', Deez called it. He wasn't wrong. My eyes hurt from trying not to blink. Human beings were not designed to stay in a state of alarm and wariness for so long, and I felt like I could drop into the bed of leaves and sleep forever. Ahead, Chief raised his hands, and we all ducked into a low crouch accordingly. He muttered something to the front pair of orcs, and they split off, creeping into the jungle to either side of us. It was equal parts impressive and frightening how easily the lumbering orcs disappeared into the wildlife, as though you'd only dreamt they were there in the first place.

"Ambush site was just up ahead," whispered Chief as he made his way back to us. "We're playing on Mr

Charlie's home-field today, never forget that."

We nodded in agreement and I felt a shiver climb all the way down my spine. Chief patted Buck and Simmons on the back.

"You two, ahead of me." He pointed at Uru, "Twenty-Seven, take point."

We assumed our positions, Uru sniffing at the air like a bloodhound. Jungle Time ticked away even slower than normal as we kept low and crept forwards. All the noises in the forest had died, its hidden creatures either focused on watching us, or long fled. Everywhere I looked, I imagined eyes, and my whole body trembled with anticipation that begged not to manifest. It could have been hours or minutes before we found what we were looking for. The jungle gave way to a man-made trail, just wide enough for a car to track through. We found ourselves at the top of a bank, looking down at the trail, its exits to our left and right. Chief took a moment to decide which way to go before eventually settling on left. We waited in our spot for Uru to relay orders to the other, hidden orcs before finally trudging onwards, staying at the top of the bank, keeping hidden within the jungle. Chief could be an asshole, but he wasn't dumb. The earlier ambush had happened on the track. It would have been easier for us to follow the same path but would make us sitting ducks for another attack. Still, it was hard to feel too grateful when leaves and branches were smacking you in the face and your forearms were bubbling up into some kind of rash.

I was busy watching the jungle and watching my feet when I bumped into Buck. Chief had stopped us, and I soon saw why. There was a body in the road, stripped and bloody. Pale skin, red from sunburn. American.

We stayed rooted to the spot, each of us looking for evidence of tracks, proof that anybody other than this body had ever been here. We might as well have been searching for bigfoot. The only tracks were boot prints on the trail, light as they walked forwards, heavy as they'd ran away. Bullet cases as they'd fired into the trees. Blood splatters from their wounds. Boot prints, bullets, and blood that matched my own. Americans left trails, Charlie didn't.

Chief got the orcs back, and the three of them headed down the slope to retrieve the body. The big one unceremoniously slung the corpse over his shoulder and began climbing back up the slope on all fours, but Uru and the other orc stayed behind, sniffing the air. Their noses led them into the other side of the bank, and when Uru dug his claws into a piece of mossy bank, it gave way, opening like a flap. Both orcs jumped back like frightened chimps.

Chief hissed out orders, so me and Deez stalked

across the trail to the opposite side of the bank. I readied a grenade to lob down, but Uru stopped me with a hand. He nodded down below and pointed to his arrow-shaped ear. I listened as hard as I could, but I couldn't hear anything except my beating heart. I'd never tried to communicate with an orc without using words, and I quickly learnt why. Me and Deez silently agreed to just lob a grenade down there to be safe, but before I pulled out the pin, Uru climbed inside the tunnel, face first. His waist barely fit, and the tunnel flap almost fell off as he forced his way inside. The other orc seemed completely disinterested, eyes fixed on the trees, nose still twitching away.

Intangible noises came from the tunnel, and me and Deez quickly shoved both our weapons into the entrance but saw nothing except darkness. I put my grenade away before I was too tempted to pull out the pin and kill Uru and whatever else was down there, simply to calm my own nerves.

We pulled back as a green head emerged. Uru climbed out of the tunnel, covered in muck and with a slash across his arm. In his other arm, he gripped a struggling child. A girl, I eventually decided. No older than six, she kicked and thrashed against Uru, but he didn't seem to care. He sniffed at the wound on his forearm and met my eyes.

"Spawn," he said, nodding towards the little girl.

Without warning, she wailed so loud I actually ducked. Uru clamped a hand over her mouth and she struggled against his grip. Chief, Buck, and Simmons appeared quickly, and the orcs were set to keep watch whilst Buck restrained the little girl. She seemed to become more slippery in his grip, and she managed to almost wrench herself free several times.

"Ow, mother fucker!" said Buck, shaking his hand and hissing in tones of outright horror. "She bit me!"

The little girl screamed something in Vietnamese and Simmons held her jaw shut, squeezing her lips together with his fingers.

"Well," said Deez, glancing around the trees, "if there was more than just her, I think we'd be dead by now."

"You made me bleed, little bitch!" hissed Buck, showing his hand to the little girl as though she might not believe him. I'd never seen a child's eyes hold so much hate.

"She's just a kid, Buck," I said, trying to pull him back.

Buck reeled and shoved me. Some part of him didn't want to hurt this child, but I was a less complex target for him. I slipped and almost fell down the bank. Buck raised his fist, I formed my own.

"Private Hill, Private Thompson," snapped Chief, stopping us both, "We have enemies to fight when you're both done fighting each other."

"I oughta kill that little bitch," said Buck, spitting on the ground.

Permission granted, Private Deez," Chief said gravely.

If his words had stopped us before, they turned us both to stone now.

"Whu-what?" Buck's voice had never sounded so small.

"We leave this girl here and we'll be swamped by Charlies before we ever see the sky again," Chief said, gaze flicking from me to Buck. I saw my own stupefied reflection in Chief's glasses. "We take her with us, and not only will she be a liability, she will be an unsolved equation."

"But, sir," I tried, "she—"

"This problem will occur again when we grab Frank. Again when we reach the Evac Point. What other outcome do you see here, Private Thompson? Are you going to take her home with you?" Chief withdrew his knife and held it out to Buck. "Be careful what you wish for, Private Hill."

Buck made no move to grab the blade. Chief stepped towards him, thrusting the knife handle out impatiently.

"Kill or be killed, Private, pick one," he spat each word with venom.

Buck reached out, took the knife, and his lips pursed as he began to steel himself.

"Buck," I blurted out, "you don't gotta do this."

As soon as the words left my mouth, I wanted to scoop them all back in. Chief snatched back the blade and whirled around on me. In his mirrored gaze, I saw a small version of myself shrink away.

"OK fine," he snarled, "we'll do this another way." His voice became cold iron. "Who's volunteering?"

My throat contorted, the air inside of me running away. "Chief," I said, "she's just a little kid-"

"A little kid who will give away our position to the enemy the moment we leave her alone. She cannot come with us. She cannot stay. Now, Private Thompson, who is volunteering?"

"Sir… " I managed, barely able to speak, barely able to form sentences in my head.

Chief removed his aviators. Inwardly, I recoiled as I was hit with the full force of his one-eyed glare. It was hard to know which was more terrible—his working eye, so full of hatred, or his dead eye, milky white and scarred. "I asked you a question, Private Thompson."

My mouth formed empty words as I tried to keep

my eyes fixed on Chief, but they kept slipping away. Around me, bodies shifted. Chief got close enough to strike me and spoke again, his voice low but quivering with rage. "Who. Is. Volunteering?"

I wanted to look at Deez, at Simmons, at Buck, at anyone, but I knew it was hopeless.

"I…"

"I will do this thing," said Uru.

Chief's unblinking glare slid away from me and took in Uru. The orc met his eyes without hesitation. "That right?" said Chief. "No rations for a week. Still interested?"

Uru glanced at me for only a second. "I will do this thing," he said.

There was a pause that would have made gods shuffle.

"Never can tell the difference between you orcs," said Chief, finally. "Guess I'll just have to dock all your rations, to make sure."

"Chief," I began, getting cut down almost immediately as Chief whirled on me, sunglasses doing nothing to hide the rage painted across his face.

"I suggest," he spat in a low growl, "you keep your opinions to yourself." The knife appeared again, a whirling glint of silver, twisting in his palm. It stopped, tip pointed at my throat. "Or I'll give you this knife and a direct order."

I tried to think of something to say, but knew it was hopeless. I tried to look at Uru, but my eyes slid to the ground. I could practically feel Chief smiling.

"Twenty Seven," he snapped, holding the knife over his shoulder, gripped by the blade. "Kill the girl and bury her body. Don't even think about eating her, I'll know if you do. I'm not having you sickfuck greenskins committing war crimes on my watch, you hear me?"

A green hand took the knife and walked away. The girl kicked and screamed as Uru took her from Simmons and carried her off into the trees. I felt tears rolling down my cheeks.

"Why no ration us?" demanded a heavy voice. The biggest of the three orcs, dead body still dangling from his shoulder like a grim ornament. I'd not heard him speak before. It sounded like he was chewing on gravel.

"Because your boy there prefers killing to eating. You got a problem with that, take it up with him," said Chief. "Rest of you, saddle up, we're moving to the evac point."

Boots trudged away, and a dull part of me followed. I gripped my rifle, feeling utterly powerless.

The walk back through the forest was somehow

worse than before. I didn't even bother to move the plants away with my hands as I stalked through the brush, catching nicks and scratches all over me that I'd only notice long after they happened. I couldn't hear the others. Maybe they were more silent than before. Maybe my senses were just dulled. We stopped for a piss and water break, and it was only when the two orcs returned to pick up the corpse that I realised they'd been gone. I couldn't see Uru. We started walking again, Simmons and Buck taking point, orcs just ahead of me. My eyes were hypnotised by the swaying limbs of the dead soldier.

Someone limped past me, walking as fast as they could to catch up to Chief. A green hand passed him a blood-stained knife. It was Uru. His face was badly beaten, his eye swollen to the point where it wouldn't open. Half of his body was smothered with jade coloured orc blood, and he had deep gashes over his arm, shoulder, and both legs.

"Put up a fight, did she?" said Chief in his slimiest voice.

Uru said nothing, resuming his limping march through the trees. He fell behind and the other orcs barged into him, almost knocking him to the floor. I noticed their knuckles and claws were stained the same orc blood colour as Uru. As they walked onwards, I dropped back.

"Uru," I whispered. "Jesus man, what have they done to you?"

His lips peeled back in an attempt at a smile. Some of his brown fangs were missing.

"Fuck, I-I'm sorry," I stammered, eyes threatening to burst with tears again.

He laid a heavy, bloodstained hand on my shoulder. "Is ok, Mike Thompson. Human not all good at killing. I see this. Some, yes. Not you."

I couldn't even bring myself to look at Uru's beaten face. I wanted to thank him but couldn't bring myself to thank him for killing a little girl for me. I kept my voice low and tried to keep it as free from emotion as I could. "She didn't suffer, did she?"

I looked up to see Uru watching me closely. We were both walking so slowly that we'd fallen far behind the others, barely visible on the freshly made trail ahead.

"Want to know secret?" he asked, as quietly as I'd ever heard an orc speak.

I nodded. After a moment, Uru smiled that same broken-toothed grin.

"Uru not good at killing too."

I stopped walking, and as Uru limped forwards, I noticed his backpack no longer had the trailing sleeve of his uniform.

"She's not dead?" I whispered, grabbing him by the arm. He winced with pain and I let go.

"Tied to tree," he said quietly. He made to turn, to keep on limping, but I stopped him.

"Uru," I said, meeting his eyes, "thank you."

He nodded, and we walked at each other's side, trying to keep up with the others.

There was a spark of electricity and Frank sat bolt upright, showering us all in soot and roaring so loud it made my boots tremble. He made a terrible effort at wiping himself clean, and Chief radioed HQ. Chopper would be at the evac point in thirty minutes, which meant at least fifteen waiting. Chief said cover was better in the old village, so we'd wait here. I sat down in the ash, and Deez joined me. Seemingly happy to take another shot at Uru, Chief ordered the orcs to set up a perimeter, all the while munching on a can of corned beef. I decided in that moment I was going to give all my rations for the day to Uru, and he could share them however he wanted.

"Transport dragon," said Deez, nudging me with his boot.

I looked up and saw what could have been a bird gliding across the horizon. It was only when my eyes adjusted that my brain could realise the scale, realise the distance. The gigantic dragon had packages strapped all across its body, yet still gracefully pierced through the air, with barely a flap of its wings. Without the fire, they were sort of beautiful. My eyes sank, head heavy. I didn't feel deserving of any beauty right now.

"Ever spoke to the orcs?" I asked Deez quietly.

He shook his head and looked at me seriously. I shook my own head and let out a sigh.

"I—"

A whipcrack came from the trees and everything went to shit.

"Contact!" someone shouted. "Contact!"

I scrambled to my feet, something hot fizzed past my ear. Everything around me was popping or banging, whipcracks sounding from every direction I knew existed. I threw myself behind a pile of blackened timber and Deez shot blindly into the trees. I leant out to fire myself, but noticed Frank stood completely out in the open, unmoving. Occasionally he'd twitch ever so slightly as he got shot.

"Frank!" I shouted, "Frank, get in cover for fuck's sake!"

The flatheaded giant looked over at me and grunted, bullets thudding into his arms, shoulders, and chest as he slowly lowered into a crouch. He was still out in the open, still getting struck on one side, and he looked over at me to check if he'd done it properly.

"In cover!" I shouted, leaning out too far and flinching back as dirt around me sprang into the air. I popped a few rounds into the trees and sank back into the soot.

Chief was shouting something, but his words were distorted. Something ahead blew up and showered us all in ash and shards of debris. Crack. Crack. Crack. I shot again, not even aiming, just wanting to do something. Deez appeared from nowhere, slamming into my timber wall and almost toppling it over.

"We gotta move, man," he shouted in a panic.

I nodded and peeked out, firing into the places I thought I could hear the shooters, but seeing nothing. Deez pushed himself up and sprinted forwards, weaving past Frank who still crouched in the middle of the burnt out village, great bloodless chunks missing from his flesh. As soon as Deez found fresh cover, he threw himself back up and began blindly shooting. I took my cue and forced my legs to move. As another explosion rocked the village, my legs stopped listening, and I hit the ground hard, skidding and scraping my forearms. Bullets whizzed past my head and I had to keep reminding myself I wasn't dead yet.

"Frank!" I yelled, "Come here!"

With a grunt, the giant obeyed. He shuffled over to me, and I pushed him forwards, using him as cover. It was stupid, but somehow it worked. The gunfire seemed to have died, but I just kept moving. As we reached Deez, I kept pushing Frank until he was hidden behind the shell of a hut.

"You OK?" I managed to gasp at Deez.

He nodded so quick I thought his neck might snap off. "Think they're falling back. One of the orcs got hit."

Throwing my head into the open, I searched for the others. I saw Chief, the big orc, and then a body.

I ran. Deez shouted something but I didn't hear him. My knees thudded into the ground at Uru's side. His chest was oozing out blood, his face locked in a confused grimace.

"Oh God," I whispered, "Uru, don't—"

Uru took my hand and squeezed. His eyes looked towards me, he tried to focus.

His mouth moved, but the air wouldn't escape him. "Buh…" he wheezed.

Uru's hand touched my chest. He kept trying to speak but could barely breathe. "Br…"

I knew then what he was trying to say, and it was my turn to struggle speaking.

"Brother," I whispered, eyes stinging.

But Uru was gone. His hand slipped from my fingers

and hit the dirt.

I don't know how long I sat there, body sagged over Uru's broken, bloody corpse. Someone tugged at my shoulders, but I couldn't get up.

"Frank," said Chief's voice behind me. It held none of his usual edge. The softness of it made my eyes sting. "Carry the body," he instructed.

Frank bent down and gently scooped up Uru, holding him like a baby. Even the monster seemed tender in that moment. I felt a hand on my shoulder.

Before I could figure out who the hand belonged to, a distant snapping of twigs made everyone look up. Something was moving in the trees ahead, and all hands went to weapons.

"Contact," boomed a voice in my ear. Man or orc, I couldn't tell, didn't care. Blood was thumping inside of me and I needed to find something to hurt. My arms moved of their own free will, and with startling ease, I had a rifle in my hands. Someone grabbed at me, tried to pull me back, but I was done running, done hiding. I could see figures moving in the trees ahead, and it felt like the most natural thing in the world to line them up in my crosshairs and squeeze the trigger.

One of the shapes dropped, as though his entire body had been given weight that his bones couldn't carry. As though someone had pushed his 'off-switch'.

My heart leapt; excitement and fear battling inside of me. Another enemy stepped out from the trees, I turned, fired again. Again. Again. Someone was shouting, but I was screaming too loud to listen.

Something slammed into me from the side, and all I could see was sky. Deez had tackled me to the ground and ripped the gun from my fingers.

It was only then I heard Chief's words, strangled and full of terror.

"Friendly fire! Friendly goddamn fire!"

R.J. HUNT is an engineer from Nottingham who enjoys writing and making things in his spare time. His cartoons 'Pokemon but with animals instead' collectively have nine million views on youtube, and his big hope is that he didn't peak with that. He has also made a bank robbery board game, and a drinking game involving wizards. Despite the nonsense, he enjoys writing dark and intriguing stories, with his favourite genres being sci-fi, fantasy and horror. He is currently working on the second draft of his first novel, THE FINAL CARNIVORE. A long forgotten god is dug out of the ground in Norway, and begins to bestow powers of mind control and immortality on people who do not deserve it. As our world begins to slip away, misfits with hidden powers of their own must come together and stop the god before he reclaims his soul, and our world is forever changed.

R.J. started writing in earnest three years ago, and it quickly washed his other hobbies away. In 2020, he hopes to complete a series of Novellas set on 'Floor Fifty-Four' - an underground facility in England that stores secrets too strange for our world.

He is often seen walking his dog (a border collie called Pepper) and getting blind drunk with the common folk.

Bibliography
ANGELS, Black Hare Press, 2019
BEYOND, Black Hare Press, 2019
JIBBERNOCKY, Black Hare Press, 2020
WORLDS, Black Hare Press, 2019

Connect
Twitter: @RJHUNTWRITES
Reddit: www.reddit.com/r/RJHuntWrites/

CHERNOBYL'S AWAKENING

By Matt Lucas

When Russian nuclear experimentation awakens dormant apocalyptic beasts, the Allied Ministry of Paranormal Defence send in their top two agents to stop Armageddon.

THE SCIENTIST

Whining alarms pierced Nikolai's ears. Flashing red lights intermittently illuminated his path as he fled through cramped corridors. The unnatural roars of what they'd unleashed resounded at his back, drawing nearer with each torturous second.

Gunfire and the shrill shrieks of his comrades alerted Nikolai that they'd failed to contain the beasts. Furthermore, a brutal cacophony of razor-sharp teeth snapping bone and tearing flesh made the scientist's stomach lurch. Ducking into a supply closet, the Russian dropped his head into his hands and sobbed.

What have we done? he lamented.

The Chernobyl experiments were designed to achieve scientific and military breakthroughs. As the lead physicist on the project, Nikolai relished the prospect of propelling the USSR past the United States. By harnessing the burgeoning power of nuclear energy, Russia would achieve god-like power.

Chernobyl was the gateway to Soviet dominance. Success meant the country would possess a monopoly on cutting edge energy production while simultaneously achieving military supremacy. The world's seat of power would undoubtedly shift from Washington to Moscow overnight.

Nikolai envisioned a world where the United States would be forced to abandon their futile Cold War. Instead, the Americans would be forced to purchase Russian energy so as to not fall behind economically. Foreseeing the prosperity his people would reap further fuelled Nikolai's obsession.

Though important, Nikolai would be remiss to confess prosperity as his primary goal. Ultimately, intimidation was his true desire. The weapons he was developing would be the ultimate deterrent to any who would oppose the expansion of Soviet communist ideology.

A vast, mobile nuclear arsenal…that was Nikolai's dream. With it, the USSR could coerce any country that dared resist communist rule to assimilate. Even when self-righteous pretenders like the Americans came as false liberators, their cities would crumble beneath the iron curtain.

Now, however, those visions of grandeur morphed into a hellish abyss. Their experiments didn't yield boundless power nor a sustainable future. Instead, they'd awakened something.

Flashes of the unholy creatures tore through Nikolai's mind. The beasts had the bodies of war horses, the barbed tails of scorpions, eagle's wings, and rows of razor-sharp teeth. Gilded manes adorned their heads, resembling fur crowns.

They were abominations, unholy demons from the depths of hell. Nikolai cowered in terror when the creatures burst forth from the earth after their last weapons test. Relentlessly they attacked the power plant, mercilessly shredding through the Soviet defences.

Earlier that day, two American spies were captured trying to infiltrate the nuclear facility. During their interrogation from the security commandant, they claimed God's wrath against Russia was imminent. Their concerns were dismissed with raucous laughter.

We should've listened, Nikolai ruminated with regret. *Now our land is teeming with vicious beasts. Our citizens are being devoured and my life's work has been undone.*

Nikolai speculated that the creatures must've lain dormant beneath the earth for centuries like locusts. Only when nuclear testing began did the swarm awaken from their slumber. Enraged, the creatures burrowed through rock and concrete, exploding in droves to ravage Chernobyl.

We've unleashed a plague upon this world, Nikolai grieved.

As the scientist cowered in the supply closet, the glass vials on the shelves began to rattle. Heavy footsteps drew near, sending tremors reverberating through the floor. The abominations approached.

Desperately, Nikolai fought to calm his breathing. However, terror's grip refused to yield. With every exhale, the scientist's throat quivered, emitting a quaking squeak.

The heavy footsteps edged closer and closer. Nikolai clutched his blood-stained lab coat and covered his mouth to muffle his distressed whimpering. Abruptly, the steps ceased next to the closet door.

Suddenly, a barbed tail burst through the barrier.

With a mighty jerk, the creature ripped the door from its hinges. Frantically, Nikolai skidded towards the back wall, curling into a feeble position.

Snarling, the beast prowled into Nikolai's midst. The scientist reeled, realising the creature's face resembled a distorted, humanoid structure. Observing Nikolai's terror, the beast smiled, putting rows of menacing teeth on display.

The scorpion tail thrust forwards, plunging the barb deep into Nikolai's chest. Bellowing in anguish, Nikolai felt the beast's venom burn through his veins. It was as if his blood were literally boiling.

When the barbed tail was pulled from his chest, Nikolai fell to the floor. He writhed in excruciating pain, yearning for death. Yet, despite the hole in his chest and toxic poison coursing through his bloodstream, death wouldn't come quickly.

Looking down at his body, Nikolai observed a new, terrifying side effect of the abomination's sting. Searing red and yellow burns began eating his flesh. They started on his arms, but rapidly spread throughout his body. Soon Nikolai morphed into a disfigured husk, begging to die.

Looking down at his distorted body, Nikolai realised where he'd witnessed this phenomenon before. These are radiation burns…

The creature responsible for the nuclear scientist's

strife seemingly smirked. Relishing the irony of Nikolai's subjection to the ramifications of his own work, the beast left to wreak havoc elsewhere. Nikolai was left in anguish, lamenting the monstrosities he'd unleashed.

...

THE AGENT

Frantically, Clay Owens tugged against his shackles, desperately battling to wrest himself free. The unnatural creatures were coming and, when they arrived, Clay feared being devoured like his Soviet imprisoners. He'd ventured to Russia knowing that something malevolent was stirring here. However, he could've never imagined the horrors lurking beneath the surface.

Twenty years battling demons, monsters, and malfeasances were rendered useless with Clay chained up within the bowels of Chernobyl's power plant. Armageddon was bursting forth from the earth and the Allied Ministry of Paranormal Defence's top agent was confined to a dank cell.

Frustrated, the strong, athletically built warrior grappled with his restraints. Sweat teemed from his olive skin and dripped from his dark brown beard. No matter how much force he exerted, the iron chains held steadfast.

"Cool your jets, kid," Clay's companion, Rick

Sherman, cautioned. He was an older, husky man with a grey, patchy beard.

"I'm not a kid anymore, Uncle Sherm," Clay snarled, "I'm damn near forty!"

"And I'm damn near sixty!" the grizzled warrior smartly countered. "So, when I tell you to cool your jets…cool your jets!"

"Sorry if I'm not content to die in this hole and leave the rest of the world to fight whatever the hell those things are!" Clay snapped back.

Uncle Sherm's tone shifted from authoritative to consoling. "Have faith. The Lord is in control. He knits everything, even the worst, together for good. Your father taught me that a long time ago."

Uncle Sherm's comment drew Clay's ire. "Don't get preachy with me! If this is God's plan…it's a bad plan!"

"Boy, you ain't seen what I've seen!" Uncle Sherman commandingly rebuked. "You weren't there in the desert when me, your daddy, and eight Allied soldiers battled Anubis' legion! I've seen the Red Sea part! I saw the Lord eviscerate the best the devil could muster!"

"And what good did it do?" Clay muttered defiantly. "You stopped one apocalypse just to suffer another. Except now, it's my kids that get to grow up fatherless!"

Uncle Sherm's lips pursed in grief. "I fought beside your father and he never lost faith…even at the bitter end.

He spilled his blood for people he'd never know so they would never have to know the horror we saw."

Clay's jaw tightened as a bitter concoction of anger and resentment consumed him. "And he never got to know me because of it."

Clay grew up listening to Uncle Sherm's war stories. But it wasn't until Clay grew older that Uncle Sherm revealed how his father died. Clay's father, Jacob, served in a battalion that investigated Nazi activity in Egypt towards the end of World War II. Hitler had grown desperate and turned to the occult, seeking the means to victory.

The Nazi's used necromancy to resurrect the pharaoh from Exodus and the Egyptian god, Anubis. The jackal-headed god raised an army of griffins and serpopards. Uncle Sherm described the griffins as lions with giant eagle's wings and the serpopards as leopards with elongated necks adorned with the heads of cobras.

After the initial onslaught massacred most of the Allied battalion, ten survivors retreated to a shanty town on the banks of the Red Sea. Ten men held off the army for a time, but they were soon overrun. Five, including Jacob, sacrificed their lives so the others might escape.

When they fled to the Red Sea, Uncle Sherman witnessed a dove fly over the waters, which he'd dreamt about in the days leading up to the mission. In an act of faith, he extended his hand over the waters and a strong easterly wind swept the sea aside. The five survivors escaped with Nazi and Egyptian forces in hot pursuit. However, once the Allied troops reached the other side, the waters collapsed atop the unholy army and boiled them beneath the waves.

Those survivors became the foundation for the Allied Ministry of Paranormal Defence. Soon the agency evolved into an international coalition bent on defending the world from supernatural threats. As they matured, the AMPD experimented with anticipating paranormal strikes by measuring unnatural energy expulsions. It was one of these anomalies that led Sherman and Clay to investigate Chernobyl.

"Well, I guess we should get a move on," Uncle Sherm unclasped his shackles and advanced towards Clay.

Bewildered, Clay shook his head in disbelief. "You were unlocked this whole time?"

Uncle Sherm shrugged, twirling a slender shard of metal between his fingers. "I picked the lock right after the commies chucked us down here."

"And when were you going to mention this to me?" Clay inquired in outrage.

"I thought we were having a moment," Sherman supposed, "ya know, a real heart to heart. I didn't want to interrupt."

Clay's brow furrowed. "A heart to heart? During the apocalypse?"

Uncle Sherm scoffed. "Don't be so dramatic. This is more of a diet apocalypse. You're like your father that way. He was always brooding, pondering the meaning of life and such. Took every drop of my comedic genius to get him to crack a damned smile when he was in one of his moods."

"You're not as funny as you think you are," Clay jested.

"I'm hilarious," Sherman rebuffed as he unshackled his nephew. "Told ya to cool your jets. You wouldn't have so much bruising if you'd have listened to me."

A few moments later, Uncle Sherm picked the cell's lock, escaping their confinement. As they neared the steel door, unaware of what might lurk on the other side, they paused to formulate a plan. Uncle Sherm scratched his jaw, pondering their next move.

"We're not gonna make it far without any weapons," the grizzled soldier considered.

"Plus, we don't really know what we're dealing with or how to kill them," Clay pointed out.

Cocking his lips to the side, Uncle Sherm wracked his brain. "If we can get to our comms, we can radio command. They should be able to give us an idea of what we're up against."

"At the very least, we need to get a lore scholar on the case," Clay pondered. "Who knows? We might even be lucky enough to get some reinforcements."

Uncle Sherm bobbed his head back and forth, unconvinced if reinforcements were plausible. "Flying over Russian airspace is going to be tricky."

"Maybe Izzy can work her magic? Call in the cavalry?" Clay deliberated.

"Well, she does have a vested interest in your survival," Uncle Sherm smirked.

"Fair point." Clay proudly grinned.

Clay couldn't help but smile at the mention of Isley "Izzy" Owens. Her father, Adam Lee, fought alongside Rick Sherman, Jacob Owens, and George Isley, who was her namesake. George was Adam's best friend and sacrificed his life alongside Jacob during the Battle of the Red Sea.

Both Izzy and Clay grew up on stories of the battalion that saved the world. While Clay mimicked his father's penchant for fighting, Izzy grew up fascinated by technology. As Clay matured as a soldier and Izzy as a brilliant engineer, they became natural fits for the AMPD.

After joining the secretive organisation, their relationship blossomed from childhood friends to romantic companions. Eventually they were married. Shortly after that, they had two sons, Andrew and Evan.

The thought of his wife and sons sobered Clay. *What if I never see them again? What if we don't even make it to the comms in time for me to hear Izzy's voice?*

Sensing the weight that loomed over his nephew, Uncle Sherm put a comforting hand on Clay's shoulder. "You're gonna get out of this place and see her again. I promise."

Nodding, Clay took a deep breath. "Let's go."

...

THE GUARDIAN

Sherman's hand clasped the door handle. His heart pounded loudly within his chest, but he refused to allow any signs of distress to reach the surface. *Don't let the kid see you sweat. You have to be strong for him.*

Slowly the door creaked open. Sherman and Clay peered into a dark labyrinth, surveying the scene. Gunfire resounded in the distance. However, that wasn't the noise that concerned the grizzled soldier.

Heavy footsteps plodded against the concrete. The abominations' snarls and screeches echoed off the cell block's walls. Sherman could hear their heavy inhales, sniffing out their next victims.

They're hunting.

With guile, the companions crept through the

concrete wilderness. Only dim, flickering lightbulbs illuminated their hazy path. Sherman looked back at Clay to ensure he was ready to descend into shadow.

Clay nodded resolutely. Sherman saw Jacob whenever he looked into Clay's eyes. Those steely blue pools of ice peered directly into the soul.

If I don't make it, take care of the boy. Jacob's plea from forty years prior emanated through Sherman's mind.

I promise, Sherman replied then and did once more within the confines of his mind.

Though they were blindfolded when the Russians bound and imprisoned them, Sherman memorised their route. Carefully the duo retraced their steps. Soon they approached the area where their comms had been confiscated. It was a small guard's booth that was now abandoned. Sherman shuddered to speculate as to what happened to the guard.

Peering around the corner, Sherman didn't see any creatures. Motioning to Clay, both men cautiously approached the structure. The front of the booth had a sliding glass window with metal framing. Though it stood at the intersection of two large corridors, the area appeared undisturbed.

Knowing a new threat could arrive any second, Sherman quickened his pace. With quiet strides, the companions rushed to the booth. On the side of the structure was a locked door. Utilising his trusty metallic shard, Sherman attempted to pick the lock.

However, his fingers fumbled with the lock under the threat of imminent danger. He dropped the lock pick and it disappeared, bouncing under the door. Cursing under his breath, the old soldier berated himself.

Clay, on the other hand, sought an alternate entry. Carefully, he slid the window open. Sherm's nephew breathed a sigh of relief, relishing their stroke of luck that the window was unlocked.

Suddenly a scorpion's tail careened through the opening. Clay recoiled, evading the venomous barb by mere inches. Instinctively he slammed the window shut with all his might.

The creature squealed in agony as the window's metal frame wedged its tail in place. Black blood dripped from the creature's wound. The bleeding only intensified the more it struggled, but Clay held firm, keeping constant pressure on the deadly appendage.

Sherman leapt into action. Throwing both his arms around the tail, he subdued its flailing. Meanwhile, Clay executed a plot of his own.

Summoning all the force he could muster, Clay repeatedly slammed the window into the creature's tail. After several strikes, Sherman felt the tail tear in two. With a final heave, Clay severed the poisonous appendage.

Despite their brief victory, the battle wasn't over. The creature burst through the open window, barrelling into Clay. They both tumbled to the floor, embroiled in a struggle for survival. Powerful hooves pinned Clay to the floor while the creature's grotesque jaws snapped at him.

Clay held the abomination at bay as it snapped wildly, seeking to plunge its fangs into his flesh. Seeing his nephew's strength waning against the vicious onslaught, Sherman rushed into the fray. Clutching the creature's still floundering tail, Uncle Sherm charged forwards.

Wielding the appendage like a spear, Sherman plunged the barb between the beast's ribs. Roaring in agony, the creature rolled off Clay. Immediately it began seizing with yellow foam bubbling from its mouth.

Unsatisfied with leaving the creature between life and death, Sherman unleashed a relentless onslaught. He repeatedly stabbed the malicious abomination until he was assured of its death. Eventually the lifeless husk ceased moving.

"I think you got him," Clay contemplated.

"You can never be too sure," Sherman cautioned, panting with exhaustion and delivering one last stab.

Stammering back onto his feet, Clay looked down upon the bizarre creature. "Any idea what the hell we're dealing with?"

"Hell…we're dealing with hell," Sherman declared with certainty. "Every monstrosity I've ever fought had the same father. His creations might take different forms, but at their core, they're all the devil's spawn."

Since the beginning of time, Satan worked tirelessly to raise immoral nations to entice and enslave humanity. Whether it was Sodom and Gomorrah, Babylon, or Nazi Germany, he would raise a spirit of corruption to seduce men to barbaric evils. His latest deceit involved cloaking his demons with monstrous flesh. That's how he'd resurrected beings of myth like Anubis and the Egyptian beasts and, now, he appeared to be at it again.

"At least we know how to kill them now . . . turn their own poison against them." Clay savoured the small victory.

Abruptly the earth quaked beneath their feet. The lightbulbs' flickering intensified. A ravenous hum like that of a stampede echoed through the dark labyrinth.

Sherman's heart sank, realising what careened towards them. "Sounds like we woke the swarm. Grab the comms, we gotta book it!"

Clay leapt over the counter and through the guard booth window. Frantically, he turned over the space in a desperate search for their radios. "C'mon, c'mon, c'mon," he begged, tearing through drawers.

"Get a move on! We don't got all night!" Sherman

started backpedalling as the horde's thunderous stampede raced in their direction.

"Got 'em!" Clay raised two radios triumphantly.

Absconding through the booth's side door, Clay tossed a radio to his uncle. Sherman caught it just as a convoy of creatures rounded the corner. The abominations galloped towards the duo with their scorpion tails poised and ready to strike.

Turning in a full sprint, Sherman and Clay sped through the cramped hallways with the creatures in hot pursuit. However, they were ill suited to outrun the demonic warhorses. As the beasts bore down on the duo, Clay radioed his wife.

"Izzy! Izzy, do you copy?" Clay shouted.

"Oh, thank God," Izzy's relieved voice replied. "What the hell is going on there? The spiritual activity readings are off the charts!"

"We don't know," Clay answered, "but it looks like the damned Soviets woke up some pissed off monsters!"

The fleeing duo turned sharply down another hallway. For all their might, the creatures' hooves lacked the traction to deftly turn on concrete floors. The manoeuvre bought Clay and Sherman precious time.

"Where are you now?" Izzy inquired.

"Trapped in the basement beneath the power plant," Sherman answered. "It's a freakin' maze down here."

"I'll pull the schematics!" Izzy replied, with the frantic shuffling of paper crinkling through the receiver.

Sherman turned back. The horde was closing in rapidly. "We gotta let them get close then change direction!" He instructed.

While Izzy searched the Chernobyl power plant's schematics for a way out, Sherman and Clay darted between hallways. At first, their tactics disoriented the creatures, but they soon adapted.

Two sects of the horde broke off from the primary group. One looped left while the other went right to form a deadly trident. With their only advantage siphoned off, the duo's chances of survival looked bleak.

"Izzy," Sherman's voice cracked, "we need a way out now!"

"Got it!" Izzy exclaimed triumphantly. "There are service elevators on all four sides of the structure! If you can get to one of those, they'll take you to the central command centre and the nearest exit!"

"You're a genius, babe!" Clay marvelled. "Now we just gotta get there in one piece!"

"Well, turning is no longer an option," Sherman theorised through panting breaths, "They've got us flanked on both sides."

"Forwards it is I guess!" Clay proclaimed with a hopeful reluctance.

Summoning all the will power they could muster, the duo forced their bodies past their limits. With death at their heels, they flew down the hallways. Soon enough, a silver glimmer of steel elevator doors manifested in the distance.

"Almost there!" Sherman cried out.

Despite having their instrument of salvation within sight, the beasts' thunderous galloping edged closer. Soon they were near enough that the duo could smell the pungent stench of the creature's blood-stained jowls. Life was racing death.

The duo reached the elevator with little time to spare. Frantically, Clay pounded the "up" button, utterly reliant on its little, white light. Meanwhile, Sherman stood guard, readying the severed tail for combat.

The horde charged with reckless abandon. Their monstrous mouths watered, and acidic poison dripped from their barbed tails. The tremors created by their powerful hooves could've registered on the Richter Scale.

Still the elevator hadn't come to their rescue. Clay quit pressing the button and turned towards the fray, his teeth gritted and his fists clenched. Their journey was at its end, but they chose not to go down without a fight.

Exchanging stoic glances, uncle and nephew nodded at each other, embracing their demise. *I'm sorry, Jacob. I tried to protect him, and I failed.*

Suddenly a deafening cacophony of shrill shrieks and collisions rocked the ground. Clay and Sherman looked on in astonishment as all three sects of the horde collided in the same intersection. Some of the creatures stumbled to the ground, while others skidded to a halt, barricaded behind their kin.

Just then, the elevator dinged, announcing its arrival. Breathing a sigh of relief, Sherman and Clay ducked into the steel carriage. Clay frenetically pushed the "close door" button, but the door remained open.

"You gotta push it," Sherman instructed.

"What do you think I'm doing?" Clay protested.

"You're going too fast!" Sherman reprimanded. "Press and hold for a second!"

Clay obeyed the instruction to no avail. "I don't know why you would think that would work. The thing's clearly broken."

"Here, let me try." Sherman interjected his hand.

"Will you give it a second!" Clay objected, batting his uncle's hand away.

"Fine," Sherman raised his hands innocently, "you deal with it."

That's when the elder agent saw one of the demonic warhorses scrambling from the dogpile. It broke free with rage blazing in its grotesque, black eyes. With a menacing roar, it charged just as the elevator doors were beginning to close.

"You gotta be kiddin' me!" Sherman bellowed in outrage.

"We gotta do something! These doors aren't gonna close in time!" Clay hollered.

Biding his time, Sherman waiting for the beast to come within range. He could smell the beast's pungent breath as it bore its fangs. Opening wide, the beast lunged at Clay.

Suddenly, Sherman thrust the barbed tail forwards, piercing through the abomination's mouth and out the back of its neck. A muffled, yet high pitched, squeal resounded from the creature's throat. It flailed chaotically before collapsing as the elevator doors closed.

Uncle Sherman inspected Clay. *Why did the creature attack him and not me?*

Sherman receded into the elevator until he reached the back wall. He slid down to the floor, panting with exhaustion. "I think we handled that well."

The radio cackled as Izzy's voice came through the speaker. "Status update?"

"Alive," Clay answered. "We made it to one of the elevators."

"Thank God," Izzy exhaled. It sounded like the weight of the world was lifted from her chest. "You guys might want to enable the emergency stop and catch your breath. I don't want you going back out there until we know what we're dealing with."

"Good call," Clay agreed, enabling the emergency stop.

Izzy cut straight to the chase. "What are you seeing out there? We've got wild energy readings, but they don't match anything we've seen before."

Resting his head against the wall, Sherman gave his assessment. "Big, scary monsters."

If an eye roll could make a sound, that was what emanated from Izzy's side. "I figured that much, Uncle Sherm, but I'm gonna need a little more detail."

"They're like enormous horses," Clay interjected with helpful commentary. "They've got tails like a scorpion and their faces look human. Plus, they've got big bird wings."

"What in the world..." Izzy failed to quell her disbelief. "I've never even heard of such a thing."

"Maybe one of the lore scholars could help?" Clay suggested.

"Probably," Izzy surmised, "and it just so happens we've got our top man on the case."

...

THE SCHOLAR

William Roberts hobbled quickly through the Allied Ministry of Paranormal Defence's library with his trusty cane by his side. His eyes darted about, seeking a specific section. When he finally reached his desired bookshelf amongst the vast, circular library, he whirled around, searching for a particular title.

His fingers grazed the worn covers until they brushed across an animal skin binding. Pulling the book off the shelf with his good hand, Roberts inspected the title.

"Beasts of Revelation," the curly haired, bespectacled scholar read aloud.

Tucking the tome under his arm, Roberts moved as fast as he could back to Izzy's command centre, filled with towering mainframes and blinking computer screens. Once there, he plopped down across from the brilliant engineer and began his study. His fingers deftly flipped through the pages as he scanned for any relevant information based off Izzy's description.

Suddenly, he came across a piece of artwork etched within the text. It depicted a grotesque creature that matched the description given by Clay Owens and Rick Sherman. "Aha!" Roberts celebrated.

"You found something?" Izzy's hazel eyes widened as

she perked up.

Roberts couldn't help but marvel at Izzy. She was a rare beauty both externally and internally. She bore her father, Adam Lee's, Korean complexion, but favoured her mother, Mary Isley's European facial features.

Roberts had fought with Lee, George Isley, and Jacob Owens in the Battle of the Red Sea. He was one of the five survivors who owed their lives to George and Jacob's sacrifices. However, he owed Jacob a debt twice over.

During the battle, Roberts was bitten in the calf by one of the vicious serpopards. His death was imminent until Jacob ambushed and beheaded the beast. Ever since, with each painful step, Roberts remembered his fellow soldier. Now, with Jacob's son in danger, he would stop at nothing to protect Clay.

"Well," Roberts began, "the good news is I know what we're dealing with."

"And the bad news?" Izzy probed apprehensively.

"The bad news is that I know what we're dealing with," Roberts lamented.

Izzy buried her head in her hands. "Alright…let's hear it."

"Then out of the smoke locusts came upon the earth and to them was given power, as the scorpions of the earth have power." Roberts quoted from the Book of Revelation. "They were commanded not to harm the grass of the earth, or any green thing, or any tree, but only those men who do not have the seal of God on their foreheads."

"Doesn't sound so bad," Izzy pondered.

Roberts continued the passage of scripture. "Their torment was like the torment of a scorpion when it strikes a man. In those days men will seek death and will not find it; they will desire to die, and death will flee from them."

Izzy's lips pursed. "Okay, that sounds a little worse. Does it say anything about how to kill them?"

Roberts perused the text and contextualised it for Izzy. "While they were created by Satan and are commanded by the Prince of Hell, Abaddon, they ultimately fall under God's jurisdiction."

Izzy's brow furrowed, perplexed. "What does that mean?"

"It means God allows them to exert punishment, but only to a certain extent," Roberts expounded. "They're temporary, more akin to a plague rather than an annihilating force."

"So this really is the apocalypse," Izzy declared, disheartened.

"Not necessarily," Roberts cautioned, "These beasts were prophesied to arrive on the Fifth Trumpet."

"And?" Izzy wasn't comprehending.

"It implies that the four preceding trumpets, or 'signs

of the end', were already blown," Roberts theorised. "Yet, the criteria for trumpets one through four haven't been met."

"In English, please," Izzy beseeched the scholar.

"The locusts' arrival is premature," Roberts revealed. "They were awakened before their appointed time."

Izzy recoiled at the revelation. "Why?"

Roberts wracked his brain. He'd studied Satan's minions for over half his life and battled them in the field as a younger man. With all that wisdom at his disposal, he knew there had to be a nugget that could help them in this fight.

Suddenly epiphany struck. "These creatures have two masters, but they can't obey both simultaneously."

Izzy leaned forward. "You said they were Satan's creations, but God holds ultimate authority over them."

"Exactly," Roberts pondered, "which means that whoever released them to wreak havoc…"

"Could send them back," Izzy finished. "But God hasn't banished them yet…why?"

The wheels in Roberts' mind were spinning. "Show me the latest energy expulsions. Where are they concentrated?"

Izzy slid a map printout across the table. "So far, the supernatural energy has been confined to this area." The engineer pointed to a scatter plot that covered the surface area of Chernobyl.

"It hasn't expanded past the city's borders," Roberts observed. "These are wild beasts, warhorses, their very nature is to roam. So why aren't they?"

Izzy slapped the table eagerly. "Because something else is keeping them there!"

"What was meant for evil, God will turn for good," Roberts gasped. "He might be allowing the attack, but he won't allow it to spread. Whatever awakened these creatures, God's endgame is confined strictly to Chernobyl."

"There's something else," Izzy rubbed her chin in contemplation. "Give me that book."

Roberts handed over the weighty tome. Izzy scanned it a few times over. Soon after, a smirk danced across her face.

The scholar recognised that look all too well. "What have you found?"

"It says that these creatures can't touch those with 'God on their foreheads'. So, if our boys are believers, the locusts shouldn't be able to touch them." Izzy theorised.

Joyously, Roberts leapt from his seat, grabbed Izzy's head and planted a kiss on her forehead. "You brilliant girl! Get on the radio and tell them!"

Beaming from ear to ear, Izzy radioed her husband and uncle. "Good news boys!"

...

THE DOUBTER

Clay stood on the cusp of a black abyss. The void pulsed with a powerful heartbeat that beckoned him to leap. At his back a voice called his name.

Turn around, a soothing voice whispered, *I'm right here, I've always been here.*

Clay heard the voice, but the void was enticing and captivated him. He wanted to listen, he wanted to turn away, but a heavy weight kept his feet firmly planted at the edge of the abyss.

Suddenly the earth quaked beneath his feet. A loud voice reverberated through Clay's ears. "Wake up! Wake up!"

Jolting back to reality, Clay roused from his slumber. Uncle Sherm had shaken him awake with news. "Your wife and Roberts have some answers."

"What do they know?" Clay asked groggily.

"Go ahead, Izzy," Uncle Sherm ordered.

"What you're dealing with are locusts, creatures straight out of Revelation," Izzy unveiled.

"Hmm, so this isn't a diet apocalypse," Uncle Sherm asserted, "this is the real deal."

"No, we think somehow they were prematurely awakened," Izzy expounded, "but God's kept the onslaught limited to just Chernobyl."

"Why?" Clay wondered aloud.

"Mysterious ways," Izzy vaguely answered.

"Aka, no idea," Uncle Sherman jested.

"I don't know how any of this is good news," Clay grumbled.

"The good news is that locusts cannot harm anyone who belongs to God," Izzy explained, "which puts you two in the clear.

Uncle Sherm shifted uncomfortably. "Do you mean they can't harm us even if they attack us or they won't attack us at all?"

"They won't attack you at all," Izzy clarified. "Any leftover Russians should be your only roadblock to escape."

Clay scoffed. "They're a little preoccupied at the moment to be concerned with us."

Izzy chuckled, clearly relieved by her and Roberts' findings. "Now override the emergency stop and get out of there!"

"On it!" Clay guaranteed with a grin.

The younger soldier moved to fiddle with the elevator's circuitry per his wife's instructions. As he activated the override, Clay noticed his uncle was irregularly sombre. "What's the matter, Uncle Sherm? I figured you'd be celebrating an easy win."

"Did you hear what your wife said?" Uncle Sherm's tone turned solemn.

"Yeah, those damned things can't attack us even if they wanted to," Clay replied.

"Then why did they attack you?" Uncle Sherm voiced the sobering truth.

Clay paused. "They attacked you too! Remember the psycho monster that tried to kill in this very elevator."

Uncle Sherman leered at Clay. "It wasn't lunging for me."

Clay's heart sank at the realisation that he wasn't privy to God's protection. He grimaced in anger. "Figures. God hasn't given me any help my entire life, why should he start now?"

"Boy, you must be out of your mind!" Uncle Sherm growled in protest. "You had a great mother, a beautiful family, and a career that actually means a damn!"

"Don't forget the father I never got to meet and his shadow I was forced to live it!" Clay spat back.

Uncle Sherm punched the elevator wall in fury. "I'm sorry your daddy died! But you can't blame God for that!"

"Then who am I supposed to blame?" Clay countered.

"Me!" Uncle Sherman roared with tears in his eyes. "I fired the shot that killed him!"

It was like Clay had been shot in the chest. A

numbness permeated through his being. "You told me Anubis killed him..."

"It took five of our soldiers to restrain Anubis," Uncle Sherm admitted in shame. "We had one opportunity to hit him with a tank gun. It was our only hope to escape. While they held Anubis down, I fired."

The truth rocked Clay to his core. Uncle Sherman, the man he'd trusted for forty years, was the reason Clay grew up fatherless. Every fibre in his being wanted to lash out. Instead, however, the hefty burden of his loss suppressed any emotion.

Before Clay could respond, the elevator began to hum as they ascended to the next floor. Uncle and nephew rode the elevator in silence. When they reached the command centre, they stepped out into the destruction.

The spacious, circular room was a highly technological hub that resembled NASA command. Rows of computer dashboards faced a large screen that monitored the power plant's facilities and external grounds.

Another horde of locusts had ravaged Chernobyl's central command. The limp bodies of Russian soldiers littered the floor. Some writhed in anguish, succumbing to the poison. Others lay still, covered in what looked to be radiation burns.

"We need to find an exit," Sherman whispered.

Setting aside his rage in the interest of survival, Clay chose to work with the man who'd killed his father. "Once we get out there and find cover, we can gauge the video footage to determine the path of least resistance."

"Here, take this," Sherman ordered, handing Clay the barbed tail.

Rigor mortis had set in, stiffening the dismembered appendage. It was a bittersweet gift. Simultaneously, the implement represented God's abandonment of Clay and his only means of defending himself.

As the duo stepped off the elevator, they were relieved to find a barrier of glass between them and the locusts prowling in the command centre. With guile they took cover behind an overturned table. Crouching behind the debris, Clay peered out into the command centre. Fixating on the security footage, Clay noticed a bizarre phenomenon.

There was an army of locusts littering the grounds outside Chernobyl's four, large nuclear silos. However, the creatures on the outside were behaving very differently to the ones on the inside. The locusts on the inside were calm and docile, having incapacitated any threats. Yet their outdoors counterparts were flailing chaotically.

"Look," Clay whispered to Sherman, "does that seem familiar to you?"

Sherman squinted, contemplating what he was witnessing. "Looks like how the locusts reacted when I stabbed them."

"Check out the soldiers," Clay instructed, "some of them have radiation burns."

"I know what woke them up!" Sherman speculated.

"What are you thinking?" Clay queried.

"What if Satan put them here, but when the Russians started testing, it woke them up?" Sherman clarified.

"Why would it do that?" Clay failed to grasp the logic.

"Think about it. Their stings cause radiation burns and the only thing we know that kills them is their own venom." Sherman elaborated. "Therefore…"

"The radiation for the Soviet's tests caused them pain," Clay finished the thought.

"So, they came up here to stop whatever was harming them," Sherman explained.

"But what about everything Izzy and Roberts said," Clay pondered, "ya know, about God turning this for good and keeping them confined here?"

Sherman shrugged. "Think about the Old Testament. God wiped out entire kingdoms that threatened the world. He rained fire and brimstone on Sodom and Gomorrah, crushed Babylon, overtook Rome, and sent a bunch of badasses to deal with the Nazi's. If you're him, who's the greatest threat to the world right now?"

"A communist nation with an unparalleled nuclear arsenal," Clay answered.

"Bingo," Sherman winked. "You saw the mission briefing. This place is the cornerstone of the nuclear advancement program. Destroying this place will cripple the Soviets for decades. As I see it, he used the locusts to wipe out the Soviet minds building these weapons and used the reactors to keep the locusts from running rampant across the globe."

Something still tugged at Clay. "So why hasn't he put an end to all this? Where's his plan to get rid of these monsters and cripple Soviet nuclear proliferation? They're still here. Chernobyl's still operational. Who stops it all?"

Sherman's eyes widened as epiphany struck. "Us."

"Come again?" Clay raised his eyebrows sceptically.

"Izzy, do you copy?" Sherman whispered into his comms unit.

"What do you need, Uncle Sherm?" Izzy replied.

"I need you to get word to the USSR government," Sherman explained, "Tell them there's going to be a meltdown at Chernobyl and that they need to evacuate immediately!"

"What are you talking about?" Concern marked Izzy's voice.

"We can cripple the USSR's nuclear program and kill

all of the locusts in one shot," Sherman elaborated. "Trust me."

Izzy reluctantly obliged. "Fine, just promise me you'll get out of there safely."

Sherman glanced at Clay, "I promise."

"What's the plan?" Clay probed.

"As soon as we get beyond that glass, those things are going to swarm you," Sherman replied, "So we're gonna need to fight our way to the control panel. Once we're there, you man the switch to overload one of the reactors and I'll watch your six."

"Like always," Clay smiled and paused for a moment. "Listen, Uncle Sherm, about earlier, about my dad…"

"Greater love hath no man than to lay down his life for a friend," Sherman interrupted. "Your father gave up his life; it wasn't taken from him."

"I know that now." Clay put a consoling hand on his uncle's shoulder.

"Now, enough of this emotional nonsense…let's go kill these unholy bastards."

...

THE SON

The time for running and hiding was over. With reckless abandon, Clay charged into the command centre with his uncle by his side. Four locusts charged from the opposing direction, bearing their deadly fangs.

The first creature lunged at Clay, who deftly dodged to the left. With the locust's neck extended, the seasoned warrior seized his opportunity. Striking upwards, Clay lodged the scorpion barb into the beast's neck.

As the initial locust fell in death, another struck from above. Swooping down, the second locust sent its tail careening towards Clay's head. Instinctively he ducked, and the barb grazed just above his hair.

Turning for a second pass, Clay readied his counterattack. The beast sped through the air towards its prey. However, its assault would be short-lived. Clutching the tail like a javelin, Clay hurled his weapon at his attacker.

The throw struck true, plunging into the locust's chest. As the beast's body rocketed towards the ground, Clay dived out of the way. Contrarily, the third locust, which had been stalking Clay from behind, wasn't so lucky.

Dead and living locusts collided and skidded across the command centre floor. Their slide came to a halt next to the main control panel where Uncle Sherm was overloading one reactor. Nonchalantly he unstuck the severed tail from the dead creature and proceeded to stab the dazed one to death.

"Head's up!" Sherm bellowed.

Clay whirled around to find the fourth locust galloping in his direction. It was advancing too fast for him to avoid. As a last-ditch effort, Clay charged headfirst towards his assailant.

Just before the locust struck with its tail, Clay slid along the slick concrete floor below the deadly barb and between the galloping feet. Caught off guard by the deft manoeuvre, the beast tried to stop its momentum. However, its hooves skidded along the floor, causing it to tumble.

With their adversary temporarily immobilised, Uncle Sherman pounced. He drove the poisoned barb deep within the creature. It wailed in agony before going limp.

Alerted by the cohorts' demise, a legion of locusts descended on the control centre. Enraged, they bashed against the metal doors. It was only a matter of time until they broke through.

Clay turned to the security screen. He couldn't even count the number of demonic creatures that assembled in the hallways outside the command centre. There would be no resistance. Two men could never stem the tide, even if the creatures were supernaturally forbidden from attacking Uncle Sherm.

More dire news came from the main control panel. "Hey kid, we got a problem," Uncle Sherm's voice uncharacteristically quaked.

"Yeah, we got a lot of problems," Clay referenced the horde of Satan's spawn battering down their doors.

"There's an automatic failsafe built into the system," Sherman explained.

"What does that mean?" Clay inquired, hoping for the best but fearing the worst.

"It means that if one of the reactors gets close to flooding, the system will autocorrect," Sherman clarified. "If we're gonna flood a reactor, someone has to stay behind and manually do it."

The choice was simple from Clay's perspective. "It has to be me. Those things can't touch you. You've at least got a shot at surviving."

"No," Uncle Sherman remained defiant. "I made a promise to your father a long time ago that I would protect you. I let an Owens man die for me once. Now it's my turn."

Tears streamed down Clay's face. "You can't do this! There's only one logical choice! You know I'm not under God's protection against those things!

"You could be though!" Uncle Sherm rebuked. "Let go of all that pent-up resentment about your father! I knew him better than anyone, he wouldn't have wanted that for you! Holding onto that anger is like staring into a black hole and waiting for the void to suck you in! If you need to blame someone, blame me! I'm the reason you're fatherless!"

Clay's dream from the elevator reverberated through is mind. The whispered message replayed. *Turn around,* a soothing voice beckoned, *I'm right here, I've always been here.*

Shutting his eyes tightly, the world around Clay dissipated. He was back staring at that dark abyss. This time, however, he listened to the whisper and turned around.

Two men were standing behind Clay. One was a warrior adorned in gilded armour. Looking at his face was like looking in the mirror. He had the same, icy blue eyes as Clay. Innately, the son knew his father.

The other was cloaked in brilliant, white light. Clay dared not look upon the brilliant visage of his face as a mere mortal. Still, despite the raw, unadulterated power teeming from his father's companion, an overwhelming, fatherly sense of love filled Clay in his presence.

In that moment, the son understood a simple truth. I've never been fatherless.

Just as quickly as it had come, the vision passed. Clay was thrust back into his reality, though it didn't feel as grim as it had moments earlier. He looked into his Uncle's tear-riddled, bloodshot eyes.

"You're wrong." Clay released his burden, "I've

never been fatherless…I had three fathers that were always there, even when I refused to acknowledge them; God, Jacob Owens, and Rick Sherman."

Clay walked to his uncle and embraced him with a newfound warmth. He knew this was goodbye in this realm. However, Clay knew farewell was only temporary.

"Now, get out of here," Uncle Sherm joked, "and take your damned emotions with you!"

Looking back with a sad smile, Clay made a new promise to replace the one Uncle Sherm had made with his father. "I'll see you again soon."

Bravely Clay walked through the doorway. The shadows of malicious beasts snarled at him menacingly, but he feared them no more. He had a father that would never leave his side…three to be exact.

MATT LUCAS writes varying forms of speculative fiction, including urban fantasy, paranormal, sci-fi, and horror. He is represented by Labyrinth Literary Agency and his debut novel, The Shadow Gospels, currently being pitched for publication.

He's had several short stories published with Black Hare Press and Blood Song Books. As his career progresses, he's always seeking opportunities to expand his resume. Writing is his passion and he hopes to spend his days cultivating captivating stories with impactful messages.

Bibliography
Angels, Black Hare Press, 2019
Apocalypse, Black Hare Press, 2019
Beyond, Black Hare Press, 2019
Forest of Fear, Blood Song Books, 2019
What If?, Black Hare Press, 2019
Worlds, Black Hare Press, 2019

Connect
Amazon: www.amazon.com/-/e/B07TKDMZWL
Twitter: @MattDLuke

WHAT IF?

ACKNOWLEDGEMENTS

 When we embarked on our Black Hare Press journey back in late 2018, we never envisioned the huge support we'd get from the writing community. We have been truly humbled by the number of submissions we've received (around 3,000 over eight publications!) and have loved reading every single one.

So, thank you to everyone who crafted tales just for us—from the tiny tales in our Dark Drabbles series to these monstrous beauties you have read here in What If?—we thank you from the bottom of our hearts.

To our families and friends, collaborators, random strangers who took pity on us, and everyone who has helped us on the way: we couldn't have done it without you.

And to you, our discerning reader, we and these fifteen talented writers did it all for you. We hope you enjoyed these tales of magical alternate history. If you did, don't forget to leave a review.

Thank you all, and see you next time.

Love & kisses

Ben Thomas & Dean Kershaw

www.blackharepress.com

A BLACK HARE PRESS ANTHOLOGY
WORLDS
DARK DRABBLES #1
edited by
D KERSHAW

A BLACK HARE PRESS ANTHOLOGY
ANGELS
DARK DRABBLES #2
edited by
D KERSHAW

A BLACK HARE PRESS ANTHOLOGY
MONSTERS
DARK DRABBLES #3
edited by
D KERSHAW

A BLACK HARE PRESS ANTHOLOGY
BEYOND
DARK DRABBLES #4
edited by
D KERSHAW

UNRAVEL
DARK DRABBLES #5
SCENE DO
edited by
D KERSHAW

A BLACK HARE PRESS ANTHOLOGY
APOCALYPSE
DARK DRABBLES #6
edited by
D KERSHAW

A BLACK HARE PRESS ANTHOLOGY
EERIE
CHRISTMAS
edited by
BEN THOMAS
& D KERSHAW